The Lady's Ghost

a Regency Romance

Colleen Ladd

PUBLISHED BY:
Marian Kelly

The Lady's Ghost
Copyright © 2014 Marian Kelly

Print ISBN: 978-1-941881-01-9
Ebook ISBN: 978-1-941881-00-2

This book is a work of fiction and all characters exist solely in the author's imagination. Any resemblance to persons, living or dead, is purely coincidental. Any references to places, events or locales are used in a fictitious manner.

Formatting by StevieDeInk. stevie1@steviedeink.com

Cover design by Laura J Miller
www.anauthorsart.com

Many thanks to Linda White (aka Regina Duke) for all her advice and encouragement over the years, not to mention the expert proofreading assistance, and to my family for believing in me even when it might have been smarter not to.

Chapter One

"OF all the dratted luck!"

"My lady!"

Portia scowled at her maid in the dim confines of the carriage. "Don't you 'my lady' me, Ellie Brown. If a horse coming up lame this close to the Hall doesn't justify a 'drat' or two, I don't know what does." It justified a great deal more than that, coming on top of a long and weary journey in the cold, musty coach. One of her late husband's favorite epithets rose to mind—Roger had not been disposed to remember his manners when he was foxed—but she refrained from voicing it, needing no further scolding from her maid.

For her part, Ellie did not hesitate to scowl back. Portia's sole ally and confidante during her brief marriage, the maid was fiercely protective and not in the least inclined to hold her mistress in awe. It was just as well. Awe would scarcely have sustained Portia through her husband's dissolute indifference, his outright contempt for the sanctity of his marriage.

"This is what comes of hiring carriages." Ellie's lips compressed to a thin line, opening a moment later to add, "And on the cheap too, I'll be bound."

Portia burrowed her hands farther into her muff and tried not to shiver. Night was coming on fast and the hot brick the coachman placed at their feet at the last stop had long since gone cold. "I'm sure Lord Ashburne did the best he could."

James Ashburne was a stiff-rumped skinflint, but Portia couldn't blame the cheapness of their travel arrangements on that. The man was badly purse-pinched, saddled with three entailed estates, two of which cost more in upkeep than they produced and the third barely squeaking by. The Ashburnes had been rich as Croesus when Roger inherited the title, but in the ten years he held it, money ran like water through his fingers. He'd already been well up the River

Tick when he pitched head-first from his phaeton while deep in his cups, and would soon have found himself in desperate straits.

Straits Portia was all too familiar with. Roger barely paid any mind to his wife while he was alive; it wouldn't have occurred to him to provide for her after his death, even if he'd had the blunt to manage it. The new Viscount Ashburne was even more down-at-heels and substantially less inclined to spend his meager funds on his brother's widow. Portia could hardly throw herself on his charity—he didn't have any. Nor any mercy, not after his wife made it clear she wouldn't be happy, or quiet, until she no longer shared her house or her title with Portia. There was nothing to be done about the latter; Portia would remain Lady Ashburne until she remarried, if she ever did. The other complaint, however, was eminently fixable.

And so Portia found herself jostling along in a cheap hired carriage, packed off to Ashburne Hall like so much unwanted baggage. Weary as she was of traveling, she did not look forward to arriving. She'd been made well aware of Roger's antipathy toward the family seat; it couldn't have suited Roger better if the Hall crumbled to the ground. Portia only hoped it wouldn't be crumbling around her ears.

The carriage swung slowly into a turn, the horses picking up their limping pace. Portia pushed aside the drafty leather window-covering and peered through the mizzling rain. An inn. The building was low and brooding, but light spilled cheerfully from the windows, casting long fingers across the yard.

When the coach drew to a halt, the postilion leapt down and walked stiffly up to hold the horses—the boy must be half-frozen. A moment later, the carriage rocked with the coachman's descent. Portia watched the man walk about the dark yard, alternately rubbing his hands together and pressing them against his lower back. Guilt settled in the pit of her stomach, though it was James who decreed they accomplish a nearly four-day trip in two. He had no intention of paying for more than one night's lodging, no matter the strain it put on man and beast.

"Coachman."

"Yes, m'lady." He took off his hat as he approached, the desultory drizzle spangling his hair. He'd been unfailingly polite and done everything in his power to see to the comfort of his passengers, though Portia knew he was not being paid overmuch for his care.

She smiled. "John, is it?"

"Yes, m'lady."

"How much farther to the Hall?"

He peered off into the distance and scratched his beard. "Not more'n half an hour's drive, I'll be bound. But this bain't no coaching inn, my lady. Can't be certain how long 'fore we get a fresh horse."

So short a distance.... If their destination had been Portia's childhood home or even Rosewood Close, the house she'd kept for Roger and the only one of his estates still solvent, she'd have left it at that, knowing the coachman would be well attended once they arrived. She had no idea what kind of welcome to expect at the Hall.

"Well then, let us go inside and wait where it's warm." Portia opened the door and allowed the startled coachman to hand her out, ignoring Ellie's shocked exclamation and scramble to follow.

"You and your boy must be half-frozen. Come inside and get something warm into you." Portia took up her skirts to keep them out of the mud and started for the door.

"Who's going to pay for it, my lady?" Ellie muttered.

"I still have a little money of my own."

"Yes, my lady. A little."

The innkeeper, a stocky giant of a man wearing an apron gray with age, met her in the chilly entranceway. His smile, when she requested a private parlor, was faintly mocking and his diction surprisingly crisp. She wondered if he'd been in service somewhere. "We aren't so fancy here. No, miss, taproom's all there is." His expression said quite clearly he expected her to take a seat in the common room and stop putting on airs. Portia couldn't blame him. Two days' travel had left its stamp on her, and her traveling dress, quite out of fashion and dyed an unflattering black, hardly gave her the look of a lady. He doubtless thought her some jumped up shopkeeper's daughter, traveling with a maid to give herself an undeserved air of consequence.

She'd never before had to *tell* someone she was Quality and was wondering how one went about it when the door banged loudly. Blowing in the cold, the coachman drew his caped coat about him with a shudder. "M'lady?"

The innkeeper blinked, and Portia fought back a smile. There was no point in aggravating the poor man. "Yes, John?"

"Ostler says it'll be most half an hour 'fore we can be gettin' on to the Hall."

"Very well. You and that boy of yours come in and warm yourselves at the fire." She glanced at the innkeeper, who was still gaping, and couldn't resist adding, "It appears I'll be joining you in the common room." Ellie made a choked-off noise.

"Miss, ah, my lady, ah—" The innkeeper cleared his throat with a noise like an avalanche, which seemed to startle him sufficiently to get him started. "I'm terribly sorry, my lady. But there really is only the common room. We've holes in the parlor roof and with the rain...." He shifted his great shoulders, looking as grossly uncomfortable as a man of his stature could.

"No matter." Portia reflected that Ellie really did sound as if she were choking on something. "Just find me someplace warm for the next half hour."

"But my lady," he protested, genuinely upset, "it isn't possible to do better for your ladyship than a settle before the fire."

"Then," Portia said, used to accepting hardship philosophically, "that will have to do."

"Yes, my lady," he said doubtfully. He dove through the door into the common room, his passage attended by the sounds of upheaval and upraised voices.

"My lady," Ellie whispered, "you can't—"

"Would you rather freeze in the carriage?"

Ellie jammed her mouth shut with an audible click of teeth and glared. Portia glared back until the innkeeper returned. "This way, if you please, my lady."

Portia stepped for the first time in her life into the common taproom of an inn and found it dark and rough-hewn, dimly lit by the fire and a few lamps that hung from the low ceiling. The close heat pressed Portia's breath back in her throat. She forced a slow breath against the suffocating feeling and was struck by the odor of the place, a pungent brew of horse, leather, and man. The innkeeper sidled over to a settle near the fire, keeping his bulk between Portia and the other occupants. They were largely silent, but their very presence filled the room with a sibilant tide of whispering and fidgeting. The noise swelled slightly once Portia and Ellie were established in the high-backed settle where they could neither see nor be seen, but didn't reach the level it had before she entered the inn. Portia's lips twitched as she considered the power of a lady's presence to silence a roomful of men.

"If I may, my lady," the innkeeper bent his great head to murmur deferentially. "Some tea?"

She mentally counted the scanty coins in her purse and decided she could just afford it. "That would be lovely." More than lovely, her empty stomach reminded her; James had given her little enough traveling money and she'd had no supper that day. "Thank you."

"My pleasure, my lady." Rather than bustling off to see to it, he stood wrapping the corner of his apron around his thumb in a nervous gesture at odds with his bulk. "My lady, if I may.... Your coachman said the Hall? Would you be Lady Ashburne?"

"I am."

"Ah." He bobbed his head. "W-welcome." It sounded strangely tentative, which might have been why he cleared his throat and said it again, his thunderous voice momentarily cutting off all other conversation in the room. "Welcome, Lady Ashburne." He bobbed his head again and left, the murmur of voices flowing in to fill the void left by his departure.

Portia leaned into the hard corner of the settle and sighed. The fire bathed her in welcome heat and she found that the odor of men and animals faded, so long as she didn't pay particular attention to it. "Do you know, Ellie, I begin to think I may eventually thaw out."

Ellie said nothing, her lips compressed in a hard line. Portia sighed again and wondered if Ellie's offended silence would last until they reached the Hall. The remainder of the trip would be more peaceful if it did.

Portia stretched her hands out to the fire, less because they needed the extra heat than to prevent herself from nodding off in the blissful warmth. She was aware of the little postilion and the red-faced coachman tentatively warming themselves at the other end of the enormous hearth, but didn't worry herself over it. It was large enough for them all, and she couldn't see standing on ceremony under the circumstances. If one set the matter of title aside, there was little difference between Portia and the men fidgeting quietly in the room behind her. Many of them likely had better roofs over their heads than she could look forward to.

Their curiosity, colored with irritation that they should be put out on her account, beat like waves upon the sheltering settle. Portia tried to ignore it, but when a pair of bright eyes peered at her around the edge of the heavy furniture, she couldn't quite restrain a gasp.

The boy flinched back, but crept forward again immediately. "D'he say the Hall?" he asked in a hoarse little voice. "D'he?"

Portia smiled. "Yes. I'm going to the Hall."

"Is Lord Ashburne with you?"

Someone alarmingly close snorted. "Don't be ridiculous, Jemmy. Giles Ashburne never leaves the Hall."

Portia nearly laughed at the nonsensical statement, but the room dropped into a silence so sudden and so deep that it quashed any such reaction.

"You're drunk, George," the innkeeper boomed, sweeping up with a steaming tea tray. "Giles Ashburne's been dead these ten years." He hooked a small table with his foot and dragged it over to set the tea tray on. Once his hands were free, he cuffed the boy lightly with one huge paw. "Off with you, Jemmy. Leave the lady alone. Terribly sorry, my lady," he said as the boy scampered away. "You'd think this lot'd never seen Quality before." He settled the tea tray in front of her, arranging the pot and cups with surprising delicacy, the odor of tea and toast making Portia's stomach grumble. "I've taken the liberty," he added, sounding suddenly so like her grandfather's butler that tears came to Portia's eyes, "of sending the potboy to the Hall to alert them to your arrival."

"Thank you..." She hesitated and he hurried to say, "Foxkin, my lady. I used to do up at the Hall, a long time ago now." He was fiddling with the corner of his apron again.

Portia smiled. "Thank you, Foxkin. You've been very helpful."

"I hope so, my lady. " Looking oddly doubtful, he took himself off.

"Well," Portia said, to herself, since Ellie was still in a snit, "that was interesting." When the toast was finished, she cradled her teacup between her hands and sat there soaking up warmth inside and out, waiting for her carriage to be ready and wondering what awaited her up at the Hall.

* * *

Ellie nudged Portia out of a light doze when the coachman came to say that a fresh horse had been found and they could be getting on.

Dozens of faces appeared in the windows of the inn when Portia crossed the innyard to her chilly carriage. Ellie tried to shield her from their gaze with her own body; not having the innkeeper's bulk, she didn't succeed. Portia kept her head high, refusing to quail under the weight of their glittering eyes, and only after the inn dropped behind them did it occur to her that they were merely trying to get a look at their new neighbor.

After all, Portia had never before been to the Hall. To the best of her knowledge, Roger had not visited the place either. He'd established Portia at Rosewood Close immediately after their wedding and visited a mere handful of times over the five years they were married, far more devoted to his Town pleasures than he was to her. It would've been exceedingly strange if he *had* bothered to visit Ashburne Hall, which was even farther removed from London. No wonder the villagers were consumed with curiosity when Lady Ashburne came to visit.

To stay, Portia corrected herself. Perhaps forever.

She wouldn't miss London. She'd spent but one Season there and barely made it through even that before she found herself a married lady. She'd passed their marriage alone at Rosewood Close and would have been happy to stay there if it hadn't been the only one of the estates James Ashburne and his wife could reasonably live in. Portia had worked hard to make it into a comfortable home, as comfortable as could be managed on the pittance Roger allowed her.

Portia loved Rosewood and in its way, it had loved her. It had glowed under her tireless hands, the servants working happily for and with her. It did not so bloom under the new Lady Ashburne, and no doubt the servants' habit of turning to Portia for direction had something to do with the decision to send her away.

Portia's eyes grew hot. She had not been *happy* at Rosewood Close, but she had been content. She angrily blinked back tears. She had to forget Rosewood. Ashburne Hall was her home now.

The carriage turned onto a deeply rutted track. Portia grabbed for the strap and Ellie clung to the seat-edge as the carriage listed into one alarming dip after another. Branches scraped the sides of the coach and tapped insistently on the top. Portia hung on grimly. The bouncing seemed endless, but they'd gone no more than half a mile when they emerged suddenly from the grasp of the trees. The coach passed through a once-clear area of wild and tangled grasses and drew up before the Hall.

Something about the looming Hall kept even Ellie from speaking as they descended from the carriage. The main house was tall and square and impressive, the hewn stone and wrought iron stern and unbending. Shorter wings swung off from either side, their dimensions lost to the darkness. Over it all hung a crescent moon, its pale light reflecting off the mullioned windows like a hundred tiny eyes. Somewhere at the top of the house, a candle flickered, solitary and cold.

Portia shivered and drew her cloak more closely about her. "Let's hope the boy reminded them to light a fire in the sitting room."

On the contrary—as Portia discovered upon entering the Hall unannounced, having been unable to discover a knocker in the dark—a welcoming fire appeared to be quite the last thing on the minds of the servants.

The grand staircase that swept up from the center of the vast, echoing hall opened out onto a gallery at the first floor landing, then split and ran up both sides of the hall to the second floor. On the landing, three people—a stripling lad, a tall narrow woman in black bombazine wearing a stiffly starched mobcap, and an older man in attire more suited to the stables—struggled to remove a large painting from the wall.

"Good evening," Portia called. The painting dipped, dropping three inches on one side. Someone gasped audibly.

"Good evening, my lady." The housekeeper broke away and dropped Portia an abrupt curtsey. She started down the stairs. The other two broke out of their paralysis, stared wildly at each other, and went back to the painting. "I beg your pardon, Lady Ashburne. We were not expecting you."

"Stay there. I'll come up." Portia lifted her dress and started up the steps, occasioning a flurry of activity around the painting, which only stopped when the housekeeper hissed something Portia couldn't hear.

Numerous doors led off the great hall, the first floor corridor and the top floor landing, many gaping open like dark mouths. Portia forced herself to turn neither to the right nor left, though the back of her neck itched strangely with the pressure of unseen eyes, but kept her focus resolutely on the housekeeper. Dust rose from the carpet runner, mixing with the pervasive odor of mold. Four steps in succession creaked when she put weight on them, each worse than the last, and she could see herself crashing through to the flagstones below. She tightened her grip on the balustrade and reached the landing safely several nervous steps later. The housekeeper met her at the head of the stairs, the other two remaining before the painting, which they'd finally succeeded in getting down. Half again as tall as the boy, it leaned drunkenly against the wall behind them.

The housekeeper faced her with blank inscrutability, but the other two had a nervous air Portia found strangely familiar. In a moment, she had it. They reminded her of her brother the time he'd knocked one of Mama's precious figurines off the mantelpiece. Tony had stood just like that, drawn stiffly erect, every muscle taut and trembling with strain, using his body to hide the gap where the figurine had stood long past the point it was clear the damage had been discovered.

She took pity on them and turned to the housekeeper. "You were not expecting me, Mrs...?"

"McFerran, my lady." She bobbed another curtsey. Her face was pulled into severe lines by the iron gray hair scraped back from her brow. "I've been housekeeper here nigh on thirty years. And much the old house has suffered. My husband and I take care of things as best we can, but there are limits, my lady. There are limits, with he and I the only staff in the poor old Hall." The man snatched off his shabby cap, his wispy hair floating uncertainly around his head as he bowed, giving Portia a glimpse of the upper third of the painting before he jerked upright. "The boy's from The Duck and Drake."

"So I assumed. Did not Lord Ashburne send word?" Now that she thought on it, Portia wasn't entirely certain James would have bothered to notify them of her imminent arrival.

"Yes, my lady. We got the letter from Lord..." A grimace flew across Mrs. McFerran's mouth. "...Ashburne this morning. But until the boy came from the inn, we didn't know exactly when to expect you."

"I see." Portia cocked her head to one side, torn between irritation and laughter. "And you thought the best way to prepare for my arrival was to remove this picture?"

"No, ma'am," Mr. McFerran said in a high voice like cracked leather. "Lord Ashburne told us to do it, and doin' it we were when the boy came. Couldn't stop then, not with it half off the wall like it were."

"Mr. McFerran," his wife snapped, "Lady Ashburne isn't interested in our difficulties."

"On the contrary; I'm fascinated. Did Lord Ashburne's letter mention *why* he wanted the painting removed?"

"Letter? Weren't no—" McFerran broke off at his wife's glare and shuffled his cap around in his hands.

"If you'll follow me, Lady Ashburne," Mrs. McFerran said with a stiff little smile, "I'll show you to your room. I won't say it's ready for you, but it'll be as comfortable as any here."

"I should like to see the painting first."

Indeed, Portia could hardly contain her curiosity. James was not likely to have ordered the painting removed. His letters were invariably as short and discourteous as he was, and Portia couldn't imagine he'd have bothered to lengthen this one with such orders when he couldn't even be bothered to mention *when* she'd arrive. Perhaps it was Roger who'd ordered them to take it down and news of his widow's arrival had prompted them to make an enormously belated attempt to obey. Though why they should be so obviously frightened was beyond her.

"Come now," she said when none of them moved. "Step aside. It can't be as bad as all that."

Their faces set in identical expressions of reluctance, McFerran and the boy stepped away from the life-size portrait. A figure of black and white stood before stormy skies, dark hair and eyes contrasting sharply with pale skin, his features too rugged to be considered conventionally handsome. The artist had painted the man's lips curved into what Portia wasn't entirely certain was a smile and captured something implacable in the flat glitter of the eyes. Not, Portia thought, a comfortable man.

"Who is he?"

Mrs. McFerran gazed at Portia for a moment too long, dark eyes calculating in her narrow, suspicious face. "Kit," she said suddenly. "Run along home now, your mum'll be worried."

"Wait a moment, Kit," Portia said on impulse before the boy could take a step. "Help Mr. McFerran put the picture back up first, will you?"

"Yes'm."

Portia turned to the housekeeper. "You can show me my room now, Mrs. McFerran."

The woman's eyes flashed and Portia feared she'd have outright rebellion on her hands, but after a moment the housekeeper turned away, taking a candle from the candelabra at the head of the stairs. Portia followed, reminding herself that the woman had been housekeeper at the Hall for thirty years. Roger only held the title ten years, none of them spent at the Hall, and who knew how often the previous lord had bothered to visit. Mrs. McFerran had no doubt become used to following her own course. Her new circumstances would take some getting used to.

"Who is he?" Portia asked again.

"That?" They'd moved out of earshot of the two struggling to lift the portrait back into position, which seemed to loosen the housekeeper's tongue. "That, my lady, is Viscount Giles Ashburne. He was lord here before Mr. Roger Ashburne took the title. You've not heard of him?"

Portia shook her head and saw something flare in the housekeeper's eyes. They reminded her suddenly and unpleasantly of the hard painted eyes of the portrait.

"I don't wonder the new Lord Ashburne chose not to spread the tale. Ten years ago," Mrs. McFerran said, lowering her voice and drawing closer to Portia, "Giles Ashburne was engaged to be wed. Beautiful, she was. Lady Amelia Holgate, ward of his Grace, the Duke of Ransley, who owns half the county. Biddable little thing with blond hair and blue eyes, as much like his lordship as a poppy is like a blackthorn. A month before their wedding date, his lordship holds a house party. Now I'm not saying it was her idea, but this house had never seen such a party since his lordship took the title. Certainly," she added, almost inaudibly, "it's seen no such thing since."

"Yes," Portia prompted when Mrs. McFerran had stood silent for a moment, staring at the portrait that was nearly back in place. "And?"

The housekeeper returned her flat eyes to Portia. "There's some say Lady Amelia wasn't so pleased with the match as her guardian, that she'd given her heart, and more, elsewhere. And there's some say a man like his lordship didn't deserve to lay eyes on such an angel. But," she went on with extraordinary vehemence, "there's no one doubts he killed her."

Portia stepped back involuntarily.

"He caught her, they say, in the arms of another man, and bided his time until her lover left." She paused until Portia's skin crawled, then added in a tone almost matter-of-fact, "And then he cut her throat."

Portia's eyes went to the portrait. Giles Ashburne scowled blackly down at her and she turned away without meaning to. "He doesn't," she said and, hearing the tremulous note in her voice, firmed it up determinedly, "look like a murderer."

"No, my lady? He vanished within the week, escaped to the Continent before he could be brought to trial. He died there, far from home. A fitting end, some say. They say," Mrs. McFerran ploughed darkly on, "he's come home: Giles Ashburne, doomed to haunt his own Hall until the Last Trumpet sounds."

An appalling clatter spun Portia around, her heart leaping into her throat, to scan the great hall. Ellie stood at the foot of the stairs, looking up at her with stolid imperturbability, and Portia could see nothing amiss. She couldn't tell if any of the doors that had been open were now closed, though that was no doubt the source of the noise. A draft, perhaps. Portia cast her eyes higher and gasped when she spied movement. A tapestry on the second floor landing swayed gently. A draft, definitely. She took in a slow breath.

"Nonsense. I'd have thought you above believing such things, Mrs. McFerran."

"As you say, my lady." The housekeeper's expression was smug, putting paid to any hope she might have missed Portia's brief fright. Mrs. McFerran headed off down the gloomy corridor and Portia followed, but not without a look back at the painting that hung glowering at the head of the stairs.

* * *

From the upper stair, Giles Ashburne watched the woman who'd invaded his home. This was the new Lady Ashburne? He wouldn't have thought her to Roger's taste. But it was ten years since Giles was borne off by death and disaster. A lot could change.

He studied the trespasser. She was small—only the boy was shorter and his growth would surmount hers in less than a month—but there was no hint of frailty about her. Quite the contrary. Her health and strength shone through her every gesture, just as her ripe curves transformed the atrocious traveling dress she wore. Her hair was caught up in a complicated knot, the brown tresses gleaming red in the flickering light of the housekeeper's candle, and her eyes when they scanned the Hall had been far too bright.

He would have to get rid of her.

Chapter Two

"HERE you are, my lady."

The chamber Mrs. McFerran showed Portia to had once been grand. Deep window casements and a high square ceiling were framed by what looked in the flickering light of Mrs. McFerran's candle to be elaborate plasterwork, though somewhat set about by spiders. The rich colors of the once-sumptuous wall coverings and window hangings were muted by age and dust.

"Hasn't been used in a decade," Mrs. McFerran said when Portia rustled the moth-eaten drapes. There'd been a superficial attempt made at cleaning, but cobwebs clung to the bedcurtains and a musty smell arose from the bedding. "No one in the house but me and Mr. McFerran, and we stick to our own."

"And the family bedchambers? What condition are they in?" For the room was clearly, by appointment and location, a guest chamber.

"Not good, my lady." Mrs. McFerran touched the flame from her candle to a battered stub sitting in a silver holder by the bed. It flared up brightly, the odor of burning dust momentarily eclipsing the damp smell of the room. "The roof leaks, most places, and there's hardly a chimney that doesn't smoke bad enough to drive out even the most stubborn."

"Poor condition for a great estate."

"For the culprit you must look to the upstart Lords Ashburne," the housekeeper flared. "No help and no money. Who can manage to keep up such a house with no help and no money?"

"M'lady?" the coachman called from the hall. "Your trunks?"

Portia went to the door to wave him in. "In here, John." It took him only a moment to lug her trunks into the tiny dressing room. Ellie came hard on his heels with Portia's one bandbox, her lips tight-pressed as she took in the straits

15

they'd come to. When he'd finished, the coachman stopped once more before her, his hat in his hands.

"Have you any thoughts about where you will pass the night?" Portia asked. "You may remain here with my blessing, if that will suit." Though Lord knew what kind of accommodations she could coax out of Mrs. McFerran.

The coachman bobbed his head deferentially. "Thank you, m'lady, the boy and I will return to The Duck and Drake for the night. I must return their horse and look after my own cattle."

"Very well. Perhaps you could take the potboy with you?" He must have come from the inn on foot, for Portia had seen no sign of a horse; the least he deserved was a more comfortable return trip.

"Of course, m'lady."

He bobbed his head again when she pressed a few coins into his hand, though they both knew it was less than he deserved. His look was one Portia would never get used to, compounded as much of pity as respect.

"Mrs. McFerran," Portia said when the housekeeper would have followed him out, her eyes narrowed as if she suspected him of having designs on the silver. Assuming there was any. "I will require supper—a cold collation will do. And send Mr. McFerran to light the fire."

"I can't speak for the state of the chimney—"

"I'll just have to take my chances, shan't I?"

Mrs. McFerran sniffed and swept out. Portia's candle sputtered in its own wax—an extravagance from a more prosperous time, which Portia had best not get used to. She had no doubt the household was otherwise reduced to tallow, or even rushlights. She looked at the shadow-draped room, her heart a weight more stifling than the tightest corset. It was a far cry from her light, airy chamber at Rosewood Close.

"A fine mess, if I do say so."

Portia turned to Ellie, a smile lifting her lips at the maid's practical tone. "It does leave something to be desired, doesn't it?"

"Spiders in the clothespress and mice in the walls, I'll be bound."

"You forgot the birds nesting in the chimney."

"I don't call this much of a welcome, I'll tell you that."

"They only received Lord Ashburne's letter this morning. Hardly enough time to prepare." Portia picked up the sputtering candle and set about searching the drawers of the small dressing table.

"So they say."

There were no additional candles in the dressing table; indeed, Portia found the drawers uniformly empty but for a layer of dust. Ah well. The search had been more a product of wishful thinking than expectation. Portia pulled open the last drawer and stifled a scream when a mouse vanished through a hole in the back of the drawer. Her heart racing, she gently slid the drawer closed.

The carpet was compounded more of dust than wool, and when Portia pushed aside the cobweb-colored drapes to look out onto the rain-swept night, she found one of the windowpanes broken. Someone had stuffed a rag in the hole in a failed attempt to keep out the wind. Three more mice took off for parts unknown when she and Ellie tossed back the counterpane, their sudden appearance less startling than Ellie's shriek.

"Well." Portia took a breath imbued with the odor of mold and let it out slowly. "It could be worse."

Her bosom heaving, Ellie stared at her as if her wits had gone begging.

"At least we have a roof over our heads." Portia stripped the blankets down to the foot of the bed. She didn't find any more mice, but the sheets were unpleasantly damp, and she pulled the blanket back up. "We shall just have to make do. We've done it before." Though Rosewood Close had been nowhere near this bad. "Any house can be made habitable with enough effort."

"And money," Ellie said darkly.

"I have a little money of my own I can draw on, as you well know." And thank heavens for her late grandfather, the Duke of Bedingfeld, whose man of business had seen to it that the modest money he settled on her was so wrapped about in protections that even Roger had found no way to touch it. Otherwise, it too would be gone and Portia would be in dire straits indeed, for she could certainly not rely upon her dower. The income from one third of Roger's lands that was her widow's portion wasn't enough to keep a mouse alive.

"Aye," said Ellie, "I know it and so does his high and mighty lordship, James Ashburne. Mark my words, my lady, he's put a roof over our heads and that's all he'll do."

"Leaving me to manage the upkeep of it."

"And a dirty trick it is too, saving him the cost of this place at your expense."

"It's not entirely unexpected." Portia smiled at her lion of a maid. "There's no good flying into a pelter over it. At least we *do* have a roof."

"Such as it is. Mice and damp and rot," Ellie muttered as she returned to the dressing room to rummage about in Portia's trunks for her nightclothes.

Portia didn't have the heart to tell her about the ghost.

* * *

They slept that night in the same bed, bundled together for warmth under the counterpane. One got used to the musty smell after a while and the sound of the rain outside was strangely soothing.

The dripping somewhere closer was not so comforting, nor could the incessant scurrying in the walls be taken for one of Nature's lullabies. Portia lay awake for a long time, wishing her companion's prodigious snoring would drown out the scramble of mice. "First thing tomorrow," she said to the blissfully slumbering Ellie, "we'll find ourselves a cat."

Her stomach rumbled and Portia wrapped her arms around herself to quiet it. The cold collation Mrs. McFerran had produced left as much to be desired as the fire that smoked and sputtered in the grate. The bread was brown and quite stale, the meat tough, and the cheese moldy. Portia had cut the green parts off the cheese, eaten as much of the meat as she could before her jaw began to ache, and foregone the bread entirely. It was a small enough meal to begin with, made smaller by removal of the inedible parts, and miniscule when shared. However, it was clear Ellie would get no better than the lady of the house, assuming she could command any food whatever. Portia wouldn't think of allowing her maid to go hungry, despite Ellie's protestation, with accompanying pat to her ample midsection, that she could more easily withstand the hardship.

Portia found herself smiling. Mrs. McFerran had certainly made her displeasure known. The woman was going to be a formidable adversary.

Much to her surprise, Portia actually managed to sleep, snuggled down in her flannel dressing gown—as soft as it was old and worn to bed for the warmth—with the counterpane drawn up around her ears. She woke, chilled and disoriented, in the darkest part of the night, her heart pounding the breath out of her before she even knew why she was awake.

"My lady?" Ellie said from very close, her voice high-pitched and tremulous.

"What is it?" Portia whispered.

The noise came from somewhere in the Hall. A scraping sound, as of something heavy being dragged. A thump. A series of bangs with no perceptible pattern, sounding first close, then far, then seeming to come from within the very bedchamber. A sudden crash of thunder startled a scream out of Ellie. For a moment, all was silent. Then the dragging noise began again.

"The McFerrans," Portia said. "It must be."

"And what would they be doing, so late at night? It's the ghost, I'll be bound."

"Where did you hear tell of a ghost?"

"John Coachman told me while he was gettin' in your trunks, and he had it from a man at the Duck and Drake who's lived in these parts all his life. Oh, my lady, we shouldn't have come. The Hall's a terrible place, it is. A terrible place."

Portia tried unsuccessfully to pry Ellie's hands off her arm. "Ellie Brown, I never took you for such a widgeon. It's the McFerrans, or a shutter come loose in the wind. Now release me."

The maid did as she was told for a moment, but grabbed hold all the tighter when Portia threw back the counterpane. "My lady! Where are you going?"

"To see what's causing that infernal racket." Portia freed herself with some difficulty and slid out of bed. She walked barefoot across the cold floor, morbidly afraid of stepping on something furry. Their tiny fire flickered occasionally, otherwise incapable of providing either warmth or light, and Portia was grateful for the sparse furnishings as she picked her way blindly across the floor. She could hear Ellie's rapid breathing from the bed, and found she had to hold her breath to prevent herself matching it. When her hand brushed the door she started back involuntarily.

Irritated at herself, Portia found the handle again, turned it silently, and eased the door open, the hinges protesting with a high whine. The noise outside ceased, and Portia stood frozen, her breath caught in her throat, until the dragging noise started up again, sounding at a distance now.

Portia took a firmer grip on the knob and peered cautiously around the door. The corridor was not nearly so dark as the bedchamber. A pale, thin light came from somewhere, turning India ink blackness into something a shade lighter but nearly as impenetrable. Portia could make out only the dimmest of shapes, amorphous and threatening. Keeping her feet safely in the bedchamber, her hand on the door, she dared to lean out and look down the corridor.

The pale light was faintly brighter in that direction, a diffuse glow that wavered like the reflection of water. The noise changed from dragging to a tapping that began and increased and echoed, rushing toward where she stood frozen in the doorway like the thunder of running feet. Something passed across the light, an enormous figure, misshapen and awful.

Portia pulled her head back and shoved the door shut. She turned the key in the lock with shaking fingers and ran shivering back to bed. Barely had she done so than something, a dragging, thumping, scraping *something* passed the door.

"A terrible place," Ellie whispered again, wrapping her arms tightly about her mistress. Portia pulled the counterpane up to her chin and lay staring at the door she could no longer see through the gloom, praying that nothing would try the handle.

Chapter Three

SOMETHING ran across her feet and Portia awoke with a scream.

She bolted upright and threw back the counterpane, sending the mouse flying. It hit the floor and vanished in a gray flash. Portia scrambled out of bed and bundled her dressing gown about her, her skin crawling. She wasn't inclined to be missish, but she dared even her brother not to feel out of sorts at being woken in such a manner. She took a deep breath to calm her nerves, wrinkled her nose at the odor of mold, and pushed aside the curtains to look out on the day.

The sky was a dismal gray that infected everything in sight, and it was still raining through a fog that slunk along the ground, muffling things near in drifting white ribbons and blotting out things farther away entirely. Portia sighed and turned to survey the room. It was no less dismal inside than out, and nearly as cold. In a proper house, a servant would have been in by now to make up the fire. Clearly the McFerrans couldn't be counted upon for such things. Portia wrapped her arms about herself with a shiver and went into the tiny dressing room.

"And what would you be about, my lady?" Ellie asked from the doorway some ten minutes later, startling Portia far more than she ought.

"Finding something to wear."

"And making a mess of my packing while you're at it, I'll be bound." Ellie took the warm stuff gown from Portia and shooed her out of the dressing room. A plate and steaming cup sat on the tiny dressing table, the odor of tea and toast floating out over the harsh smell of cold ashes and decades-old miasma of neglect. "You sit there and break your fast—though how you can keep body and soul together on so little is beyond me—and leave the clothing to me."

Portia seated herself at the dressing table, tucking her dressing gown as closely about her as she could, picked up the cup, and sipped her blissfully hot tea before starting on the toast. "Thank you, Ellie," she said when the maid emerged from the dressing room a few minutes later. "You're a wonder."

"What's a wonder is that that woman ever had the running of the Hall when there *were* a lord in it." Ellie frowned about the room and finally laid Portia's gown and underthings on the bed with visible reluctance. "Stared at me like I'd a second head when I asked for tea and toast to break your fast. Took her so long, you'd have thought she had to bake the bread right then and run to India for the tea. Then she burnt the toast and looked daggers at me when I told her it wouldn't do."

Portia laughed. "It's probably the hour that's put her off. Early even for country folk." A habit she learned her first year at Rosewood, when there were never enough hours in the day to do what was needful to make the house comfortable. It would no doubt stand her in good stead now.

And wasn't that a facer, as her brother would have it? Years making Rosewood Close a comfortable home, and now the new Lady Ashburne would have the comfort of it, while the old Lady Ashburne got packed off to start again somewhere else. It was enough to.... No, Portia told herself, firming up her chin, crying never solved anything. At least here she was free of James and his wife. Free of their poorly concealed irritation that Roger's death should have brought them, in addition to the title and lands, a legion of debts and a widow to support. Free of the unfriendly curiosity that peered out from behind their looks. One could almost hear them asking themselves, *what possessed Roger to marry the chit in the first place? Must be something wrong with her to drive him to London and the arms of every bird of paradise that caught his fancy.*

"There's no call for her to act all high and mighty about it."

Portia shook off her black thoughts. There was no point dwelling on her situation. She was stuck here, with no relatives to depend on but her husband's family and her brother. James had already proven how little he cared to do for her by dropping her in this bumblebroth in the first place. And her brother was still at University. She knew Tony would do anything he could to help if he knew of her straits, but he didn't have any more money than she did. She must simply make the best of it. "Give it time, Ellie. After ten years, the McFerrans have no doubt grown rusty. Even the best gate squeaks if it hasn't been used for a while."

Ellie considered this as she helped Portia into her chemise and petticoats. "You're suggesting that I try a little oil."

"Something like that."

Ellie snorted. "I'd have to tip the butter boat for certain to get that dragon on my side."

"That's as may be." Portia smoothed down her skirts. The gown was neither elegant nor fashionable, but it was sturdy, warm, and comfortable, and a perfect dress for staying home in, as it had not escaped the dye pot when she went into mourning, nor taken the dye evenly. There were doubtless some situations in which it would be useful to look as if she were molting, but Portia couldn't bring any to mind. "We are no more likely to rid ourselves of her than she of us, so we'll have to learn to scrape along together."

"Yes, but does *she* know that?"

Portia let herself be steered to the dressing table, and waited until Ellie fell into a familiar rhythm with the brush before saying, "We must at least try. There's a tremendous amount of work to be done." Rosewood, when she had first come to it, had suffered Roger's neglect, but not yet forgotten what it was to be a gentleman's manor house. The Hall, from what little Portia'd seen of it, was another matter entirely.

"His lordship ought to be ashamed of himself, packing his brother's widow off to a crumbling, ghost-ridden—"

"Don't be a ninnyhammer," Portia told her as sternly as she could while still remembering the fear that had overtaken her the previous night.

"I was that scared when the ghost dragged itself past our door." Ellie's brushing became ferocious before she recollected herself and lightened up, running one hand down Portia's long brown hair in wordless apology.

"It was only the McFerrans. I'm certain of it." By the light of day, the horrible shade she'd glimpsed seemed a thing of air and darkness, the product of something no more terrifying than a man walking in front of a candle. "However, if you would prefer to seek better employment...."

"Are you turning me off?" Ellie twisted Portia's hair up, securing it in place with a few expertly placed pins.

"Just offering you something better than a roof over your head. I may be stuck here, but you don't have to be."

"If you're staying, so am I."

"Well then," Portia said, hiding her relief in a show of brisk efficiency, "we shall take on the Hall together, and the mice and dragons and ghosts had better watch out. Now. Did you break your fast? I thought not. Go down and eat. I'm afraid you'll have to shift for yourself, but better that than take Mrs. McFerran's cast-offs. Send her up to me. Our first task is to move rooms."

She did not wait for the housekeeper in her grudgingly bestowed bedchamber, but started down the hall, opening doors as she went. The drapes were all drawn and the dismal light swimming through the thunderclouds left a great deal to the imagination, though it was clear the chamber she'd slept in was far from the worst of the lot.

She had reached the landing and stood looking at the portrait of Giles Ashburne when Mrs. McFerran joined her, puffing audibly up the stairs until she caught sight of Portia, at which she slowed her pace. Portia did not turn from her contemplation of the painting. The man was, without doubt, glowering.

"He didn't like Lord Ashburne much, did he?"

"My lady?"

Portia turned. "The painter."

Mrs. McFerran's eyes flicked to the painting and away, her expression passing so quickly it was near impossible to read. Was that distaste? "I believe the portrait was considered handsomely done at the time."

"Why did you not take it down?"

"As my lady knows, we were attempting to do so when—"

"Before I came." Portia remained before the painting when Mrs. McFerran would have shepherded her downstairs. "You might have taken it down anytime. Why leave it there if you dislike it so?"

"Some might have objected." Mrs. McFerran hovered two steps down, as if she could draw Portia with her by will alone. Portia continued to study the portrait.

Who, she wondered, would have objected to its removal? The master of the house had himself ordered it taken down, if the McFerrans were to be believed. But why? Portia couldn't believe James would have bothered. That left only Roger, though why he should have cared what paintings hung in a manor he never intended to visit was beyond her. With an effort, she drew herself away from the mystery and turned to the housekeeper.

"I wish to inspect the Hall, Mrs. McFerran. We will start with the servants' quarters." Mrs. McFerran drew breath as if to argue, then started abruptly up the stairs.

They began at the top of the Hall and worked their way down, through servants' quarters, all except the McFerrans' draped in cobwebs, dust, and rodent droppings; the nursery and schoolrooms, where a window had broken some time ago, letting in the damp to turn many of the books green while the rest simply moldered away; and down again to the first floor and the family apartments. Mrs. McFerran lingered overlong in some rooms and tried to rush Portia through others, withal showing her displeasure in every action.

The rooms in the family wing were in slightly better condition, though no less dusty. A flurry of skittering attended the opening of many a door, though there were never any mice in sight when they went in. Portia looked everything over carefully; the eerie light she'd seen the previous night had come from either this wing or down in the hall itself. The explanation for her ghost lay somewhere around here.

They made their way to the end of the hall and back, stopping last at the two chambers that lay close upon the landing. The size, the richness of the appointments, and the dressing closet they shared proclaimed them the master's and mistress's private chambers.

The predominant color in the mistress's chamber was a watery blue, a dispirited shade not improved by the wavering light from outside, but the furniture was a golden oak that made the room feel brighter than it might. The carpet was moth-eaten and there were mice in the bed—there were doubtless mice in every unoccupied bed in the house. It was not her light and airy bedchamber from Rosewood Close, but Portia could picture herself there.

Besides, it appeared to be the soundest bedchamber in the house.

"This will do," she said, more to herself than the housekeeper. Then, to that woman, who was staring at her oddly, "You will please have Mr. McFerran shift my trunks."

"You can't," Mrs. McFerran protested, as shocked as if Portia proposed staying there with the master next door. She quickly collected herself. "This was Lady Ashburne's chamber."

"And it will be again." Portia reflected that there were a few too many Lady Ashburnes about. And definitely too many Lord Ashburnes.

"I meant Mr. Giles' beloved mother," Mrs. McFerran said repressively, adding "my lady" as an afterthought.

"You're not going to tell me this room's haunted too?"

She was hardly bowled over to hear Mrs. McFerran mutter darkly that she wouldn't be surprised. "Nevertheless," Portia said, "I will take this room."

She didn't wait for a response, but walked through the large shared dressing closet, which still contained a surprising amount of men's clothing, its half-tenanted state giving it an air of abandonment greater than that of the rest of the house, and into the master's bedroom. This was undoubtedly a man's room, done up in colors that looked black under their covering of dust, but were probably deep hues of blue and green and red. The furniture was large and solid, of a dark wood that shone even through the dust. The rug, like the others, was gritty and threadbare, the drapes little better. In stark contrast to the rest of the rooms she'd seen, the dust here had been disturbed. There was a confusing array of footprints where a rudimentary cleaning had obviously been attempted.

"We thought to make this room ready for you, my lady," Mrs. McFerran offered when Portia continued to survey the room, which she found strangely pleasing.

"And?"

"We stopped when it began to rain." She indicated a battered bucket near the window. It was half full of murky water, the carpet around it dark. The leak must be of recent vintage, for it hadn't yet colored the ceiling plaster. Portia tried to remember which room was directly overhead, but had seen so many she wasn't certain. It made no matter, the rain could easily be running down the outer wall and across the ceiling without showing itself upstairs at all.

Portia didn't ask why they'd attempted to make the master's bedroom habitable when the mistress's chamber would have been more suitable. First, because she had no doubt there was some fault in the mistress's chamber which the McFerrans knew or suspected and which Portia would discover only when the chimney started falling about her ears. And second, because just at that moment, a sharp noise startled the breath out of her.

It was repeated a moment later, and again, resolving itself into the measured tread of footsteps. Mrs. McFerran gasped, her hand flying to her throat. For all Portia suspected her of making up ghost stories to drive her new mistress away, there was no denying the housekeeper looked frightened. Someone was walking about upstairs.

The footsteps seemed to be making for the door, so Portia did as well, following them out the door and down the hall. There was no carpet runner in the upstairs hallway and his boots echoed off the bare floor and walls. Portia broke into a run and reached the stairs before he did. She stood staring at the upper landing as the footsteps approached, beating as hard upon her ears as her heart did upon her ribs, washing over and around her like the sea, until they were directly overhead. Still, she saw no one.

Then, so suddenly her heart missed a beat, they stopped.

Chapter Four

PORTIA stared at the upper landing, silence ringing in her ears. She counted out twenty beats of her heart without seeing or hearing anything from upstairs, then called for Ellie until her maid dashed into the hall below.

"Have you been in the kitchen all this time?" Portia called down.

"Yes, miss. My lady."

"Have you seen Mr. McFerran?"

"Sommat the matter?" that gentleman asked, coming into the hall behind Ellie.

"Where have you come from, Mr. McFerran?"

"Stables," he said readily enough and without any trace of the breathlessness he'd surely have evinced had he run down the back stairs and around the Hall to arrive blameless on the ground floor after walking about loudly in the upper stories. Even assuming he could have done all that in a few short moments and without making a sound.

Portia turned to Mrs. McFerran, who stood watching her with a faint quirk to her thin lips. She scarcely seemed the same woman who had, only a moments before, looked so terrified of the noises overhead. "Who else is in the Hall?"

"No one, my lady." The quirk turned to a narrow smile. "Excepting the ghost."

Refusing to dignify that with a response, Portia called down to the other two to go on about their business, which Ellie did with obvious reluctance, McFerran without even a shrug.

Then Portia climbed the stairs to the upper landing. He, whoever he was, had had plenty of time to sneak off, though how he could have managed it without making even so much noise as a mouse, Portia didn't

26

know. But of one thing she was certain, he could not have come down the hall without leaving tracks.

There were no footprints in the dust that lay thick on the floor of the hall but Mrs. McFerran's and her own.

* * *

Portia rejoined Mrs. McFerran on the landing, the older woman wisely keeping her peace. Giles Ashburne's portrait smirked at her from over the housekeeper's shoulder, and Portia turned away before Mrs. McFerran could interpret the direction of her gaze as proof she believed this talk of ghosts.

"Now then, Mrs. McFerran, for the ground floor."

Portia barely saw the parlor, the sitting room, the conservatory full of the husks of dead plants and the smell of rot, and only noticed the billiard room insomuch as it struck her that her brother would have wept at the condition of the table. The breakfast room made no impression whatsoever, assuming the housekeeper even showed it to her, and the dining room was memorable only for the layer of dust and cobweb that lay so thickly on the table she at first thought it a tablecloth.

She did notice the library, for Mrs. McFerran at first walked past the door, and only returned to it when Portia did not follow. For a moment, it appeared the housekeeper had mislaid her key, but finally the door opened. Portia walked into the large room like a woman in a dream. Papa hadn't held with society's ideal of feather-headed ladies; until illness took him from them, he'd seen to it that Portia had as good an education as her brother. Tony had surpassed her now, having gone off to University while Portia rusticated at Rosewood Close, but her love of books had never left her.

The cases ran from floor to ceiling, and the ceilings—like all of those on the ground floor, though this was the first Portia had made particular note of it—were very high indeed. The books ran wall to wall to wall with a gap barely wide enough for the door and breaks for two tall, narrow windows. Portia had not been aware of the rain ending, but as she stood staring, the sun threw itself through the windows to light up the bookcases in a blaze of glory. Whole shelves of books had matching leather bindings—the kind rich gentlemen bought by the foot to fill out their libraries and left eternally unopened, the pages uncut—but the rest, oh the rest, were a miscellany of bindings, a riot of colors. Books bought for the pleasure of it, for reading rather than looking at. Books to be avidly devoured, consumed with pleasure and a touch of desperation that, some day, all would be read.

"Oh my." Portia's voice was little more than a whisper, and that hard enough to squeeze through a throat tight with something other than breathing dust. How far from expecting this she'd been. Rosewood had a small bookroom, a couple hundred books of various stamps, of which James Ashburne had permitted Portia to take a small handful. The decision of which to take could not have been harder if a mother had been told to pick which of her children to keep. Had Portia but known what she was coming to....

"My lady?"

Portia took quick halting steps to the nearest case, moving stiffly on legs that had forgotten how to obey her. She stroked the rich leather binding of a folio of William Blake, his beautiful engravings rising into her mind. Nearby was a rackety copy of Burns, the spine much abused. And there Coleridge.

"My lady, we'd best be getting on."

And down away to her left, two whole shelves of Shakespeare, pray heaven the mice hadn't gotten to them!

"There's the kitchen and stillroom yet."

Portia made herself step back, swallowing the rebuke that rose to her lips. The books had waited ten years; surely she could school herself to patience a little longer. There were, sad to say, greater calls on her time.

"Yes, let us get on." But she couldn't stop herself looking back wistfully at the door Mrs. McFerran had locked behind them.

Ellie jumped up from a plate covered with breadcrumbs when they entered the kitchen, which was neat, clean, and as sound as they come. The McFerrans clearly knew where their priorities lay. Mrs. McFerran allowed Portia a quick look into the well-stocked root cellar and the scullery, pointed out the sadly abandoned stillroom, then stood with her hands clasped primly before her and fixed Portia with a gimlet eye.

"And that door?"

"That's the butler's pantry, my lady."

"Open it."

Her lips pressed into a thin line, Mrs. McFerran found the proper key and fit it to the lock. She swung the door open on a room black as pitch.

"Get me a candle, would you Ellie?"

When the maid returned with a flickering tallow candle, Portia stepped into the cramped, windowless pantry. Flames reflected from a million pale eyes, wavering across the family silver that had languished ten years without the touch of a butler's busy polishing cloth. Hundreds of pounds' worth of plate, and Roger had left it to tarnish in the Hall. He must really have hated the place, else this wealth of silver would have been unearthed and sold long ago.

"If need be," Portia murmured to herself, and perhaps Ellie, "we can always pawn the silver." What James didn't know wouldn't hurt him. He'd spout the silver himself, if he but knew it was there.

The housekeeper drew an angry breath, nearly choked on it, and locked up the butler's pantry with a sharp twist of the key.

"I'll need her late ladyship's keys," Portia said, and the tight line of the housekeeper's lips whitened further. "Or his lordship's. Whichever you can lay your hands on." She would be a fool to leave herself at the mercy of a hostile housekeeper. Mrs. McFerran had everything locked up tighter than the Tower, and Portia would be dashed if she was going to meekly ask the housekeeper to open the library for her. Or anything else, for that matter. "Now, if you will, have Mr. McFerran shift my trunks, and one of you get a fire started under the wash tub. We're going to make this place livable again, starting with my bed chamber."

She'd never have spoken so to the housekeeper at Rosewood Close, but even at Rosewood there'd been underservants, scullery maids and footmen and a washerwoman who boiled all the laundry twice a month. Here, there were only the four of them, and they would all have to pitch in if they were to get anything accomplished.

They worked straight through the day with only the briefest of pauses to eat a simple nuncheon of bread and cheese (the bread slightly less stale than last night's, the cheese no less moldy). By the time they were done, the furniture had been shifted, the carpet turned, and the draperies, bedding, and cotton from the mattress boiled and laid out to dry in the sun with many a muttered imprecation against sudden rain showers. Mr. McFerran—whose entire vocabulary seemed to consist of "ar" and "yes'm"—had cleaned out the hearth and thrust a long-handled brush up the chimney, knocking loose large quantities of soot and the disintegrating remains of several bird's nests. The afternoon was well advanced when Portia wiped the last of the dust off the delicate dressing table and looked about her with satisfaction.

The room looked bare without its draperies, but the warmth of the sun falling through the windows was welcome. Though the carpet had clearly been turned previously, before the Hall fell on hard times, the underside was now in better shape than the top, being only a bit threadbare around the edges. And if the weather kept clear, there'd be clean, mouse-free bedding to retire to that night.

Ellie finished sweeping the hearth and propped her hands on her hips to survey the bedchamber. "Not a bad day's work, if I do say so myself."

"If you don't, I will." Portia laid down her dusting cloth and ran a finger over the elaborate inlay that scrolled across the top of the dressing table. "Lovely. Now to get you settled in. Have you a room picked out?"

"Aye; at the end of the hall near the stairs. Mrs. McFerran added the bedding into the washing pot after your own. And not best pleased to do it, either," she muttered in tones which made Portia glad she'd not seen the confrontation between her maid and the dragon. Mrs. McFerran was taller, but Ellie was twice as wide, and it was anyone's guess which of them was more stubborn.

"Let's go give it a good cleaning."

Ellie whisked a bit of stray soot into the hearth. "You've no need to worry your head about that, my lady. I'll see to it once you're settled in here. There's your trunks yet to be unpacked."

Portia sighed, knowing it would be futile to argue. Surely other women didn't have this much trouble with their ladies' maids. It was her own fault. She'd needed an ally far more than a properly deferential servant when her husband of less than a week packed her off to Rosewood Close. On her own head be it that she'd thereby lost all pretense of cowing her own maid. It was just as well. A cowed maid would have been a colorless companion.

While Ellie finished up in Portia's bed chamber, Portia set about clearing space in the dressing room. Giles Ashburne had clearly left in a hurry. Coats still hung in the wardrobe, their gay colors sadly moth-eaten. Shirts here, trousers there, all in dire need of pressing and streaked with dust. A hat occupied a high shelf, so covered in cobwebs it looked like gray felt. Portia shifted everything into one wardrobe and closed the door, sneezing at the dust and the smell of neglect.

A silver-backed brush lay abandoned in one corner. Portia picked it up and rubbed absently at the tarnish. What kind of man had used this? A murderer? Truly?

"Now you know there's little enough room in here for me and your trunks," Ellie said as she bustled in with a broom and dustmop.

"All right, I know where I'm not wanted."

Ellie set about unpacking Portia's gowns with a care better suited to more delicate materials. Portia watched her cluck over smudges and smooth out wrinkles. There was little enough to exclaim over when all was said and done. Most of Portia's wardrobe she'd brought into the marriage with her, and it was depressing to realize that the dresses had outlasted her husband. Even more lowering that Roger had been so often absent he'd seen no more than half her small collection of gowns.

Too many of Portia's dresses had suffered the dye bath when Roger died, for there was no money for widow's weeds. Nothing new there. There'd been no new dresses for years. However much James wanted to blame Portia for the state of the Ashburne finances, he had to admit that the money certainly hadn't gone for her clothes.

Portia went into the master's bedroom, still clutching the silver brush. Her feet balked for a moment at the doorway before she forced them onward. When she discovered she was holding her breath, listening for footsteps, she shook herself angrily. It was dark in the chamber, and she pushed open the drapes to let in the light. Here, too, was evidence of hasty packing, still visible where the McFerran's superficial and quickly interrupted cleaning had not reached: a scum of lather and whisker dried in the washbasin where a man had stood shaving, a snowy cravat abandoned on the floor by the dressing table, the top drawer of the heavy writing desk sitting open, paper poking out higgledy-piggledy. All stood as it had the day Giles Ashburne left, not even a servant come in to tidy up. Why bother, after all? The lord of the house had gone for good.

She wondered if Roger had been at Ashburne Hall when it happened. He'd never talked about it. Never mentioned the Hall at all except to wish it to perdition. One was hardly likely to make a talking point of one's cousin murdering his fiancée and fleeing to the Continent, of course, but Portia'd married into the family, for pity's sake. She deserved to know what happened.

Portia sighed. She'd deserved a lot of things. There was no point in falling into a brown study over it. She put the brush down on the writing desk and peered into the open drawer. His correspondence lay within, untouched and imbued with the warm odor of fine tobacco. Feeling suddenly like a trespasser, she slid the drawer gently shut and went to have a word with Mrs. McFerran about supper.

* * *

It was no cold collation this time, despite the hours the housekeeper had spent toiling over a hot wash tub. Portia had made it quite clear that would not suit.

Mrs. McFerran had responded in her own particular manner. The meat pie was a marvel of the cooking arts: overcooked on the inside with a crust so undercooked as to be soggy. There was little to no seasoning, the meat was tough as old shoe-leather and the vegetables limp, stringy, and unidentifiable. In short, supper was edible only to the extent that Portia was starving.

When Portia had swallowed all she could, she took up the candle by which she'd dined and went to the library.

It took her five minutes to find the proper key. Mrs. McFerran had handed the ring over when she laid supper before Portia, her face pinched with disapproval. She hadn't vouchsafed a single word, which Portia took to mean she could sort out the keys on her own. She made a note to find the one for the butler's pantry first thing in the morning, just to be certain she had it.

Using the tallow candle in its simple brass holder to light her way, Portia found a small volume of Byron's works and took it up to her new bedchamber. It wasn't until she'd sent Ellie to bed and was settled in with clean sunlight-scented linen pulled up close about her, warmed and lighted by a fire that did not smoke overmuch, that she realized the book smelled impenetrably of tobacco. She hadn't noticed before, as the candle reeked rather of the barnyard.

Portia stared for the longest time at the door leading through to the master's bedroom. "What kind of man were you, Giles Ashburne?"

Chapter Five

SHE woke from blissfully uninterrupted sleep when Ellie drew open the drapes to let in a beam of buttery sunshine. They wouldn't have to worry about leaks today.

It wasn't until Portia was sitting up in bed drinking her morning tea, the coverlet pulled up to ward off the chill, that she remembered what was so strange about a sound night's sleep.

"Did you sleep well, Ellie?"

"Yes, my lady." Ellie flashed her a quick smile and went on into the dressing room, her voice floating back. "A quiet night."

Indeed, Portia thought as she reached for a piece of toast. No midnight noises. No footsteps. No ghost.

The toast was burnt on the underside and put on the plate just so, so Ellie wouldn't notice. Portia ate it anyway, though the housekeeper had somehow managed to leave the unburnt side distastefully soggy. If she left any, Ellie would know something was wrong and Portia didn't need anyone fighting her battles for her. She sipped her tea, which Ellie had clearly made herself, as it was hot and sweetened to perfection. Once a poor substitute for the morning chocolate she'd never done without before her marriage, tea had become such an integral part of breaking her fast that Portia wondered if she'd take to chocolate again if ever she had it. She gave an unladylike snort. Little chance of finding out.

She finished the last of her tea and set the tray aside. Her slippers were precisely where her questing toes expected to find them. Shivering, she pulled on the wrapper Ellie had left across the foot of the bed and went to look out the window onto the glistening day.

It had rained again during the night and the trees shimmered with it. Fog rose tentatively from the ground under the early morning sun, but it would soon burn off. It bade fair to be a lovely day.

Portia sat quietly at the dressing table while Ellie brushed her hair vigorously enough to make her eyes start from her head. Finally, Ellie set the brush aside. "What today?"

"The sprigged muslin, I think."

"Yes, my lady." Ellie went into the dressing room to retrieve what used to be Portia's favorite walking dress. It had been green, once, but had come from the dye pot a deep gray. Though it was no more fashionable than any of her dresses and, indeed, somewhat more worn than most, at least it wasn't black. One inevitable conclusion Portia'd reached in the past year was that she didn't like black any better than it suited her. It rankled that she'd been forced to sacrifice half her gowns to the memory of a man who hadn't given her a single thought after the vicar pronounced them man and wife.

Why hadn't he wanted her? He'd talked a great deal of love before their marriage and shown little enough of it after. And yet, if not for love, why had he wanted to marry her? Portia may have been the granddaughter of a duke, but Roger gained neither money nor prestige by taking her to wife. If a man didn't marry for money or a title, why did he marry, except for love or lust? Even were it that last and most low of reasons—and Portia had no illusions about that; she was no ravishing beauty to drive a man wild—Roger had certainly slaked his desires quickly, coming to her bed but a handful of times over their marriage. Had she been so lacking, so inept at pleasing her husband that he lost interest in the marriage bed as soon as he attained it? Portia shook herself from such lowering and unproductive thoughts, eyes skimming along the elaborate scrollwork of the dressing table for a distraction. Her gaze lit on a silver-backed hairbrush that had certainly not been there when she went to bed. Portia's old serviceable wooden brush lay where Ellie'd left it, looking poor and disreputable next to the elegant silver brush. Portia picked it up and turned it in her hands, inspecting the tarnished back.

"Where did this come from?" she asked when Ellie returned, the sprigged muslin draped over her arm.

"My lady?"

"This silver brush, where did it come from?" She knew, of course; she'd carried it from the dressing room into the master's bedroom only yesterday and left it on his writing desk. The mystery was how it came to be on her dressing table. "I may be poor, Ellie, but not so poor as to need to—"

"Begging your pardon, my lady," Ellie said stiffly, "but it was there when I came in to wake your ladyship. I wouldn't have—"

"No." Portia sighed. "No, of course you wouldn't. I don't know why I suggested it." Except, of course, that the idea had occurred to Portia herself: how ridiculous it was for this beautiful brush to sit in the gloomy master bedroom, waiting for a man who would never return, while Ellie used a creaking wooden brush on her mistress's hair.

Ellie gasped, her eyes round as saucers. "My lady! The ghost—"

"There is no ghost." Portia absently rubbed at the tarnish with her thumb in slow counterpoint to her racing thoughts.

"But—"

"The door wasn't locked. Neither the one to the master's chamber nor my own. All the McFerrans need do was sneak it out of there and in here while I slept."

"But why?"

"Mrs. McFerran wants to run this house as she has for ten years now, without interference. Obviously, she intends to drive me off." Portia laid the brush gently on the dressing table. "She won't succeed."

"What are you going to do, my lady?"

"Nothing." Portia shrugged her wrapper off into Ellie's hands. "We'll put the brush back where it belongs—"

"In the master's chamber? Oh, my lady, I don't know if I—"

"*I'll* put it back," Portia said, trying not to be irritated at Ellie's foolishness. The maid couldn't help being easily taken in by such things, her head having been thoroughly filled with ghosts and goblins and wee beasties when she was a child. "She's expecting a reaction, and I'll be demmed if I give her one."

"My lady!" Ellie exclaimed, shocked.

Portia sighed.

* * *

Twenty minutes later, Portia went through the dressing room into the master's bed chamber. She could feel Ellie's eyes on her back, could even imagine how wide and round they must be as the maid watched her nervously from the dressing room door.

Portia had forgotten to draw the drapes the previous day and sunlight spilled into the room. It made all the difference in the gloomy chamber. She could see it in her mind's eye—cobwebs and dust banished, furniture polished, a fire roaring in the hearth: a man's retreat from the world.

Portia put the brush on the shaving stand this time. She twitched her skirts aside as she slipped past the bucket by the window, glancing into it to find it no fuller than the day before, the carpet around it dry. She looked up, but still couldn't make out where the water had come from. Unfortunate. It was a lovely room, a place she felt at home, for all its masculine flavor.

Portia locked the hall door and the door from the master's chamber to the dressing room. She couldn't lock the door to her own chamber or Ellie would be unable to carry out her duties, but at least no more of Giles Ashburne's belongings should go wandering.

"Now," she said to herself as she started down the hallway, leaving Ellie to finish tidying up, "to beard the dragon."

Mrs. McFerran was ensconced in the little room off the kitchen that would have been the terror of the undermaids had the Hall run to them. The housekeeper's sitting room was, like the kitchen, largely untouched by the general decay of the Hall.

"Good morning, Mrs. McFerran, no need for you to rise," Portia said pleasantly, though the housekeeper's only response to her entrance was to lower her darning to her lap. "This will take only a minute. My," she went on, looking around the snug room as she settled into the chair opposite Mrs. McFerran's, "but you've done wonders in here. Quite cozy, isn't it?"

A flush sprang up on the housekeeper's sharp cheekbones and she clutched her sewing closer. "What can I do for you, my lady?"

"Why, I wished to go over the week's menus with you." Portia looked at the other woman with as much wide-eyed expectation as she could summon, catching Mrs. McFerran flat-footed, but not for long.

"Lord Ashburne left such matters to me."

"Lord Ashburne is not here." A gross understatement no matter *which* Lord Ashburne one was speaking of. "I will want to go over the menus with you each week. We cannot have," she added with pointed gentleness, "a repeat of last night's supper."

Mrs. McFerran took an audible breath.

Portia rose. "We all have our talents, I suppose, and not everyone can cook. Perhaps a cook might be found somewhere."

The housekeeper let out her breath with a hiss, her mouth working, though nothing came out. Once again, she recovered herself quickly. "If my lady feels the need, I'm certain one can be hired in the village," she said with such apparent calm that Portia knew she believed there to be no hope of success. Either there were no suitable cooks in these parts or, more likely, the housekeeper knew Portia couldn't come up with wages for another servant.

"Excellent. I'm certain the means for hiring a suitable cook will present itself."

When Mrs. McFerran's sole response was a superior-looking smile, Portia couldn't resist allowing her eyes to drift toward the wall the sitting room shared with the butler's pantry. Mrs. McFerran's whole body jerked, propelling her halfway to her feet, her mending sliding off her lap. She changed direction just as suddenly, plumping back down in her chair and bundling it into a tight ball against her spare frame, but not before Portia saw that it was a man's coat. Though no expert on men's clothing, Portia could clearly see it wasn't Mr. McFerran's; it was far too large to fit his bent shoulders and the fabric too good besides. How little did James pay the McFerrans that she must take in mending? A hot rush of pity and humiliation overtook Portia. It was insupportable that Roger should have thrown tens of thousands of pounds to his horses, drinking, and mistresses while the Hall and its caretakers fell to wrack and ruin.

She remembered at the last minute that she had to set herself above Mrs. McFerran or live forever pinned under the housekeeper's thumb, and swallowed back the conciliatory words that hovered on her tongue. "Oh, and I shall want to look at the household accounts. One can't make proper menus, after all, without knowing what's in the pantry."

* * *

"Blast and damn!"

Ellie jumped, squeezing one of Portia's gowns to her bosom. "My lady!" she exclaimed when she saw Portia. "I was that scared!"

Indeed she must have been, not to scold Portia for absolutely scandalous language. Portia plumped herself down on the side of the bed with a sigh. "Roger made an absolute mess of things here."

"Nothing new about that, is there?" Ellie spread out the gown she'd been clutching and clucked. "Look what you've done, making me crush your gown. Now it'll need ironing."

"Like as not, everything in my trunks needs ironing." Portia picked at a mouse-hole in the counterpane. "Not that it would matter if I was a mass of wrinkles."

"Of course it would matter," Ellie said stoutly. "There's some kind of society even in this dismal place, I'll be bound. Although I don't see how your ladyship can be visiting just yet, what with the parlor unfit for man nor beast." To visit one's neighbors implied that one's own house was open to visitors. Which Portia couldn't see happening for quite some time. She might as well take up holy orders and become a nun.

"The parlor's the least of our worries. What we really need is a cook."

"Aye. You can't feed Quality burnt bread and moldy cheese." Ellie picked the dress up and scowled at it. "Or entertain them in wrinkled gowns."

Portia gave up. There was no point in expecting sense from Ellie when she was fussing about Portia's gowns. Portia ought to be used to it by now; Ellie'd been fussing about her wardrobe the better part of five years. Were the world a fair place, Ellie Brown would have found herself in service to a woman with an endless and ever-changing wardrobe, instead of a confirmed country mouse with superb lineage and no prospects whatsoever. Portia stood and shook her skirts into place. "Well, there's nothing for it. I'll have to write Mr. Burnsides."

Ellie so far forgot herself as to drop the dress. "My lady, you can't!"

"I see very little alternative."

"But, my lady! To ask your solicitor for funds is, is—"

"Is?" Portia prompted, reaching for her traveling desk, which Ellie'd aligned neatly with the back corner of the dressing table. "Blast and damn," she said again, quietly this time, when she found it devoid of even a scrap of writing paper. There were her brother's letters and the solicitor's, but she could hardly use the back of one of those. James had packed her off so quickly she'd forgotten to replace her stationary or refill the inkwell. She closed the traveling desk and began searching the dressing table without much hope. She wasn't surprised to find it empty except for her meager complement of toiletries.

"It's playing right into his hands, that it is!"

"Whose hands?" Portia asked absently. Lord Ashburne must have engaged in correspondence from his country house on at least a few occasions. If not from the library, which was completely given over to books, then where?

Ellie stamped her foot. "His high and mighty lordship, James Ashburne."

Of course, how stupid of her; the desk in his bed chamber. "Do you think it would suit his purposes any less well if we were to starve?" Actually, it might, if only because Society would frown upon his treatment of his sister-in-law if they came to hear of it. But he would hardly mourn the return of her jointure, such as it was. "No, Ellie, we must look after ourselves, and if that means I must petition Mr. Burnside for release of funds, then so be it."

Ellie moaned and wrung her hands as she followed Portia into the master's bedchamber. Portia seated herself at the heavy writing desk, tugged the chair up close, for the desk was made for a much taller person, and began opening drawers. She found paper in the first she tried and an inkwell and pen in the second. A mouse ran across her hand when she reached for the ink and Ellie's scream scared her nearly as badly as the pinprick of claws.

Portia drew in a careful breath and suggested that Ellie had other matters to attend to. She was forced to be unusually firm when the maid proved stubborn, and it was only with some difficulty that Portia managed to shoo her off.

When she was gone, Portia braced her elbows on the desk and said into her cupped and still shaking hands, "I have *got* to get a cat."

She took a steadying breath, looked the drawer over carefully, and retrieved the inkwell and pen without further incident. The quill had seen much use, but it wasn't so inclined to sputter that she couldn't write clear copy. Portia was sadly accustomed to writing such letters, and the words came easily enough. She remembered to include her new direction, as James was certain to take advantage of any monies arriving on his doorstep whether or not they were his to appropriate, made liberal use of the blotting paper, and found an unused wafer in the desk to seal the letter. Mr. Burnside would not be surprised to receive such a missive from her—he might not even be surprised at her change of address—and he was in the habit of responding quickly, thank heavens. Thank heavens, too, that it was the recipient who paid the postage, for she had only the smallest of sums left in her reticule.

Portia recorked the inkwell and found a stained rag to wipe the pen on. She neatly replaced both pen and ink, and reached for the blotting paper. The mirror-image blottings of other writing than her own caught her eye and she turned the paper to look more closely, warm memories of idle afternoons rising in her mind. Hiding in her grandfather's library with her brother after their parents' death, trying desperately to keep Tony out of the trouble that dangled at his coat tails wherever he went, she'd made a game of reading the old duke's blotting paper, trying to make sense of reversed and fragmented words and phrases, most of them entirely too dry to be of much interest aside from the challenge of puzzling them out.

Giles Ashburne's handwriting, for she supposed it could only be his, was distinct and spiky, only touches of the round Copperplate hand his tutor had no doubt tried to beat into him still evident. A phrase here clearly pertained to estate business, one there addressed some crony who owed him money, and this one.... She turned the blotting paper around twice, looking at it from every angle without success, and finally accepted that if she was going to snoop into a dead man's affairs, she might as well admit it and read his letters.

His business correspondence was filed away neatly in a drawer on the left, copies without salutation or signature and blotted originals kept for his own records. She scanned through them, discovering from the dates and the sheer volume of correspondence that Giles Ashburne had, much to her surprise, made Ashburne Hall his principle seat. He'd sent off frequent directions regarding Rosewood Close and the third Ashburne estate, both entrusted to the hands of an estate agent, but apparently spent little time at either estate. If there was a house in London, it received no mention whatever. It was the Hall that formed the center of his existence and the heart of his correspondence.

The letters to his estate agent showed undisguised respect for the man's opinion, as often asking the man's advice as issuing orders. Ashburne was clearly no novice himself, the plans laid out in his letters both comprehensive and intelligent. Portia had learned how an informed and interested lord ran his estates from her grandfather, a great deal about how not to manage one's interests from Roger, and had spent the better part of the last five years struggling to bring Rosewood Close up to snuff. She recognized in Giles Ashburne's correspondence a man devoted to his home and tenants, full of brilliant plans for its future. How little the Ashburne Hall of today resembled the home of his past, less yet his vision of its future.

"Oh my Lord Ashburne," Portia murmured, "if you only knew the hands into which you tumbled your estates." Perhaps he had not cared, so full of murderous rage he could not look beyond his actions to their consequences.

She straightened the edges of the stack and put it back where she found it, then opened the drawer that had been ajar the first time she entered the room. Here were letters of a different stamp, the hand rushed and inelegant, words crossed out, rewritten, and crossed out again, whole paragraphs lined through so violently she wondered if the letters were ever recopied and sent. A man struggled on these pages, trapped in an awkwardness of love utterly alien to Portia. She'd neither experienced it herself, nor had it offered her. Certainly, Roger had never been less than polished in his pursuit, nor more than perfunctory after their marriage. To love so deeply, to *be loved* with such frenzy....

Portia realized suddenly that her hands were shaking. She shoved the letters back into the drawer and closed it with a bang, in such a pelter to escape her confusion she nearly forgot to take her own letter with her.

"I'm going to the village." She took the pelisse Ellie had just finished folding and tugged it on.

"One moment, my lady, while I get my bonnet."

"I have no need of a chaperone."

"But—"

"I'm a widow of mature years, Ellie—"

"Aye, all of five and twenty and halfway to your grave."

"—and I can certainly get myself to the village and back. If you've nothing to do, you may begin cleaning the morning room."

She reached the front door before realizing she didn't know *how* she was going to get to the village. With a curse—one of Roger's favorites, which would have driven Ellie into spasms—Portia stalked across the great hall and out through the kitchen to the stables behind the Hall.

"Mr. McFerran," she called when she reached the ramshackle building.

Receiving no response, Portia ventured inside. Dust motes danced in the thick shafts of sunlight that fell unimpeded through the roof, and she was assailed by the odor of stale hay and horse dung. No gentle wickers greeted her entrance, the smell apparently the only thing of an equine nature the stables contained.

At one end of the empty stalls, a carriage had pride of place, its once-elegant body sagging on the frame. Portia brushed its dusty side, paint flaking off under her fingers. How low it had been brought. Even lower than Portia herself, for she still served some purpose, though sometimes she wondered if it was any greater than simply making her way from one day to the next. Even should the carriage's broken wheels be mended, however, there was no purpose it could now serve without even a pony to pull it.

"Yes, m'lady?" Mr. McFerran said from behind Portia.

She turned, her heart pounding, to see him standing in the doorway, and smiled despite herself at sight of the man, as ramshackle as the stables. What position might he have held at the Hall when it and he were young? "I'm going to the village, Mr. McFerran. Is there a trap or dog cart?" she asked in a spirit of unfounded optimism, blinking as she emerged into the sunlight.

"Sorry, m'lady." He belatedly remembered to sweep off his cap, sending his thin hair dancing in the light breeze. "The Hall don't run to such conveniences. Ain't done for nigh on four years."

"Surely you haven't been living here without any means of transportation."

"Aye, since Maisie—that were the mule, m'lady—died. The tenants," he added in his cracked voice, "they bring the little whatnots nec'ssry to life, and that's all we've need of."

Portia bit back a demand to know how she was supposed to take care of the necessities of *her* life without a single concession from James, the McFerrans or Fate itself, and instead asked how far it was to the village.

McFerran pulled on his cap, cocked his head to one side, and scratched a jaw blue with stubble. "Seven miles by the road, I'll be bound."

Portia's heart sank. "Seven miles?"

He glanced at the house, then, his face softening, said, "Be 'bout four if you go through the fields," with a confiding air.

"Thank you, Mr. McFerran." Filled with a feeling of genuine warmth for the fellow, Portia patted his bony shoulder. He wheezed dreadfully, snatching his cap off, and Portia thought that if his skin had not been tanned to leather, he'd have blushed.

* * *

Whatever McFerran said to her, his head falling into the habitual bob that reminded Giles of nothing so much as an old horse heading for the barn, caused her to look up at the house. Giles stepped back from the window, forgetting she couldn't see him from where she stood. He moved forward again in time to see her set out determinedly for the home wood, the sun striking sparks from her hair where it peeped out from under her bonnet.

Damned interfering female.

He swung around to the cool darkness of his bedchamber. Sticking her hands and her inquisitive nose into all that was his, the unprincipled baggage. His house, his room, his servants, and *by God*, his letters!

Two long strides took him to the desk. He yanked open the drawer that held his personal correspondence and pulled it all out, folding the pages together without looking at them. He had no desire to see his own familiar hand, much less read a single word. He knew what a cake he'd made of himself, unexpectedly in love with a slip of a girl who'd no idea she'd captured his heart, nor any idea what to do with the paltry thing. He thanked God he'd never been able to bring himself to send Amelia more than conventional fripperies and proper notes of affection. He was grateful he'd never opened his true heart to her faithless love, and yet some part of his mind asked—had asked for ten years now—if she'd have run to another man's arms had she known how he truly felt, beyond the conventional forms of courtship. Perhaps, had he bared his heart to her, she'd yet live.

Giles shoved the papers into his coat pocket and slammed the drawer. There was a fire in his unwanted guest's bedchamber; he could smell the smoke.

The maid had taken herself off, and he passed easily through the dressing room into the bedchamber that had once been his mother's and would have been his wife's. She had done good work here, he admitted grudgingly and with no little surprise. How different she was from the ladies he'd once known. Not only would they have fled the Hall at the first hint of its true state, but not one of them would have lifted a hand to straighten so much as a crooked picture, let alone work from dawn to dusk alongside the servants. The bed chamber had been returned to the cheerful, airy sweetness he remembered as a child, down even to the sharp clean scent of lavender. He followed his nose to the source of the scent and found that either she or her maid had spilled over a bottle of it on the dressing table and not noticed, or not cared. He set it upright and wiped up the spilled lavender oil with his handkerchief. Then he crouched by the hearth and fed every single misbegotten letter to the small, ravenous fire.

He knelt there a long time after the last scrap of paper curled and blackened and fell to ash, warming himself over the tiny flame. He was always so cold. He ought never have returned.

He ought never have left in the first place. At the time, with Amelia dead and the countryside in an uproar—with her guardian, the Duke of Ransley, his one-time friend, breathing fire and calling for his blood—there seemed no other choice. Ransley was powerful and respected, Giles a mere viscount, with few friends and only money to recommend him. The House of Lords did not often put one of their own on trial, but if Ransley had asked, they would have. If Ransley had demanded vengeance for his ward's death, they'd have given it. Giles had no illusions as to the outcome of such a trial. He would be convicted, and that conviction taint his blood and that of his heirs. The title and lands would be forfeit to the crown. It was too bitter a pill to swallow. He could have borne his own execution—might even have welcomed it, so deeply had his heart sunk upon Amelia's death—but he could not allow the House of Lords to take everything. He held his title and lands in trust, handed down from his father and his father's father, safeguarded for his son and his son's son. To protect it, Giles had met death with open arms.

He couldn't bear to lose the Hall.

And yet, for all his sacrifices, he'd lost it anyway.

Giles closed his eyes, held his hands out to the warmth, and tried to lose himself in memories of the Hall as it was. Tried not to notice the odor of mildew, the water that dripped fitfully somewhere, the faint sounds of movement that never quite stilled in the walls. It was easier here, where she'd been at work.

How could Roger have failed so utterly to protect the estate Giles left in his trust? Roger had never been as fond of Ashburne Hall as Giles, but that was no excuse. He could remember every second of the night he left, his young cousin—no, not so very young, even then; as old as Giles had been when the title came to him—eyes shining as he took Giles' hand and swore to protect all that Giles was forced to flee. He couldn't have known how very soon word would come that Giles had perished at sea, how quickly the title, estates, and money would fall to him. And yet he had pledged to protect all that belonged to the Ashburnes with what little he owned and everything he was.

He had failed miserably, even after he had all the money and power of the title behind him.

Giles opened his eyes and stood. The past was past. It could not be altered, only regretted. The present, though, was mutable. Her arrival in a hired coach with a single maid and a small collection of dowdy dresses had been unforeseen. She had to be got rid of before she settled in more determinedly than she already had. Whatever it was she thought she was escaping—some perceived insult or plan of her brother-in-law's she found unpleasing—was nothing to what Giles had in store for her.

She'd been stubborn so far, but Giles was more stubborn still. Portia Ashburne would be out of his house before the rest of her baggage could arrive.

Chapter Six

PORTIA was used to walking. Rosewood Close ran to slightly better equipage than Ashburne Hall (not a difficult feat), but the cattle were so often in demand by the estate agent or the tenants that it was generally less hassle to go by foot. That was especially the case this last year, with James and his wife gathering everything of value about them like magpies.

The home wood was dark and overgrown—she wouldn't want to attempt passage at night—but soon gave way to areas thinned by tenants seeking firewood and then to neatly cultivated fields. The tenants' apparent disinclination to approach the Hall was mirrored in their reaction to Portia. She saw quite a few men out in their fields, but none so much as waved. The boy herding sheep gave her a wide margin, as did the little goose girl whose path crossed hers. Not even Rosewood's resident madwoman, eking out her living selling cures and salves to the tenants and generally thought to be a witch, was given such a wide berth. Obviously word had spread that Lady Ashburne was at the Hall. It was equally obvious the locals were not enamored of the idea.

Well, they would simply have to get used to her.

Thank heavens the innkeeper Foxkin appeared free of the local suspicion. He ushered her into the inn with the proud deference of the best butler, and installed her in the parlor with a genial comment about the cloudless skies—no need to worry about leaks on such a fine day. When he brought her tea and some of the most delicious-smelling scones she'd ever been offered, she didn't have the heart to send the food away, though the cost would eat up her last remaining funds. At least Mr. Burnsides could be relied upon to act quickly upon her request; she need not be penniless more than a sennight.

Like the taproom, the parlor was low-ceilinged and a bit dark, but there the similarities ended. Clearly, not only did Foxkin know from his years in service what the Quality desired in a private parlor, but business was profitable enough to allow him to provide it. Though not of the first stare, the furniture was good, of sturdy construction and lovingly polished. A small fire burned in the grate to keep off the chill, and the painting over the hearth was pleasing to the eye. Even the tapping of someone working on the slate roof was pleasant to hear, indicating as it did that the parlor would be habitable come the next rain.

When the innkeeper came to remove the tray, Portia asked him how much farther it was to the village and learned she was right on the outskirts; a few hundred yards by the road would find her in the village proper. In addition, Foxkin gave her to understand that, while it bore little resemblance to London or Bath or Brighton, the village did boast several eating and drinking establishments, a butcher's, a baker's, and a modiste who might not have been all the rage in London, but was much in demand locally.

"Is there somewhere I might post a letter?"

"Right here, my lady. The mail coach stops at the Duck and Drake for passengers and I can get a letter on it right enough."

She handed over her letter and watched him tuck it into his apron. "Thank you, Mr. Foxkin. Would you have a free moment?"

"Of course, my lady." He settled more solidly on his feet, giving the appearance of being rooted until the Last Trumpet. She wished she could ask him to sit, but it wasn't done, and while she wouldn't have minded, she had the impression he would.

"Can you tell me about the area?" It would take her ages to get a feel for it herself if she were limited to walking. If she set out in the wrong direction from the Hall, she might walk all day without leaving Ashburne's park.

"I'd be most happy to oblige, my lady. Can I freshen your tea?" He lifted the steaming pot to refill her cup and when he'd done, cleared his throat with a sound like grumbling thunder. "There's Tynesfield, the Duke of Ransley's estate, that marches with Ashburne Hall on the east. He's a powerful man is the duke, and known for his fairness. Folk hereabouts take their disputes to him, if it's not a matter for the law. He's got a ward you might encounter." The innkeeper cleared his throat again, a smile twitching at his lips. "Lady Clarissa Seabrooke, she is, and a right handful too."

"Sister to the lady who—?"

"No, my lady," he said, looking shocked.

"I do have ears, Mr. Foxkin. I could hardly remain ignorant of the tragedy at Ashburne Hall." Especially when her own housekeeper was quick to acquaint her with the tale, and with such relish that Portia could only assume the woman had little liking for her late master.

"Yes, my lady." His hand slid the length of his apron, large fingers alternately pleating and smoothing the corner. "Terrible, it was."

"I have no doubt." Portia sipped tea and gently turned the conversation. "And to the west of the Hall?"

"T'other side lies Lord Courtland's estate."

"Courtland?" Portia frowned. The name was vaguely familiar. Something to do with Roger.

"Yes, my lady, Lord Simon Courtland."

"Ah yes." Portia had never met Courtland—she'd been introduced to few of Roger's set before they wed and none after she found herself packed off to Rosewood Close—but his name was ever on Roger's lips on those occasions he deigned to visit her. "He and my husband were friends of long standing, I believe."

"Yes, my lady, though Lord Courtland was no more often at home than Mr. Roger Ashburne was at the Hall."

"No doubt the same state of affairs persists." Lord Courtland was doubtless no less fond of Town now than when he had cavorted about it in company with Roger.

Foxkin's lips twitched. "I've a mind that's true, my lady." He did not need to say that Courtland was only at his country home when he had reason not to be in Town, which was to say, when the money ran out and the duns got too importunate.

There were few other families of note in the area, and Foxkin quickly gave her to know their names and titles, whose sons were at University, whose daughters were due to come out, which were expected to make brilliant matches, which were despaired of. There was nowhere like a taproom for gossip and no one like an innkeeper for remembering it. Unless, of course, it was a society matron.

"Tell me, Mr. Foxkin," Portia said when she'd heard enough about the local gentry to last her a good while, especially as she could hardly mix with them socially unless she could contrive to appear less obviously without a feather to fly with.

"Yes, my lady?" He leaned solicitously towards her and Portia was again reminded of her grandfather's butler, though that personage had been far too conscious of his employer's worth to bend in any but the stiffest breeze.

"What did that fellow mean the other night, when he said that Giles Ashburne never leaves the Hall?" She'd been wondering about it ever since. At the time, it seemed completely nonsensical, if only because she'd never before heard of Giles Ashburne. Mrs. McFerran's talk of ghosts had made it strange in an entirely different way.

Foxkin took the corner of his apron in a tight grip. "I wouldn't pay George any mind, my lady. He was in his cups and making as much sense as men in that state generally do."

"But what do you think he meant?"

"Nothing to signify, my lady."

All right then, Portia would try another approach. "How long have folks hereabouts thought the Hall haunted?"

He released his apron and smoothed it with a convulsive movement of his hand. "Haunted, my lady?"

"Cut line, sir. I'm not so cloth-headed as that."

Foxkin looked, for a moment, as if he thought he ought to be shocked. Then a twinkle appeared in his eye. "No, my lady, I don't suppose you are. As for haunting, I don't rightly know. I suppose it was inevitable, given what happened."

"I suppose." Portia rose and he helped her into her pelisse. It occurred to her that the only version of events she had was from Mrs. McFerran, who was hardly the most unbiased of storytellers. Foxkin had said, when they first met, that he used to work at the Hall. "What do *you* think happened?"

"I try not to think about it, my lady." Foxkin guided her out of the Duck and Drake, every bit the polished servant. She forced herself not to inquire what position he'd had at the Hall. Ten years ago, Foxkin wouldn't have been old enough for the exalted responsibilities of a butler, and he was much too large for a footman. Most households preferred their footmen matched in height, if nothing else, and the thought of finding two men of Foxkin's stature boggled the mind. He'd no doubt played some far less exalted role, which it would only embarrass him to dredge up. "I do know one thing, Lady Ashburne."

"Yes?"

"Lord Ashburne was innocent."

Chapter Seven

GILES seated himself at the delicate dressing table that used to be his mother's, his tall frame fitting awkwardly into so feminine a space, and opened Portia Ashburne's traveling desk.

He drew the letters out and arranged them, first by sender, then in order by date. One stack was clearly business, the sender tending towards convoluted legal phrases and a dryness that turned the ink to dust on the page. They were universally responses to requests for money. How like a woman to so constantly overspend her allowance.

The second stack were different. The hand was the same on all the letters, the references to a young man's amusements, and the tone so familiar as to be insultingly casual. It was clearly a long-standing relationship and the letters made frequent reference to previous assignations and hopes for future ones. The writer promised on many occasions to come see her as soon as he could and signed himself by his first name only, and with love.

Giles put the letters from him and rubbed his fingers together to shed the feel of the paper. He hadn't thought it possible, but he could find it in himself to feel sorry for his cousin, despite the destruction he'd wrought on the Hall. The poor fool had married a woman who'd made a cuckold of him throughout their marriage and not even had the decency to wait out her year of mourning before returning to the relationship. He'd been wrong in thinking she'd come to Ashburne Hall to escape something. She was not in flight, but in exile. James had obviously sent her to the Hall to keep her indiscretions out of the public eye. Giles remembered James as a prating prig, tattling on Roger when he wasn't dogging his footsteps, but he appeared to have this situation, at least, well in hand. Except he'd dumped the shameless female on Giles.

Giles put the letters back in the traveling desk and closed it. He couldn't resist lingering in the bedchamber a moment more, appreciating the clean, comfortable serenity despite the woman who was author of it. Then he went back through the dressing room. Her unfortunate wardrobe was explained now too. James had wisely sent the woman away with only her cast-offs, knowing she could hardly take even to country society in gowns so sadly worn.

He'd have owed Roger an apology were his cousin still alive to receive it. Roger may have been a scapegrace, but the state of Ashburne Hall could not be laid entirely at his doorstep. There was one obvious reason for a woman to marry one man when she was in love with another, and Roger had had sufficient of the ready to tempt any woman. He'd been a damned fool to pour money into his wife's every whim while the principle Ashburne estate went begging, but then, men were often fools over women.

Giles had been just such a fool, once. He fancied now his heart was as smooth and hard as any stone.

* * *

"Careful, my lady." Foxkin deftly shunted Portia out of the path of a carriage that dashed into the inn yard with a deal of shouting and noise. As if in response, a loud whinny rent the air, and a large bay hunter bolted out of the stable, several men hot on his heels. For a moment, it looked as if there would be a horrific collision between the carriage and the escaping horse. Then Foxkin calmly stepped into the path of the stallion and grabbed his bridle, hauling him to a stop with an effortless application of strength. The animal tried to rear, but Foxkin pulled him back down to all fours, where he stood quivering.

"Oh my," Portia breathed. She approached cautiously, aware of the animal's rolling eyes and restless feet. He was all energy and strength, quivering under her hand when she stroked his shoulder. There was something elemental about him that reminded her, oddly enough, of the figure of Lord Ashburne standing against stormy skies.

"A little more care, if you please," Foxkin told the man who came to collect the horse. The walk back to the stable was accomplished with a laughable combination of prancing (the bay's) and foot-dragging (the man's).

"A beautiful horse. Does he belong to one of your lodgers?" The Duck and Drake was, after all, an inn, and more prepossessing by light of day than it had appeared the night she arrived. Any traveler would be fortunate to break his trip here.

The skin around his eyes crinkled. "Not exactly. I'm putting him up for a gentleman staying in the area."

"Will he be here long?" Portia wouldn't mind seeing the bay in action again. She'd mind even less seeing the man who could sit that horse.

The lines at the corners of Foxkin's eyes deepened. "Not long, the gentleman said, but I've a mind it may take longer than he planned."

* * *

Portia was halfway to the Hall when she realized she'd forgotten to ask Foxkin where she might find a cat.

"Blast!" She stopped walking and stood looking back the way she'd come. She'd just passed into the home wood and didn't relish returning across the fields under the suspicious eyes of the tenant farmers. On the other hand, she really didn't want to keep finding mice in beds and drawers and whatnot.

Portia seated herself on a stump in a leafy bower by the side of the narrow track, took off one of her half-boots, and shook it to dislodge the stone that had begun paining her a good mile ago. Nothing fell out, and she sighed. Like as not, the problem was in the boot itself, but as she couldn't afford new ones, she was just going to have to make the best of it. She dropped the offending boot and set about rubbing her aching foot.

Thank God there was a shortcut. But of course there had to be, didn't there? The potboy from the Duck and Drake had made it to the Hall on foot before Portia's carriage. She'd spent some time waiting for a new horse to be harnessed, true, but the coachman had got her to the Hall with alacrity once he had a team to drive. To get there before her, the boy had certainly not gone around by the road. But if he took this shortcut, Portia reflected, he must have reached the Hall a good quarter hour before her. Yet Mr. McFerran said the boy's arrival interrupted them in the act of taking down Lord Ashburne's painting. Which they were still struggling with almost fifteen minutes later? It made no sense. Clearly, it was only after the potboy burst in with the news that Lady Ashburne was at the Duck and Drake that the McFerrans began to remove the painting. Why had it not been done earlier? And why, given that it hadn't been done earlier, did they think it so important to get it down before she arrived?

For the life of her, Portia couldn't think what purpose it would serve the McFerrans to remove that painting, nor why, after trying so hard to prevent Portia from seeing it, the housekeeper no longer seemed interested. She ought to have the painting moved to her bedchamber, if only to see Mrs. McFerran's reaction. It would go well over the mantel shelf.

On consideration, perhaps not. It would not be a comfortable thing to have Giles Ashburne looking down at her from above the hearth. There was something unsettling about that painting. Some portraits seemed to follow you with their eyes. My Lord Ashburne's eyes never shifted, but he seemed to be following you nevertheless. It was too large a price to pay merely to discomfit Mrs. McFerran.

A pity, really. So far, they'd drawn up about even. Mrs. McFerran had gotten her licks in in the matters of dust and mice and especially food. But Portia'd contrived comfortable living quarters for herself, refused to be frightened by things bumping about in the dark, and she thought she'd touched a nerve on the cooking issue. She couldn't follow up on her threat to hire a cook—even when Mr. Burnsides sent the money she'd requested, she'd be unable to spare enough to hire a good cook, and it would serve no purpose to hire the kind of cook she *could* afford. Why waste her money paying for the same quality cooking she was getting now for free? But Mrs. McFerran had not liked having her cooking disparaged. It might prove harder for the housekeeper to continue swallowing her pride than for Portia to continue swallowing her cooking.

Portia gave her foot a last rub and slipped it back into her half-boot, where it immediately rubbed up against whatever had been paining her the last mile. She took a resigned breath. Perhaps Ellie could do something about it. If not, Portia would just have to learn to live with it. As she'd have to learn to live with Mrs. McFerran. She still held out hope that it could be done on peaceful terms, but if not.... Portia huffed out her breath and stood up.

She heard the thunder of hooves a moment before the gray gelding rounded the corner, his rider mounted astride, blond hair flying behind her like a pennant. Portia stepped quickly back, fetching up hard against the trunk of a tree. Before she could get away, the horse was on her, passing so close its mane whipped her face and the rider's booted toe caught her in the ribs, driving her to her knees.

The horsewoman cursed, sawing on the reins, and the gelding drew up short, rearing with an angry whinny. He was back on all four feet in a moment, the rider dismounting so fast, Portia at first thought she'd been thrown. But the woman landed on her feet and dashed over to Portia, while the horse, proving itself far calmer than the last few moments suggested, began to quietly crop grass.

"Terribly sorry," the woman gasped. "I didn't see you there. There's never anybody here. I didn't see you."

She was, Portia saw now, more girl than woman, her face terribly white. Portia forced her hand away from her side. "No harm done," she said in a credibly even voice. It hurt no worse than some of the tumbles she'd taken with Tony when they were children; bruises were doubtless the worst of it. She stood, using the tree for balance.

"I'm so terribly sorry," the young woman said again, bending to brush leaves off Portia's skirts. "I shouldn't ride neck or nothing through the woods, I know I shouldn't. But there's never anybody here, and even though they said Lady Ashburne'd come, I didn't think she'd, you'd, be walking about in the home wood and really—"

Portia took in the thick honey-colored hair tumbled about the young lady's shoulders, the brilliant blue eyes blazing above a field of freckles, and the men's riding breeches, and said, "Good afternoon, Lady Clarissa."

Lady Clarissa Seabrooke gaped at her a moment, then threw her head back and laughed uproariously. "Didn't take you long to get the lay of the land." The look she gave Portia as she offered her hand was frankly appraising. "You'd be Lady Ashburne then." Her fingers were strong and callused from the reins, her handshake far from the fade-away grip of the usual milk and water miss awaiting her come out.

"I would." Finding herself on the receiving end of a scrutiny that could only have been intensified by the use of a quizzing glass, Portia didn't hesitate to respond in kind.

Lady Clarissa was a good head taller than Portia, her figure showing far too well in the men's riding breeches. Portia judged her not more than a year shy of her first Season, which made her appearance doubly surprising. That a duke's ward might tear about the countryside in a manner more befitting a boy, Portia knew well could happen (having done precisely that herself when she was younger), but that said duke should not have taken his ward in hand well before she reached her come out was something of a surprise.

"Funny. I thought you'd be older. I don't know why." Lady Clarissa gathered up her mount's reins and dragged his head out of a mound of clover. "I suppose because Roger Ashburne seemed so old to me when he came into the title. Of course, I was eight at the time."

Portia smiled. "He must have been all of twenty." She wondered what Roger had been like at twenty. Probably not all that different from at thirty— racketing around London, deep in his cups and gaming away everything he owned. She remembered the charming man who had wooed and won her and wished, as she had so often over the years, that he hadn't been a lie.

"Old," Lady Clarissa decreed, the twinkle in her eye fading slightly as she added, "Though not so much as Lord Ashburne, who was frankly ancient."

"What," Portia asked, "twenty-five? Twenty-eight?" The man in the painting was mature, but were he still alive, he wouldn't be older than many looking to marry chits in their first Season.

"Ancient to a girl of eight." She began walking down the trail, the gelding ambling along at her shoulder. Portia joined them, overcome with contrition as she remembered far too late that Clarissa's sister was murdered, and by all accounts by the very man Portia had just spoken so lightly of.

"My sincerest apologies, Lady Clarissa, I fear my wits have gone begging. I should never—"

"Pray, do not refine upon it. I'm the one who brought it up." Lady Clarissa kicked at a rock in the path. "My uncle won't talk about it, the subject is entirely to be avoided around him. Even the servants keep mum. If the stable boys hadn't been full of the news of your arrival, I'd not even have known *that*."

"It appears we'd have met in any case."

Lady Clarissa looked briefly contrite, but seemed utterly unable to resist returning to the forbidden subject. "No one talks about it. At least, not to me. It's like... like when some country mushroom shows up at a ball. Everyone knows, and everyone knows they all know, and no one says anything, or even looks too long at them. They act like they can shield me by not talking about it. They forget I was there.

"I was, you know," she said when Portia prudently kept silent. "Uncle had said I could attend the ball, but he sent me home when they found her."

There was more pique than sorrow in the young woman's voice, and Portia couldn't help herself. "You weren't close to your sister?"

"Half-sister." Lady Clarissa sighed. "I sound horrible, don't I? I'm sorry she's dead—no one deserves to die, not like that. But it's been ten years and everyone expects me to weep and wail every time her name comes up, if it ever does, or take the veil or something. They forget I barely knew her. Amelia's grandmother—her father's mother—brought her up after Mama remarried. I didn't even meet her until I was eight. Uncle Ransley took me in when the influenza carried Mama and Papa off." She sniffed and swiped the back of her hand across her face. "Mama was his sister. It was the same year Amelia was set to come out, and her grandmother thought she couldn't do better than to launch her here. Who wouldn't be impressed by the Duke of Ransley's niece?"

The comment spoke volumes about a lonely little girl looking for someone to fill the hole left by her parents' deaths. Lady Amelia had not, apparently, wanted a half-sister. It was understandable, perhaps. What girl preparing to come out wanted a schoolroom chit dangling along behind her? Especially one who'd just lost her parents and her home and was looking for reassurance.

"He always scared me a bit," Lady Clarissa said suddenly, and Portia thought she was referring to the duke until she added, "Giles Ashburne. Always looked like thunder's next of kin. I don't think I ever saw him smile. He frightened Amelia too, I think. Or maybe she just didn't love him very much. She always seemed so cold."

"Then why marry him?"

"Uncle Ransley's idea, not that I ever heard Amelia complain. Lord Ashburne was only a viscount, but rich as Croesus, and the estates march. Tynesfield's not part of the entail, you know. If my uncle chose to, he could have left it to Amelia's son, once she had one, and combine the estates. Besides... Uncle Ransley liked Ashburne. Not that you'd know it now."

Rich as Croesus and Ashburne didn't go in the same sentence in Portia's experience. Roger'd been very much pockets to let at the time of their wedding, though he'd been careful to ensure it didn't show before the knot was tied. If he'd thought her dowry sufficient to bail him out, he'd grossly miscalculated. Such thoughts had been devastating the first time they occurred; now it was merely lowering to think Roger had likely never loved her.

How must Giles Ashburne have felt when he realized his bride to be didn't return his affections? Portia felt a flush rise under her skin when she recalled the letters she'd read, letters that had fallen (if sent at all) on deaf ears. *You can have no idea what the sight of you does to me, for I have no words to tell you here, and no breath to speak them when I'm in your presence.* Portia squeezed her eyes briefly shut in a futile effort to banish the words she'd fled the Hall to escape. Even at his most charming, Roger had never made her feel the way this man's letters had. And there was something, Portia scolded herself, decidedly perverse about being envious of a murdered woman.

"Do you think he did it?" Portia blurted, proving herself even more lacking in the social graces than the wayward chit beside her.

Lady Clarissa looked sidelong at her. "I don't know. He intimidated me as a child, but was he really a man of such terrifying jealousies? I honestly don't know. Pray God Uncle Ransley never hears me say so!" She glanced around, half in jest, half as if she might actually see him emerge from the trees that now hemmed them in.

"He believes in Lord Ashburne's guilt?"

"He's steeped in it. You'd have thought, when word came of Ashburne's death, that God himself had denied him his revenge. I don't think he's ever quite gotten over it." She stopped walking abruptly as if realizing how near they were to the Hall. "I shouldn't go any farther."

"I very much doubt it's actually haunted." Portia smiled.

"It's not that. What my uncle would do if he knew I was even this close…. Do you know," she said, momentarily diverted, "the first I heard anything about Ashburne Hall being haunted was a month ago? I overheard one of the stable boys talking about seeing lights at the Hall. The head groom would have turned him off without a reference if he knew I heard."

"I should think, with the McFerrans about, that there are usually lights at the Hall."

"Oh, but this is different. A light burning through the night in Ashburne's bed chamber, just as it did the night—" Lady Clarissa broke off, perhaps realizing how ghoulish she would be to continue.

Remembering the eerie light she'd seen that first night, and furthermore that her bedroom now adjoined the chamber in question, Portia shivered, and was thoroughly irritated with herself for doing so.

"At least, that's what the stable boy said." Lady Clarissa scowled. "And my uncle would turn him off for the mere mention of Lord Ashburne. You see how ridiculous it is? He's ten years dead, and I'm only just now hearing about the haunting, but just try to make my uncle see what I really need protecting from."

"Which would be?"

Lady Clarissa sighed gustily and plunked herself down on a fallen log. "My uncle's always so busy with estate business and Town business that I don't think he ever really sees me. I know I'm a hoyden," she said with a frankness that only proved her point. "I'm not a ninnyhammer. I'm eighteen. I know I'll be labeled a quiz and a ramshackle female, or worse, when I'm launched in Town. I'll be the laughingstock of the *ton*. Uncle Ransley thinks, if he thinks about it at all, that all he has to do is have some modiste dress me in the first stare of fashion and everything will come out right. I know better."

Portia found herself at a loss. Lady Clarissa was entirely right—she'd never pass Society's scrutiny as she was—but it simply would not do to say so. "I'm certain everything will be—"

"It will *not* be all right and I'll thank you not to pretend it will." Clarissa heaved a sigh that originated somewhere around her ankles and buried her face in her hands. "You see how hopeless I am?" It was not a lengthy fit of the dismals. Her head came up almost immediately and the gleam in her eye made Portia take a step back. She'd seen that look before. It invariably graced Tony's face just before he landed himself in the suds, as often as not dragging Portia right in there with him. "You could teach me!"

"Beg pardon?"

"*You* know how a lady's supposed to act. I mean, look at you—no one would ever take you for less than a lady, even if your dress isn't fit for a—" She clapped a hand over her mouth and stared at Portia out of wide, horrified eyes.

Portia couldn't help herself. She began to laugh.

Chapter Eight

"MORNING room's swept and dusted." The glow of perspiration on Ellie's skin and the dust smudging her nose made Portia feel like her eight mile walk was nothing but an idle entertainment. It also made her feel guilty for her earlier sharpness with the maid. "Windows need washing yet, and the drapes aren't fit for the rag bag."

"I expect you could say that about every curtain in the house," Portia said ruefully. She followed Ellie into the morning room. The drapes indeed weren't fit for hanging; what the mice hadn't got, the sun had faded into cobwebs. However, the furniture was dusted and the grate cleared out, the lamps shone, and everything that could glow with polish did. "Very nice, Ellie. You've done wonders."

"Carpet needs to be turned," Ellie said as dourly as possible while glowing with pride.

"We'll get Mr. McFerran in to help with the furniture. Yes, a very nice job." She was laying it on a bit thick, but it was for a good cause. Ellie would never permit Portia to say a word about coming over the lady at her; compliments were the only coin she could apologize in. "You'll never guess who I met coming back through the home wood," Portia said as they went upstairs together. "The Duke of Ransley's ward."

Ellie stopped dead halfway up the stairs. "Not she as what was murdered!"

"Of course not!" Portia refrained from comment on either Ellie's tortured phrasing or her gullibility. Ellie's grasp of proper King's English suffered when she was frightened and her superstitious nature, it seemed, deepened the longer they remained at the Hall. "Her sister. Half-sister. She wants me to teach her how to act like a lady."

Ellie snorted inelegantly.

"I'll pretend I didn't hear that." Portia swept into her bedchamber without daring to look at the maid for fear she'd break out laughing.

She knew immediately that something was awry, though at first all she could say for certain was that the smell of lavender was a bit strong. She'd have to remind Ellie to be frugal with it; she couldn't afford to be extravagant with her little luxuries. Ellie bustled about while Portia stood in the middle of her bed chamber and tried to put her finger on what was different.

It took several minutes to realize the chair was pushed out from the dressing table and her traveling desk wasn't quite as far back as it had been. She seated herself at the table and opened her desk.

Someone had been in her letters and whoever it was had done nothing to hide the fact. Her first unreasonable thought was that it was a form of retaliation for getting into Giles Ashburne's correspondence, as clear as if he were saying "just see how you like it." *She*, Portia corrected herself. The culprit must be Mrs. McFerran, and the timing proved the housekeeper had been spying on her.

"Ellie." Portia was surprised to hear her voice come out mild and even. "Please go fetch Mrs. McFerran up to me." Ellie startled her by dropping a curtsey before rushing out. Perhaps her tone hadn't been as mild as she'd thought.

By the time Mrs. McFerran arrived, Portia had managed to impose a surface calm over her seething irritation. Every one of her letters had been handled, not only all the correspondence with Mr. Burnsides but her precious few letters from her brother as well. It was lowering to think of a mere servant making herself privy to Portia's financial woes and beyond insulting that she'd read Tony's letters.

"Ah, Mrs. McFerran," Portia said when the housekeeper presented herself. "I don't know how Lord Ashburne ran his house or what you've become used to in his absence, but I do not expect you to enter my private apartments when I am absent. I certainly do not expect you to avail yourself of my personal correspondence." She closed the lid of her traveling desk with a bang that startled a twitch out of Mrs. McFerran.

"I'm certain I don't know what your ladyship is speaking of," Mrs. McFerran said after a minute of tight-lipped silence, her jaw so stiff it was a wonder she got the words out at all.

"I am quite certain you do. Just as I am perfectly aware you don't want me here." Had the situation been different, Portia would have given Mrs. McFerran to understand that one could always hire another housekeeper, but she was certain she'd never convince a respectable housekeeper to work under the conditions at the Hall, let alone at the pittance of a salary James would allow, assuming he'd let her turn the woman off in the first place. "You can be well-assured that I will not be leaving under any circumstances. *Any* circumstances, Mrs. McFerran. There is no point, therefore, in these shenanigans with footsteps and hair brushes, nor to your making yourself free of my personal belongings. Do I make myself clear?"

"Perfectly, Lady Ashburne." Far from appearing intimidated, Mrs. McFerran allowed a thin-lipped smile to flicker across her mouth. "Though I might suggest that your ladyship is speaking to the wrong person."

"I have no doubt you will inform Mr. McFerran how things stand."

"I was referring to the ghost."

"There is no ghost."

"As you say, my lady," Mrs. McFerran said serenely. "Will that be all?"

"No, that will not be all," Portia snapped. She reined in her irritation and continued in a softer tone of voice, though not so soft that the 'please' was not an order, "You will please hand over your key to this chamber."

"As you wish, my lady." Mrs. McFerran drew forth her chatelaine and selected a key from it, handing it over expressionlessly.

"Is this the only key aside from my own?"

"I believe Lord Ashburne had his keys with him when he left," the housekeeper said with a disturbing little smile.

"Ghosts don't need keys," Portia said to herself after Mrs. McFerran left. Nonetheless, she found herself going into the dressing room to make certain that the door into the master's bedchamber was still locked.

* * *

When Ellie returned some little time later, she found Portia standing in the musty dressing room, surveying her gowns with her hands on her hips.

"They won't get any better for being glared at."

"No, they won't," Portia said without taking her eyes off the pitiful collection of dresses. Lady Clarissa's thoughtless words had come back to her as she passed through the dressing room and she'd ended up staring at her tiny wardrobe as if, if she only looked long enough, there might somehow be one dress, just one, she'd missed. Something less than five years old, something that wasn't black or gray, something a lady might wear without looking down at heel. Something that did not make her look a veritable dowd, or worse.

It had been a long time since she'd indulged in the kind of self-pity that resulted in scanning her wardrobe for a single fashionable gown, even longer since she'd had any chance of finding one. Even Ellie's talent with a needle could no longer bring about that miracle. Already, the best parts had been clipped and saved and cobbled together, a patchwork poverty of a wardrobe.

"Nothing left to remake," she said, mostly to herself. And nothing left to wear. Lady Clarissa had put her callused, hoydenish finger directly on it. Portia's gowns weren't fit for a scullery maid.

Country society around Rosewood Close had known her and the straits her husband had left her in. They'd accepted her. Not without pitying looks and whispers behind fans, it was true, but they had invited the penniless Viscountess Ashburne to picnics, to afternoon teas, to socials. That was before Roger died, of course, sending Portia into mourning and the best of her gowns into the dye pot. After that, she was reduced to the society of James and his wife, the vicar and one or two others who looked on her circumstances with such pity that she soon stopped entertaining altogether. But in this new place, with these people used to Ashburnes rich as Golden Ball, Portia very much feared she'd be unable to go about in society at all.

"Unless..."

"My lady?"

"What is the one place in the Hall we have not yet investigated, Ellie?"

"Oh no," Ellie said, with what Portia considered to be an unnecessarily trepidatious expression.

"The attics."

"Oh my."

"Oh my, indeed. Bring a candle."

Ellie obediently followed Portia out of her bedchamber, which Portia was careful to lock behind them—no point in having Mrs. McFerran's key if she didn't lock up. She gave the spare key to Ellie so there would be no difficulties about the maid getting in to take care of her duties. They went up to the second floor, through the doorway on the upper floor landing, and up a narrow enclosed staircase into the attics.

"What are we looking for?" Ellie asked when they reached the dark and cluttered space, her voice hushed as if she feared being overhead by someone. Or something.

"Trunks, bandboxes, wardrobes," Portia said, louder than she'd intended. Lifting up her candle, she headed off to the left. "Clothes, Ellie. Preferably the dowager Lady Ashburne's. Preferably free of moths and mice."

"Not asking for much, are you?"

"Stubble it and start looking."

"Lord Ashburne was a bad influence on you, my lady."

"Yes, well, he could hardly have been a good one." Portia held her candle high to shed more light on the old furniture, boxes, trunks and various odds and ends that loomed formless in the gloom. The light did nothing to give the place any semblance of cheer, so shrouded in dust, cobwebs and darkness was it. It did, however, clearly show that someone had been there, and quite recently, judging by the sharp-edged marks in the thick dust. Curious, she followed the footprints, but was unable to come to any conclusion about what whoever made them had been doing. There were neither markings in the dust where something had been removed nor anything so clean it could have recently taken up residence.

"Over here, my lady." Portia joined Ellie in lifting a birdcage and dressmaker's dummy off a large, steel-banded trunk. When they opened it, however, it contained only old draperies and a large colony of mice.

Ellie's scream ringing in her ears, Portia closed the heavy lid and picked up her candle. The wardrobe listing awkwardly against the chimney looked promising, but contained only an old gentleman's coats and cloaks, out of style by fifty years or more and fit now only for the cloud of moths that flew out of them. Portia closed the creaking doors with a sinking heart. She hoped whoever packed the dowager Lady Ashburne's belongings had done a better job, or this was a fool's errand. Assuming that lady's clothes were even there to find.

Ignoring Ellie's banging and muttering, Portia ducked under a low beam and surveyed the next attic, her candle sending shadows crawling aimlessly about in the gloom. There was light somewhere off to the left, a pale and eerie glow. Portia opened her mouth to call Ellie, but nothing came out. Very nearly despite herself, she moved toward the light, each step shorter and slower than the last. A soft finger brushed her cheek. Portia clamped her jaw on a shriek. Cobweb. It was only a cobweb.

A large trunk stood on end in the middle of the narrow aisle, surrounded by a wavering nimbus of light. Portia laid one trembling hand on the corner of the trunk and paused a moment, breathing deeply. She forced herself to step around it and nearly screamed when something flickered across the light. When she saw what it was, she took a deep breath and tugged viciously at her hair, quite out of countenance with herself. What a ninnyhammer! It was only a hole in the roof, which a sparrow had taken advantage of.

She peered in the neat nest tucked up by the eaves, finding three small eggs, then studied the hole sourly, shielding her candle from the draft with a cupped hand. No wonder the master's bedroom leaked. Carefully avoiding the rotting floorboards where the rain had come in, she turned and came face to face with a wavering white figure.

Portia screamed.

By the time Ellie thundered over, Portia had regained most of her composure and was starting to get her breath back, though her heart still beat nine to the dozen. "Careful. You'll put a foot through the floor."

Ellie stopped short. "What happened? I was that scared when you—"

"Came face to face with myself in that mirror." Portia indicated the cloudy pier glass someone had stood against a stack of bandboxes. "I swear, Ellie, I'm getting as bad as you. I thought for a moment I'd found the ghost."

Ellie made a humphing noise and went back the way she'd come. Portia thought briefly of apologizing, but decided against it. Ellie might take it for encouragement, and Portia didn't need her maid any more steeped in superstition than she already was. She surveyed the ancient furniture and acknowledged that while it might have witnessed the late dowager's birth, it was too old to be contemporary with her death. She was clearly in the wrong part of the attics. Portia picked up the candle she'd dropped in her fright and started back the way she'd come, making her way by the wan light coming in through the hole in the roof and wishing she'd realized her candle had gone out before Ellie stomped away.

Ellie hadn't gotten far. When Portia inched her way around the trunk blocking the narrow aisle, she found her maid flailing around, distressed huffs coming from her clamped lips. Portia stepped under a wild swing and took the candle from Ellie before her gyrations could extinguish it.

"Ellie! It's just a cobweb."

"Aye, and who knows what's creeping around in it." Ellie gave a convulsive shudder and began brushing jerkily at her dress.

"Whatever it was, it probably ran off when you started waving your arms around in its home." Portia used Ellie's candle to light her own and turned to survey the trunk she'd slipped around twice now, finally taking occasion to wonder what it was doing right in the middle of the path into the next section of attic.

Portia handed Ellie's candle back and bent to look at the catches. Though it was possible to open the trunk while it was on its end, it would perhaps not be advisable, and she got Ellie to help her push it over. It fell with an awful bang, raising an enormous cloud of dust. Coughing and waving her free hand before her face, Portia tried not to get her hopes up as she set about opening the trunk, which in addition to the usual catches had been wrapped about with rope. The knots were beastly.

When they lifted the heavy lid, Ellie standing well back in case of mice, Portia was struck by the strong odor of camphor. She began to smile. Someone had looked after the contents of this trunk. It boded well. It boded very well indeed.

She gave Ellie her candle and wiped her hands on her filthy skirts, then reached into the trunk. The first dress she lifted out was velvet and satin, heavy with the weight of the voluminous skirts popular before the turn of the century. It was entirely intact, untouched by mice or moths or mildew.

"Oh, lovely," Ellie breathed.

"Very." The style was hopelessly out of date—even worse than Portia's own clothing—but that didn't signify. It was the fabric Portia wanted. The large trunk was full of dresses and underslips and nightrails, Portia saw as she delved deeper, all in excellent condition and neatly packed. Someone had handled these with love; it was as palpable as the camphor that made her want badly to sneeze.

"Oh, my lady," Ellie breathed, "what I could do with these…. But how are we to get them down?"

"Not the same way they came up, I'll be bound." They couldn't possibly get the heavy trunk down that steep narrow staircase without the assistance of at least two strong men. They'd have to carry the contents down an armful at a time. Portia thought of the condition of her dress and winced. "Here, Ellie, give me one of those candles and go fetch the sheets off my bed." At least they weren't covered in dust and cobwebs.

Ellie dashed off, leaving Portia alone in the gloomy attic, her candle throwing wavering shadows on the looming boxes and discarded furniture. Careful not to drip tallow into the trunk, she folded back one dress and then another, her throat tight as she took in the deep soft fabrics, the rich colors.

How carefully someone had packed this trunk, how very much they must have cared. "She won't miss them," Portia whispered to the waiting attic. "She doesn't need them anymore, but I do. More than you could ever imagine."

* * *

It took several trips, but eventually the entire contents of the trunk was spread out on Portia's stripped bed, a riot of color glowing in the light of the setting sun. Lady Ashburne, it appeared, had been a woman of strong and bold tastes, unwilling to sink quietly into the aged background of life. Washed clean of cobwebs and attic dust and changed out of her filthy walking dress, Portia picked up a gown of burnished copper and held it against herself.

"Oh yes, my lady," Ellie breathed. "Peel away the fusses and furbelows and narrow the skirts, and you'll be the toast of even a Town ball, let alone these country socials."

"Never mind the balls, Ellie. What I need are morning gowns and walking dresses." She reluctantly put the ballgown back on the bed.

"Oh, but my lady—"

Portia forced a smile. "Let's get me outfitted like a proper lady and leave the fancy dresses for another time. I believe we'll start with this one." She chose a walking dress of dove gray silk that would be the easiest to alter to fit both her and current fashion.

"Yes, my lady." Ellie's face screwed up in a mulish expression that was all too familiar.

"Later, Ellie."

"Yes, my lady." Ellie began shuttling gowns into the dressing room a few at a time, treating them with exaggerated care. The limited airing they'd received so far had already greatly reduced the smell of camphor, but Portia reflected with some amusement that she could rely on her dressing room, at least, remaining free of vermin for a while.

Most of the dresses still lay out when Mrs. McFerran tapped on the door. Her dull black eyes moved quickly over the bed and her lips compressed.

"Yes, Mrs. McFerran?"

"Supper's ready."

"Thank you, I had quite lost track of the time. We'll need to get the various bell pulls and dinner bells working again and save you the walk up the stairs." Portia swept the housekeeper out the door ahead of her. She had the impression that the woman would as lief snatch up the dowager's gowns and hide them away somewhere. Let her disapprove. Portia was mistress of the house now and Mrs. McFerran would just have to get used to it.

When they reached the landing, Portia made a deliberate point of looking at the portrait. Mrs. McFerran mustn't think she'd scared Portia with her gruesome stories and pretend ghosts. And if Portia felt a vague sense of defiance as she met Giles Ashburne's flat painted gaze, it had nothing to do with the dresses, and certainly nothing to do with the letters she'd read or how unsettled they'd left her.

It was as Portia set foot on the grand staircase running down to the great hall that she glanced up and saw a figure on the second floor landing. "What the devil?"

From two steps farther down, Mrs. McFerran eyed Portia incuriously. "My lady?"

"Who is that?"

The housekeeper turned to look where Portia pointed. "Who is who, my lady? I see no one."

As she spoke, the man turned, a figure in black trousers and waistcoat, his linen snowy white, and vanished up the hall. Portia ran across the landing to the next set of stairs and, snatching up her skirts, took them at a most unladylike pace. She reached the upper landing only to find both it and the hallway empty. There was no way he could have reached the nearest door before she got to the top of the stairs, not without making a hellish noise. The floor was bare wood. She was certain she'd have been able to hear him run across it, even over the pounding of her heart.

There was nowhere he could hide and nowhere he could have gone.

Chapter Nine

PORTIA swept down the stairs past Mrs. McFerran without a word. She did not particularly look at the housekeeper, but was aware of the woman's expression nonetheless. Smug. Most housekeepers would be mortified to discover the new lady of the house prone to strange starts, but Portia could distinctly feel Mrs. McFerran's triumph. If she thought Portia could be frightened into decamping and leaving her in possession of the Hall, she was sadly mistaken.

"Is there something the matter, Lady Ashburne?"

"Nothing at all," Portia said repressively. "There's a hole in the roof of the east attic. Have Mr. McFerran see to it."

With that, she went in to eat her supper in solitary splendor. Or rather, in the moth-eaten majesty of the dining room.

The vegetables were overcooked and the meat underdone, but nothing was burnt and supper was, while not good, at least edible. Evidence of the salutary effects of threatening to sell off the silver. It was something to remember. Mrs. McFerran was so stubborn as to be guaranteed immune to any threat to turn her off, even could Portia carry it out, but she evinced toward the Hall all the overprotective instincts of a doting nanny.

Sitting at one end of the long dining table, Portia looked around the decaying room and resolved to eat her meals in the breakfast room in the future. It was already more habitable and would certainly be less guaranteed to make Portia feel as if she were quite alone in the world. It was one of God's petty ironies that she'd spent most of her childhood wishing to escape her brother's near-constant presence and all her adulthood to date wishing for a little companionship.

Portia swallowed the lump in her throat and scolded herself for dwelling on her misfortunes, especially as she was doing so in a transparent attempt to not think about what had just happened.

She was as certain of what she'd seen as she was that Mrs. McFerran had looked directly at him and seen nothing. Certain he could have reached no hiding place before she caught him up. Certain he'd moved without making a sound. Certain he was no other than Viscount Giles Ashburne.

Portia set aside her fork, unable to swallow another bite. She took the three-branch candelabra by which she'd eaten and started resolutely up the staircase. She did not look at the portrait at the head of the stairs, though she was aware no matter how she tried not to be of the light of her candles ebbing slowly over and away from his dark form. As she started up the upper staircase, her skin crept with the feeling of his eyes on her back.

When she reached the upper landing, she stood for some minutes without moving, surveying her surroundings in the wavering light. The threadbare carpet extended a few feet in each direction, no doubt to keep children's and servants' footsteps from echoing all the way down into the great hall. It was so worn and moth-eaten, however, that even in her light slippers, Portia's every step resounded.

Portia bent to inspect the floor more closely, bringing the light down to shine directly on the tracked-up dust where the carpet ended. The nearest door was at least ten steps farther along the hall; perhaps six for someone as tall as the man she'd seen. She and Mrs. McFerran had left their mark while inspecting the house the first day, their tracks running all the way up and down the hall. No footsteps had been added to theirs. The area just to the right of the landing was swept nearly clean of dust by the trips she and Ellie had taken in and out of the attics, but she didn't see how he could have vanished quietly up those stairs. Not the way the door squeaked and the stairs creaked. Besides, he'd disappeared to the left—she'd stake her best dress on it. Though that wasn't saying much.

Portia searched for anything that could explain the man's appearance or disappearance until the candles were burnt nearly to the socket, her fingers were stiff with cold, and she was so aware of Giles Ashburne staring at her from his portrait that she nearly jumped out of her skin at every slightest noise.

She finally gave up and headed down to bed. Either there really was a ghost or she had mice in her attic in more ways than the literal. Neither thought was particularly comfortable.

* * *

"Oh, my lady, you're that cold, you are." Ellie herded Portia over to the fire that flickered weakly in the grate and added another log. In a moment, flames leapt up in profligate delight. At least keeping warm wasn't a problem. Portia couldn't afford coal to heat the Hall, but there were a prodigious number of trees in the home wood. It would be years before they ran out of firewood, if ever.

"You shouldn't have waited," Portia scolded. Ellie pushed her into a chair and wrapped the coverlet around her. "I can get myself to bed."

"Of course you can, my lady," Ellie said without leaving off her fussing. "Now will you be wanting some tea or a hot posset?"

"No, Ellie, thank you. I believe I shall just read a bit."

"Yes, my lady." Ellie retrieved Portia's book for her and tucked the blanket more securely about her feet.

Portia sat before the fire and attempted to read while Ellie bustled about, for all the world as if there were a hundred little chores that needed doing in the room. Her inability to make any progress could not, however, be laid at her maid's door, but on something that had been niggling at Portia ever since her meeting with Lady Clarissa Seabrooke.

Lady Clarissa, after her gaffe about Portia's dress, had gone on to shove her foot even more firmly in her mouth by intimating that she had a generous allowance and would be happy to pay for Portia's assistance. She had not, much to Portia's surprise, turned an even deeper shade of red and apologized for the implication that Lady Ashburne would sully her hands in Service, but instead looked her straight in the eye and said, "Ladies hire themselves out as companions and governesses every day when they've nowhere else to turn. Why shouldn't you receive some recompense for making an impossible hoyden into a lady?" She'd swung astride the great gray horse with an injunction to think about it and galloped off as impetuously as she'd ridden down on Portia in the first place.

The idea had haunted Portia ever since.

Roger had left her in a pitiful state and James was hardly likely to improve the situation. He was not the rakehell his brother had been, but even a nip-farthing like James would be hard-pressed to make anything of the mare's nest Roger left. A large infusion of money was all that would save the Ashburnes now. How unfortunate James was already wed, or he might have married money and bailed the Ashburnes out of River Tick. As it was, the Ashburne finances, and with them her widow's jointure, were extraordinarily unlikely to improve. The modest portion settled on Portia by her grandfather was so set about with protections that even she could request only the most meager of funds at any given time—a fact which had saved the money from Roger's hands, but made it of extremely limited use in her current situation. Once the Hall was more habitable, the money might be enough to live on, but not when there was so much that needed repair. And then there was the question of servants. A small house might be run by a maid of all work, but a grand estate like the Hall required more servants if it was not to go entirely to rack and ruin. Servants Portia simply could not afford.

She had a lot more latitude as a widow than she'd had as an unmarried chit, ripe for seduction and the ruination of her reputation, but there were still too few avenues of support open for a penniless lady. There were, as Lady Clarissa had point out, positions as companions and governesses which a lady in her reduced circumstances might have no recourse but to take, but neither offered much hope for Portia. She did not delude herself that she'd paid enough attention to her own governess as to be able to take on the education of some sprig of nobility, nor was she sufficiently self-effacing to quietly accede to the querulous demands of those *ton* matrons who believed themselves in need of companions. Besides, she suspected she'd be considered too fair of face to have much chance of being offered either position, not being a *complete* dowd. Dowagers did not like to be shown up by their companions, and ladies did not hire governesses who showed the slightest chance of being able to turn the heads of their sons, or worse, their husbands. Never mind that Portia'd been unable to keep the attention of her *own* husband; it was the impression that counted. All of which was moot, for though he'd go not one step out of his way to support her, James Ashburne would fly into the boughs with a vengeance if his sister-in-law set her feet on such a path.

That left only remarriage, and Portia's experience of that state was such that she'd never willingly put herself at the mercy of another man.

Which really left her only one option. She was going to have to turn Clarissa Seabrooke into a lady.

* * *

Portia couldn't sleep.

Ellie had gone to bed some time ago, after tucking her mistress into her nightrail and then between the sheets. The Hall was dark and, for once, quiet—even the skittering of mice seemed to have stopped. She supposed she could credit their taking themselves elsewhere to the odor of camphor, which she could still smell even though the dressing room door was closed.

Her thoughts wandered in circles, returning over and over to a single subject. Even after all the events of the day, any one of which ought to be enough to keep her occupied, every time she closed her eyes she saw Giles Ashburne's strong slanted handwriting and awkwardly passionate words.

Finally it was just too much, and Portia slipped out of bed. She couldn't find her slippers and didn't spend much time looking for them. She lit her candle with a spill from the fire, took her keys from the dressing table and made her way through the dressing room and into the master's bedchamber.

It was, perhaps, the lack of a fire in the grate that made the darkness in Ashburne's chamber seem so much deeper than in her own. Gone was the masculine warmth she'd felt by light of day. The gloom that closed in about her was stern and unbending, hard and chill with disapproval. She had invaded his room, read his letters, and felt so little shame that she was back to do it again. Portia kept her eyes on the tiny flame of her candle, certain that if she lifted them, she would see him sitting in the corner of his room. Or worse, not see him, though her prickling skin knew he was surely there, seething. The wind she'd barely heard in her own room rushed hissing outside, pushing freezing drafts across the floor, biting at her toes. She could scarcely hear her own breath, and when the wind suddenly slapped hard at the Hall, she jumped.

The candle flickered and nearly went out. Portia cupped her hand around the sputtering flame and waited for it to steady, calling herself seven kinds of fool. It was just the wind, and this was just a dark room, and there was no one watching her from the shadows.

She walked, stiff-legged, to the writing desk and pulled out the drawer that held his personal letters, her fingers unsteady, only to find it empty of everything but the smell of tobacco. Portia sank slowly into the chair and stared into the empty drawer. They were there only that afternoon, letters full of passion and pain, letters she could not for the life of her forget. Knowing it was non-sensical, and with a feeling much like desperation, Portia opened every drawer and even rifled through the neat stack of business correspondence, as if she could have somehow misplaced the letters. Finally, her mind whirling with confusion, she picked up her candle and went back through the dressing room, remembering that she hadn't relocked the door only once she was standing by the hearth in her own room. Stiff with a strange reluctance, she went back through the dressing room, sneezing at the miasma of camphor, and locked the door to his room. Then, though it was not the least bit necessary, the door from the dressing room into her room.

Finally, she crouched before her dying fire, her nightrail tucked about her freezing feet, and stared into the glowing coals, trying hard to think. She certainly hadn't moved the letters. Her superstitious Ellie wouldn't have even entered his room on her own, let alone looked in the writing desk. Which left Mrs. McFerran. But why now? She'd had ten years to decide, for whatever reason, to make off with his letters.

The obvious answer sent cold fingers up Portia's spine. Mrs. McFerran knew.

Portia huddled over the glow of the fire, its tiny flame producing a faint warmth worse than no heat at all, and shuddered herself nearly to pieces before common sense got hold of her once more. She forced herself up and into her flannel dressing gown, and climbed into her bed for warmth.

Reason was what was needed here. Mrs. McFerran couldn't have known that Portia read the letters. Though Ellie might have seen her from the dressing room door, her presence there would have prevented the housekeeper from doing the same and Portia could not possibly have failed to notice the hall door opening while she was in the master's bedroom. It was only her sense of guilt at having shamelessly read what was so very personal that made her think Mrs. McFerran somehow knew of it.

The housekeeper had merely taken advantage of Portia's absence from the Hall to enter the master's bedroom and remove those items she thought too personal for Portia's perusal. For all her stern satisfaction at the story of Lord Ashburne's crime and the divine punishment meted out to him, Mrs. McFerran's love of Ashburne Hall extended to defending not only the Hall but everything in it from interlopers. What else, Portia wondered, was missing? And how would she ever know?

She blew out her candle and composed herself for sleep, though she was even less inclined toward that state than she'd been before her unrewarding incursion into Ashburne's room. She forced herself to lie still through the slow count of ten minutes before she got up again. She should have accepted Ellie's offer of a hot posset.

The bellpull was broken, but even if it hadn't been, Portia wouldn't have roused her maid at this hour for anything short of an emergency. She relit the candle, spent another couple of minutes fruitlessly searching for her slippers, then left her room, not without trepidation. Her feet wanted to hesitate at the door. Two nights ago, there had been something moving about in the dead of night. Portia forced herself to unlock her door and step out as if there were no cause for alarm. The hall was empty, her candle the only light.

She headed downstairs, not stopping to look at the portrait of Giles Ashburne, indeed doing her best to forget it was there. She reached the kitchen without incident, neither seeing nor hearing anything untoward and managing, even, not to stub her bare toes on the uneven floor, though they were so cold, she might not know if she had. As she'd hoped, there was a banked fire in the stove. Mrs. McFerran was too savvy a housekeeper to let her kitchen fire go out and suffer through the inconvenience of getting it restarted. Portia put a small log on the fire and set the kettle on the stove to warm.

She was in the midst of looking for tea when she realized there was a light under the door of the housekeeper's sitting room. Portia had nearly reached the door when her good sense caught up with her. Demanding the return of Lord Ashburne's private letters was simply out of the question.

She turned back to her tea, glad she'd conducted herself quietly enough not to rouse the housekeeper, when a man's voice uttered a profanity she would never have expected from the soft-spoken Mr. McFerran. She lingered despite herself to hear Mrs. McFerran's set-down, for that woman would scarcely allow such language in her hearing, even or perhaps especially if it came from her husband. Instead, she heard the housekeeper say, "That's as may be, but we *will* have her out, mark my words."

Portia couldn't make out the response, only the deep rumble of the voice.

"She's resourceful, I'll give you that," Mrs. McFerran said, fugitive respect in her voice. "I had thought to scuttle her the first night. Few ladies of her stamp would do aught but run screaming at finding mice in their blankets."

More masculine rumbling. Portia inched closer to the door, but still could not make out Mr. McFerran's part of the conversation.

"Of course I knew there were mice in the bed when I put her in there. I'm not a ninnyhammer, you know. ... No, more's the pity. She's stubborn. You've as much evidence of that as I. Yes, even about the food. She wants to go over menus and the household accounts now. ... Not yet, but if she begins haunting the kitchen, she'll tumble to it sooner rather than later. She's not as clothheaded as we'd hoped. ... I think we'll have to try something else. It's difficult enough to produce separate meals; if she does begin to make time in the kitchen, it will become entirely impossible."

Ha! So the McFerrans *had* been eating better than Portia. It sounded, however, as though she would soon see a marked improvement in her meals. Portia made a mental note to haunt the kitchens if there was a future dip in quality. She shifted from one icy foot to the other and glanced longingly at the kitchen fire, glowing nicely now.

"That's a thought," Mrs. McFerran said in response to some lengthy pronouncement of Mr. McFerran's. "There's only so much that even the most stubborn woman can take. Mark my words: one way or another, we will send her ladyship packing." The certainty in her voice sent chill fingers up Portia's spine. For the first time, Mrs. McFerran seemed more threat than nuisance, and Portia backed slowly away from the door.

"I've a few things in hand myself," Mr. McFerran said, the deep voice so close he might have been standing directly behind her, though still so muffled by the thick door as to be hard to recognize.

The log Portia'd placed on the fire gave a loud pop and her heart lurched. She shoved the kettle off the stove, snatched up her candle, and raced away before anyone could reach the door and catch her out.

It was only after she'd achieved the great hall that Portia realized she'd allowed herself to be routed by her own nerves and a noise the McFerrans could doubtless not even hear. For a moment, she hesitated. Knowing what her tormentors were planning might make all the difference to her ability to stick at the Hall. In the end, however, her childhood training held firm and she continued on her way; there was nothing more lowering than to be caught eavesdropping on the servants.

* * *

From the shadowy depths of the Hall, Giles watched her climb the stairs, her candle glowing pale around her. She was barefoot, and he couldn't help but notice, as she lifted the trailing hem of her nightrail, that she had a nicely turned ankle. A nicely rounded figure, as well, when her nightclothes shifted and pulled snug enough around her to show it as she climbed. It came in momentary glimpses that left him wanting more. By and large, her shapeless flannel dressing gown turned her into a midnight drab, and Giles found himself wishing James had not sent her off without her silk nightrails and satin peignoirs. He longed, with a heat that surprised him, to see her in nightclothes that clung lovingly to her curves and welcomed the revealing candlelight. Denied her body, the light of the candle glowed through the rich brown hair that hung in loose disarray down her back, and Giles was put strangely in mind of angels.

He didn't believe in angels any longer, if he ever had.

He watched her all the way to the top of the stairs before he managed to wrest himself from her spell. No need to see her all the way to her bedchamber. The damage was already done. Just how much had the little minx overheard?

He would give her an hour to fall asleep and then he'd set to work. There was much to be done.

Chapter Ten

PORTIA spent an unsettled night. Sleep came only fitfully, and at one point she bolted upright in bed, certain she'd heard footsteps. But no matter how she strained her ears, there were no further footfalls to be heard over the sound of the mice racing about in the walls.

She'd lain awake a long time. She'd overheard nothing she hadn't already suspected, but still, it was deeply unsettling to know she was indeed at daggers drawn with her housekeeper. She spent some time composing a letter to James in her head before admitting that her brother-in-law would never agree to turn the McFerrans off. They were stuck with each other, and the sooner she convinced them of that, the better.

"Morning, my lady," Ellie chirped, startling Portia out of an uneasy doze. She threw open the drapes, letting in a shaft of sunlight that speared through Portia's sleep-dulled eyes with painful brilliance. "It's that beautiful out today, it is."

Portia agreed wordlessly and sat sipping hot tea and eating perfectly browned toast while Ellie bustled cheerfully about the room. She tutted over Portia for sleeping in her dressing gown, scolding her for not telling Ellie to add another blanket to the bed before she retired if she was cold. When she finally took herself off to select a gown for Portia to wear, Portia was nearly as startled as Ellie herself when the door failed to yield. It took Portia a minute to remember locking it, and a further few moments to recall where she'd left the keys. Ellie did not seem to think it odd that Portia'd locked the dressing room door; in fact, she seemed relieved her mistress was taking the ghostly threat so seriously.

The assumption irritated Portia, and she'd have taken exception to it had she been able to clearly state just why she *had* locked the dressing room door. Not for fear of ghosts, surely.

She stumbled blearily out of bed and seated herself at the dressing table as Ellie returned, one of the old black gowns draped over her arm. "I've nearly got the new one done," she said apologetically. "You'd be surprised how hard it is to find needle and thread around this place. You're a slow top this morning, if I do say so. It's what comes of being up half the night, sorting your new gowns. I'd have helped you with it, my lady, and happy to," Ellie chattered on, making Portia wish she'd found herself a quieter maid. "What, if I may ask, did you do with the ballgowns? No need to tuck them away, my lady, you know I wouldn't be working on them without your say-so."

"I did nothing with the gowns, Ellie. Make some sense, do."

"But you must have, miss, they're not there."

The news startled Portia into fully opening her eyes for the first time that morning. The first thing they fell on was the silver hair brush.

Portia's entire body seized up in a moment of superstitious dread. Twice she'd returned that brush to the master's bedchamber and twice it had reappeared on her dressing table. This time through two locked doors. She stared at it so long even Ellie noticed something amiss and fell silent.

Finally, Portia gathered her courage and reached for the brush, unsurprised to see her fingers trembling. When her index finger made contact with the gleaming silver, she jumped despite herself. The dread broke in a spurt of anger. Portia muttered one of Roger's favorite epithets. What a peagoose she was! Of course it was real, and of course there was a reasonable explanation for it.

"Ellie, you didn't by any chance—"

"I thought you—"

Portia shook her head stiffly and Ellie clammed up with an audible gulp. Portia reached for the brush again, forcing herself to wrap her fingers around the cool surface. It felt perfectly ordinary. It *was* perfectly ordinary. And perfectly untarnished. Someone had given it a good going-over with a polishing cloth since yesterday.

"Very well, then, Ellie. If we are to keep finding this on my dressing table, we might as well make use of it." Portia handed the silver-backed brush to Ellie, who shrank momentarily away before nerving herself to take it. "Now," Portia said as Ellie started to brush her hair with a much more tentative hand than usual, "what was that you were saying about the dresses?"

"All the beautiful ballgowns, my lady, they're gone! Not a one left in the dressing room."

"What? You must have—"

"I looked and looked, and where could they go anyway? The morning dresses and walking dresses and nightrails and such are still there, but all the ballgowns, my lady!" Ellie stopped brushing abruptly, her hands shaking as she realized that Portia didn't know a thing about it. "You didn't move them, my lady? Only... if you didn't move them, then, oh Lord, oh my lady, who—"

"Not a ghost," Portia cut in before Ellie could get even more worked up. "What need does a ghost have for ballgowns?"

A giggle forced its way through Ellie's lips and she began brushing again. "Then who did it, my lady?"

"Who else is in the house?" Portia said sourly, calling herself seven kinds of fool. She'd demanded only her room key from Mrs. McFerran. But there was another door into her room, and the housekeeper had a set of keys that no doubt encompassed every door in Ashburne Hall. She could come and go as she liked, locked doors or no.

* * *

When Portia went downstairs, she fully intended to have it out with the housekeeper then and there. But Mrs. McFerran was not to be found in the kitchen, the stillroom, her sitting room, or anywhere else Portia thought to look. Not willing to spend the morning hunting her housekeeper through the Hall, Portia retreated to the library to wait for the woman to put in an appearance.

She paused a moment after fitting her key to the lock, anticipating the pleasure all those books gave her—the only real treasure she'd ever been vouchsafed. When she pushed the door open, the sight that greeted her stopped her heart like a blow.

Portia stared at the empty bookcase, her breath congealing in her chest. It was nothing but bare shelves from floor to ceiling, nothing but dust and cobwebs and mouse droppings. Portia shoved the door wide and some small portion of her heart returned when she saw it was the only case so denuded. The rest settled uneasily into place when she caught sight of the chaos of books scattered over the floor.

Portia stumbled into the library and stood staring at the books stacked in the middle of the floor, everything tumbled together without regard to subject, author, or the proper care of the valuable volumes. As she knelt next to the first pile, she was struck by the feeling that there was some kind of order to the placement of the books, but she couldn't put her finger on quite what.

She picked up a book that had fallen on its spine and gently closed it, stroking her fingers over its misused binding, tears starting in her eyes for the poor cracked leather. She set the book carefully atop one of the stacks and reached for the next mistreated darling, wedged between two piles, its covers sadly scuffed. Slowly, she began straightening and sorting the books into some semblance of order, mourning the harsh treatment they'd received, seething at the thought that it was done to hurt *her*.

Mrs. McFerran had the gall to seek her out while she was engaged in this activity.

"I do not know," Portia said when she looked up to find the housekeeper in the doorway, "what you hoped to accomplish with this wanton destruction, but you have not succeeded." She carefully smoothed a creased page. "I will have your keys."

"You cannot turn me off, Lady Ashburne."

"Perhaps not, but I can take your keys. You may keep the ones to the pantry, the stillroom and your sitting room. The rest you will give to me."

The housekeeper's back stiffened. "I will then be unable to attend to my duties."

"The only rooms in the Hall that will be locked are those you need have no business in." Portia looked at Mrs. McFerran until she averted her gaze. "If you believe yourself unable to fulfill your obligations, you may, of course, choose to resign."

There followed a moment of thick silence. Finally, Mrs. McFerran withdrew her chatelaine, took three keys, and handed the rest to Portia, who compared the ring to her own to verify that the keys the woman kept were the ones specified. "That will be all, Mrs. McFerran."

Portia deliberately waited until the housekeeper had turned to add, "Oh, and Mrs. McFerran? I expect to see all the dresses you took from my dressing room returned by the time I retire for the night."

"I don't know to what you're—"

"Cut line, madam. " Portia rose, smoothed her worn skirts, and swept the housekeeper out of the library, favoring her with one last thought before she closed the door on her. "I will have new gowns, Mrs. McFerran. If I do not have the dowager Lady Ashburne's gowns to make over, then I will simply have to spout the silver and buy some."

* * *

Portia spent the morning sorting books and returning them to the shelves. Unable to discern any common ground in type or subject, she settled for putting them in order by author. Histories, farming treatises, plays and novels ended up rubbing covers and Portia promised herself she'd bring some order to the chaos when there was more time.

She was relieved to discover that, by and large, the books had not been as badly used as she had first feared. A few had been mistreated, but most were in as good condition as if they'd never been off the shelves. She might have known. Mrs. McFerran wouldn't irretrievably damage anything in her precious Ashburne Hall, even to get at Portia.

The top shelf was too high for her to reach, even with the library stairs. She was perched at the very top of the steps, putting books on the next shelf down and wondering what she could do with the last stack, when a whirlwind burst into the library.

"Lady Ashburne! I'm so glad I caught you. I saw you from outside, and— Whoa!" Lady Clarissa grabbed for the library stairs, steadying them under Portia, who pried her fingers free of their desperate grip on the shelves and quickly descended to solid earth. "I'm terribly sorry," Lady Clarissa stammered. "I had no idea you were so close to the door."

"No matter," Portia was able to say with a degree of sincerity once she was no longer in danger of falling. She dusted off her drab black skirts, vaguely wishing her new gown was finished, though she wouldn't have been wearing it to haul dusty books around even if it were. "What can I do for you, my lady?"

The boldness that attended Lady Clarissa fled of a sudden and she fell into concentrated study of the nearest shelf of books. "I was, I just, I—"

The hamper Lady Clarissa had dropped when she grabbed the library stairs protested its rough treatment with an irritated mew. "I thought," Lady Clarissa said, with the air of someone who had *not* just desperately latched onto the first subject that presented itself, "that you could use a cat. This place must be overrun with mice."

"How very thoughtful of you, my dear." Portia knelt to unhook the lid of the basket, which was rocking with its occupant's efforts to free itself. A black paw with white-tipped toes poked out, soon followed by the rest of the cat. He immediately sat down and began licking his ruffled fur, which sported random splotches of brown, as if he'd run under a painter's worktable. He was in that stage of adolescence that made even the sleekest of animals awkward.

When Portia picked him up, he blinked slowly at her over a broad white nose. "Does he have a name?"

"Not unless you count 'hey you' and 'scat.'"

"All right." Portia stared into the pale green eyes. "I dub thee Thomas. Go, Sir Thomas, and hunt mice." She put him down and he dashed immediately out the library door, much to Portia's amusement. "Thank you."

"You're most welcome."

"And now, my dear. Your real reason for coming?"

Lady Clarissa flushed. "I was hoping you'd made up your mind about teaching me," she blurted.

"I have. Shall we retire to the morning room?" It would be as comfortable as anyplace in the Hall, excepting Portia's own bedchamber. The carpet wasn't turned yet, true, but Ellie hadn't said anything about mice in the furniture, so at least there was someplace to sit.

"Oh, but—"

Portia took pity on her. "Of course I'll teach you."

"Oh, thank you!"

"I haven't done anything yet," Portia said wryly, reflecting that Lady Clarissa's appreciation for the lessons would no doubt suffer in direct proportion to their tediousness. She ushered the young woman out of the library, securely locking it behind them, and led the way to the morning room.

Portia went directly to the window and pushed back the threadbare drapes, letting in the late-morning sun. Though dimness would have hidden the worst of the furnishings' faults, Portia had always believed things looked better when properly lit. Even, she thought with an inward wince, when they looked worse.

Lady Clarissa stood with her riding boots planted firmly on the worn carpet, her fists propped on her hips, and surveyed the room. "It's the first I've been back since it happened. I had no idea it'd gotten so bad, the poor old house. You wouldn't credit, Lady Ashburne, how much I liked Ashburne Hall. Or how much," she added, almost inaudibly, "I envied Amelia."

"I thought Lord Ashburne scared you." Well done, Portia scolded herself. How is the young lady to learn proper manners from you when you perpetually demonstrate the most rag-mannered behavior yourself?

"He did. But at least... At least if you marry someone, they have to pay attention to you. Don't they?"

"I wouldn't count on it," Portia muttered. "All right, Lady Clarissa—"

"Clary, please."

"Lady Clarissa, if we are to practice proper Society forms. For the moment, however, let's leave that aside and indulge in some plain dealing. You need someone to give you a little Town bronze and I, as you so accurately pointed out, am so far up River Tick I haven't much chance of coming out again."

"Oh, but I didn't—"

"Don't come over all missish on me now. You were absolutely right. If I want to have any chance to making the Hall livable, I shall have to earn some money somehow. So I'm going to take you up on your offer—I will endeavor to teach you the manner the *beau monde* expects from a duke's niece and you will pay me for the lessons. Agreed?"

"Oh yes!"

"Very well then." And thank heavens! Once she realized this was her only recourse, Portia had spent every free moment since worrying that Lady Clarissa would change her mind. It was well the girl had come to the Hall or Portia should soon have had to go looking for her.

If Portia could make Clary shine for her coming out, the young lady's success would bring other girls to her door. If Foxkin was to be believed, Clary wasn't the only chit in the neighborhood whose behavior was unsuitable one way or another. Portia wasn't cut out to be a companion or governess, but she had one thing she *could* sell: she'd been brought up by a duke and knew the manners expected of the highest in the land. It was not only the hoydens like Clary that she could help, but the daughters of the lesser lights of nobility, who needs must appear quite proud and polished to make good matches. But if Portia was to avoid being tarred with the brush of Service, she could not go from house to house. She must accept girls into her home for the lessons, and that meant relying on Clary not only to show well, but to pay her well. Lady Clarissa was willing to accept the Hall as it was, but it would produce no good effect on other prospective customers. The morning room, dining room and great hall, at a minimum, must be made to look like a proper lady's country home.

Portia stepped to the bellpull and gave it a delicate tug. It did not, thank heavens, snap off in her hand, and she thought she heard the chime of the bell from deep in the house. With any luck, Mrs. McFerran would put in an appearance, for it would be too lowering to have to go in search of her housekeeper. "The first lesson," she told her new pupil, "is that a lady doesn't enter a house uninvited, let alone go poking around on her own. She gives her card to the butler or housekeeper or footman, and waits for her hostess to send word whether she is receiving or not."

"I *do* know that," Clary objected. "But there's no door knocker and—"

"No servant to answer the door in any case. Just remember that you're going to have to get over your impetuousness if you don't want to be labeled a quiz or worse. Next, I will ask you to dress appropriately the next time you come. That means a morning gown or walking dress, Lady Clarissa."

"But—"

"There's no point to teaching you how to act like a lady if you persist in attending your lessons in men's clothing."

Clary opened her mouth to protest, then thought better of it. "I take your point, Lady Ashburne. I'm to learn to be a lady, which means dressing like one."

"Precisely."

Mrs. McFerran tapped at the open door and went away again with her lips pinched when Portia said, "Tea, please." Now what was that about? Mrs. McFerran went about with a permanently sour expression, and Portia wouldn't be the least surprised if she felt put about by being asked to fulfill her duties, but that had actually looked more like disapproval. Why should the housekeeper care if Portia had Lady Clarissa at the Hall? "Besides, I'm quite certain you don't show up at table with the Duke of Ransley in riding breeches."

"Not that he'd notice if I did." Clary sighed and plumped down on the nearest chair. "I don't think I can do it."

"We've only just started."

"Yes, but to sigh and simper and flutter my eyelashes and hide behind my fan..."

"Good lord! There's no need for all that." Portia seated herself in the chair nearest Clary's. "All you need do is follow the proper forms and meet the expectations of the Society sticklers, thereby ensuring you receive plenty of the invitations, your vouchers for Almack's, and—"

"Offers from eligible gentlemen."

"Those too."

"But if I don't sigh and simper and so forth, how will I capture one?"

"If you do sigh and simper and snabble yourself some cloth-headed husband who thinks that's what he wants in a wife, then where will you be? No, Lady Clarissa—you have to be yourself and find a man who loves you for who you are."

Assuming there was such a thing. Portia kept the thought to herself. It was not her place to discourage Clary's romanticism. A good marriage was vital to a lady's well-being; not even the niece of a duke could afford to drift into spinsterhood.

They got through tea without major mishap, Clary proving that her manners weren't nearly as bad as she made out by not commenting on the lack of dainty pastries to go with the tea. Portia found herself almost grateful that James and his wife had descended on Rosewood Close after Roger's death, forcing her to brush up on her manners, grown rusty from five years' lack of exposure to Quality.

"I think," Portia said when tea had come off almost without a hitch, "that's enough for our first day. If it will suit—" A thunderous crash from upstairs made her jump. Portia ignored it with an effort, Clary following suit after her first involuntary flinch. "—perhaps you might return tomorrow?"

"Oh, thank you, Lady Ashburne, I—" At Portia's look, Clary cut off the effusive flow and composed herself. "Tomorrow would be quite acceptable, Lady Ashburne. Thank you."

They emerged into the great hall the same moment Ellie came dashing pell-mell down the stairs, in a state even a maid should not succumb to. "Oh my lady," she gasped, hanging on the balustrade, "oh come quickly, do! He's fallen through the ceiling!"

Chapter Eleven

FOR a moment, Portia thought Ellie was talking about Giles Ashburne. Then she came to her senses. For one thing, Ellie'd be in a quite unimaginable state if a strange man had fallen through the ceiling. And, much more to the point, Ashburne was dead.

Portia dashed after her maid, taking the stairs at a pace even Clary in her men's riding breeches couldn't outstrip. She was in too much of a taking to reflect on how badly such behavior undercut her ability to teach the young lady decorum.

Ellie led her to one of the servants' rooms on the second floor, where Mrs. McFerran was attempting to help her husband out of a litter of moldering lathe and plaster. As soon as he saw Portia, Mr. McFerran corked up the groans and curses that had been audible from the landing, but he was dead-white and utterly unable to put any weight on his right leg. Portia rushed forward to take his free arm and help Mrs. McFerran get him gingerly perched on the bed.

Portia took one look at his rapidly greying complexion and said, "Where's the nearest surgeon?" The housekeeper didn't seem to hear. "Mrs. McFerran," she snapped, "the nearest surgeon?"

Mrs. McFerran looked at her with strangely dazed eyes and murmured, "The surgeon? Yes, Mr. Millbank."

"Can you take care of Mr. McFerran until I get back with the surgeon? Ellie will help."

Mrs. McFerran stared at her without comprehension, looking wholly human for the first time since Portia entered the Hall. In the next moment, something had broken open in her eyes, and Portia had to turn away from the helplessness she saw there.

"Well," Portia said, mostly to herself. She squared her shoulders. "Well then. I'll go find this surgeon."

"Pardon me, Lady Ashburne," Clary said from the doorway, startling Portia, who had forgotten her. "But it'll be quicker if I go. I know the way and besides, my Gunpowder's faster than any horse you have here."

Especially as they didn't have any. The thought chimed strangely against something already in Portia's mind, but she couldn't think what and now, she acknowledged as Mr. McFerran groaned through clenched teeth, was not the time. "Yes, please, Lady Clarissa. Go."

Clary was off like a shot, and Portia turned back to the McFerrans. "There must be laudanum somewhere in the house, Mrs. McFerran. Where is it?"

The housekeeper slowly dragged her eyes away from her husband. "Stillroom, my lady."

"I'll get it. In the meantime, Mr. McFerran can't remain in this room." The gaping hole in the ceiling would prove problematic if it rained and generally unhealthy even if it didn't. "How far is your room?"

"It's just a few doors down," Ellie said when Mrs. McFerran didn't immediately answer.

"Mr. McFerran, do you think if we hold you up, you can hop to your room?"

"Yes'm." He began to struggle to his feet, and Mrs. McFerran quickly put her arms about him.

"Let me, my lady." Ellie pushed forward before Portia could move to McFerran's assistance. "I'm taller."

Portia ran ahead to open the McFerrans' door, then downstairs to get the laudanum. She felt as completely useless as ladies of Quality were expected to be, doing nothing more helpful than running to get the laudanum, though it was patently obvious that moving Mr. McFerran must be left to Mrs. McFerran and Ellie. Not because Portia was a lady, but because she was not of a height to offer much support, even to a man of Mr. McFerran's moderate stature.

The stillroom shelves were full of crocks and bottles and jars, some broken, others containing only a crystallized remnant of whatever mixture they'd once held. It seemed like she fumbled in the dimly lit stillroom for ages before she at last lit on the right bottle. She dashed back up the stairs to the McFerrans' room.

Having regained some measure of control, Mrs. McFerran took the laudanum from Portia and administered it to Mr. McFerran, who grimaced at the taste, but drank it down. Portia stayed long enough to see the laudanum begin to take effect, smoothing the distress from Mr. McFerran's face, before returning downstairs to wait for the surgeon.

He took an eternity to arrive, during which Portia paced on the carriageway, barely noticing the weeds reclaiming the white gravel, the unkempt trees leaning ominously over the drive. Finally, a trap pulled by a proud, if somewhat shaggy, gelding crunched up the drive, a tall spare man in black at the reins.

"Mr. Millbank?" Portia asked as he reined in his horse before her.

"The same. Lady Ashburne, I presume."

Well, thank heavens he hadn't taken her for a servant in her dowdy black dress. "Where's Lady Clarissa?"

Mr. Millbank descended from the trap and lifted down his bag with a grave dignity quite out of keeping with the station of a mere surgeon. A physician might, perhaps, be forgiven for such self-importance. As it was, Portia could only guess that he must be the sole medical man in the area or his pretensions should have been deflated some time ago. He turned a penetrating look on her, finally unbending enough to say, "I sent her home."

His tone was that of a man who'd rescued some impressionable young chick from bad influences, and Portia had to remind herself that in her experience Ashburnes *were* bad influences. Still, it was difficult not to bristle at being relegated to the same company. "This way."

Mr. Millbank ascertained from her which room the McFerrans were in and headed up the stairs with the terse pronouncement that she need not trouble herself further. Fuming, Portia went into the library to finish putting the books away and try not to fret over a man toward whom, despite hearing him plot against her with his wife, she could wish no ill.

* * *

"The leg is broken."

Thankfully, Portia was not on a ladder this time. She picked up the book she'd dropped, straightened the pages, and slid it onto the shelf before turning to Mr. Millbank. "How badly?"

"He may walk again, if he keeps still and receives proper tending." His tone suggested it wasn't likely in such surroundings.

Portia ignored the slur. "You have informed Mrs. McFerran what needs to be done?"

"I have."

Portia gathered her courage with her next breath and said, "If you would be so good as to send me your bill, I will be able to pay it within the month." It never got any easier to admit her empty pockets, though one would think after all this time, she'd be quite good at putting off tradesmen and running up tabs. Certainly, it had never seemed to bother Roger.

The surgeon's lip curled. "I will *leave* you my bill, Lady Ashburne," he said, handing her a neatly written sheet of paper. Portia set it on the library table, all the lessons of her childhood going into keeping her face impassive when she saw the amount he was dunning her for a bare half-hour's work. "I will also take the liberty of informing you that I shall be unable to attend your servant further until this bill has been paid."

With that, he donned his hat and marched out of the library. She heard the front door bounce off the jamb and swing back open with a spine-grating creak. Her head high, though there was no one to see it, Portia went out to close the door properly. She slumped against it, her hands on her burning cheeks, and didn't notice Ellie until the maid huffed, "What a skinflint, the beak-nosed old bastard."

Portia dropped her hands and took a slow breath before turning. "I can't blame him," she said wearily. "When the Quality run out of money, it's never other Quality who go unpaid." A man couldn't hold his head up if he failed to discharge his gambling debts, but there was no shame in letting his tailor, chandler, or doctor go begging.

No one in the village was likely to be in any doubt about the state of Lady Ashburne's finances—the Hall's condition could not but be a byword in the neighborhood and the gossips would surely have spread the sad state of her wardrobe to all and sundry by now. Mr. Millbank had probably only come because it was Lady Clarissa who fetched him, not wanting to appear in a bad light before the Duke of Ransley's ward. He'd obviously come prepared to ensure he wouldn't suffer for Portia's financial woes, and Portia truthfully *couldn't* blame him, though he'd never have dared speak so to a man, even a badly strapped gentleman with his accounts well in arrears.

"Still, my lady—"

"Never mind, Ellie. I'll see he's paid, somehow." She started for the stairs, Ellie at her heels. "Now, how *is* Mr. McFerran?"

"Sleeping like a baby. That surgeon strapped his leg up good, dosed him with laudanum, and lectured Mrs. McFerran like she were a half-wit afore he took himself off. And dared charge you dear for it, I'll be bound." More dearly than if he had been a physician. Though a physician would have been of little use in the instance, as most would refuse to sully their hands with such injuries.

Ellie trailed Portia into the bedchamber Mr. McFerran had fallen into and stood watching her survey the patch of blue sky visible through the hole. Unless Portia very much missed her guess, or the roof was worse than she feared, it was the same hole she'd spotted in the attic the day before. The floorboards under it had indeed rotted away from the constant wetting, though Portia wished Mr. McFerran had not proven it the hard way.

"Fetch me a candle, will you Ellie? We'll have to get into the attics again."

It took them the better part of an hour to stretch enough oiled canvas across the hole Mr. McFerran had left in the attic floor as to render it mostly rainproof. It required the shifting of some remarkably heavy furniture to hold the canvas in place, and Ellie was muttering under her breath by the time Portia decreed it would serve. She stayed after Ellie had squeezed back through to the door and spent several precarious minutes determining how much she could see of the roof through the hole in it.

When Portia rejoined Ellie at the attic door, she was in lower spirits than at any time since she first saw Ashburne Hall looming out of a gloomy night.

"What is it, my lady?"

"I'm afraid that's not the only hole in the roof." Portia started down the stairs, holding her candle high as she navigated the steep steps. "Nor will our patch hold for long." She sighed. The money she'd sent for would not only not cover both the roof and the doctor, she was very much afraid it wouldn't pay for either one. "There's nothing for it. We'll have to pawn the silver."

She opened the door to the second floor landing and came face to face with Mrs. McFerran. Gone was the all-too human woman fearing for her husband. In her place, a flat-eyed gargoyle met Portia with an expression that could turn flesh to stone.

"How is Mr. McFerran?" Portia asked.

The housekeeper didn't appear to have heard. "If you pawn the silver," she said stoutly, "I shall have to inform Lord Ashburne."

Portia was taken aback. It was for Mr. McFerran's sake, in part, that she was even considering such a course. How dare Mrs. McFerran take her to task for it! Portia lifted her chin, her voice icy as she said, "If you feel you must. Of course, Lord Ashburne has two other estates to keep up, plus the expense of his Town entertainments, while I need only support this one establishment. I will pawn only what I must, but Lord Ashburne.... Well, I really don't know *what* he will do." She made herself smile sweetly and said, "I feel quite certain, Mrs. McFerran, that you will do what is best for the Hall," and left her impotently fuming.

Chapter Twelve

DAMN her, how dare she! She deserved all the horrors of Hell.

Giles paced up and down the great hall, his boots on the bare stone raising a racket that echoed off the high ceiling. He contemplated disturbing her sleep with a different racket, filling the Hall with a wailing that could wake the dead. But no, Mr. McFerran didn't deserve to have his painful sleep interrupted.

Portia did. By God, she did. How dare she see the old man injured like that—because *she* could not be bothered to get proper workmen in—and still think of nothing but her dresses? The doctor had barely left when that woman and her maid were back in the attics looking for more gowns to make over. And when she didn't find any....

The Ashburne silver was the only thing besides the library that had survived these last ten years. Damned if he was going to let her turn it into fripperies.

He took himself off to his bedchamber and went from there into the dressing room, where a strange noise startled him. He lifted his candle in time to see an awkward-looking cat disembowel a mouse. "Where did you come from?"

The animal stared at him, reflected candlelight shining from its eyes. Now there was an idea....

But first. He surveyed the dressing room, her dresses and his mother's hanging side by side. He'd already taken much of it back—the fancy ballgowns he remembered from his youth, his mother bending her sweet-smelling cheek for his kiss before she went out. He'd given Portia no opportunity to rip those apart for her selfish vanity. But he'd been too easy on her. He'd left the day dresses and shifts and other odds and ends.

It took him half an hour to spirit away the rest. She would take the last of what was his? He would take all that was hers.

When he was done, he shielded the candle flame with his hand and walked into her bedchamber. He stood a long while in the dark, her lavender scent filling his lungs and his head, looking anywhere but at his candle until he'd grown accustomed to the dark and could see the room clearly. In all that time, there was no movement from the bed. He approached and stood watching her peaceful sleep, untroubled by the noise of his activities or the voice of her conscience, if she had one.

How, he wondered, could she look so sweet and innocent in her sleep— her hair fanned across the pillow, her face turned softly to one side—and yet be so heartless? How could he, knowing what he knew, still find himself attracted to the soft cloud of her auburn hair, the pale sheen of her skin? Quite without meaning to, Giles reached to brush one finger lightly over her downy cheek.

She stirred and woke, looking at him through sleep-blurred eyes. He waited for the moment when she woke fully, terror stretching her eyes wide.

He snuffed out the candle, her scream echoing in the dark room.

* * *

Portia huddled in her bed all the rest of that night with the blankets drawn close about her, her eyes endlessly scanning her bedchamber. Hard as she tried, she couldn't bring herself to get up and light her candle from the coals of the fire, assuming there were any. The blankets were no protection at all, but she couldn't make herself let go of them.

He'd been so close she fancied she could feel his breath. Giles Ashburne and no doubt about it, his face the face of the portrait, though somewhat racked about with the years. And wasn't that the proof of it? Proof she hadn't just dreamed it, for if she had, she'd have imagined him exactly as he was in the painting, not aged betimes by hard days and foreign climes.

Portia shuddered and drew her blankets closer, eyes uselessly scanning the room, ears straining. Again and again she heard, or thought she heard, some stealthy sound, audible only by the desperation with which she listened. Nothing so obvious as footsteps. But he was coming for her, she knew he was.

He'd been surrounded by a ghastly shuddering light that vanished the instant she saw him. She could see nothing now, but she knew he was still there, invisible to her straining eyes, for she could hear him. Yes, and smell him, the rich scent of his tobacco clinging to her senses as it clung to the pages of his books.

Portia didn't draw a full breath until dawn began to slowly gray the inky shadows. She didn't close her eyes for even a moment until Ellie unlocked her door—the noise of the key scraping in the lock shuddering over her straining nerves—and came in with jaunty good cheer.

"Good morning, my lady. I've finished your walking dress, and the first stare of fashion it is too, if I do say so myself." She draped it over the dressing table chair on her way to bring Portia her morning tray and open the curtains. Something leapt onto the bed and Portia screamed before realizing it was the cat.

Ellie whirled, her hand at her throat. "Oh, my lady! You frightened me."

"Well, *he* frightened *me*." The cat settled himself on the counterpane and wrapped his tail unconcernedly about his paws, as if screams were a usual morning greeting. "Did he come in with you?"

"I don't believe so, my lady."

"You," Portia said to the cat, reaching to rub his broad forehead, "are a sneak." Well, at least the stealthy noises were explained. Somehow, Thomas had gotten himself locked in the bedroom with her.

Too bad it did nothing to explain the apparition she'd seen. She tried to tell herself it had been only a dream, but could not make herself believe it.

"Are you well, my lady? You look that done in, you do."

Portia doggedly poured her tea, managing somehow not to spill it, and lifted the cup to her lips, cradling it between her hands to get the warmth of it. "I'm fine," she told Ellie after she'd swallowed several scalding mouthfuls. "I didn't sleep well." On no account would she tell Ellie what she'd seen—Portia was not capable of dealing with a hysterical maid on top of the night she'd had.

"It's what comes of not having a proper supper, that's what I say."

Supper had been a cold collation, managed without stale bread and moldy cheese this time and assembled by Ellie and Portia herself, as Mrs. McFerran was needed at her husband's bedside. Given the circumstances, it had not been a bad effort.

"May I use your keys, my lady?" The question was perfunctory, as Ellie already had the ring Portia'd left on the dressing table and was fitting the key to the lock on the dressing room door. Portia sipped her tea with her eyes closed and had nearly succeeded in nodding off sitting up when Ellie screamed.

Tea went all over the counterpane, and Portia barely caught the cup before it rolled off the bed. Her heart pounding, she scrambled out of bed and padded barefoot across the floor.

"Oh," Ellie moaned, "all gone, they're all gone."

With a sense of weary fatalism, Portia looked in to find the dressing room bare of all but the most basic of underclothing. Everything had been removed, from her recent acquisitions to her oldest gown. He was determined to leave her nothing, she thought numbly, to leave her shivering in her shift. She did shiver then, and something in her woke up.

Why did she persist, in these moments, in thinking of a man? It was, again and always, Mrs. McFerran who found a way through locked doors, who would do anything to see Portia out. Well this effort was self-defeating; Portia could hardly vacate the Hall in her nightrail. Perhaps the housekeeper intended to scratch at her door once the full import of Portia's situation was borne home to her and offer the return of her dresses if she'd leave. If so, she'd grossly miscalculated. Besides, she'd missed one.

"Well," Portia said, giving Ellie a smile that only shook a little, "it shan't be hard to decide what to wear. Come along, Ellie, let's get me ready for the day."

"But, my lady!"

"Once you do, we'll go looking for my gowns." Portia seated herself at the dressing table and stared defiantly at herself in the mirror. At the edge of the reflection, she could see Thomas lapping milky tea off the counterpane. "And we won't stop until we find them."

Portia closed her eyes while Ellie brushed her hair, and found it difficult not to let her head nod with weariness. What connection, she wondered, did the missing gowns have with Ashburne's... visitation? Was it only coincidence that she had seen, or dreamt, a ghost the same night Mrs. McFerran was walking off with her entire wardrobe? Unbidden, the sight of him came back to her: skin pale, hair and clothing so dark they merged with the night, assuming he had a body at all and didn't just fade away into nothing. Flames had flickered in his black eyes as if he carried all the fires of Hell inside him.

Portia shuddered, and Ellie rushed to wrap her in her dressing gown. No, Portia thought, firming her spine, she would not succumb to a fit of the vapors. She was strong; she had to be. They would not drive her out. Not Mrs. McFerran, nor her mice and thievery and ghost stories.

Not the ghost himself.

* * *

The day did not get any less wearisome.

Portia began it with a visit to Mr. McFerran. His wife watched with smoldering resentment and said not a word while Portia touched her fingers to the sleeping man's brow. He was overwarm, sweating in the grip of laudanum and fever, his braced and bandaged leg an unwieldy lump under the blankets. Fever was to be expected, but if he did not improve on his own, a return visit of the doctor would be required.

Portia left without a word about the gowns. She had no doubt Mrs. McFerran would look at her with her flat black eyes and say she hadn't any idea what Portia was talking about. It would be less infuriating to find the missing gowns herself.

Except they were nowhere to be found.

Ashburne Hall contained a vast number of hiding places, and Portia and Ellie had poked into all of them by tea time. Every room in the servants' quarters but the McFerrans' own, which in any case contained no hiding place large enough to conceal an entire trunk-full of gowns. Every guest room. Every one of the family apartments. Every inch of the attics and every box, trunk and wardrobe. They looked in the musty conservatory, under the billiard table, in every nook and cranny of the kitchen. And the breakfast room. And the dining room. Portia set Ellie to searching the housekeeper's sitting room and the stillroom and went herself to check the library and butler's pantry, which Mrs. McFerran ought no longer have keys to. But then, Portia had believed the woman no longer had keys to her dressing room until she woke to find it ransacked.

Ellie joined her in the butler's pantry, panting that she'd found nothing, but thought she could hear footsteps on the stairs. Portia collapsed into the hard, straight-backed chair the butler had used when polishing the silver and tried to think. She was tired, hungry, and growing depressed at consistently receiving less than nothing for her pains. Not just the effort to find her gowns, but the struggle of simply living at Ashburne Hall. If she thought James would take her back, she might well have hied herself back to Rosewood. She could hire a coach at the Duck and Drake. If she had the money for a coach, which of course she hadn't.

Portia picked up a Russian samovar, squat-legged and pot-bellied, heavier than it looked and ugly as sin. "How could anyone possibly care what happens to this?" she asked Ellie. "What do you suppose it would bring?"

Mrs. McFerran swooped suddenly into the butler's pantry and snatched the samovar from her. "How dare you!" she gasped, clasping it awkwardly to her bosom.

"How dare *you*, madam?" Portia snapped back. "I don't know what you've done with my clothing, but it serves no purpose to take it. You might as well return it and save yourself the trouble that will surely follow if you do not." Her mother would never have spoken to their housekeeper thus. Her mother would never have had to; Father would have turned the woman out at the first sign of trouble. Pity Portia could not do the same.

"And if I do not? You shall simply take this—" Mrs. McFerran shook the samovar at Portia. "—and trade it for gowns and jewelry and fancy trinkets. You would take this and all the rest and sell it for your own pleasure."

Portia gaped, thrown momentarily off. It was only then she remembered her threat the previous morning, that if the stolen ballgowns were not returned by evening, she'd sell the silver to buy some. Never mind the doctor and the hole in the roof, this was what Mrs. McFerran thought she was about. The truth knocked at Portia's teeth, but even if Mrs. McFerran would have believed her, which was debatable, Portia could not bring herself to tell the woman that if they wanted the doctor back, they'd have pay him first. She was as proud, in her way, as the rest of the *ton*—it was one thing to drown yourself in debt for ballgowns and fancy finery, but to admit you hadn't the blunt to keep life and limb together.... No, it was too lowering to be borne.

Portia stood and lifted a silver cruet stand from a nearby shelf, turning it this way and that. "It doesn't bear the Ashburne crest, so it's safe enough to spout. There won't be any talk to sully the family name." *Further*, she might have added. "And you must admit it's particularly ugly. Though not nearly as ugly as that samovar."

Mrs. McFerran clutched the offending urn closer. "You can't."

"I can and will."

"You'll be selling the library next."

It was true the books might fetch a higher price than the silver if spouted in the proper place. Portia shuddered at the thought. Ashburne Hall could afford to lose a few ugly pieces of plate, but Portia could not bring herself to part with a single volume from the library.

"No," Portia said, almost gently. "But I will be selling this." She handed the cruet stand to Ellie and took the samovar from her housekeeper, who let it go without a struggle, either too startled or too smart to tussle with her mistress, however brazen she was in speaking to her. "And this." She handed it to Ellie as well, locked the butler's pantry, and started down the hall.

"And," Mrs. McFerran asked, "if your gowns reappeared?"

Portia did not turn. "I would still sell it."

* * *

She took Ellie with her to the Duck and Drake. It was one thing to walk about the countryside by yourself, another to do it while lugging several valuable pieces of silver. She found a couple of burlap sacks in the dilapidated stables to hide the gleam of silver in, and together they set off through the home wood.

Portia half expected to be run over by Clary, racing late to her second lesson, but there was no sign of the girl. She ought to have shown up at the Hall in the middle of Portia's clothing-hunt. It was just as well she hadn't, but the young lady was now so late it was quite clear she wasn't coming. Portia fretted uselessly over what Mr. Millbank had said to drive the chit off and, worse, whether he'd carried the tale to the duke, who was so set against the Hall that Clary'd hardly dared approach it that first day. Portia couldn't afford to lose her first pupil. She was relying on Lady Clarissa's example to bring in more students after she went on to have a (hopefully) brilliant Season. It really was her only hope. She certainly could not continue to spout the silver—sooner or later it would run out, or James would discover what she was doing, or Mrs. McFerran would murder her in her sleep.

She allowed Foxkin to bring them tea—she was famished, and in any case would soon be able to pay for it—and waited until he came back to take the tray to ask if he knew where she might be able to sell a few pieces of silver. It was the first time he'd seen her in suitable clothing and Portia hated to extinguish the look of approval that had sprung into his eyes when he saw her in the gray silk walking dress, but she had no one else to ask.

Foxkin looked the samovar over, rubbing his chin with one hand. If he recognized the monstrosity, he chose not to mention it. Nor did he ask if she was certain she wanted to sell it or give her a look either condemning or pitying, for which she was grateful.

"Well, my lady, there's no one closer than a day's ride who'd give you fair trade for a piece like this," he said finally, dashing her hopes. "Still." He stepped back, as if a different angle would make the samovar less hideous. "I fancy I know a gentleman hereabouts who would be interested in such a piece."

Portia couldn't imagine why. "Could you direct me to him?"

"I could, but your ladyship shouldn't be walking about the neighborhood with such a heavy burden." Nor would it do her reputation any good to show up on a gentleman's doorstep with something to sell, like a common gypsy. "If I may... I could keep this piece, and the other, and contact the gentleman I have in mind. If he proves as interested as I'm certain he will, I can arrange the matter. Would that suit?"

"Yes, thank you." It didn't suit, but it would have to do. It was not that Portia didn't trust Foxkin. The innkeeper had been nothing but beforehand with her so far and she couldn't afford to start mistrusting him now. But the money would be, she feared, several days in coming, by which time the attic and servants' quarters might well be flooded and who knew what state Mr. McFerran would be in.

"I believe I know what he would offer, my lady," Foxkin said slowly, choosing his words carefully. "May I advance you part of that sum, purely in good faith?"

Purely in pity, Portia feared, but she couldn't afford to turn it down. "That would be most agreeable of you, Mr. Foxkin."

He excused himself, taking the silver with him, much to Ellie's unspoken consternation. Portia was careful not to meet her maid's eye. She didn't need scolding, she needed the money, and if whatever Foxkin gave her was all she got out of the silver he'd just walked off with, it would still be more than she had. He returned with a modest bag that jingled with coin. She tucked it directly into her reticule; she would not embarrass either of them by counting it in front of him.

"I find myself curious, Mr. Foxkin," Portia said, once she'd drawn the strings on her reticule.

"Yes, my lady?" he said with such avidity she knew he would be as happy as she to embrace some less embarrassing subject.

"Was Lord Ashburne liked?" He looked startled, and she added, "Before." In some ways, she was nearly as startled as he that the question had left her lips. In others, she understood herself quite well. She was looking for some reassurance that the dark figure bending over her in the night wasn't evil by his very nature.

"Well, my lady," Foxkin said cautiously, as if feeling his way through dangerous territory, "yes. Yes, he was. He wasn't always a comfortable man." Portia started at hearing the very thought that had come to her when she first saw the implacable black eyes of Ashburne's portrait and nearly missed the rest. "But folks hereabouts liked him. More, probably, than the duke. His grace is honest and fair, but... unbending, while Lord Ashburne...." Foxkin seemed suddenly to recollect himself. He straightened his shoulders and took one corner of his apron in his large fingers. "Is there anything more I might do for you, your ladyship?"

"Yes," Portia said, reminding herself she had no call to stick her nose into a crime ten years dead and gone. "Can you direct me to Mr. Millbank's place of residence, and who would you recommend to repair a roof?" Even with the money he had advanced her, she didn't have enough to cover both expenses, but with any luck she soon would.

Foxkin looked taken aback, but recovered quickly. "Certainly, my lady."

Mr. Millbank's house was located on the other end of the village. The last time she was at the inn, Portia had been careful to return home the same way she came, not wanting to be seen any more than necessary in her disreputable gown. Today, with her new walking dress, more fashionable than anything she'd had for years for all it was made over from a dress last worn in the previous century, she did not hesitate to step out toward the village. She might have only the one dress in her closet, but she needn't act like it.

Foxkin had kindly left her alone in the parlor long enough to count her money. It wasn't much, not a tenth what the silver was worth, but it was enough to pay the doctor and still buy a few items to eke out the limited contents of the pantry. Accordingly, Portia gave Ellie a certain sum and a list of things to buy and sent her off to handle those purchases, the maid protesting all the way. Ellie sometimes forgot that Portia was no longer the innocent chit who'd married a man she hardly knew. Being seen without a maid would do less to harm her reputation than being seen haggling with the butcher.

The state of the village spoke well of the Duke of Ransley. As the highest-ranking nobleman in the area, it was doubtless his influence that kept the buildings along the high street in good repair and the people in accord with each other, at least publicly. Aware of the eyes on her, Portia walked with her back straight and her head up, and no one went so far as to stare, at least not obviously.

She made it to Mr. Millbank's without incident, paid him, much to his obvious surprise, and left with the expressed hope that it would not be difficult to engage his services in the future.

Partway back down the street, Portia stopped to look in the modiste's prettily decorated window. One dress in particular caught her eye: a ballgown of severe beauty, its simple lines designed to show the wearer's figure to best advantage. So far from London, it was not likely to be the first stare of fashion, but it was sharp and elegant and the deep shimmering blue of its bodice and skirts couldn't help but catch her eye. Portia could never afford such a gown, but she couldn't help noticing how it was cut, or imagining making that copper-colored ballgown from the dowager Lady Ashburne's trunk over into the same pattern. If she still had it.

She turned away from the window and was nearly bowled over by Lady Clarissa, who came pelting out of the shop dressed in a pretty gown of seafoam green, pins in the shoulders and skirts where the modiste was still working on it.

"Lady Ashburne! How wonderful to see you." Clary grabbed Portia's hand and dragged her into the shop before she could either protest or return the gabbled greeting. "I must speak with you," Clary hissed, tugging Portia toward the back of the shop, where a woman of middle years waited. She was pretty in a peculiarly French way and dressed in the perfect pattern-card of fashion, the best of advertisements for her shop.

"Lady Clarissa, we must get on," she said, her accent quaintly punctuating the words. "Your uncle, he will be most displeased if we are not completed in time."

"Yes, yes, Madame Fanchon." Clary took a position with her feet together and arms outstretched with long-suffering patience. "May I make you known to my old friend, Lady Portia?"

Clary's eyes pleaded with Portia, and she allowed the modiste to greet her by that name. The woman looked her over with a quick judgmental eye and did not dismiss her out of hand, which was a credit to Ellie's talent with a needle. Portia didn't want to think about the reception she'd have gotten in one of her old gowns. Or if she were introduced as Lady Ashburne.

Thus trapped, Clary's "old friend" watched while the modiste poked and pinned, measured and mended. Clary's eyes remained on Portia's face throughout, the intensity of her gaze such that if she could have conveyed whatever was the matter by the force of thought alone, Portia would surely know in an instant why she was watching as her would-be pupil fidgeted her way through the fitting of half a dozen dresses, all pretty, but not quite the thing for a girl's come out. Portia would have expected the duke to make use of the local modiste to create his niece's wardrobe for the Season; her prices were doubtless more reasonable than those in Town. But then, Ransley had the money to pay a fashionable dressmaker straight from Paris once they got to London.

"Out with it," Portia said as soon as the modiste had declared herself satisfied and disappeared into the back room. "I've never seen you so skimble-brained." Not that she'd had much opportunity to observe the young lady, but Clary hadn't struck her as inclined towards histrionic displays. "What's got you in such a taking and why did you not introduce me as Lady Ashburne?"

"Because," Clary hissed, "Mr. Millbank, that interfering old fusspot, emptied his budget to my uncle." She turned about so Portia could do up her dress. "Oh, Lady Ashburne! He's forbidden me to have anything to do with you."

Chapter Thirteen

"HAS he?" Portia was grateful Lady Clarissa could not see her face, and for her steady fingers, still automatically doing up the young lady's dress. Clary had no idea how vital her lessons were to Portia—less for the money she was willing to pay than for the start her success could give Portia on a new livelihood—and it would be entirely too lowering for her to discover it now that the duke had dashed those hopes.

"Oh, my lady!" Clary spun and grabbed Portia's hands. "Portia, please! You must help. You have to do something."

"Turn about, you're not done up yet. What do you expect me to do?"

"Convince him!" She fidgeted until Portia had done up the last button, then whirled on her again. "If I don't have you to teach me, I'll be the laughing stock of the *ton*. I will, I know it!"

"Take a damper, child."

Clary scowled and stamped her foot. "I'm not a child."

"You're certainly acting like one."

With a sigh, Clary plumped down in the velvet chair. "I know. I'm sorry. But I was so happy. So certain it would all turn out right, now that I've got you to teach me." She turned liquid blue eyes on Portia. "I was even looking forward to my Season."

"You still should." Portia took a breath and threw her hopes to the wind. "You proved yesterday that you know how to comport yourself. You've a governess, I'm sure, and a good one. You've just let yourself forget her lessons. Put your mind to it and you'll do fine."

"No. I need you! I'm a hopeless hoyden, Lady Ashburne. Without you, I'll make an absolute cake of myself, I just know it."

"You will if you keep on like this."

"Please, Lady Ashburne." Clary clasped Portia's hands again and turned the most perfectly pleading look on her. "Please talk to my uncle. I'm certain you can convince him, if you only try."

"What do you suggest I do? Present myself at Tynesfield and ask for an audience with his grace?"

"Oh, I knew you'd do it! I knew it!" Clary leapt to her feet and caught Portia in a rib-bruising hug. "He's coming in his carriage to pick me up. He'll be here any minute."

With that, she dragged Portia to the door and Portia, all too aware of the flaccid state of her so-recently filled reticule, the exorbitant cost of fixing her roof, and the fact that she currently had but one dress to her name, allowed herself to be led. She hadn't the foggiest idea what she'd say to the duke and she wasn't looking forward to finding out. She had only one thing going for her: she was not impressed by his title. She was a duke's granddaughter, and dukes did not intimidate her.

"Oh dear," Portia murmured when the Duke of Ransley's curricle came into view, its black lacquered sides shining like polished silver. He was younger than she'd expected and tall, as fair of hair as his niece, with a strong face and piercing, almost colorless eyes. If Clary hadn't been squeezing her hand so tight, Portia might well have faded back into the modiste's shop. The man was the very definition of formidable.

Ransley drew his horses, an impressive matched pair of grays, to a prancing halt and sat looking down at them. Portia felt his eyes on her, as sharp as the modiste's and more measuring, and lifted her chin to stare him full in the face. His lips twitched, his expression almost approving, but he had not missed the grip his niece had on her hand, and the first words out of his mouth were, "You did not tell me you were meeting a friend at the dressmaker's, Clarissa."

Lady Clarissa made a sound very like 'eep' and seemed to dwindle before Portia's eyes. "Well, Your Grace," Portia said when the girl seemed unable to do more than blink mutely at her uncle, "it appears we have no one to do the honors."

"A pity. We shall have to shift for ourselves." He made a credible bow from the seat of his curricle. "Ransley, madam, at your service."

Portia curtsied, hoping her trepidation didn't show. "Lady Portia Ashburne, Your Grace."

His eyes shuttered, every hint of affability evaporating from his face. If she'd thought Mrs. McFerran a past master at coming over the gargoyle, it was only because she hadn't yet met the Duke of Ransley. "Give you good day, madam," he said in a voice like ice. "Lady Clarissa, if you would climb up, please. We have much to do."

Portia unobtrusively tightened her grip on Clary's hand when she felt it begin to slip away. Once the chit got into Ransley's curricle, he would give his team the office, and that would be the end of it.

If she ever hoped to have a comfortable life, or a house that wasn't crumbling about her ears, she would need a solution more long-lasting than spouting the silver. Lady Clarissa Seabrooke was her entrée into that life, the only chance Portia might have to prove herself worth hiring. The young lady didn't shrink from calling herself a hoyden, wouldn't hesitate to give credit where credit was due, and could be relied upon to spread the word that here was a gentlewoman who could take a wayward chit, of whatever parentage, and turn her into a lady. If she let Ransley take that away from her without a single word spoken in her defense, then she deserved Ashburne Hall and all its discomforts.

"Beg pardon, Your Grace, but have I done aught to offend you?"

He stared stonily at his horses as if her voice was but the buzzing of an insect.

"I understand that you have reason to mislike my house and my name, but I assure you, sir, I have done nothing to earn your enmity."

"You live, madam. That is enough." Still he did not look at her. "Turn loose of my niece this instant."

She released Clary, who'd recovered enough from her initial fright to plant herself at Portia's side, a mutinous gleam in her eyes. "You misjudge me, Your Grace, if you think I would hold her against her will. And you misjudge your niece if you think she would let me. She came to me for lessons; I could do no less than teach her."

"What has she to learn from such as you?"

He might have accosted her with the basest Billingsgate and cut her less deeply. But his contempt only stiffened her spine. She glared at his aristocratic profile, turned to her as if she were so far beneath his notice he didn't owe her even the courtesy of looking at her. "I am the granddaughter of a duke. I am a lady in my own right and was raised with all the manners of my class. You may choose not to bother yourself with the raising of your niece, but someone has to see to it she becomes the incomparable she should be, and not the laughingstock of the *beau monde*."

"Beware, madam. You dare too much."

"Someone must. Someone must see your niece for who she is and what she may be." In a moment, they'd begin drawing a crowd. Portia hated to make a spectacle of herself. She hated even more giving up without a fight.

"My niece will have nothing to do with any of your cursed name, or with that double-damned place." Ransley turned, and when his eyes fell on her, it was all she could do not to back away from the hatred in the pallid depths. "Do you understand me, madam?"

"I am not an Ashburne."

"You are worse. You were not born to the name, but chose to take it upon you."

"What does that signify? That I wed Roger Ashburne, the more fool I? That might prove me to have been a want-wit, but it doesn't make me cursed. You know nothing about me, Your Grace."

"You allied yourself with that family. That is all I need know. I have lost one niece to the Ashburnes, I will not lose another. You may rely upon that."

Somewhere in her anger, Portia found an uncomfortable pity. "Giles Ashburne is dead, Your Grace, and Ashburne Hall nothing but a crumbling wreck." Portia dared to step closer and put her hand on the polished armrail of his curricle, her voice unconsciously gentling. "Giles Ashburne is dead," she repeated. "He can do no harm to Lady Clarissa. I would not want to. She needs help, Your Grace, and you must—"

"I must nothing, madam. My niece will have nothing to do with you or yours." His gloved hand came down on hers, trapping it hard against the curricle. "If Ashburne had not fled justice, he'd have been found guilty by the House of Lords, his title and lands stripped away and all those of his blood tainted with his crime. He fled man's justice, but he could not flee God's." The pressure of his hand numbed her fingers.

"I am no threat to your niece." Portia dragged her hand free. "I am no descendent of Lord Ashburne. You cannot penalize me for what he did." It seemed to her that something came over her then and she hardly knew what she was saying. "Assuming he even committed the crime with which you are determined to tar his whole line."

"You forget yourself," Ransley growled, his face incandescent with rage. Portia stepped hastily back, half-afraid he would strike her with his whip. How badly it might have gone from there she was never to know, for a canary-yellow curricle drew suddenly to a halt next to the duke's equipage and the driver, a strapping man dressed in the peacock colors of the sporting set, his red hair cut *à la Titus,* threw the reins to his tiger and leaped down. "Lady Clarissa, if I may be so bold...." Without waiting for a response, he kissed her fingers and handed her into Ransley's carriage with a flourish.

"Courtland," Ransley said, barely more civil than he'd been to Portia. He gave the reins a slap and his horses bounded away, Clary shooting Portia a despairing look as she was carried off.

"And Lady Ashburne. A pleasure." Courtland took her hand and pressed a kiss to it that was as disconcerting as it was surprising. She withdrew her hand in some confusion. Gloves. She really must get some gloves. "My dear Lady Ashburne," Courtland said with an engaging smile, "my deepest apologies, but you must forgive my familiarity. I feel I know you, Roger spoke of you so often."

"I find that hard to believe," Portia murmured, unable to imagine why a man who'd hardly ever thought of her could possibly be moved to speak about her. "However, he most certainly spoke of you." She watched Ransley's carriage pass from sight. "I have a bone to pick with you, sir."

"For interrupting your discussion with Ransley? Think nothing of it, my lady. I was happy to assist." Without so much as a by your leave, he tucked her hand into the crook of his arm and walked her to his curricle. "Allow me to see you home."

Portia was tempted to decline, and hotly too, but it would hardly help her reputation to brangle with two local noblemen on the same afternoon. Besides, she'd told Ellie to go directly to the Hall once she'd seen to her purchases, and it would be better not to be seen trudging home alone like the veriest peasant after making such a spectacle of herself with the duke. She allowed Courtland to hand her into his curricle and waited until he clucked to his team to say, "I had not finished my discussion with the duke."

"You have if you know what's best for you, my dear Lady Ashburne. The stand you took was not like to make you popular with the duke, or anyone else in these parts."

"I should thank you for your interference, is that it?"

"I certainly hope so. I'd hate to find myself in your ladyship's black books." He smiled sidelong at her, and Portia wished she had not only the gloves but the parasol so beloved of fashionable ladies, for it would have given her something to do, for all that she'd always thought fidgeting with such items the province of ninnyhammers.

She turned her eyes to the road, and after the silence had drawn out a little too long, said, "I was given to understand that you do not often visit your manor, my lord."

"Not a sennight here and already listening to gossip," he teased. Courtland slapped the reins, drawing a little more speed from his cattle. "I like the countryside well enough. There are such beauties to be seen." He frankly stared at her until a bend in the road required his attention. "But in truth, I found it necessary to rusticate for a time."

"Your creditors?" Portia knew too well how it went. It had taken her half her marriage, the more fool her, to understand why there was never any money and why Roger would come now and again to Rosewood, acting as if he enjoyed his country visit while all the time looking for a way to get back to London.

"Are best left unmentioned," Courtland murmured. "For they are unmentionable creatures indeed, are they not?"

"Perhaps," Portia said, though she might have pointed out that his life would be circumscribed indeed were there no one to loan him money. She adjusted the brim of her bonnet for want of anything else to do. "Does no one doubt Giles Ashburne's guilt?"

Courtland drew his team to a halt in the middle of the road and sat looking at her until her nerves were stretched unbearably. "If they do," he said finally, "they're smart enough not to mention it. You've seen how passionately the Duke of Ransley believes it, and he's a hard man to cross. Besides." Courtland got his horses started again. "I know nothing to suggest that Ashburne did *not* kill Lady Amelia, much as I wish I could say otherwise, for he was a friend. However I try, I cannot see why he would have fled were he innocent."

"I see," Portia murmured. "How did he die?" Mrs. McFerran hadn't said, assuming she knew herself.

"The packet whose captain he bribed for passage to France sank off the coast with all hands on board. They never found all the bodies."

Portia frowned. "Then—"

"There were enough," Courtland said in a hard voice. "I went to France with Roger to identify his cousin—the House of Lords would never have taken his uncorroborated word. But I own I'd have gone in any case, for Roger's sake. He was in a bad way." Courtland fell silent long enough to make Portia's face burn for her curiosity. Finally, he shook himself. "So, you see, Ashburne's fate was sealed by an act of God and no one now doubts his guilt. I suppose there might be a few here and there who dare think otherwise. That great oaf of an innkeeper, perhaps. And that poor soul at the Hall who could see no wrong in her master no matter what he did. But they're few and far between, and even they know to keep their peace."

If by "the poor soul at the Hall," Courtland meant Mrs. McFerran, then he was very much mistaken in her feelings on the matter. She delighted too much in speaking of Lord Ashburne's misfortune to have ever held him in high regard. He'd hit the nail on the head with Foxkin, though. The innkeeper had flat-out told her he believed Ashburne innocent, an act of astounding trust on his part, she now realized.

Courtland made no comment on the state of the drive, though he was forced to slow to a crawl to navigate it without overturning his fancy equipage. When he pulled up before her door, he did not give her an opportunity to descend on her own, but leapt down and gave her his hand.

"I should like to make myself free to visit, Lady Ashburne," he said, his leaf-green eyes holding her as captive as his warm fingers. "There's little enough good society in the area. We must needs stick together, don't you agree?"

Meaning, no doubt, that one door was already firmly closed against Portia and she shouldn't dismiss him out of hand. "I have always thought, Lord Courtland, that one should never cut one's neighbors without sufficient cause."

He laughed. "I think I shall take that as an invitation, Lady Ashburne." He leapt back into his curricle and took up the reins, pausing to doff his hat to her. "Until later."

With that, he was off, traversing the drive at a faster pace now that he didn't have to worry about bouncing his passenger out of her seat. She watched him go, aware of the Hall brooding at her back and trying unsuccessfully to decide what she thought of Lord Courtland.

She could see why Roger had liked him. Courtland was an engaging scamp. A man very much in Roger's line, she reminded herself—a gambler and a libertine and overall a man of little account. She'd have to be featherbrained indeed to tie herself to another faithless lord.

Chapter Fourteen

IT stormed that night.

The first crack of thunder occasioned a deal of rushing about, as Portia and Ellie snatched pots and buckets from the kitchen and ran about in the upper floors, sticking them under leaks. The hole Mr. McFerran had inadvertently made into the servants' quarters required three large pans all by itself when the rain began seeping through the canvas stretched over the damaged ceiling. Portia imagined water was building up atop the canvas, a lake of it stretching out across the attic, engulfing wardrobes and trunks, seeking another way down. She wished her imagination were not so good.

She even dared enter the master's bedroom, but saw no need to add a second bucket to the one that already stood under the leak. It was no fuller than it had been previously, and there was no sound of dripping even with the renewed downpour. Perhaps the leak was intermittent, or the new hole in the attic had drawn water away from the route it had previously taken into the room.

Supper that night was shepherd's pie, which Mrs. McFerran had insisted on taking time away from her husband's bedside to cook. She was quick about it, the result much more the thing than her previous pretense at ill-cooking, and they somehow managed to eat every bite, though when Portia was in the kitchen collecting pans she'd thought Mrs. McFerran had enough food going for six. Ellie kindly offered to do the washing up. Rather, Ellie turned Portia out of the kitchen when she offered to help, the maid turning into a virago of offended sensibilities at the thought of her ladyship washing dishes in her smart, new (and only) gown.

Portia drifted about the old house a while, listening to the thunder outside, the plink of rain inside. Eventually, she took her candle into the library, which by some miracle escaped the worst of the leaks, and read until her eyes burned and the candle flickered low.

When Ellie had popped in some time previous, Portia sent her on to bed. Now she wished she hadn't been so adamant that she could get herself into her own nightrail. The thought of retiring to her dark and silent bedchamber did not appeal. Nor the idea that she would be utterly alone as she climbed the stairs, walked down the hall, and turned the key in her lock.

Portia put down her book with a sigh, finally admitting to herself that she was afraid to sleep in that room. By light of day, she could listen to reason and believe it nothing but a vivid, terrifying dream. How could it be else? But reason and logic faded to nothing when the sun went down. Portia shivered to think of waking to find him bending over her. And if the next time he appeared to her not as a man, but a drowned corpse, bloated and faintly glowing? Portia shuddered and scolded herself for allowing her imagination to run away with her.

She put her book back on the shelf, locked the library, and went upstairs, barely giving Giles Ashburne's portrait a glance when she passed it. Nor did she look up or down the hall, but continued up to the servants' floor. The McFerrans' door was closed and Portia tapped lightly before pushing it open.

Dimly lit by a single, guttering candle, Mrs. McFerran's face was a study in fatigue, a dozen years older than the woman who bore it. Mr. McFerran tossed restlessly, making pained sounds whenever his movements shifted his splinted leg. For all they'd done to her, Portia could feel nothing but pity.

She went to Mrs. McFerran and laid a gentle hand on her shoulder. "Let me watch a while. You can do him no good if you fall ill yourself."

Mrs. McFerran stared, then nodded slowly and hoisted herself out of her chair like a woman of ancient years. It occurred to Portia suddenly to wonder just how old the McFerrans *were*—the woman seemed so vigorous in her antipathy, the man timeless in the way of all woodsmen. Portia saw Mrs. McFerran to the door and closed it behind her—she trusted the housekeeper could find an untenanted bed for the night, or would not mind sharing with mice. Then she went back to the bedside and sat watching Mr. McFerran twist in the grip of fever until her eyelids drooped, the only thought in her mind the dread certainty that Mr. Millbank must be sent for first thing in the morning.

* * *

Giles found her there sometime after midnight.

He had stopped in to see how Mr. McFerran was doing, expecting to see the old man's wife at his side, and the sight of Portia nodding in the chair by the bed so startled him that he stood for some minutes watching her from the doorway, though she might wake any minute and see him. He wouldn't particularly have minded scaring her out of her wits again, but her screams might wake the invalid.

Still he stood and watched. He'd not thought her the kind of woman to pay such attention to a mere servant, nor to step one iota out of her way to demonstrate even a lick of kindness. Gowns and jewels and hair were all her sort cared for. He saw he'd inadvertently left her one of the dresses she'd stolen. He'd make sure not to miss it again tonight. His eyes drifted down over her. The gray dress clung invitingly to her curves, and the sight of her sleeping there, her bosom rising and falling with each soft breath, kindled a growing heat in his chest. He forced his eyes away. No, perhaps he would leave the dress. He could imagine far better than he liked her drifting about the place in her shift and it did nothing for his peace of mind. It was infuriating to find the exterior so appealing when everything about the interior disgusted him.

Indeed, she might almost be taken for an angel of mercy, dozing peacefully in a chair by the old man's bed.

How fortunate he knew better.

* * *

Portia stirred and blinked open unwilling eyelids. She hadn't meant to drowse at Mr. McFerran's bedside. She was glad to see he'd fallen into deeper slumber. Fever still dewed his brow, but at least he no longer hurt himself with shifting about.

She stretched and looked around, surprised to find the door open. She was certain she'd closed it. Perhaps it had not quite latched.

But it seemed to Portia that she'd heard something, just as she woke. Something muted and repetitive. Footsteps, perhaps, retreating down the hall.

She went to the door, hesitating a moment before she could bring herself to look out. Her eyes fell on a figure in the hall and her heart leapt into her throat. It was only with a mighty effort she prevented herself from screaming the house down.

"Ellie Brown," Portia scolded when she got her breath back, remembering to keep her voice low, "you took ten years off me."

"You, my lady? What about me?" Ellie scurried the last few feet and darted in at the sickroom as if she were escaping the storm that still crashed and muttered without. "I 'bout near died when you stuck your head out sudden like that," she whispered. "What were you looking for?"

"Nothing." Portia glanced at Ellie's slippered feet. She was as certain as could be that the footsteps had been shod. Even, perhaps, the peculiar muted crack of boots. "You didn't see anyone in the hall?"

Ellie's eyes popped. "Who should I meet in the hall?"

"Mrs. McFerran, perhaps," Portia lied to calm her.

"No, my lady. No one."

"No matter." Portia stared irresolutely at the door. Perhaps she'd merely imagined the footsteps.

"You need your sleep, my lady," Ellie said, in much the same tone she'd used when Portia was a little girl. "Go on. I'll watch here." There was no arguing with Ellie in this mood. Portia went, her candle flickering dreadfully, threatening to leave her lightless in the draughty hall.

Even held as high as she could stretch, the candle's feeble light could not penetrate all the corners of her bedchamber at once, and Portia was not satisfied she was alone until she'd poked into every nook and cranny and checked three times that the doors were locked.

She used her candle to light the fire Ellie had laid in the hearth and did not climb into her bed until the flames sent fingers of light probing into every corner of the room. Then she changed quickly into her nightrail and climbed under the blankets, determined to stay awake.

No dripping phantom would sneak up on her tonight.

Chapter Fifteen

PORTIA was awakened by a horrendous crash.

She bolted upright in bed and found herself looking into curiously flat black eyes. She scrambled wildly back and tumbled ignominiously off the bed.

"My lady!" Ellie gasped, rushing to help her up. "Oh, I'm terrible sorry, my lady, but I was that frightened, I was!"

"What the deuce is going on?" Portia demanded. That Ellie didn't immediately scold her for her language showed it was serious indeed. Portia rubbed both hands over her face, trying to reach some middle ground between drowsiness and terror, and forced herself to look around.

The fire she'd lit before turning in had burned down to nothing. A lacquered tray and its contents were strewn across the floor just inside the door, tea from the broken pot seeping into the rug. Someone had pulled the chair from the dressing table close to the bedside and Giles Ashburne's portrait leaned rakishly against it.

"How did you get it in here, my lady?" Ellie asked, rushing to wrap her shivering mistress in her dressing gown. "And all on your own, too."

"I didn't," Portia managed. "It wasn't there when I went to bed."

The admission frightened Ellie into a fit of hysterics so profound that Portia was at last reduced to shoving the maid onto the bed and digging out the vinaigrette Ellie insisted she keep in her toiletries, no matter she'd never needed it. She was glad for it now, for two good whiffs of the awful thing, and Ellie collapsed in a shuddering, thankfully *quiet*, heap.

Portia left her there, alternately moaning "oh, it's the ghost, oh my poor lady" and sniffing gingerly at the vinaigrette with the determinedly martyred look of those taken suddenly ill. Portia rather doubted her sturdy maid would faint, even in an excess of superstitious nonsense, or that the foul-smelling stuff could possibly be helping, but at least it kept Ellie mostly quiet. She tried the door to the dressing room and found it still locked. The door into the hall, of course, stood open as Ellie had left it. Portia thought briefly of how the maid's shrieks must have echoed throughout the house and hoped it had at least shaken Mrs. McFerran's nerves a bit. Then she remembered Mr. McFerran and hoped that, by some miracle, he had managed to sleep through the ruckus. Portia picked her way through her spilled breakfast and removed the key still stuck in the outer door lock.

"Is this your key?"

"Yes, my lady. I'd just got the door open when I saw...." Ellie broke off, shuddering, and took such a deep whiff of the vinaigrette that she fell into a coughing fit.

"The door was locked when you got here?"

Ellie nodded, her eyes watering.

Portia handed the key to her and went to stand before the portrait. It seemed much larger now that she looked it straight in its painted eyes than it had hanging at the head of the stairs. It was placed deliberately so it would be the first thing she saw when she woke, and Portia shuddered to think of waking in the night to find it staring unblinking at her out of the gloom.

She walked around it, but there was nothing to see. Just the portrait, which had proven so difficult for the McFerrans and the potboy from the Duck and Drake to handle the night Portia arrived, leaning negligently against a chair as if it had taken a stroll up the hall to prop itself there. "How did you get here?" Portia murmured. The doors were all locked, and though Mrs. McFerran had shown herself adept at circumventing locks, she wasn't strong enough to shift the large painting all by herself.

"Oh, it's the ghost," Ellie wailed. "Oh, my lady, this is a horrible place. We can't stay here. We'll all be murdered in our beds, we will."

"I've never heard of a ghost killing anyone, Ellie. Come to that, why would it want to? It would just make more ghosts to clutter up the place."

It was an unfortunate attempt at humor, and Ellie wailed, "Oh, oh, oh, we'll be murdered, we'll all be murdered. We have to leave, my lady. We must, oh we must!"

"And go where? What do you suggest we do, sleep under a hedgerow?"

Her tone had a more salubrious effect on Ellie than the vinaigrette. The maid stood and shook out her skirts in a huff. "I'll just see if my lady has any dresses left, shall I?"

"If I have, they're not going to be in there," Portia said when Ellie picked up the key to the dressing room.

Ellie made a show of looking about the room, her pantomime somewhat undercut by the fact that she wouldn't look directly at the portrait that dominated the space. "Nor out here, either," she said, her mood shifting towards maudlin again. "Your beautiful new dress. All that work. And now it's gone, and your ladyship has nothing to wear."

"Did you think I was fool enough to leave it where someone could walk off with it?" Portia lifted her pillow to show Ellie where she'd hidden the gown before composing herself to sleep.

Ellie gave a cry and caught up the dress, shaking it out and holding it up. "It's all over wrinkles, it is."

"Yes, but it's still here." Portia ignored the much put upon look her maid directed at her and slid her feet into her slippers. "Now, I suggest we repair to the kitchen, where I can have my breakfast and you can press my gown."

"But, my lady." Ellie made a helpless gesture toward the painting.

"If it's still there when we return, then you and I will see if we can't move it back to the landing."

"If it's still..." Ellie trailed off with an audible gulp.

"Who knows, we might be lucky and it'll go the way it came." Portia shooed her maid out into the hall, and struck off toward the kitchen, not bothering to lock the door behind her. Not only would things be quite a bit easier if the portrait was, in fact, removed while they were downstairs, but it seemed foolish to continue engaging in such a useless gesture.

Someone continued to get in regardless.

* * *

Fed and dressed at last, Portia climbed the stairs to the servants' floor. The first floor landing looked empty without Giles Ashburne glaring down upon it.

Mrs. McFerran sat stolidly beside her husband's bed, watching him twist and turn. If it hadn't been for her emotional reaction when he was first injured, Portia could almost have believed the woman didn't care, so blank was her expression.

"No better?" Portia asked quietly.

Mrs. McFerran looked at her for a long moment before shaking her head.

"I'll send for the surgeon."

Portia went back down to send Ellie after the doctor. She hated to send the maid out in such weather, for it was still pelting down rain, but there was no one else and Portia could not go herself. Nothing harmed a lady's reputation like being seen splashing through the rain on foot, presenting the overall appearance of a drowned rat.

Unless it was being seen wrangling in the street.

Portia sighed. She went into the library, the cat greeting her with a much put-upon yowl the moment her key scraped in the lock.

"How did you get in here?" Surely she hadn't locked the cat in when she went upstairs last night. Thomas mewed again, stropped himself vigorously about her ankles, and trotted off in the direction of the kitchen. Portia went on into the library and sighed again. Someone had gotten in here as well. This time, it was the second case from the door that was empty. The books were once again piled into stacks all over the floor, and the overall mess was, if possible, worse. Some of the stacks looked so precarious they might go over any minute, and there were loose books scattered about the floor, as if tossed there by someone in a tearing hurry.

Anger rose briefly in Portia's breast, then fell away again, conquered by fatigue and a touch of the dismals. Could nothing go right? She set about putting the books back with dogged persistence and was still at it when Lord Courtland called.

He didn't bother with the front door. Or, if he did, she didn't hear him. Portia ought, perhaps, tell Mrs. McFerran to reaffix the knocker, assuming she could find it. It may well have been taken down some time ago, for who was welcome here? Instead, Courtland rapped on the library windows, startling Portia half to death. He smiled unapologetically and headed back to the front of the house without any apparent doubt she would let him in.

"Good morning, Lady Ashburne," he said when he was inside, shaking rain off his beaver hat and caped greatcoat. "I hope you don't mind that I availed myself of your invitation so soon."

"I don't remember extending an invitation." Portia took his hat and draped his coat over the hall table to dry.

"No? I was quite certain you had." Courtland strode to the center of the great hall and stood staring about him, for all the world as if he owned the place. He paused for a long moment on the blank spot at the head of the stairs. "A pity," he said without looking away from where Ashburne's portrait had hung until sometime during the night. "I tried to tell Roger he couldn't let the family seat go to rack and ruin, but he was never disposed to listen." He turned to her. "If I'd known that fixing up the place would fall to you, I'd have tried harder to convince him."

She wasn't in the mood for his flirting, not least because his words only reminded her that she hadn't the money to make this place livable, nor now any prospects of getting any. "Yes, indeed, I'm certain you'd have dragged him away from his clubs and his cards, from racing meets and pugilistic bouts. You'd have seen him free of his lightskirts and demireps, and—"

Courtland raised his hands in surrender, a smile dancing around his mouth. "You win, Lady Ashburne. Roger was a man, not a boy, and I'd no call to interfere with his pleasures, nor truthfully any interest in doing so. Forgive me? I'd as lief be friends with such a beautiful woman." He stepped back on his heel and looked her over with frank appreciation. "You must know that's a lovely gown."

"Cut line, sir."

"I'm quite serious, my lady. I have it on good authority that it's all the rage in London."

"Spanish coin, sir. It's the same dress I wore yesterday."

"It was lovely yesterday, and it's lovely today."

Portia turned with a sigh, weary of sparring with him, and headed for the library. Atrocious manners, but then why should her manners not go with her house? He caught her up within a few steps, laying his hand on her arm.

"I cry pardon, Lady Ashburne. I only meant to tease a little."

"It's a touchy subject, sir."

"So I see." He walked with her into the library and seated himself without seeming to notice the stacks of books scattered about the room, nor the dust that dulled every surface. "What's got you so Friday-faced?"

"Not much to signify." She stooped to pick up a book. "The roof is disintegrating. There are mice in every wall and moths in all the linens. The housekeeper's husband broke his leg falling through the ceiling and is coming over feverish. My wardrobe's five years out of date, when it can be found. And the Duke of Ransley's taken an instant dislike to me."

She turned to find that he had his hands up in surrender again, and snapped her mouth shut. She set her book on the top of a nearby stack and picked up another.

"Well," Courtland said, "I'm afraid there's little I can do to help, aside from pointing out that Ransley's like to take anyone in dislike for any reason. It's got nothing whatever to do with you, so why fadge yourself over it?"

"It's certainly got to do with me now, hasn't it? I did, after all, tell him to his face that I thought Lord Ashburne innocent."

"He'd have cut you for your connections regardless of what you said. What difference can it make whether you exacerbated the situation?" Courtland leaned back in his chair, crossing his legs and lacing his fingers.

Portia sighed and sank into the chair opposite him. "I had hoped to alter my situation—"

"By marrying the old bastard?!" Courtland hooted in a most uncivilized manner.

"Really, sir!"

He regained control of himself with a cough. "My apologies, Lady Ashburne. Pray continue."

Portia took a breath. If he were like Roger, laying her cards on the table would only make him laugh. But he'd been helpful, not twitting her (or at least not overmuch) for the state of the Hall or her twice-worn dress or even her brangle with Ransley. And she was so very tired of having no one but servants and chits barely out of the schoolroom to talk to. "I had hoped that, if I taught Lady Clarissa proper manners before her come out, I might be able to offer such services to others in the neighborhood." She sighed. "But I can see now that it will not serve. Even were I able to bring Ashburne Hall up to snuff, no one would allow their daughter to visit. Not when they believe Lord Ashburne a murderer. Especially not if they think he still haunts the place."

Courtland sat forward suddenly. "Do they?"

"Your estate marches with Ashburne Hall, my lord. Surely you knew."

"I haven't often been here since Ashburne died." Courtland sat back, his eyes focused somewhere in the middle distance. "It never occurred to me he might return..."

"His loyal retainers certainly want me to believe he's here. You wouldn't believe the pranks that have been passed off on the 'ghost.'"

"Ah, so that's what you meant about your wardrobe, 'when it can be found.'"

"That doesn't matter," Portia said, realizing how true it was only as she said it. "These things, they're minor discomforts, down to the leaky roof and the mice. Even were they dealt with, my situation would not materially improve. Not if people are put off by the reputation of the Hall. *That's* the thing I've got to fix."

"Tall order."

"Not really. I just need to prove Lord Ashburne innocent."

A stillness came over Courtland, and she realized that she had his full attention for the first time, but all he said was, "Tall order," again.

"For all I might have acted like one of late, I'm not a want-wit," Portia snapped. "I know it's quite the assumption, but it's the only thing I can afford to believe. If Lord Ashburne was guilty, then Ashburne Hall's reputation will never change, and I'll be stuck with mice and rotting damp—"

"And ghosts."

"—forever. Don't you see," Portia went on, leaning towards him as she fell into the grip of the outrageous idea, "if he was guilty, then I'm lost. But if he was innocent...."

"Yes." Courtland ceased the pretense of lounging indolently in his chair. "That would change everything, wouldn't it?" He dragged a hand through his hair, disarranging the damp red locks. "Mayhap he was. I couldn't believe it when I heard he killed the chit. We all knew something was awry—there were rumors about her that no man could be sanguine about in his bethrothed—but that he should have killed her when he might have simply broken the engagement—"

"There, you see!"

"He was also the last man I'd have expected to do a flit, so you see how far *that* takes us. Besides, even if he was, in fact, innocent, how are you going to prove it now? Ten years is a long time."

"If Giles Ashburne did not kill his fiancée, then someone else did. Someone must know something. And you know everyone in the area." He began shaking his head and Portia leaned forward to touch his hand. "I will do this with or without you—you must see I have no choice—but I own it would be easier with your help."

"You ruddy fool! Has it not occurred to you that there's nothing you could do more guaranteed to ink yourself permanently into Ransley's black books?"

"Only if Lord Ashburne turns out to be guilty."

Courtland continued to stare, still slowly shaking his head, though more in wonder than negation, Portia thought.

"Well, are you with me or not?"

Courtland stared a moment more, then began to laugh. "Might as well be," he said when he regained his breath. "What have I got to lose? Ransley hates me already."

* * *

Giles leaned on the railing at the second floor landing and watched her show Courtland out. Where he was, they'd have to look almost straight up to see him, and even if they did they'd likely not spot him. The murky light was so bad he could barely make out Courtland's ruddy hair, which glowed like a flame even by weak candlelight.

And what the devil was *he* doing at the Hall?

Lord Simon Courtland. Rake. Libertine. Gambler on dice and cards and what raindrop will reach the windowsash first and which woman's virtue will fall next. Always with pockets to let and always somehow coming up with the blunt for another hand, another roll, another bet, jaded with a life of wagers, wins and losses.

But Giles had much to thank Courtland for. The man had stood friend to him when all others had forsaken him, helped him escape the country when it became clear he must either flee or lose everything he held dear. Courtland stood now in the lower hall—the man who helped Giles flee, arranged passage to France and saw him safely on his way—and leaned his gleaming head toward Portia's as they exchanged words in voices too soft for Giles to make out. She tipped her head back to look up at him and smiled at something he said.

Giles scowled. He watched Courtland kiss Portia's hand and duck out into the rain. Whose friend was he now?

Portia had closeted herself in the library with him for some time. A merry widow, she, taking what advantage came to her. Even in this place. If James thought to curtail her licentious behavior by exiling her, he had failed signally.

Giles leaned on the railing, his mind taking him, however he dug in his heels, to the library, the endless minutes they'd spent there alone. Had she burrowed her fingers in Courtland's hair while they kissed? Guided his head to her ripe bosom? A large drop of rain spattered on Giles' brow. He tipped his head back to look sourly up at the roof—at this rate, the attics were like to come tumbling down the stairs any day. The Hall was crumbling while that woman played around with gowns and fripperies. And Courtland. Giles pulled out his handkerchief and wiped his face, suffering in the sudden sweet scent of lavender. Hells bells, would nothing get the scent out of his linen? It haunted him.

The door banged, startling Giles out of his thoughts, and Portia's strapping shepherdess of a maid flew in, bringing a cloud of rain and a black-cloaked figure with her. They must have just missed Courtland in the drive. If they'd met up with him, someone would have ended up overturned in the mud. Mr. Millbank peeled off his sodden cloak and dripping hat, exchanged a few words with Portia, then followed the maid upstairs.

Giles faded back from the railing and retreated down the hall to the servants' stairs. The attics and upper floors were denied him by the rain and the doctor respectively, and Portia was in the library. Giles headed for the family apartments.

It was time she learned that things didn't only happen at night.

* * *

Night came early, the rain bringing a premature end to the day.

Giles slipped out of the Hall, a voluminous cloak wound round him though there was no one about in such weather to see him go, and headed into the home wood. Trees creaked and groaned, tossing in the wind and dripping unerringly on him, rain running down his face and under his collar until he bent his head against it, pulling the hood of his cloak far forward.

The route he took was familiar from a lifetime's use. Not even the passage of years could dull it in his memory, though it had been difficult at first to find his way through the thick underbrush that had grown wild while the Hall lay vacant. Giles left the path before it intersected with the high street and worked his way by slow degrees around behind the Duck and Drake.

The stable door creaked terribly when he teased it open, but the stable hands were all inside, warming their hands at Mrs. Foxkin's kitchen fire and their innards with her good supper. Giles pushed the door closed behind him and shook the dripping hood back from his face. He gave a low whistle and a horse, one of the many that stamped and shuffled in the thick darkness, whickered in response.

Giles made his way toward the sound, one hand running lightly across the stall gates while his eyes accustomed themselves to the darkness, and rubbed the velvet nose that pushed out at him. "Evening, Bayard," he whispered. "How are you, boy?" One hand on the stallion's neck, he slipped into the stall and spent some time stroking the eager horse, who refrained from dancing while they were pressed into such close quarters, contenting himself with quivering under his master's hand.

The warmth and great breathing life of the animal lulled Giles' senses, and he almost missed it when someone entered the stables. When he did realize that he was not alone, he was alerted not so much by some faint creak of the door, but a moment's utter stillness, a breath of night air pricking through the thick warmth.

The other made his way through the dark with a sure-footedness equal to Giles' own, his progress measurable only by the quiet nicker of horses as he passed. He stopped outside Bayard's stall and, like Giles, rubbed the stallion's soft muzzle.

"Well?" Giles said, his voice barely louder than the soughing of the wind in the trees.

Foxkin's teeth showed white in the dark. "Well what, my lord?"

Giles cuffed him lightly. "Did you bring me anything to eat, you daft jackstraw?"

Foxkin handed over a piece of beef squashed between two thick cuts of bread. "It's not your fancy Frog cuisine, but I trust it'll do you."

"It'll do well." Giles set to with a will, saying between bites, "With Mr. McFerran down sick, his wife hasn't much time for cooking. I've been shifting for myself."

"Lucky you haven't starved to death." Foxkin handed him a tankard of ale, the contents slopping over Giles' fingers in the dark.

"I've spent ten years fending for myself, sirrah."

"Aye, ordering your pints in pubs and your meals in fancy restaurants."

"Not so fancy as all that," Giles murmured, more amused than offended. Foxkin had a saucy tongue on him that Giles had never suspected when the man was in his service. Came of being his own master. He'd made good use of the money Giles left him against the certainty he'd be turned out of service once Giles' flight was discovered. Had Giles but known, he'd have provided for all the servants, but he'd never thought Roger capable of beggaring the Hall. "Did you find out where she took the silver?"

"To me, my lord. Where else?"

"That makes things easier. Is it close at hand?"

Foxkin was shaking his head. "I can't just give it over to you, my lord."

"No, of course not. I've nowhere to take it but back to the Hall, and if she found it again.... But then, she's had no luck finding her gowns."

"And it's right rude of you to have taken them. My lord, you really must—"

"No, I mustn't. You've let that female pull the wool over your eyes, and now you'd have the whole world looking at her through lambskin."

Foxkin sighed gustily. "You're a mistrusting bastard, that you are, my lord. Especially of women. All on account of Lady Amelia and her—"

"Daniel," Giles said between his teeth, "if you're looking to have your cork drawn, go ahead and finish that sentence."

"Beg pardon, sir," Foxkin said quickly. He was a deal broader than Giles, but they were nearly of a height, and Giles' temper was up. "I'm sure I didn't mean to—"

"Yes, you did, but enough. Can you keep the silver here a few days?"

"Just like I'm keeping Bayard 'a few days'? Yes."

Giles ignored the gentle jab. "Excellent. Thanks to you, I won't have to ransom my silver from some cent-percenter."

"You brought the money?"

"Of course I did. Didn't know what I would find."

"Hand it over, then." Foxkin said it while rubbing Bayard's strong neck, and for a moment, Giles couldn't make sense of the soft words.

"Are you dunning me?"

"The lady's expecting me to arrange sale of the silver, my lord. Not pack it away in my root cellar."

Giles swore under his breath, viciously and vividly, finishing with, "Hell and damnation, but you're right. If she doesn't get the money from you, she'll just go elsewhere, and I'll be chasing my silver all over the county." He fished in the voluminous pocket of his cloak and tossed the bundle of coin to Foxkin. "Damned if I thought I'd hand my blunt over for that vixen to fritter away on geegaws and fripperies."

"You don't know she'll—"

"Of course she will. She'll want to look her best with Courtland running tame at the Hall." The memory of their heads bent together soured the ale in Giles' stomach. Not only for the feeling she roused in him, try as he might to banish it, but for the threat Courtland represented. He of all men was in a position to guess that Giles still breathed. If he suspected.... Worse if he told her....

"Lord Courtland's at home?"

"Isn't he ever?" Whenever Courtland got to *point non plus*, which was often, he headed for the country to rusticate until he talked someone into paying his shot or his creditors had forgotten sufficiently that he might show his head in Town again. For years, Giles had wanted to drain the bottom lands to produce more arable land for his tenants, but they crossed into Courtland's property and if Courtland did not also drain his side the effort would be in vain. Could he get Courtland interested in even so small an improvement? Not bloody likely. The only use Courtland had for his country estate was as a place to mark time until he could get back to Town.

"I've seen little of Lord Courtland these last ten years and heard less."

"His luck's been running better than usual, I suppose. And isn't it just *my* luck that *his* has run out now? Having that unprincipled baggage dumped on me by James was bad enough."

"Found anything yet?"

"How can I with her constantly underfoot?" Giles gave Bayard a last pat and slipped out of the stall.

"My lord," Foxkin said before he reached the door. "If you weren't so blind, you might see the surgeon at your door."

"What the deuce is that supposed to mean?"

"You might also have noticed the holes in your roof."

"I bloody well know I've got damned great holes in the roof. Blister it, man! What's that to do with anything?"

"I gave Lady Portia Ashburne money enough when she brought me that silver t'other day that she might have bought several gowns. Now, she's had Mr. Millbank out to the Hall, and she's asked me to send someone to see to the roof, but I haven't heard she's ordered so much as a scrap from the modiste. But," Foxkin said in an infuriatingly mild tone, "no doubt your lordship knows better."

Chapter Sixteen

PORTIA sighed and stretched her aching back.

All the books were now back on the bookcases, excepting those that went on the top shelf. She'd stacked them neatly next to the cases they went in, in readiness should she ever get anyone to put them away. Courtland was tall enough, but one could hardly ask a visiting lord to mount a ladder and help out. The lamp guttered on the table—heaven only knew when last it was filled—and her eyes burned.

She needn't have whiled afternoon into evening setting the library to rights. There was no one to notice or care if she left things as they were. But Courtland left without materially adding to her small store of knowledge about Lady Amelia's murder, and Portia could either put herself to work reshelving the books or she could spend the time brooding over the task she'd set herself.

Little had she known when she opened her mouth to the Duke of Ransley what kind of mess she was getting herself into. And yet... What else was there to do but prove Lord Ashburne's innocence?

Pray heaven he *was* innocent!

If he wasn't, Portia might as well pack herself up bag and baggage, and throw herself on James Ashburne's mercy, for the Hall would never become livable on her tiny income and only in London could she spout enough of the plate to effect any appreciable change. If it came to that, the quality of James' mercy being strained indeed, Portia might as well throw herself on Ransley's mercy, though she was more than half convinced he had none at all.

He must though, mustn't he? The locals, after all, looked to him to solve disputes fairly. Portia snorted—fair-mindedness was hardly the impression he'd made on *her*. Still, she had to believe that, if she could only get him to speak with her, he could be brought to see how much good she could do Lady

Clarissa. But how could she make the man see reason when she couldn't even get him to listen civilly? Pray heaven proving Ashburne's innocence would somehow sweeten the duke's disposition. Assuming he *was* innocent—

"Oh for God's sake," Portia said aloud and blew out the tarnished lantern that sat in such high state on the huge library table. She wished she could snuff out her thoughts as easily.

Carrying the stub of a candle she'd lit from the lantern, her tired eyes watering at the stench of the tallow, Portia nudged the cat out the door with her foot, locked the library, and headed up the stairs. She hesitated at the landing, empty without Ashburne's portrait glaring down upon it, and thought briefly of going up to check on Mr. McFerran. But Ellie was sitting with him now and the surgeon had said he was on the mend before leaving another outrageous bill.

Portia turned down the hall to the family apartments. Time to see if Giles Ashburne was still her guest.

The portrait was not leaning against the chair by her bed. Portia let out a careful breath, surprised to feel a touch of loss in her relief. It was the uncertainty, she decided. If it wasn't on the landing and it wasn't here, where was it?

She knew a moment later, when the feeble light of her candle reached the cold hearth. It picked out his eyes first, gleaming in the dimness, and Portia stepped back before she could help herself.

"Don't you know it's discourteous to linger in a lady's chamber, Lord Ashburne?" Perhaps Portia oughtn't have thought about having the portrait hung over her mantel shelf to disconcert Mrs. McFerran. It seemed now like tempting Fate. Portia scowled at herself and knelt to light the fire from her candle. It was slow to catch, and she had to force herself to keep at it, the feeling of him staring down at her raising the hairs at the nape of her neck. She shivered, the cold fingers walking up her spine having nothing to do with the storm that blustered outside or the damp chill of her chamber.

Portia bounced to her feet the moment the kindling caught, her eyes darting to the portrait. Not surprisingly, neither it nor its subject had moved. Giles Ashburne still stood immoveable before a lowering sky, as if unaware of the storm that gathered at his back. She hadn't been certain whether he was smiling when she first saw the portrait. She was certain of it now. It was an oblique smile, amusement without welcome. She thought, irrationally, that he was pleased with his recent efforts.

"Well, my lord," she made herself say aloud, her voice going some way to disperse the gathering clouds of superstition. Much more of this and she would become as flighty as her maid. "Have you at last found a place you like, or will you be wandering off when the mood takes you?"

Portia made herself look away from the portrait before she could begin searching it for similarities with the face she'd seen bent over her but two nights gone. That visage was burnt into her mind, and she found herself looking for it in the portrait, as if it might be hidden inside the smooth implacable glare of the man in the painting. Of course it could not be there. The man in the painting was not the same man who'd labored over letters to his lady love, pouring out his heart on the page to a woman doomed to betray him. Not the man who'd fled his home to die on some distant shore. How embittered Ashburne must have become.

Portia shook herself free of useless speculation and imagination. It *was* all imagination. To believe otherwise was to fall into Ellie's brand of mindless superstition. The fire had done little to warm the room and there was no point in standing around growing cold when she should be preparing for bed.

When her light fell on the dressing table, the candle wobbled in her hand, dripping hot tallow across her knuckles. Portia barely felt the burn. Her traveling desk was open, letters spread across the table. Her breath grew tight in her chest, outrage filling her at Mrs. McFerran's audacity. How thankless the housekeeper was, how unmoved by Portia's efforts on her husband's behalf.

Portia put the candle on the corner of the dressing table and wiped the back of her hand on the dressing gown that was draped over the chair. Her singed knuckles smarted at the rough treatment, but she was beyond noticing. She began gathering up the letters, and was brought up short when she came to a single letter placed dead center on the table. Her hands shook so badly the others scattered from her grasp. Slowly, she sank into the chair, reaching trembling fingers for the letter.

It was one of Tony's and must have been smoothed flat with some care to avoid tearing it at the folds, which had grown thin with much handling. Someone had marked red ink in a hard bold hand across Tony's familiar handwriting.

"Who can find a virtuous woman? Her price is far above rubies." And, below it, in a vicious scrawl, "Get out of my house!"

This handwriting, too, was familiar. It was Giles Ashburne's.

The letter fluttered to the floor. Portia folded her hands under her chin, pulled her feet up under her, and sat huddled in the dressing table chair, curled into the tightest ball she could manage.

Eventually, she made herself move. Made herself change out of her dress and into her nightrail, turning her back to the portrait as she disrobed without asking herself why she did so. And then, as if movement had been an end in itself, she ground to a halt in front of the fire and stood staring into the flames until her feet were blocks of ice. Finally, she spurred herself into motion once more, put on her dressing gown and slippers, took up her candle, and went out of the room.

She did not look at the portrait over her hearth.

Portia shooed Ellie away from Mr. McFerran's sick bed, only realizing after the maid was gone that she ought to have mentioned that Ashburne's portrait now hung over her mantel shelf. She sighed, for it was too late to call her back, and resigned herself to more smashed crockery in the morning.

Mr. McFerran slept quietly, his brow dry, his color good. Portia settled herself at his bedside and watched through the night, taking comfort in the clear signs he was on the mend, finding a kind of peace in his soft, gentle breathing.

Some endless time later, she had the impression of rising through fathoms-deep water to see a man clad in black standing opposite her, looking down at the invalid. As Portia stared, the man looked up and saw her. His face was expressionless, but there was something in his eyes that was not in his portrait, like a door softly opened. He put one finger to his lips and walked out, making not a sound, though he wore scuffed top boots.

Portia blinked, coming fully awake, and dashed after him, but when she gained the hall, he was gone.

* * *

Finding Portia once more nodding by McFerran's bedside was the last straw.

Giles had come home wet to the skin, the wind-whipped rain seeping inexorably under his cloak, and went straight up to the attic. He found the oiled canvas stretched over the hole in the attic floor by splashing into the water that built up on the edge, and investigated the extent of the hole by feel, impressed by the effort it had taken to shift the furniture into place to hold the canvas.

Foxkin's scold marched through his head, as it had all the wet walk home.

Giles stripped off his sodden cloak and went down to check on the invalid. He found her there, as he had once before, nothing but peace in her sleep. "All right," he said to himself and to the specter of Foxkin that rode him, "so I've misjudged her. In this at least."

She caught him there, and he found her charming despite himself, so muzzy with sleep that she let him walk out without a word spoken. He wondered with some amusement how much she would think she'd dreamt.

Then, for he was, at least some of the time, a fair man, he waited through the long hours, shivering until his clothes dried on him, for her to hand her merciful duty over to Mrs. McFerran and retire to her bed. And an hour after that to make certain she slept, for he did not mean to frighten her this time.

When he had finished filling her dressing room—all the dresses he'd taken and more besides—he found himself hesitating before her chamber door. He'd done all he need do, plus some by way of apology and guaranteeing she'd not need money for clothing in the near future. He'd stripped her of her wardrobe for pawning his silver; it was only right to return it when he discovered that she hadn't bought fancy ribbons and expensive French lace but surgeon's visits and shingles. But there his debt to her ended, for though she was better than he'd painted her, her correspondence showed her to be a woman of easy virtue and broken vows. He would not permit himself to regret the note he'd left her.

He found the key that matched her bed chamber and turned it silently in the lock, slipping into the darkness where she slept, as he had long-since discovered, as deeply as any child.

His eyes already accustomed to the dark, he could see the letters he'd left on her dressing table, now strewn over the floor. He gathered them up, placed the one he'd written on at the top, and tucked them away in her traveling desk. For a minute, he allowed himself to be distracted by the sight of his own portrait looking down from above the softly glowing fire. For that, and for sending her screaming in the night, he did feel regret. There were other ways to achieve his ends.

Finally, responding to the lure of her, which he'd felt even on the other side of the dressing room door, he drifted to the bedside, standing well back so she would not see him if she woke.

Her hair lay strewn across the pillow, surrounding her face in an inky cloud. He remembered how it had looked when he stood there last, light from his candle flickering in the mahogany depths. His fingers itched to touch, to find out if her hair was as silky as it looked, to brush the impossible softness of her cheek. But to touch her would be to wake her. He allowed himself to imagine her as he'd seen her, climbing the stairs by the light of her candle, her worn dressing gown clinging to her ripe curves. He wanted to peel back the counterpane and watch the dim firelight touch her body as he could not, stroking her through her thin shift, brushing the soft mound of her breast, the curve of her hip.

Giles tore himself from her side, cursing. Just because she wasn't the grasping harpy he'd thought her didn't mean she was a woman he could allow himself to want.

Chapter Seventeen

ROUSED the next morning by a terrible crash, Portia rolled over and sighed.

"Oh miss," Ellie gasped, her tone as near to a shriek as she could get without raising her voice, "it's... it's..."

"Over the mantel shelf. Yes, Ellie, I know." Portia sat up, yawned and stretched.

"You—"

"It was there last night, and therefore reasonable to expect it might be there still."

"Nothing in this house is reasonable," Ellie muttered, crouching to pick up the scattered toast and shattered tea service.

Portia ignored the maid's grizzling and slid out of bed, dancing on the cold carpet until she found her slippers. "I put the grey walking dress under my pillow again." She didn't apologize for it—Ellie could complain all she liked; nothing would convince Portia to risk finding herself with only a shift to wear come morning.

Ellie pulled it out with a long-suffering sigh. "It'll be down to the kitchen with us again this morning, my lady."

"Let me at least get into my chemise first. I'm not fond of shivering in my skin in the kitchen."

"I'll just get your ladyship a fresh shift." Ellie went to get the keys from the dressing table and Portia remembered the mess of letters she'd left there the night before. If Ellie saw the one with Lord Ashburne's writing on it, she'd have a fit so profound even a liberal application of the vinaigrette wouldn't let them get on with the day for some time. She reached the dressing table at the same moment as Ellie and stood gaping at the clear surface of the table while Ellie walked off with the keys. Portia lifted the lid of her traveling desk just far enough to see that the letters were there. Someone had been in her bedchamber again during the night. Portia shivered, though this felt different from the rest. Her ghost had done a superb job so far of tearing things apart. This was the first time he'd tidied up, which was almost more unsettling. She wondered if it was the start of a new tactic.

Her relief that Ellie hadn't seen the letter was tempered somewhat by the belated realization that, having never seen Giles Ashburne's handwriting, Ellie would have made little of the letter. It was also, apparently, premature. Portia's heart kicked into a gallop when Ellie screamed.

She only realized it wasn't terror when she joined the maid in the doorway and found herself gaping at a dressing room crammed full of brilliant, expensive gowns. Her own looked mousy and very poor indeed tucked away in one corner.

"They're back," Ellie gasped.

And then some, Portia saw, but did not say. She only hoped they wouldn't vanish again before she had a chance to wear them. Ellie must have had the same thought, for she was gathering finery into her arms in a flurry of activity that paid little mind to color, quality or purpose, morning gowns next to ballgowns next to silk shifts, gray with green with burgundy.

"If you wouldn't mind," Portia said, trying very hard not even to smile for fear she'd burst out laughing, "I think I would prefer to dress—" She plucked out one of her old gowns. "—before I go down to breakfast."

* * *

Portia descended the stairs in a brown study, not certain whether the reappearance of her dresses was some kind of peace offering or the next step in a campaign that would see them vanish again just when she could least afford it. Did it mark a sea change or just an ebbing of the tide?

She found Mrs. McFerran in the kitchen. Asked for tea and toast, the housekeeper provided it silently, but for the first time not sullenly. The toast was neither burnt nor soggy, the tea dark and hot. And when Portia thanked her for it, she swore she saw a touch of humanity flash across the woman's eyes. Perhaps there was hope for them yet.

The surgeon's visits and Portia's turns at the old man's bedside may have at last cracked the ice. And in that context, the return of Portia's dresses made sense. Mrs. McFerran was of course responsible for that, as she'd been responsible for their disappearance in the first place. After all, what made more sense, an angry housekeeper, or a vengeful ghost with a predilection for stealing lady's dresses?

What did *not* make sense was the letter. The handwriting was without doubt Ashburne's, but the very ease with which Portia could identify it after only a brief acquaintance with his correspondence meant it was so individual in character as to be simple to mimic. Any of his retainers might have learned how. But how, in a single night, had Mrs. McFerran gone from penning so hostile a message to filling Portia's dressing room with the dowager Lady

Ashburne's gowns? What had Portia done in the intervening hours to bring about a change of heart?

Sat at Mr. McFerran's bedside? She'd done that before—why should it make such a difference now?

Portia tried not to dwell on what she'd dreamed as she nodded over Mr. McFerran's sickbed. She couldn't fathom why she would dream of Giles Ashburne standing over Mr. McFerran, watching him sleep. It was disturbing enough to conjure up vengeful ghosts; she hadn't the slightest idea what to make of the softening she felt in him. Rather, in her imagined version of him. For of course he wasn't real, and if he was no longer frightening, it was nothing to do with him. Perhaps her mind was trying to tell her something? Oh bother!

She banished such considerations. Rather than growing easier in her mind, the more she told over all her reasonable explanations, the more uncertain she became. It was too easy to brush logic and reason aside and blame these pranks on *him*. Her ghost. She wasn't certain she liked the drift of her thoughts.

That morning began a new trend. Where nothing Portia'd tried since she came to the Hall had gone right, now it could not seem to go wrong. Mr. McFerran was on the mend, Mrs. McFerran cooked mostly edible meals, Portia had a surfeit of things to wear, the weather came over warm and clear, and if none of that fixed the hole in the roof, at least it didn't get any worse.

The next day, Ellie was working on a new morning dress and Portia attempting to make over the copper ballgown after the style of the dress she'd seen in the modiste's window when Mrs. McFerran showed Foxkin into the morning room.

"Presented himself at the kitchen door, my lady. Asked to see you." And instead of telling him to remain in the kitchen and asking Portia for direction, Mrs. McFerran had brought a common tradesman into the morning room like any titled visitor. If she thought to insult Portia—which of course she did—she was sadly mistaken.

"Thank you, Mrs. McFerran." Portia caught the gleam of thwarted spite in the housekeeper's eyes when she turned to go, and restrained a sigh. They were not out of the woods yet, the cordiality of the last two days but a brief respite. She gave Ellie a look and her maid rose, curtsied, and left, not without showing a flash of defiance—it doubtless offended her sense of the proprieties for Portia to see a tradesman alone. "Good morning, Mr. Foxkin. What brings you here?"

He looked absurdly smaller without his apron and woefully ill at ease, crushing his hat in his hands as he fidgeted in the morning room. For that, more than any slight against her, Portia could cheerfully have strangled Mrs. McFerran. "Lady Ashburne." He stopped, gulped a breath, and shifted on his feet. "Terribly sorry to intrude, my lady. Only, I've got, that gentleman I mentioned, he, here." He pushed a worn leather satchel at her, looking away the moment it left his hands. It wasn't every day a man in his walk of life brought money to a woman in hers.

"Thank you," Portia said, and felt it to be inadequate, but didn't know what else to say. Her lessons in etiquette and deportment did not cover a situation such as this. She mastered the desire to look inside and poked the satchel down beside her in the chair. "You've been most helpful, Mr. Foxkin."

"A pleasure, my lady." When he turned to her, Portia saw the sheen of tears in his eyes. While he may have glanced away to save her embarrassment, it was another impulse that kept him gazing at the moth-eaten draperies.

"How long were you in service here?" Portia asked quietly.

Foxkin brushed the back of his hand across his cheek. "I was the age of my oldest boy when I came here, my lady, strange as it is to remember now." He looked around again, without any pretense at discretion. "The poor old place."

"It is that."

"You wouldn't have credited it, my lady…" Foxkin's eyes were focused on some distant vision only he could see. "…how grand Ashburne Hall was then. Even the Duke of Ransley envied Lord Ashburne the Hall."

"Did he?"

"Yes, my lady. I overheard him tell Lord Ashburne as how he'd have to marry his line to Ashburne's to even come near such a place." Realizing suddenly who he was talking to, Foxkin's shoulders shot up toward his ears, his eyes flicking to Portia. "Never mind me, my lady. My mind wanders."

"I'm all ears, Mr. Foxkin. You said…" Portia paused, finding her way cautiously back into a conversation interrupted several days ago. No more than interesting then, now it was vital. "…you knew Lord Ashburne to be innocent of the crime he was accused of."

"Yes, my lady."

"How so?"

The innkeeper blinked and glanced away. His fingers slid along his pantleg. Finding nothing to fidget with, he settled himself more solidly on her faded hearthrug and said, "I'm certain it's nothing your ladyship would find interesting."

"On the contrary. I'm very interested."

"It's ten years dead and gone, my lady."

"Of course it isn't," Portia said reasonably. He blinked, and blinked again when she added, "If it were, people wouldn't be so loathe to talk about it. Now, how do you know he was innocent?"

For a moment, it appeared Foxkin would stand mute. Then he shifted suddenly on his feet and said, "Because I knew Lord Ashburne, my lady." He seemed not to see Portia's disappointment. "He was reserved, unbending, and downright difficult, if you'll pardon me for saying so, but he was a good man and a good master."

Insight burst in upon her and Portia blurted, "You were his valet!"

Foxkin flushed. "Took a country boy still wet behind the ears and trained him up to be his own master and anyone's man." He became suddenly intense, quite in contrast to his assertion that the tragedy was ten years dead and gone. "Mark me, my lady. Lord Ashburne didn't kill Lady Amelia. He couldn't have."

Nearly breathless with excitement, Portia asked, "Were you with him at the time?"

Foxkin shook his head. "I only wish I was. I attended Lord Ashburne early in the evening, but later he sent me to oversee the arrangements for the ball. I didn't see him again until after... after the body was discovered. I wish to God I'd been there."

"Yes," Portia murmured, much deflated. She agreed when Foxkin offered to send over a couple of fellows who could see to the roof and thanked him for bringing the money himself, which brought a fiery flush to his cheeks and set him back to wringing his hat as he bowed himself out.

* * *

The satchel, which Portia opened once Foxkin was well gone, contained a surprisingly large sum of money for two ugly pieces of silver. The sight of it quite took her breath away.

Her solicitor's contribution to the coffers arrived a few hours later, less lavish but no less welcome. For the first time in her life, Portia was flush with money. Before she wed, she had only to ask for what she needed from her father and then her grandfather. Any amount greater than her pin money was a matter of the most nebulous imagination. It was only after her marriage that she handled any significant sum on her own—significant not in quantity but necessity, for funds were so short that amounts greater than her pin money were *still* more imagined than experienced. She thought long over where to keep the money safe until it could be used, the leather satchel hidden in the meantime under the folds of the gown she was working on, and finally took it into the library when no one was about and hid it in the second bookcase behind the books on the next shelf down from the top. It was one her "ghost" had gone through already, and he'd not so far done any backtracking, so she supposed it safe. Certainly, no one else would think to look there.

The workmen sent by Foxkin presented themselves that afternoon and set immediately to repairing the largest hole in the attic, hauling wood in and out that day and the next and hammering away from breakfast until supper, working with a will to finish before it came on to rain again. Portia dared any ghost to rest peacefully through that ruckus.

Apparently, however, he did. For three days, nothing moved, disappeared or moved of its own accord. There were no unexplained noises. Portia met no figures roaming her halls but the workmen. She was even getting used to seeing Giles Ashburne glare down at her from the portrait above her hearth.

On the third day, she discovered he'd been at the library again. Her first intimation of it was when Thomas ran out with a meow the moment she opened the door. Her money—what was left of it—was still there, but the fifth and sixth bookcases were now empty, their contents stacked in the middle of the room. Why had he skipped the third and forth, Portia wondered? She studied them and thought they looked less dusty than the others, but that hardly seemed to signify. She found it difficult to be too angry. She was wearing a new morning dress of green sprigged muslin, delicate and fashionable, her ghost had stacked the books neatly this time and, wonder of wonders, he'd not only reshelved the books that went on the top shelves of the newest disturbed cases, but those from the first two cases, which she'd been unable to put away.

She was engaged in sorting the books when Clary stalked in wearing a determined expression and, Portia was pleased to see, a dress.

"To blazes with my uncle."

"Good afternoon, Lady Clarissa," Portia replied, as imperturbably as possible. She picked up a book, looked at the spine, and put it in the appropriate stack for shelving. Her ghost was still leaving the books in piles, sorted by what rationale Portia could not guess. There seemed little purpose to the activity, especially when all the other "ghostly" incidents had ceased, though Portia thought she might be beginning to grasp the reason for it.

Clary threw herself down in a chair. "*He's* not the one who'll end up spilling a glass of ratafia down the front of his dress while everyone snickers up their sleeves."

"True," Portia said, trying very hard not to imagine Ransley in a ballgown.

"I'll risk his wrath if you will."

Portia needed only a moment to decide. The money from spouting the silver could only go so far to rehabilitate the Hall's condition, and do nothing to fix its reputation. She was going to need both Lady Clarissa's money and her good example to get anywhere. Proving Ashburne innocent might take some time. Time neither Clary nor Portia had. The Season would be upon them before they knew it and there was much to do to bring the chit up to snuff. "All right."

They were not fifteen minutes into their lesson—on the subject of not ripping up at a duke in public, regardless of the provocation—when a man said from the hall, "What's that great gray beast doing pulling up weeds in the drive?"

"He's not a beast." Clary scowled, heading into the hall despite Portia's gesture for her to stay put. "He's Gunpowder."

"Lady Clarissa," Courtland exclaimed, whipping his hat off. "I hardly expected to find you here."

At sight of Lord Courtland, Lady Clarissa turned into a blushing mute, and it was Portia who said, "And now that you have?"

Courtland winked broadly. "I wouldn't dream of betraying my fellow conspirator. Why is the front door open?"

Portia jumped at the change of subject, hoping Clary wouldn't ask what he meant. "Because of the sparrow."

"The sparrow."

"It's flitting about up there somewhere and we hoped if we opened some doors and windows, it would find its own way out." Truth be told, Portia didn't particularly want it out. It had a nest in the attic, after all, and the hole it was in the habit of using was now boarded up. But the day was fine and warm, and the bird made a good excuse to let the sun in.

"Best be careful, Lady Ashburne. While you're waiting for the bird to leave, other creatures might just find their way in."

"Yes," Portia said, watching him put his hat and cane on the hall table without waiting to be invited, "they might."

"Like that gray gelding." Courtland turned to Lady Clarissa. "How do you do it, my dear? My horse needs must be tied or hobbled to keep it where I left it, while that high-strung animal of yours wanders tame about the yard like a dog."

Clary muttered something about training and turned a shocking white when Courtland gallantly congratulated her on her skill as a horsewoman and kissed her fingers.

"To what do we owe the pleasure, my lord?" Portia smoothly appropriated Clary's hand from Courtland and led the girl into the library. Who could have guessed her outspoken, headstrong pupil would turn into a blushing schoolroom chit at a few compliments from a gentleman? Portia clearly had her work cut out for her.

Lord Courtland sauntered after them and stood looking at the scattered books. "A never-ending task, I see. Another of your ghost's pranks?"

Portia shot him a quelling glare. "I am merely attempting to bring some order to the room." She seated herself on a green couch that had seen so much use the knap was worn off the velvet and patted the cushion next to her. Clary plumped down with all the grace and refinement of a five year old and Portia surreptitiously pressed her hand to the center of the girl's back when she began to slouch. "My sincerest apologies, Lord Courtland. I'm afraid we're at sixes and sevens around here this afternoon, and I am unable even to offer tea." First, because the library bellpull was broken off at the ceiling. Second, because Mrs. McFerran was sitting with her husband. And third, because Portia didn't want Lady Clarissa and Lord Courtland to spend any more time together, even chaperoned, than absolutely necessary. Courtland was an engaging scamp; it would not be hard for Clary to develop a *tendre* for him. Besides, the twinkle in Courtland's eye did not promise circumspection, and as easy as Clary appeared about her half-sister's death, she might take it ill were she to discover Portia was attempting to clear the murderer's name.

"I regret to say I would be unable to accept in any case," Courtland said gallantly, seating himself in a chair cater-corner to the couch. "I have time enough for only a short visit."

Good. He was treating this as an ordinary social call, though there was a gleam in his eye Portia mistrusted. "You rode here, my lord?"

"Indeed. It's a fair day, though the roads are all over mud. However did you get here, Lady Clarissa, without spoiling that beautiful riding habit?"

Clary said something perfectly inaudible, and Courtland smiled as if he could hear her. He obligingly switched his attention from the blushing girl to Portia and carried on a perfectly correct, and perfectly trite, conversation for the requisite fifteen minutes before taking his leave.

Portia closed the door behind him and returned to find Lady Clarissa striding up and down the library in a fever of irritation. "You see?" she demanded when Portia came in. "You see how hopeless it is?"

"It's not hopeless at all, my dear. Sit, please," Portia said, returning to the couch, "and cease pacing about like a caged animal." She waited until Clary plunked back down next to her. "It's merely a matter of practice. We'll go over the proper forms and practice polite conversation and—"

"I shall forget every shred of it the moment a gentleman looks my way."

"Well certainly, if you convince yourself you will."

"Oh, Lady Ashburne." Clary threw herself on Portia in an excess of emotion. "However will I manage? I can't speak with even one gentleman without turning into a blushing widget. However will I face a whole ballroom of them?"

"Practice, my dear." Portia patted the girl's heaving back. "Practice. Come now, get control of yourself, Clary."

"I can't help it," Clary snuffled. "Oh, my lady, he must think me a complete ninnyhammer!"

Oh dear.

* * *

Courtland knocked on the library windows not fifteen minutes after Lady Clarissa left, much easier in her mind and completely unaware Portia was near to despairing. Even if she successfully taught the girl everything she knew, if it all went out of Clary's head the minute a man paid her the least attention, the results didn't bear thinking on. What Clary needed was practice conducting herself under a gentleman's eye, and that Portia could not provide. The only gentleman in the vicinity that she knew was Courtland, who barely qualified for the title, and with whom Clary was already far too taken. Portia'd be damned if she'd see the girl attached to a worthless rake, no better than Roger. And *Ransley*.... Ransley'd be incandescent with rage. She cursed the duke for being so little aware of his ward that he didn't realize she was hopelessly inept in society, and blamed him in no small part for his niece's shyness around the opposite sex. It was doubtless her guardian's imposing demeanor that put the seal on Lady Clarissa's nerves.

"Have you been watching from the home wood?" Portia demanded when she opened the door to Courtland.

"Is that any way to greet a gentleman?" He'd obviously been home, for he was no longer dressed in riding clothes and from the drive came the sound of wheels rocking over gravel as his team stamped and fidgeted.

"Oh, do gentlemen rap for entrance on library windows?"

"Baggage," he said without heat. "If you had a knocker on the door, I might not be reduced to circling the house in search of you. And what do you mean by asking if I was watching?"

"You've missed Lady Clarissa by a mere quarter-hour."

"How unfortunate. Had I come earlier, I might have escorted her home. At which point," he went on sardonically, "Ransley would doubtless have come after me with a whip." He thought her jealous, which was lowering, but better that than he realize how very much he concerned her when it came to Clary.

"What have you done to anger him so?"

"Not one whit more than you, my lady." Courtland laughed suddenly. "Which is to say, plenty. No, my lady, it's you I wanted to get alone, not Lady Clarissa. I had thought we might go for a ride in my curricle, but it clearly wouldn't have done to interrupt your lesson. I trust now is a more appropriate time."

"You were on horseback earlier." Which would have made it a great deal easier for him to see Clary home. Had he really stopped at the Hall to see Portia, or had he another goal in mind? Lady Clarissa no doubt had a substantial dowry and that horse of hers was eminently recognizable. He couldn't have seen it from the road, but the road was not the only approach to Ashburne Hall.

"I was on my way back from the village earlier. And furthermore, I hadn't been in your stables then."

"What the deuce were you doing in my stables?"

"Not finding anything. After that, I thought it best to bring my curricle. I'd have brought a pretty little mare from my stables, but I wasn't certain if you had a riding habit." He looked her over with an appreciation that made her grateful for her new dress, then ruined it by saying, "I take it you found your wardrobe."

"It's an excellent thing you made yourself scarce earlier. Lady Clarissa would learn nothing about manners with you around."

"I should say the same, but I make it a habit never to insult a lady. Come now, Lady Ashburne, will you ride with me? I would be happy to wait while you collect your bonnet." The sun shining in through the open door turned his hair into a flame-tinted halo that gave him a less than angelic look. He leaned in until his breath stirred her hair. "I thought to share what I've learned in the village."

It was the work of a minute to get her hat and join him on the drive. The hat was several years old, but Ellie had adorned it with some of the lace she'd removed from the dress Portia was wearing and it suited well enough. She only remembered that she still didn't have gloves when he handed her into the carriage, holding her fingers longer than necessary, or proper.

"Ho," Courtland called to his tiger when he had the reins in hand. "Plant yourself, George." And with that, he took off down the drive without giving the tiger time to climb on behind. "Better if we have no witnesses, I think."

"Oh?" Portia hung onto the edge of the seat, relaxing only when they reached the main road, where Courtland could spring his horses without throwing her off.

"It's an unpopular task we're engaged in, Lady Ashburne. Folks hereabouts aren't fond of Ashburnes, especially Giles Ashburne."

That didn't jibe with what Foxkin had told her, but the innkeeper's perceptions may have been skewed by his obvious fondness for his master. "Oh?"

Courtland slanted her a look. "What does that mean?"

"Tell me about him."

"Why the interest?" He turned toward the village, his horses trotting along at a brisk clip. The hedgerows were high, the sun warm on her back. It had been an eternity since Portia had ridden along a country road with a handsome lord, and it was only with an effort she remembered she had more pressing concerns.

"How am I to prove the man innocent if I haven't a clue what he was like?" When he continued silent, she sighed. "Or tell me what you've found in the village. It's why we're here, isn't it?"

"It may be why *you're* here, Lady Ashburne." Courtland let up on the reins until the horses fell into a smooth walk, and his free hand found hers. "I had hoped to take a pleasurable ride with a beautiful widow."

Portia was not blind to his implication, nor unaware that he'd chosen the word widow deliberately. Roger had introduced her to the marriage bed, though he'd given her precious little reason to regret his disinclination to return overmuch to it. Carrying on the family line had not been as important to Roger as carrying on in London. If he had not married to produce an heir, however, she was at a loss as to quite why he'd bothered. Certainly, it hadn't been for money, or out of love, or even an appreciation for such attractiveness as she might have, though he'd been most convincing about those last two before they were wed. The realization that the man she'd wed—the man she thought she loved—neither loved nor desired her had been among the most lowering of Portia's life.

As for Courtland's proposition, while as a widow she could dally without sullying her reputation, so long as she was discrete, she failed to see any reason she should. She needed Lord Courtland's assistance, however, so she didn't free her hand from his and said merely, "It *is* a pleasant day, isn't it?"

"All right," Courtland said with a laugh, releasing her to take up the reins again. "I know when I'm out-maneuvered. What do you want to talk about: Giles Ashburne, or what I found in the village?"

"Lord Ashburne, if you please."

"There've been two of that title since Giles Ashburne, but I expect in the village there's only the one Lord Ashburne, even yet. For a mere viscount, Ashburne was demmed top-lofty. He was fortunate to be so tall. It meant he didn't have to stick his nose in the air to look down at you."

Courtland didn't sound much like a man describing his friend. Then he smiled. "He was also loyal to a fault. Where he trusted, he trusted, and where he did not..." He hitched his shoulders. "Take Ransley. Now there's an untrusting old bastard." Ransley hadn't seemed particularly old to Portia. No older than Giles Ashburne at any rate, and not much older than Courtland himself. "Liked Ashburne, though."

"What does that have to do with Lord Ashburne's loyalty?"

"He agreed to marry the chit, didn't he? She was pretty, I'll give you that, but a demanding baggage. And he didn't love her. I don't think he even particularly cared for her. When they danced, he might as well have been squiring his sister around the floor. If he'd had one."

To touch you is sometime more than I can bear. I have lived so long in hopes of one day finding the dearest treasure of my heart, that I do not quite know what to do now that my hopes bid fair to be fulfilled.

Portia opened her mouth, then thought better of it. Not only would it reflect poorly on her to have read Ashburne's personal correspondence, she couldn't feel right about sharing something so intensely private. Even if he was dead. "Why did he agree to marry her, then?"

Courtland shrugged, the horses surging briefly into a trot at the shift of the reins. "Ransley's idea, combine the estates. He promised to settle Tynesfield on Amelia's son if he died without an heir of his own getting. Told you, they were friends. Have you seen him?" he asked suddenly.

"Who?"

"Your ghost. Have you seen him?"

"*My* ghost?" Portia said, feeling unaccountably flushed. "The Hall's ghost, you mean. If there is one."

"Then you have seen him."

"Of course not." Dreams didn't count, however vivid. Portia ignored the fact that the first time she saw him, she was wide awake.

"What sort of things has he done?"

"I told you, it's the servants. They want me out of the Hall, God knows why, and they're willing to do anything to make that happen. What did you find out in the village?"

Courtland made a face and slapped the reins, drawing a little more speed from his horses. "Not a demmed thing."

"But you said—"

"No one wants to talk about it. No one wants to even think about it. They're scared."

"Of Ransley?"

"Him or the ghost."

"That's nonsense. Someone must know something."

"If they do, they're not talking." Courtland turned onto a track barely wider than the curricle and reined in on the edge of a lovely green meadow. The sun drifted down in a languorous haze that matched the sleepy drone of bees. A lark warbled in greeting.

"Now I wish I hadn't left my tiger behind. I might get you to walk with me if I had someone to hold the horses." He wrapped the reins loosely around his fist and turned to face her. "Lady Ashburne, you must leave off."

Portia glared at him. "You said you'd help."

"I've had time since to consider the matter. My lady, if you don't leave off, someone will get hurt. And I'm very much afraid it might be you."

"Nonsen——"

"For Christ's sake, woman! Do you really think, if someone other than Ashburne *did* kill Lady Amelia, that he's just going to sit back and wait for you to unmask him?"

She hadn't thought beyond clearing Lord Ashburne's name so she had a chance of living at the Hall in peace. Certainly she hadn't thought asking questions about a ten-year-old murder could be dangerous. But if the murderer wasn't Lord Ashburne, and if he was still around, still watching.... She shivered, and was immediately disgusted with herself. If she gave up before she even started, what then? Was digging into Lady Amelia's murder really any more dangerous than living in a house like to fall down about her ears any moment? "What happened the night Lady Amelia died?"

"Dammit, woman! Haven't you been listening?"

"What happened?" Portia persisted. Courtland swore, dragging his free hand through his hair. "You were there."

"Yes," he said through clenched teeth.

"Tell me."

"What's there to tell?"

"What happened? How did it happen? Who found her? Who was there?"

Courtland stared at her so long that Portia was convinced he wouldn't answer, when he suddenly said, "Everyone who was anyone in the neighborhood was there *and* half of London besides. Ashburne had the hosting of it, but it was Lady Amelia who chose the guests, less to celebrate the betrothal than to prove to the bride to be she wouldn't be moldering in Ashburne Hall for the rest of her life, no doubt."

"Cynical."

"I told you, she was a demanding little thing. Not the least happy to be foregoing her Season just because she was already spoken for." He laughed suddenly. "Oh, how I'd have loved to be a fly on the wall when Ransley told her she was to be wed. I wonder if she dared show him her claws." Courtland turned an earnest look on her. "You see how useless it is to pursue this? Ashburne Hall was full to bursting and dozens more were guested at Tynesfield. People who'd never been here before, nor have been since. Your murderer could be anywhere, assuming he's not rotting at the bottom of the sea."

"All the better for us if the real murderer's not nearby. He won't know his danger until too late."

"And if he *is* close at hand, he might take your head off before you even know who to fear, puss." He shook his head. "It's no wonder you led Roger a merry dance."

Portia swallowed an angry denial. If Roger was dancing during their marriage, in any sense of the word, it wasn't with her. "Go on. "

"I wasn't staying at Ashburne Hall. Not with my own house so close. Roger was with me—said he couldn't stand tripping over people morning, noon and night. God knows how Ashburne was holding up; he was never much for doing the pretty. The bride to be went home to Tynesfield every night. That's Ransley for you. A house full of chaperones, but his ward would not spend one night under her intended's roof until they were wed. Much good it did. Ashburne wasn't the one Ransley needed to worry about. Lady Amelia had already bestowed her favors elsewhere."

"How do you know?"

His expression mocked her. "Everyone knew."

"Did everyone likewise know the name of her beau?"

"I never did learn who was enjoying her." He was deliberately crude, but Portia didn't let him put her out of countenance. In truth, what shocked her was not what Lady Amelia may have done, but how certain everyone had been that she'd done it. Without, it appeared, a scrap of evidence.

"Did Lord Ashburne know?"

"That she was sharing her favors? I don't see how he could have missed the gossip. As to whether he knew who it was, that I couldn't say. If he actually caught them together, as the story goes, then he must have."

"That assumes he killed her."

"Lady Ashburne," Courtland said, faintly mocking, "you're the only one making the assumption that he *didn't*."

"Who found her?"

"The house party had been together more than a week. Lady Amelia's dainty little hand was everywhere. Breakfast picnics. Battledore and shuttlecock on the lawn. Forfeits and crambo and charades at night. Though there was dancing most nights, she'd insisted on hosting a grand ball with all the trappings. You've seen the ballroom at the Hall, of course."

Portia vaguely remembered a large room echoing with old footsteps, dust an inch thick on the floor. She hadn't concerned herself with it—it had no furnishings to speak of and there was no need to set it to rights. for there could be no chance of it being put to its proper use while she was in residence. She nodded.

Courtland leaned back against the squabs, staring sightlessly over his horses' twitching ears. "Decked out with flowers and shining lace. Musicians on the dais. Lobster and I don't know what all in the supper room. Lord, the blunt that must have taken to lay on. All gone to waste. The bride to be never appeared. Her maid helped her change into her ballgown in an upstairs bedroom some half-hour before the neighboring families were to arrive, and that was the last anyone saw of her. We all turned out to search."

His voice fell and Portia leaned closer to hear.

"It was Ashburne found her. Out on the green where there was to be yet another picnic the following morning. Carried her back to the Hall himself, golden hair spilling over one arm, the ballgown a cloud of silver lace over the other, and all in between red as red. When he laid her before Ransley in the great hall, his shirtfront was covered in blood." He turned and something dark swam in his eyes. "Her throat was cut ear to ear."

Portia flinched. She looked away from him and swallowed. "That's all? That's the only evidence against him?"

"There were no gypsies in the area. No tramps or vagrants. She'd been robbed of neither her jewelry nor her virtue, assuming she still had it. It wasn't the work of someone outside the Hall."

"Then one of the guests...."

"Who else had cause?" Courtland untangled the reins, flexing the hand that had been clenched around them. "Ashburne fled justice a week later."

It was a long and silent ride back.

Chapter Eighteen

HE wasn't watching for her return.

Where Portia Ashburne went and what she did was no concern of his. So long, of course, as she was not pawning his silver, and he'd already given Foxkin additional monies in anticipation of that eventuality. As for anything else she might take it into her head to do.... Giles hated to see whatever shreds of respectability the Ashburne name still bore trampled into the mud, but he could hardly chase around the countryside after her.

No, he wasn't watching for her return. The room in the servants' quarters where he'd taken refuge from that bustling Amazon of a lady's maid merely overlooked the drive. That he was looking out when Courtland drove off with Lady Ashburne was the merest coincidence. That he was looking out when they returned, purest chance.

Courtland's tiger, whose loitering about the drive for the past hour guaranteed that whatever Portia Ashburne was about, it would not add any countenance to the family name, ran to take the near horse by the headstall. Courtland—still partial to peacock colors, Giles saw—leapt down and came around to lift her down, his hands lingering too long on her waist, as of course they would. Why should Courtland be any more immune to Portia's slim waist and pleasing curves than Giles? He cursed himself for returning the gowns he'd taken, but how could he know Portia and her maid would turn his mother's cast-offs into such flattering fare? Courtland said something to her, and she turned her cheek for his kiss, which he bestowed with unmistakably passionate fervor.

Damn him! What the hell was Courtland about? Did he think he could give her a slip on the shoulder, help himself to her favors, and walk away when he'd had his fill, as he doubtless would, flying back to Town as soon as he was flush again? The hell of it was that he probably could. Portia Ashburne had shown little delicacy of feeling when her husband was alive, even carrying on under his very nose. Why should she display any better morals now he was dead?

Giles turned and walked out of the tiny bedchamber without remembering to check the hall first. Thankfully, Lady Ashburne's maid was not still flitting about the servants' quarters, squirreling away gowns in every room in the wing. Giles had found that amusing, earlier.

He reached the landing and stood looking down as Portia came in alone. She walked to the center of the great hall and stopped, staring down at the heavy flagstones polished smooth by ages of Ashburnes. She stood so near where Lady Amelia had lain, and looked so long upon the flagstones, that Giles felt a crawling begin under his skin.

She finally looked up, an audible gasp escaping her lips when her gaze lifted to the first floor landing. He'd taken advantage of her absence to return his portrait to its usual place, and she stared at it, for all the world as if she expected it to move of its own accord.

"My Lord Ashburne," she murmured, and Giles' heart froze. "How you must have bled to find her there. No wonder they believe you haunt the Hall. How many of them know in their hearts that you're innocent?"

Giles was so startled he nearly let her catch him out.

* * *

"Blast!" Carefully, Portia began to unpick her stitches. She oughtn't be working on the copper gown by candlelight, and most assuredly not when she was so distracted as to sew the hem of the skirt to the bodice. Thank heavens she'd sent Ellie to her bed hours ago. The maid had driven her to distraction, fluttering about her bedchamber in a perfect agony of indecision, not certain which to be more excited about: that she'd hit upon a method of keeping Portia's wardrobe out of the ghost's hands, or that Portia was, to Ellie's mind, already well on her way to attaching another gentleman. Portia didn't have the heart to dampen her enthusiasm, but neither could she bear her maid's blithe assumption that marriage was her mistress's best option.

Portia dropped her sewing into the old workbasket she'd found playing host to a family of mice under the drawing room couch. Emptied and cleaned, it proved in surprisingly good condition, given it hadn't been used since the previous Lady Ashburne last sported the gown Portia wore. Thomas hissed and batted free of the gown's encompassing folds.

"My apologies, Sir Thomas," Portia told the cat, who fixed her with an accusing eye. "But you ought to know better than to sleep in a lady's workbasket."

He stalked off in high dudgeon and Portia turned her eyes to the fire with a sigh. It was no use attempting to concentrate on anything when her mind was full of broken vows and creeping blood. She'd seen nothing of the countryside on the ride back to the Hall and missed entirely whatever rote words of courtesy Courtland had extended when he helped her down from the carriage. His kiss had come as a shock, and she'd instinctively turned so it landed on her cheek. He laughed, but his eyes had snapped with something that looked a great deal more like irritation than amusement. Covered in confusion, she'd retreated into the Hall, where Giles Ashburne's portrait glared unexpectedly at her from the landing. She felt both unsettled and reassured by his presence.

For the first time, Portia could truly believe the Hall haunted. She could see Lady Amelia lying in the great hall in a pool of blood. She could feel a presence lurking in the flat black eyes of Ashburne's portrait, doomed for all eternity to stare at the place his fiancée had lain.

"Oh for pity's sake," Portia said aloud. The portrait wasn't alive. Nor, for that matter, was it doomed to stay in one place, as had been most emphatically proven of late. If she kept on like this, she'd fulfill Mrs. McFerran's fondest dreams and run *herself* out of the Hall with superstitious nonsense.

Lady Amelia died horribly, choking on her own blood. Portia had already known that. The entire neighborhood believed Lord Ashburne guilty. She'd known that too. The only one who *didn't* believe Lord Ashburne a blood-soaked fiend was Foxkin. And Portia herself. Though she hardly counted, as her belief was more a matter of expediency than knowledge.

Portia did not believe in premonitions or visions. She did not believe that spirits, guilty or otherwise, reached out from their graves. And she did not believe that something was watching her, however much her nerves pricked. There were no spirits haunting the Hall.

And there was no earthly reason for her to feel lonely in her room now that Giles Ashburne's portrait no longer hung over the hearth.

Portia picked up her candle and left her room. If she wasn't going to be able to sleep and she couldn't be trusted with a needle, she might as well read. Something reasoned, rational, logical. Plato or Aristotle, perhaps.

From his frame, Giles Ashburne watched her approach the landing and Portia deliberately turned her body to shield her candle rather than let the dancing flame imbue the portrait with any more life than the painter had already given it. It was not until she was halfway down the stairs, his painted gaze heavy on her back, that she saw light in the depths of the great hall. Instinctively, she cupped her hand around her candle and shrank down against the stairs. She froze, her breath caught so hard in her breast that her ribs ached with it, trapped between the painting behind her and the man before.

He stood by the library door, limned in a pale wavering light that picked out his harsh profile and dark hair and left the rest of him to fade into the night. He was all in black but for the patch of white where his linen showed at the neck. If he was wearing a cravat, it was white as well, though she rather thought he wasn't, this man who showed himself most often in waistcoat and shirtsleeves, as if such undress was standard for spirits.

Portia forced herself down one step, then the next. She lost sight of him when she reached the foot of the stairs, and hurried round to find he'd vanished. The moldering green baize door that led to the kitchen was too far. The doors to the parlor and morning room had been under her eye the whole time. There was nowhere he could have gone but the library.

Portia smiled. "I've got you, my lord ghost."

The library door was locked. Portia fumbled out the key, cursing under her breath when it stuck in the lock. The hinges creaked horribly when she teased the door open and, hissing in frustration, she threw it wide, only to find the library cold and dark and silent.

Portia advanced cautiously, her candle casting a dancing light that ebbed and flowed, now stretching as far she could reach, now pooling around her feet, cold in worn slippers. Afraid that the door might slam behind her, Portia deliberately closed it herself, even going so far as to lock it, though her heart constricted at the soft click. She took her legs on a stiff, unwilling circuit of the room, poking her candle into the recesses and dark corners, the high-backed chairs, and everywhere a man might hide.

Nothing.

She reached for the curtains with a hand that shook, holding her breath against the bump of her fingers against something solid. Nothing lurked behind the curtains but the windows, through which the half-grown moon peered furtively, its light silvering the furnishings. Portia made a second circuit, this time looking under the desk, the couch, even the chairs, finding only the cat, whose eyes flared at the candle's approach, frightening Portia near to death. Portia bit her tongue hard and continued the search, wondering why she'd wanted the blasted animal in the first place. She found herself once more by the high, black windows, her candle reflecting off the window-glass in a golden pool of light.

Portia sighed, defeated. He'd come into the library—she was certain of it—but there was no sign of him now. A light flashed outside. Not a reflection. It was definitely outside, moving and flickering on the grounds. She put both hands to the window, spilling hot tallow down the glass, before she remembered it didn't open.

"Well, he got out somehow," Portia muttered. She sped back through the library, her candle fluttering weakly in her shaking hand as she fought open the locked door, raced down the hall and through the kitchen door into the chill night. Portia took a stifled breath, wispy clouds and a pale moon pushing the cold down upon her like a wet blanket. She shivered, wishing she had her cloak. No time now. She hurried around the corner of the house, one hand shielding her candle, careful not to look at it for fear she'd set a legion of ghostly lights dancing behind her eyes and miss the real one in the throng.

There wasn't even a shred of wind. The night held its breath, even the little night creatures falling still as Portia stood with Ashburne Hall looming at her back and strained to see into the thick blackness of the home wood.

Nothing. He was here; she knew he was. The wood drew her with its pretense of emptiness. He was here, and this time she wasn't going to be put off. She walked slowly, finding her way with blind determination. Lightning burst without warning off to her right and something hissed by her head. Portia stumbled, her heart leaping into her throat.

Though there was no rain, no grumble of thunder, another burst of flame exploded nearby with a close, flat crack. Something hit Portia hard, throwing her to the ground, driving the wind out of her. The candle fell from her hand and went out. Something went hissing and rattling through the brittle tangle of dead rosebushes. Portia could barely breathe. She got her hands up and pushed against the weight that covered her.

"Hold still," he muttered in her ear, his breath stirring her hair. She shoved him hard, and he shifted, only to lie heavier against her. "Lie still, you fool!" His voice was vicious, near soundless. "He's shooting at *you*."

Portia gaped up at him, making no sense of the words. The moon tipped his hair with silver and burned in his eyes as he glared at her from far too close. Her chest rose against his with every breath. She was stifling. She flattened her hands on his chest and pushed. His coat was open, his linen warm with the heat of his body. "Get off." Her voice was appallingly weak.

He cursed, something she couldn't make out for the softness of his voice but knew by its ugly sound, and swooped down, blocking out the night sky, kissing her as Roger never had. There'd been sweet innocent kisses before their wedding, short perfunctory ones after. Nothing like this. His mouth was demanding, as hot and hard as the body that trapped her. Portia made a noise in her throat even she wasn't certain was a protest and pushed at him, but he might as well have been made of stone.

Warm stone. With lips that burned like fire. Her very bones were melting. She was going to dissolve into a puddle and soak into the cold earth beneath her. Or, more likely, the hard body that covered her. Her hands slid up to his shoulders, but she couldn't have said whether she was pushing or pulling. He broke off suddenly, leaving her breathless, and stared down at her with eyes that no longer burned with the moon, but with a fire hotter and darker.

Portia licked her lips, tasting him there. He laid his fingers on her mouth. "Quiet," he whispered, and she could feel his breath on her face. "Listen."

At first, she could hear nothing at all over the pounding of her heart. She was aware only of the touch of his calloused fingers, rough as Roger's had never been, the hard heat of his body bearing her down with a determination Roger had never shown, even in their marriage bed. For the first time, she saw Roger as not only a faithless libertine, but a weak and ineffectual man. As the thought slid into her mind, taking her away from the moment and the feel of him over her, she heard movement in the home wood, sounds so soft and faint they might have been the shuffle of small creatures, the sighing of the wind.

He moved not a muscle, his fingers stilled on her lips, head cocked slightly away from her as he listened. She strained her ears all the harder, finally realizing that what she heard were careful footsteps, catching the crack of a branch and, just at the edge of her hearing, a muttered curse.

The noises grew steadily fainter and died away completely, but he remained frozen through several dozen beats of her heart before letting out a slow breath that relaxed him against her. By the time he brought his eyes back to her face and removed his fingers, Portia had recovered both her voice and her sense.

"Giles Ashburne, if you would be so good as to get off me?"

Chapter Nineteen

"KEEP your voice down, madam." His low voice rumbled through his chest and set up an unsettling reverberation in her own.

"Whoever it was is gone," Portia hissed.

"Mayhap he's not gone far." This time, when she pushed, he yielded, though not by much.

Portia took in a fuller breath than she'd managed since he knocked her down, the cool air doing less to clear her mind than she'd hoped. She realized suddenly that she had one hand pushed up under his coat, the other tangled in the thick dark hair at the nape of his neck, and felt a hot flush paint her face. Impossible for him to see her blush by the thin moonlight, but he must have felt her face heat, for he showed his teeth in a sudden smile that flashed white in the darkness. Portia looked quickly away and removed her hands as casually as possible. The hand that had been under his coat felt strangely warm, even after she no longer touched him and, when she held it up, she saw that her fingers were painted black in the moonlight.

"I think," Portia said in a remarkably calm voice, "we'd best get you inside, my lord, and bind up your wound before you bleed to death."

"I'm already dead," he said in a voice equally calm. "Or hadn't you heard?"

"I had not heard ghosts could bleed."

"Ghosts can do a lot of things." Ashburne showed no inclination to move and Portia's heart lurched as she imagined him sinking down and dying where he lay, trapping her under the weight of his body. She scolded herself for being a complete goosecap. He would not be so calm if he were badly injured. A moment later, he lifted himself to his knees in one quick movement that left her breathless with surprise and the sudden chill.

When she would have risen, however, he held her down with one broad hand while he looked around. Finally, he stood and reached to hand her up. He did not show a gentleman's courtesy in brushing the grass and leaves from her skirts, nor give her a moment to do it herself, but started for the Hall with her hand still clasped in his. She had to trot to keep up with him. He didn't falter when a cloud covered the moon, but kept on through the blackness with surefooted familiarity, not pausing until they were in the kitchen with the door locked behind them.

Only then did he let Portia go. She didn't waste time shaking feeling back into her fingers, but went straight to the stove to poke up the fire and add another log. There ought to have been a candle somewhere near the stove, but she couldn't find it. She turned to Ashburne, who stood watching her from the door, the light of the growing fire licking tentatively at his features.

"Find some candles and light them. You'll know better than I where they are. Then take off your coat and sit down. And if you vanish on me, I'll rouse the whole house looking for you."

Five minutes later, Mrs. McFerran walked in on her as she searched the stillroom. The housekeeper looked much less formidable blinking over her candle with her nightcap drooping over one eye.

"Spirits," Portia said, before the woman could ask what she was about. "There's a wine cellar, of course, but where do you keep the hard liquors?"

Mrs. McFerran's lips compressed. Portia ignored her, making a soft sound of triumph when she found the healing ointment she remembered seeing in her earlier search of the room. She hoped Ashburne wouldn't be in need of the laudanum, which was still in the McFerrans' room. She gathered up the ointment, needle and thread, and strips of linen bandaging she'd already discovered. "Well?" she said when she saw the other woman still in the doorway. "What are you waiting for? Spirits, Mrs. McFerran, get me some. Not sherry. Scotch, brandy, port if you must. Hurry."

She left the woman gaping after her and returned to the kitchen, not acknowledging the fear that he'd be gone when she got there until she pushed open the door with her hip and found him adding more wood to the fire. Ashburne whirled at her entrance, taking an extra step to catch his balance. Portia dumped the supplies she'd gathered on the table and went to take his arm.

"I am quite well, madam." He tried to pull his arm out of Portia's grasp and she tightened her grip on his sleeve.

"You didn't remove your coat."

"I saw no need."

Portia turned back his collar with her free hand, revealing a shirt seeping with blood. *When he laid her before Ransley in the great hall, his shirtfront was covered in blood.* Portia banished Courtland from her mind and said, "Come, sir—" just as Mrs. McFerran returned, a dusty bottle in her hands.

"Oh!" she exclaimed, very nearly dropping the bottle. She plunked it down on the table and went to take Ashburne by the arm. His injured one, as it happened, and Portia wasn't the only one to notice how he paled. "Oh," Mrs. McFerran exclaimed again, releasing him. "My lord, what—"

"Nothing to worry yourself over." Portia was astounded to see his stony expression soften. "I'll be fine, Mrs. McFerran. Go on back to your husband."

"I'll do no such thing, my lord. You'll be needing care, I'm thinking." Mrs. McFerran gave Portia a withering look as much as to say that certainly *she* couldn't manage it, and went to fill a pot with water from a bucket near the door.

"*I'm* thinking," Ashburne said, "you had both better get on to bed." He extracted his sleeve from Portia's grasp and went to take the pot from Mrs. McFerran, setting it on the stove with a bang that slopped water over the rim, raising a furious hiss from the fire.

"But my lord—"

"Of all the cloth-headed—"

"Out." Ashburne's voice was no louder than theirs, but it was as effective as a roar. Mrs. McFerran turned without another word and headed for the door. Portia stood her ground, but not without a quaver.

"Leave the bottle," she said when the housekeeper picked it up on her way out. The woman hesitated, distributing her glare equally between Portia and Ashburne, then put it down and swept out, not quite banging the door behind her. "Why does it not surprise me that she didn't faint dead away at the sight of her 'ghost'?"

"I've no idea. Why haven't you?"

"I don't believe in ghosts."

"No?" he said with an unpleasant smile. "Why haven't you come looking for me then?"

"And have no better luck than I did searching for my dresses? No thank you, my lord."

Ashburne dipped his fingers in the water, which could hardly be more than lukewarm yet, and shook them off. "I believe I told you to get out."

"I have no intention of doing so."

He growled. "I don't need any female flutterings, nor anyone to fuss over me. Why do you think I got rid of Mrs. McFerran?"

"Come, sir, be reasonable. You can hardly stitch up your own wound. Sit here and let me tend you." Portia tried to guide him to the table, where half a dozen candles flickered in various holders, but he was as immovable as a rock.

"I need no tending, madam."

"Yes, I know; you're dead." Portia clenched her teeth and breathed out hard through her mouth rather than voice some of the words that rose to her tongue. Then, as sweetly as she could, she said, "Forgive me if I'm mistaken, Lord Ashburne, but it seems to me that you've been shot. Though I'm aware that, on the whole, dead men don't bleed, you might want to do something about that before you ruin more than your shirt, coat, and waistcoat."

"I was shot," Ashburne said, deftly removing his arm from her grasp, "because of you, you damned interfering woman."

"Me?"

"You. God save me from goose-brained females who haven't got the sense not to go running out into the dark."

"I was running after you," Portia said between her teeth. "If you hadn't been playing this stupid game—"

"It's not a game, and as I wasn't outside, you can hardly have been following me, madam."

"Stop calling me that." She didn't know how he could invest the word with more venom even than Ransley, but it was grating. "If you weren't outside, then who was?"

"Whoever it was, I'd wager a monkey he doesn't like you."

"Me! He was shooting at you. Given how fondly you're regarded in the area, it's preposterous to assume anything else."

"Yes," Ashburne purred, stepping entirely too close, "but *I* am wearing black, while *you*..." He fingered the sleeve of her pale green gown. "...were quite visible, even in the dark. Whoever was lurking in the home wood could have had no doubt he was shooting at a woman. So unless you're going to suggest that Mrs. McFerran has recently made a mortal enemy—"

"I wouldn't be surprised if she had," Portia muttered.

"—it was you he was firing at."

"Then he was a demmed poor shot."

"Not as poor as all that. He'd have hit you if I hadn't pushed you down."

Which meant, of course, that he *had* been shot because of her. Furthermore, that his covering body, hiding her pale dress with his black coat, had saved her life. Portia tried not to think about it, which was as impossible as not noticing that the blood on Ashburne's shirt was creeping slowly towards his buttons. "Then I owe you, sir. And if you are a gentleman, you will allow me to repay my debt. Sit down."

He stared at her for a long moment before sighing and seating himself. "You're impossible."

"And you, sir, are infuriating."

Portia got him out of his coat, which was thankfully not cut to the snug height of fashion, wincing at the blood that painted his left sleeve from shoulder to elbow and crept inward from his shoulder. "Can you get the rest off on your own?"

"Of course," he growled, and began tugging his waistcoat buttons open one-handed.

"Good. Drink this." Portia handed him the bottle Mrs. McFerran had brought and went to drop the needle, thread, and bandages in the water that boiled fiercely on the stove. God alone knew how long they'd been in the stillroom gathering dust and worse. She turned when he gasped something even Roger had never said in her presence and began coughing. "What?"

"What the devil is this?" Ashburne demanded, glaring at the bottle from which he'd taken, if his continued coughing was any measure, a large swallow.

"I asked Mrs. McFerran to bring me a bottle of spirits."

"Did you tell her who it was for?"

"Of course not." Portia used a ladle to fish the bandages out of the pot and hung them in front of the stove to dry, then began the difficult task of retrieving her needle and thread.

"Ugh." He wiped the back of his hand across his mouth. "If I'd known I had such swill in my cellars, I'd have used it in the lamps years ago."

"Hoist by your own petard," Portia said without sympathy. If he hadn't conspired with Mrs. McFerran to drive her out, the housekeeper wouldn't have made a point of finding her the worst bottle in the cellars. She took it from him and helped him out of his shirt. Blood ran freely down his left arm from a ragged gouge in the thick muscle of his shoulder. Portia concentrated on wiping away the blood, trying to notice neither his powerful chest nor the heat rising off his skin. Even seated, he was very nearly as tall as she, and he hadn't the grace to look away while she inspected the wound, his direct black gaze reminding her that this body had crushed hers to the ground not a quarter-hour ago. This chest had pressed against hers. This mouth....

Ashburne shifted his legs so he could bring her in closer, resting his hands on her waist. Drowning in the heat of his body, Portia reached for the bottle of alcohol and poured it over his shoulder. The resulting roar ringing in her ears, she slipped away to check on the bandages.

"You," he said between his teeth, "are a heartless hell-cat." Already, new blood spilled down his arm.

"If it's not worth putting on the inside of you, my lord, then it might as well do some good on the outside. Your shoulder needs to be sewn up."

"It does, does it?" Ashburne mocked. "And your vast experience in these matters arises from?"

"It's not a vast experience," Portia said impatiently, "but I have seen such injuries and I do know what to do." Never a bullet-wound, of course, but Ashburne's injury didn't look so different from when Tony had fallen off the banister when he was ten and gouged his calf on the corner of a stair. The surgeon had required her presence, though she was then still a schoolroom miss, because Tony would be calm for no one else. "Or I could send for Mr. Millbank." He glared. "Well then?"

Ashburne picked up the bottle Mrs. McFerran had brought, looked appraisingly at it, then put it down again. "I should like something more palatable. There's a bottle of brandy in Mrs. McFerran's sitting room, if you would be so good?"

It wasn't a question and Portia left him holding his ruined shirt to his shoulder to stem the blood. The bottle was easy enough to find, tucked in Mrs. McFerran's workbasket under a coat Portia now recognized by size and cut to be Ashburne's. When she brought it to him, he drank directly from the bottle.

"I can get the laudanum," Portia offered.

"You can get out."

"No."

"Get on with it, then. I suppose you're good with your needle."

"Good enough."

He snorted and took another long swallow from the bottle. "Not that it signifies."

It was more difficult than the doctor had made it look. Pushing the needle into his bloody skin was impossible until she forced herself to think of it as the fabric for a new dress. Even then, she nearly couldn't bring herself to do it. It didn't help that he was watching, no expression on his face as she drew needle and thread through his flesh. He didn't flinch, nor make any sound, and he drank steadily from the bottle without a sign the alcohol was having any effect whatever.

When the slow, gathering silence had plucked up Portia's nerves so badly she could feel her hands begin to shake, she said, "Why are you here, my lord?"

"Ashburne Hall is my home."

"Dangerous place to be," Portia murmured. "If the Duke of Ransley finds out—"

"Is that a threat?" he asked, his tone so low and vicious that the words at first meant nothing. Then they sank in, and Portia's jaw clenched.

"Merely an observation, my lord. You must have a very good reason for taking the risk. Why are you here?"

"Ashburne Hall is my home," he repeated. He drank again from the bottle, and for the first time she noticed how white his knuckles were. She hoped he wouldn't break the glass.

"It has not been your home for ten years."

"I don't give a bloody damn who owns it—"

"I wasn't talking about the succession. Don't expect me to believe you've been lurking here the past ten years. I'm far from a widgeon, my lord." It got easier as her stitches closed off the wound. The blood came slower and she could sometimes get two in before she had to stop to blot it away so she could see. "If you'd been in residence—assuming you could risk it, not knowing if or when Roger might take it into his head to visit—the ghost stories would have begun a great deal earlier than a month ago. *And* I wager the Hall would be in much better shape."

"Instead of the disaster you've made it."

"I?" Portia said, startled to hear accusation in his voice. "You must look to Roger for that. I have had all I could do to keep Rosewood Close habitable."

"Rosewood?" He turned, halting with a muttered curse when the movement twisted the needle out of her fingers. "What's wrong with Rosewood?"

"Nothing a concerted application of money wouldn't fix." Portia wiped blood away to verify that he hadn't torn out her stitches. "If there were any to apply."

"What the devil are you about? I left more money than could be spent in a lifetime. How could Roger possibly have made ducks and drakes of it all?"

"Drinking, dicing, demireps."

Ashburne took a long swig of brandy and produced a lengthy string of muttered curses.

"Why *are* you here?" she asked when he appeared to be finished.

"The devil take it! To prove myself innocent."

"Are you?"

"Yes, damn your eyes!"

"Nice to hear," Portia murmured. "I rather thought you might be."

"How very kind of you to tell me so. Would I be here risking my life, my title, and my lands if I weren't?"

She wiped away blood and surveyed her work. The wound was only seeping now, blood oozing through the neat line of black stitches. She set about tying off her thread. "Beg pardon, my lord, but to the best of my knowledge only the first still belongs to you. James Ashburne owns the rest."

"Not for long, he doesn't."

"What do you mean to do?"

"I mean to take back what is mine." His glittering eyes followed her across the kitchen.

Portia laid the dry bandages on the table and used his shirt to wipe blood away from the wound one last time. He hissed when she dabbed the healing ointment on the outraged skin showing red between her stitches. "How do you mean to do that?"

"That, madam, is my business. And I'll thank you to keep your nose out of it, Portia Ashburne." She could feel him watching her and resolutely kept her eyes on the bandage she was winding about his arm. His mood changed so quickly she nearly reeled with the sudden damping of hostility. His free hand brushed her cheek, and Portia forced herself not to flinch away from the too-close smell of blood. "Portia," he murmured. "Unusual name."

"Father was enormously fond of Shakespeare."

"Naturally." Now he was laughing at her, though he wasn't even smiling. "*The Merchant of Venice*. A very intelligent and just lady, Portia. Can I expect that same justice from you?"

His tone brought her eyes to his. "I should hope so, my lord."

"Can I now?"

She had the distinct impression he didn't believe her.

Chapter Twenty

GILES woke to the sun warm on his face and knew he wasn't in the priest-hole he'd occupied since Portia Ashburne barged into the Hall. His head ached almost as abominably as his arm.

He forced his eyes open, the late-morning light spearing into his head, and found himself looking at his own bedchamber ceiling. He remembered then: dragging his coat on over his bare chest and leaving her in the kitchen. Expediency as much as exhaustion led him here—little point in hiding from her any longer. Though that maid of hers.... Giles closed his eyes again. Damn it all.

He gingerly probed his left arm through his coat. His shoulder was tender and itched dreadfully where she'd sewn him up. *Bloody hell*, chased itself across his drink-thick head. *You couldn't have just let her get shot?* It would have solved the most pressing of his problems. Even as the thought rolled around his mind, bumping up painfully against the parts of him that had been too brandy-sodden the previous night to be anything but miserable now, he recoiled at it. He couldn't have done anything less than put himself between her and what threatened her; what's more, he'd do it again if he had to.

He wished he could convince himself that his certainty on that score had nothing to do with the soft give of her body under his, the cool trembling response of lips that had warmed quickly, parting under his to allow—

"Bloody hell," he said aloud, and worked himself upright.

He'd gotten no farther than the edge of his bed when a key scraped in the lock. He had barely enough time to realize there was nowhere to hide before his dressing room door opened and Portia Ashburne came in, attired in a sapphire gown that made her eyes shine like jewels. Giles was so startled, he forgot to catalog just which of his late mother's gowns it was.

"How the devil did you know I was here?"

She smiled sweetly. "You snore, my lord."

"I do not."

"How would you know?" Portia walked toward the bed, picking up a bottle from the bedside table. He could smell the crisp scent of lavender water that clung to her. "I can assure you, my lord, that when you've been imbibing...."

Giles didn't remember bringing the brandy upstairs. He scowled at her, not liking the cool condemnation in her eyes. How dare she judge him? He took the empty bottle, slammed it down on the bedside table, and stood, not caring that it would put him entirely too close to her until her startled breath fanned his bare chest.

Mrs. McFerran chose that moment to let herself in through the hall door. Giles sat down abruptly on the bed while Portia moved to open the drapes, letting more light in to pierce his aching brain.

"My lord," Mrs. McFerran said, bobbing a neat curtsey. From the tray in her hands came the smell of tea and toast and the hot bran and rank herb odor of some kind of poultice. The combination turned his stomach. She nudged the bottle aside so she could set the tray on his bedside table, plumped his pillow against the headboard and said, "Let's get that coat off you, my lord."

Knowing from long experience that there was no point in arguing with Mrs. McFerran in this mood, Giles obediently let her help him out of his coat, leaned against the headboard so she could put the tray across his lap, and did not, however much he wished to, flinch when she stripped off the bandages and applied the steaming poultice to his throbbing shoulder. Then, after enjoining him to eat, she whisked herself off with a promise to return that, in his current mood, he felt was more a threat than anything else.

"Good Lord, that stinks," Portia said after the housekeeper had gone.

"Yes, thank you." Giles poured himself some tea and attempted to ignore the smell. Thank God she'd only brought him toast. He didn't think he could manage anything more in the miasma rising from the poultice. "Where's your abigail?" Pray God she wasn't out warning the neighborhood.

"It's her free day. I shooed her off to the village as soon as I rose this morning." Portia turned dancing eyes on him. "She could hardly have missed your snoring otherwise."

Giles bit back his response and addressed himself to his tea. Mrs. McFerran returned with his clothes and shaving kit and a basin of warm water, checked under the poultice, and left with a satisfied look. At no point during the whole process had she looked daggers at Portia. Nor had she said a word about the impropriety of that woman's presence in his bedchamber. Giles wasn't skimble-brained; he knew he'd lost his primary ally against Lady Ashburne. Her pleased expression after seeing the job Portia had done stitching him up gave him a good idea why.

As soon as he was certain Mrs. McFerran had gone for good, he scraped the poultice off onto his breakfast plate and used his napkin to wipe up the worst of the mess.

"Mrs. McFerran will be disappointed," Portia observed.

Giles set his breakfast tray aside and climbed out of bed. "Mrs. McFerran won't know unless you tell her. And if you do, I shall see to it that every dress in your wardrobe vanishes, including the ones your maid thinks she's got safely squirreled away."

She wet a cloth in the washbasin. "This will need to be rebandaged." She began dabbing at his shoulder.

"You were quick to winkle yourself into Mrs. McFerran's favors. Give me that."

Portia stepped out of his reach. "I merely asked if she wouldn't mind helping me tend to you this morning."

"I am quite capable of tending to myself. Give me that," he said again when she went back to gently cleaning his arm.

"I'm nearly finished."

"You're a stubborn baggage."

"She was much relieved," Portia said as if he hadn't spoken, "when I assured her I wouldn't be bruiting your secret all about the neighborhood."

"I knew you wouldn't when you opted to sew me up instead of running for Ransley," Giles said with more assurance than he felt. The last woman he'd trusted had betrayed him. And got herself killed into the bargain. Gooseflesh rose on Giles' skin at the memory of bullets hissing so close by Portia's head that one had taken him in the arm when he wrapped them around her.

He looked down at her head, bent in concentration as she cleaned and rebandaged his wound. She didn't even come up to his shoulder. Though Lady Amelia had been taller, she'd possessed a doll-like fragility Portia lacked. And not one-tenth of Portia's stubbornness, for all Amelia had been bull-headed as anything. "Did you never believe I was a ghost?"

"I'm not so cloth-headed as to believe everything I'm told. Though I own you gave me some bad moments, my lord." Portia tied off the bandage and smoothed it lightly. "I trust, now that you're back among the living, you'll have the courtesy to stay out of my bedchamber."

Giles' first impulse had nothing to do with courtesy and everything to do with the memory of how she'd looked when abandoned to sleep. The second was to defend his right to not only enter any room in the Hall, but invade her chamber and her privacy if she had no more shame than to read his private correspondence. He mastered both impulses and instead said, "I notice you've no compunction about entering *my* bedchamber."

"Someone had to see to it that you were in good health. Besides," she said, sitting on the end of his bed and drawing her legs up under her, "I wanted to speak to you before you vanished again."

"You think I'm likely to?" Giles concentrated on sorting out his shaving things one-handed, most emphatically *not* thinking about her perched on his bed.

"I thought it possible. Though I would hope you know I'm not fool enough to believe I imagined it all, even if you had vanished by the light of day."

"Of course." Giles said, at a loss. Hard to believe he'd held his own on the floor of the House of Lords when he couldn't even keep his countenance before this one spirited woman. Blame it on the vicissitudes of a decade in exile. He'd sailed all the seas of the world and done well enough for himself to be able to undo some, at least, of the damage to the Hall, but he'd been careful to avoid the company of Englishmen and the places they gathered, and he hadn't spoken to an Englishwoman of his own class in years. Add to that the hardships of the last month: sneaking back into England by the poorest, most uncomfortable means possible so he might not be recognized by any member of the *ton*; heartbreaking weeks spent searching the Hall in constant, mind-numbing disbelief at the infamous condition of his home; reduced finally to prowling his own halls by night, rarely seeing the McFerrans and almost never speaking to them for fear of being seen or overheard. It beat a man down, made him feel as if he were, indeed, more spirit than man.

And this woman, whose beauty cut him like a knife, who spoke so plainly and was so unintimidated by him and so infuriatingly stubborn.... He had no defenses against her.

Not against her persistence, nor her intelligence. Far from the usual air-brained society miss, Portia plowed on with unflagging determination, doing whatever was necessary. He had to look no further than the work she'd already done at the Hall to see she was a woman who would survive any indignity. How very different she was from the women he'd known, from Amelia, who'd been unwilling, or unable, to exchange more than mere commonplaces, who wanted gallant gestures and speeches like overblown roses, things he'd never mastered except on paper, and even then found himself unable to send.

Heat rose up Giles' neck as he remembered afresh that Portia had had the gall to read those stumbling attempts to relieve a heart overburdened with love. He could remember now only a shadow of that feeling, though it had been powerful enough at the time. Not powerful enough to keep her from flying to another man's arms. However Giles twisted and turned, he could not escape fault for her death.

"How, pray tell," Portia said, giving Giles an unpleasant start, "did you end up 'dead'?"

He realized he'd been lathering up his shaving brush for several minutes, and began applying it to his face. "I fail to see what business it could possibly be of yours."

"Even Mrs. McFerran agrees I did an excellent job sewing you up. The least you can do is satisfy my curiosity."

He might have said they were even, as he wouldn't have been shot if it weren't for her. Instead, he found himself saying, "If I stayed, Ransley would have had not only my neck, but my lands and title. Had I simply fled, he might well have had me tried in absentia, with nearly the same results. The only way to save the title and lands was to "die" so they could pass, unstained, to Roger." Portia gave a most unladylike snort. Giles picked up his razor, trying not to see the dust and decay around him, even here, where the McFerrans had tried to set things right. "A friend helped me escape and arranged passage for me. Once on the Continent, I intended to bribe some official to send word of my demise."

"But the boat sank off the coast of France," Portia murmured.

"Who—"

"Courtland."

Giles paused, startled. He couldn't imagine why Courtland should have taken time away from courting her to tell tales about him. "Fortunately, I have always been a strong swimmer." He wiped the razor and started on the other side.

"And the ghost? How long had you planned that?"

"Not at all. Some of the more superstitious villagers began to talk of spirits when they saw new lights moving about the Hall at night. Foxkin thought it best to encourage the stories."

"And when I arrived?"

"If we'd gotten the portrait off the wall before you arrived, we might have passed me off as a servant or some relative of the McFerrans. As it was...." He tipped his chin up a bit to get at his throat.

She laughed and his hand wavered at the sound. "I could never have mistaken you for a servant, my lord, even if I hadn't seen your portrait. Though you might, I suppose, have passed yourself off as a cousin, or even your own by-blow."

He grimaced. "How should I have convinced you not to mention my presence to anyone in the village?"

"Upon reflection, my lord, it's probably best you were a ghost."

Giles wiped streaks of lather off his face. "And now that I'm not?"

"I told you, I won't be bruiting it about the neighborhood that Lord Ashburne is back at the Hall. Not that anyone would believe me if I did."

"Ransley would."

"Perhaps. The duke seems possessed of the idea you're only one step removed from Lord Lucifer himself. But I doubt he'd believe me if I told him the sun rose in the East."

"What the deuce have you done to upset him?"

She made an unbecoming face. "I'd like to say it was all your fault, and certainly my association with you did not turn him up sweet—"

"What association?"

"The name. As soon as he heard it, I was as good as consigned to Perdition." It hurt to hear that his one-time friend's animus against him was still so strong. Giles feared the pain showed on his face, for Portia stood and went to look into the bucket Mrs. McFerran had cooked up under the supposed leak in his ceiling as an excuse to look away. Her consideration touched him nearly as much as it irritated him. She toed the bucket and said, "No wonder it never got any fuller when it rained. An infamous trick, sir; you should be ashamed. Of course," she went on in a different tone of voice, "I only further consigned myself to Ransley's black books when I told him you were innocent."

He almost dropped the shirt he was pulling over his left arm. "You did what?"

"No doubt I shall give him a complete disgust of myself as soon as he learns I've convinced Lord Courtland to help me prove it."

Giles sank into the chair by his writing desk and gaped at her, only realizing he was staring when she flushed. "I think you had best tell me precisely what you've been up to."

It took her less than five minutes to tell him, and nearly twice that long before he found his voice afterwards. "And yet," he said, and saw her flinch at the edge in his voice, "you don't believe it was you he was shooting at?"

* * *

She had to get out of the house. It felt even more haunted now than it had before. Perhaps it was this new worry, this utterly unfathomable idea that someone wanted to harm her. Perhaps it was just Lord Ashburne.

Portia snorted, tightening the strings of her bonnet when a stray breeze threatened to take it off. There was nothing "just" about Giles Ashburne. She'd understood in part when she saw his portrait, but it wasn't until she met him in the flesh that she fully grasped why he intimidated Lady Clarissa. And Lady Amelia too, if Clary was to be believed. Ashburne was a powerful man, strong and confident in his ability. Though his features were too harsh for a chit like Lady Amelia to call handsome, there was an aura of strength about him that made him powerfully attractive. It was no wonder she'd always known he was there, even though she hadn't believed that the Hall was haunted.

His presence permeated every inch of the place.

"Why the brown study, my lady?"

Portia gasped, her hand flying to her throat. She glared at Lord Courtland, who sat smiling down at her, his arms crossed on his saddlebow. She must have been far gone in thought not to have heard him ride up. "For shame, sir! You frightened me."

His smile widened. "And here I was thinking that nothing could. Not ghosts nor mice nor murderers."

"Good morning, my lord. Shall I ask what you're doing on Ashburne lands, or merely assume you're up to no good?"

"Of course I am, my lady." Courtland swung lightly out of the saddle, neat in a bottle-green coat and buckskin breeches. "For I've most assuredly come to see you." He took her hand and bowed over it, the sun striking flames from his tousled hair. Then he bent to kiss her, and this time she allowed it.

The clear-water taste of his mouth was pleasant, but she had in her memory a kiss flavored with smoke and nightfall, and it simply did not compare.

"*Do* you have a riding habit?" Courtland asked when she drew herself out of his arms.

"Yes," Portia said, confused.

"Good. We may yet share a most enjoyable ride." He winked at her, then took up his reins and dragged his horse's head out of a clump of clover. "Where to? The village or the Hall?"

"Neither. I am merely out walking."

"Then I will join you, with your permission." He tucked her hand in the crook of his arm and walked slowly along the path, the horse following dutifully. "Tell me, Lady Ashburne, has your ghost come to visit again?"

"I told you, my lord, there is no ghost."

"Isn't there?" He looked sidelong at her, his mouth tugged into a smile. "You have rather the look of a woman who's been... consorting with spirits, if I may say so."

"You may not," Portia snapped, blood rising into her face. Ashburne had only kissed her, not— She turned, ostensibly to follow the trilling of a songbird that sang somewhere nearby, the brim of her bonnet hiding her face. "What you may do, Lord Courtland, is tell me what happened after Lady Amelia's death."

"For God's sake!" He took her chin and made her look at him. "I told you how dangerous it is to pursue this, did I not?"

"You told me you thought it dangerous," Portia allowed, lifting her chin out of his grasp. "What you have not told me is how I am to live here if I do not pursue it."

Her situation had undergone a sea change overnight. Ashburne's need to prove himself innocent was fathoms deeper than Portia's. She had no idea how he intended to clear his name, let alone retrieve his title and lands, but she knew beyond any doubt that, if it were possible at all, he would do it. And when he did, Portia's position would become even more precarious. Even if Ashburne could be convinced to let her stay, it would not be proper for her to live at the Hall with a man who was no relation to her. She might, perhaps, persuade him to let her return to Rosewood Close, but she wasn't the least bit certain how far his sense of familial obligation would extend. He had no legal or ethical responsibility to provide for her. Once he regained the title, Portia might even lose her jointure. Could her widow's dower be paid from Ashburne coffers, such as they were, if it were proved that Roger had never truly been Viscount Ashburne?

Portia's only hope was to place Ashburne in her debt. Which, ironically, required that she continue the task she'd already embarked upon. A task both Courtland and Ashburne had tried to warn her away from. If she could help prove Ashburne innocent, perhaps gratitude would keep him from turning her out without a shilling.

"Come now," Courtland said, "it's not as bad as all that. You have money of your own, after all."

Portia was startled into a bark of laughter. So that was the explanation for his interest. "Wherever did you get that idea, my lord?"

He had the grace to look abashed, and rubbed his ear with the hand that held the reins. "I believe Roger...."

Portia laughed again, not caring that she sounded brittle. "He was ever convinced I was keeping something from him. Make no mistake, my lord, there is a very little money, doled out in even littler dribs and drabs by a solicitor who is in no way susceptible to entreaty." That would put paid to Courtland's interest. A man like Courtland was invariably on the prowl for either someone pretty to warm his bed or someone with deep pockets to pay off his debts, and preferably both, could that but be arranged. He would not continue to waste his time on a drab little wren without a feather to fly with.

Much to her surprise, he smiled down at her. "Then we are very much in the same boat, my lady. I can only venture to hope you derive as much enjoyment from the company as I."

Either she'd underestimated his requirements for a bed warmer, or he didn't believe her. Portia released a relieved breath. She still needed his assistance, after all, if she was to get into Ashburne's good books. "The company is charming."

"I strive to satisfy, my lady."

Flustered, Portia looked away from the predatory gleam in his eye. "Why was everyone so certain Lord Ashburne left of his own accord?"

Courtland sighed. "You're not going to leave this alone, are you?"

"I can't afford to." She waited, walking quietly at his side, and finally said, "For all anyone knew, Lord Ashburne was murdered by the madman who killed Lady Amelia."

"My dear Portia, the madman who killed Lady Amelia was Giles Ashburne."

Portia ignored his use of her Christian name. It was entirely too coming of him, but she couldn't afford to give him the set down he deserved. "How can you be so certain of that? There were others who might have done it."

He watched a hawk soar overhead. "None with so great a reason."

"There must have been someone." Portia had to believe that. If she was sharing a house with a devil who could cut a woman's throat, one who moreover had keys to every room.... She'd been there nearly a fortnight, Portia reminded herself, and he'd done nothing but try to frighten her.

"You are forgetting that he fled justice. Ashburne booked passage for France. If he'd made it, he would no doubt have vanished into the Continent."

Booked passage. Lord Ashburne had used the same phrase to describe his flight. It was common enough. She'd have made nothing of it if she hadn't heard it twice that morning. Or if Ashburne hadn't ordered her, before she took herself out of the house for much-needed air, not only to stop poking her nose into his business, but to leave Courtland out of it. "Why are you so insistent that he did it? You must have known he was innocent or you'd never have helped him escape."

Courtland whirled on her. "For God's sake, don't let Ransley hear you say that!"

"You did help him, then!"

"Where the devil did you hear that?" Her grabbed her arms and shook her. "Who told you?"

"No one." Portia tried to pull away, but his fingers only bit deeper. She forced herself not to shrink back. "You're hurting me, my lord."

Courtland released her with a curse. He spun about, scanning their surroundings as if he expected to find someone lurking in the bushes. "It was that wretch Foxkin, I'll be bound—"

"It wasn't Foxkin," Portia snapped. "This is outside of enough! I figured it out for myself. You said you were his friend and—"

"Damn me, is that all?" He released a shuddering breath. "For God's sake," he said again, in quite a different tone of voice, "don't let the duke hear you say that. He wouldn't wait around for the House of Lords to deal with the likes of me. He'd cut out my liver and lights himself." Courtland took her arm, his grip gentle this time. "You must see you can't keep on with this. It's deuced dangerous."

"Don't you think I know that?"

"I'm not certain you do."

"For pity's sake, my lord, I'm not a complete want-wit! If it were safe, someone wouldn't have tried to shoot me last night."

"What?"

Portia winced, cursing her foolish mouth. She hadn't meant to open her budget like that. Her wits really had gone begging, despite what she'd told him. "It's nothing to signify, my lord. Just someone trying to scare me off."

"Blister it, girl, don't you see that's demmed good proof you shouldn't keep on?"

"No, my lord Courtland. What it is, is demmed good proof someone's got something to hide."

Chapter Twenty-One

"WHERE the devil have you been?"

Portia finished untying her bonnet strings and put it on the hall table. She brushed loose strands of hair back from her face and wished there was a mirror; she must look a complete fright. "I take it Ellie hasn't returned yet," she said to Ashburne, who glowered at her from the library door, casually dressed in shirtsleeves and coat. Portia was beginning to think he'd forgotten how to tie a cravat.

"Perhaps you were not perfectly attending, madam. I said, where the devil have you been?"

"It's no wonder you intimidated Lady Clarissa, my lord. Your language leaves much to be desired." When she came in, Portia had wanted nothing more than a hot dish of tea, even if she had to make it herself, but she could see through the open library door that Lord Ashburne had cleared several shelves of yet another bookcase, and drifted that direction instead.

"My language has been ten years out of English society. And I have plenty of call to swear when you persist in being so dam— dashed thick-headed." The drapes were closed and a profligate number of candles burned in the candelabras to offset the gloom. She knew Ashburne couldn't chance anyone seeing his "ghost" making free of the library, but Portia couldn't help but think he was using up their entire precious store of candles on one sunny afternoon. "Wait. Lady Clarissa? Little Clary, Ransley's ward? What have you to do with her?"

"Hopefully, preparing the poor girl for entrance into Society." Portia took the top book from one stack and looked at the spine. "She's woefully inept." Like you, she nearly said, but thought better of it. "What have you been doing with these books?"

"*You're* going to teach her manners?"

Portia regretted holding her tongue. "I'm the granddaughter of a duke, sir."

"And she's the niece of a duke."

"Little good it's done her. Ransley doesn't even show her enough attention to realize she's been galloping neck or nothing about the neighborhood in riding breeches." She picked up another book. "You're not still trying to frighten me off, so what's the meaning of this?"

"Breeches? Ransley's ward? Lord." Ashburne sank into one of the library chairs. "He barely let Amelia out of his sight. I'd have thought, after what happened.... How could he be so cavalier with Clary?"

"He doesn't want to admit that she's growing up. As if denying her a proper wardrobe for the Season and the polish to properly acquit herself will keep her a child forever."

"And you're going to teach her that polish." It was said without sarcasm this time.

"I had hoped to. But Ransley made it clear that no ward of his would have anything to do with any member of the Ashburne family."

Ashburne leaned back, his hand going to his injured shoulder, black eyes searching her face. "Why do I suspect you paid him no mind?"

"I wouldn't know, my lord."

"Would it be because you're a demmed contrary chit who hasn't the sense to keep her nose out of other people's business or even stay inside for her own safety?" Though his voice was mild, the tone was pure acid. "I told you to remain in the Hall, Lady Ashburne."

"It may have escaped your attention, my lord, but you are not my guardian. Nor my husband. As such, I fail to see why you claim the right to tell me what to do." She picked up a book and flourished it under his nose. "What exactly are you about in the library? Why take down case after case of books?"

Ashburne's calloused fingers closed around her wrist and tugged. The book went flying as Portia sprawled across his lap. His chest and thighs were hard under her. Her breath caught in her throat and her stomach flipped. The heat of his body beat so strongly against her that she couldn't tell whether the flush spreading through her body came from embarrassment or from him. Mortified, she tried to squirm away, forgetting about his shoulder. "In case it's escaped *your* attention, my lady, someone is trying to kill you. I will confine you to the Hall, personally if need be—" His grip tightened, as if he meant that literally. "—to keep you from drowning in a welter of your own blood somewhere on the grounds."

Portia froze. "You need not concern yourself, my lord," she said, pity gentling her voice. "It's broad daylight. Why would anyone harm me at a time when he would likely be seen?"

"Likely is not the same as certainly. You might easily vanish into the home wood with no one the wiser." Ashburne lifted Portia off his lap and set her on her feet as if she were a doll. Her skin burned with the imprint of his hands. "Overgrown as it is, your body mightn't be found for years. If ever."

Portia went cold. Why, she wondered in a strange distant part of her mind, had the murderer not done the same with Lady Amelia? The home wood would not have been so overgrown then, of course, but there were all the Ashburne lands on which to hide a body. Not to mention Ransley's, or even Courtland's, both of which abutted Ashburne's property. Why leave the body where it would so easily be found? Unless someone *wanted* it found.

Ashburne dragged a hand through his hair. "You're not listening to a word I say."

"Of course I am, my lord."

"Then you'll cease this foolishness. Stay inside where it's safe and stop nosing about the neighborhood for clues." His glare made it clear he was not asking but ordering, and Portia might have said nothing—though she had no intention of obeying—if he hadn't added, "And leave Lady Clarissa to her uncle."

"Of course I won't!" Portia blurted, forgetting that it was now more important to stay on Ashburne's good side than to teach Clary how to comport herself. If Ashburne could be convinced to let her stay at Rosewood, Portia might limp along on her small income. If he could not, then Portia would find herself in straits from which even Clary's influence could not rescue her. But she'd promised the chit, and she wouldn't abandon her now. "The poor girl is in desperate need of assistance and her uncle hasn't the first idea what to do, or even that something must be done. I can't—"

"You can't bring her into the Hall."

"She's already been, on three occasions, with no one the wiser. I don't see what—"

"Portia!" Startled, she glared at him for his presumption, and he pinched the bridge of his nose between thumb and forefinger. "What you do not seem to see, my lady," he said with the careful diction of someone on the verge of raging, "is that you've already cost me nearly a fortnight. I have spent," he went on over her protest, "the better part of the last two weeks skulking in the shadows to avoid you rather than doing what I came here to do."

"I fail to see what harm having a young lady here a few hours a day will have."

"No? When the young lady is Ransley's ward? When he'll roar like an Atlantic gale if he finds out she's even set foot in this house? When the barest intimation that I'm still alive, let alone at the Hall, will bring him down on this house like the hand of God?" He stalked to the second bookshelf, took down the books from the next-to-highest shelf without need of the library stairs and pulled out the brown leather satchel she'd hidden there. "Take it," he said, shoving it at her. "Buy whatever fripperies you can't do without. I'll pay for the surgeon, the roof, and anything else that comes up. You do whatever you like with this; it's the last monies you'll get from me. Don't even think of trying to pawn my silver again." When she didn't take the bag, he tossed it on the library table, knocking over a silver candlestick.

Portia snuffed out the candle before it could damage the table. She did not turn around until the burning in her cheeks subsided. "It's your money, my lord," she said stiffly. "I wouldn't dream of—"

"I said take it. Take yourself off to the modiste or the milliner or what you will. Just get out."

Portia unclenched her teeth far enough to say sweetly, "I thought you didn't want me to leave the house."

"Hell and damnation! Take your maid, take the main road, stay out of the home wood, and stay away from Ransley. *And* Courtland."

Shaking so hard she could barely stand, Portia watched him remove books from the case he'd already half-cleared, taking them down a few at a time and stacking them by a chair. Much as Portia wished not to, she saw how he favored his left arm, the painful hitch in his movement whenever he forgot, and pity and curiosity got the better of her anger.

"What *are* you looking for?"

"I told you to get out."

Portia gritted her teeth. "Perhaps I could help."

"You've done enough, madam."

"For which you are most welcome." His shoulders twitched, but he did not otherwise respond. Portia stepped up to relieve him of the next armful of books. He watched her put the books with the rest, then went back to removing volumes from the shelves. "You are looking for something, of course."

Ashburne knelt to sweep up an armful of books bound identically in burgundy leather, dumped them next to the other stacks, and went back to the shelves without vouchsafing Portia an answer. She didn't let it put her off.

At first, Portia'd taken the mishandling of the books for a gambit like the rest, an unsettling trick designed to drive her out. But that theory went by the board after Mr. McFerran was injured and Mrs. McFerran did not have the time to engage in so useless an exercise. Yet it happened anyway. Portia knew then that, unless she really *did* have a ghost, there was some purpose behind removing the books greater than simply annoying her. It couldn't have taken all night to clear a single bookcase, yet only once had he taken down more than one. In the three day gap when none of the bookcases appeared to have been touched, he'd simply been returning the books as he went, leaving the cases looking the same, if less dusty. Then, frustrated at his slow progress, he'd taken down two cases at once and left her with an even larger mess than usual. Obviously removing the books was the least of it. "What precisely are you looking for?"

Ashburne turned with the last armful of books, his eyebrows lowering when he found her already seated in his chair. He put the volumes down and stood for a moment glaring at her before pulling a chair up for himself. Portia reached for the book atop the nearest stack and fanned the pages gently.

"A note, obviously," she said. Ashburne picked up a book and began going through it with painstaking care, even going so far as to hold the book by the spine and give it a gentle shake. She could see why it had usually taken him a whole night to go through a single bookcase. "I doubt pressed flowers would help your case."

When he didn't answer, she searched the book she held again, more carefully, and set it aside, then reached for another. She trusted she was right about the note; if not, surely he'd have told her what to look for.

Portia discovered the aforementioned pressed flowers and the occasional butterfly or moth, which had either found itself within the pages by accident or been shut up there by some schoolboy. The first time she found a folded square of paper, Portia's heart kicked hard against her ribs. She saw Ashburne's hands slow and stop on his book as she teased open the thin folds of the letter. The disappointment when she found it was to "Dearest Matilda" from "your loving Randolph" was deep enough to bleed all the breath out of her. Even not knowing quite what she was looking for, she had no doubt that this was not it. Portia reminded herself that there were plenty more books, and no doubt plenty more notes, and put the earnest and tender letter back where she found it. Ashburne's hands began to move again and Portia fought off a fit of the dismals at the thought that this rush of hope, and the crushing disappointment that followed, was a familiar thing to him already.

When the silence had stood between them long enough that Portia's ears had become accustomed to the whisper of paper and the soft cadence of his breathing, Ashburne spoke.

Chapter Twenty-Two

"SHE was beautiful. A china figurine of blue and gold." Portia glanced up, but Ashburne's eyes were on his hands, and she returned to her task. She nearly looked up again when he said, "And I let myself believe she could find it in herself to consider me... acceptable." The letters she should never have read rose into her mind (*I would worship at you as at an altar, bringing myself as offering.*) and it was suddenly as impossible to look at him as to speak.

"I knew, when the rumors first reached my ears, brought by someone who thought he was doing me a kindness, that they could not be true." Ashburne's voice remained quiet and steady, and Portia could not tell if he still felt all the pain and grief of Lady Amelia's betrayal and subsequent death or if it had faded in him, as pressed rose petals faded to pale shadows, hardly more substantial than the stain they left upon the page. "And so I told him, and anyone who dared voice the gossip in my hearing. I thought at first that, despite my best intentions, denial of the rumor merely fed it, but came eventually to understand that it had other meat to grow on. She was young. She wanted...." He stopped. Looking sidelong at Ashburne, Portia saw him trace the embossed title of a book bound in burgundy leather, an expensive edition of *Romeo and Juliet*. "I am not a pretty fellow. I could not give her the pretty words she wanted."

Portia savagely bit her lip to prevent herself speaking. It was he, of course, who had removed the letters from his desk. And perhaps—pray God it was so!—he did so without knowing she'd already read them. Whether he knew or not, he would certainly not thank her for speaking of them. It came to her, with a pain that filled her chest, that she had been right in thinking the letters had never been sent. And *that* was as great a tragedy as the death of the woman to whom they were written. She forced herself to take the book he held.

159

"Perhaps, if I had, she would not—" He stopped himself, making a curt gesture with his left hand that must have hurt his shoulder, for he took in a quick breath.

Portia found another letter and opened it, her fingers trembling though it was too time-stained to be anything to do with an event only ten years gone, and found the paper covered in lines of close, crabbed, utterly illegible handwriting. Silently, she handed it to Ashburne, who looked briefly at it and handed it back.

Portia returned the note to the book and closed it. "How old is this library?"

Ashburne made a small sound, perhaps of amusement. "Some of the books are as ancient as the Ashburne name itself."

"So we may yet find a note from Queen Boadicia?"

The sound was definitely amusement this time, short and soft. "Mayhap we will." It was several minutes before Ashburne spoke again, and when he did, his voice had lost the soft reflective cadence of a man speaking to himself. Though Portia regretted breaking his mood, she was relieved. The gathering weight of his words had filled the library with a tension like the thick heat of a summer storm. He would tell her less now than he might have, but at least she could breathe. "The day of the ball, one of the footmen handed Amelia a note from her lover after breakfast."

"How can you know it was from her lover?" Assuming she had one, which Portia seemed alone in questioning.

"When I came into the library some minutes later, I found her here, where she'd slipped away to read it in private, a book in her hand to excuse her presence."

"Come, my lord, such light evidence! I've often come in here for a book, and I have no secret lover."

Ashburne gave her a hard look she couldn't understand. She found herself strangely reluctant to meet his gaze. "You have an appreciation for books Lady Amelia sadly lacked. She had no use for my library." Portia mechanically set aside one book and took up the next. "No, she picked up the book so she'd have an excuse for being here should anyone come in. Had she merely wanted somewhere quiet to read a blameless letter, she wouldn't have bothered. The ruse showed a guilty conscience. The note was from her lover."

"Granted that," and Portia had to admit his reasoning was convincing, "why look for it here?"

"She had a book open under her nose when I entered the library. When she saw me, she jumped a mile and snapped the book closed."

"You think she closed the note up in the book."

"I would stake my life on it." He paused over the book in his lap and gave another of those unamused laughs. "I *have* staked my life on it. That *billet doux* set up an assignation. Amelia met her secret lover that night and it was he who killed her. With that note, I may yet be able to prove my innocence. I will, at least, know whose hands are stained with her blood."

"But how can you possibly know he killed her? How can you know she didn't just meet up with some dastard?"

"She would not idly have left the Hall, already gowned and coiffed for the ball, less than an hour before it was to start. Not her own ball, an event she'd planned for weeks." Ashburne idly turned a few pages of the book, but his eyes were not on it. "She was wearing her dancing slippers when I found her." He took in a harsh breath and turned his penetrating eyes on Portia. "No. She went out to the picnic green because her lover arranged to meet her there, out of sight of the house but close enough she might easily slip away."

"The assignation, if there was one, need not have been made in writing," Portia pointed out. "She might have left the house with someone. No one saw her leave."

"I did. I told no one. Not then—what purpose would it serve but to expose her perfidy? Though I could not bear to attach myself to a woman who would betray me even before we were wed, I would not betray her. Once the house party was over, I meant to go to Ransley. Between us we could arrange the end of the engagement with the least damage to her reputation. Later.... I did not dare reveal that I'd seen her leave and could have followed. It would only have put the noose more snugly about my neck."

Portia teased apart two pages stuck together by the flower pressed between them. She didn't particularly expect to find a note affixed there as well, but it gave her something to do as she said, "Do you truly think— I'm sorry, my lord, but can you honestly believe she left that note in the book, in your library, under your very nose?"

"It would have taken a chit more brazen than Amelia to remove that note from the book in front of me, or even to have walked out with the book, knowing what was in it. What if I asked her what she was reading?"

"Guilty conscience," Portia murmured.

"She couldn't know that I wouldn't have questioned her." Ashburne gathered up the set of burgundy-bound Shakespeare folios and went to put them back on the shelf. "The last thing I wanted was to force her to face me with it. I still hoped to sever the connection without further harm to her reputation. I could not forgive what she'd done, but... I did not wish her to suffer." He'd finished reshelving the Shakespeare, but he continued to kneel with his back to her. "If I'd been the sort of man she wanted, the sort to give her pretty words and prettier things, perhaps she would not have gone with him. If I'd confronted her that day, in this room, she would not have died."

Portia stared at him for some moments before finding her tongue. "You cannot know that, my lord."

"Perhaps not." Ashburne returned to his seat and took up the top book off the next stack.

"If he was determined to kill her, he would have done so whatever obstacles came between. Another day, if you thwarted him that one." Portia smoothed a wrinkled page and closed the book. "But what reason did he have?"

"That she was marrying. That she would no longer be his. That she could betray him."

"His reputation would not suffer so much as hers."

Ashburne gave an awkward one-shouldered shrug. "Who else could have killed her? Who else had reason?"

Courtland had said the same of Ashburne. "Surely if she left the book here then you must know which it was, or at least which shelf she put it on. Why search the library from one end to the other?"

Ashburne was shaking his head. "I began where I believed it to be the first day I arrived. It was not there. I got through that wall," he said, gesturing at the shelves that bracketed the windows, "before you came, with no luck. I was not perfectly attending, I admit." He snorted. "In fact, I deliberately turned my head so she could put the book someplace she thought safe. So I would not know where it was. I suppose I did not want to face the temptation to read it. If I'd known how important it was...." He shook himself. "At any rate, she had no opportunity to retrieve it. There were too many people about, too many activities in which she must, as hostess, take part. It's still here, somewhere. And it's my only chance to clear my name." He looked at the bookcases stuffed full from floor to ceiling and wall to wall. "And so I find myself in the unenviable position of finding a teardrop in the ocean."

"Why not ask the footman who gave her the note? Surely he knew who sent it."

"Assuming he didn't find it on the hall table, that he wasn't bribed not to tell, that he can even still be found? He could be anywhere in the world. No, merely knowing her lover's name will not serve. I must have proof he arranged to meet her at the time and place she died."

Portia picked up another book. "I have heard it said, my lord," she said delicately, "that you caught them together, and killed her after her lover left."

His head came up sharply. "If I can find the man and shove his own *billet doux* under his nose, I promise you, my lady, I will make him confess his crime."

It seemed to Portia an awfully thin thread to hang his salvation on. "Can the note still be here after so many years? Roger—"

"Never bothered to step foot in this room while I was master of the Hall. Why disturb it once he was viscount?"

"He might have sold off all the books."

"He had no reason to." Ashburne's jaw shifted. "He ought to have had no reason to."

"But why wait all this time? You might have cleared your name years ago."

"If, at the time, I could have found a single, quiet moment to think, to understand the significance of that note, perhaps I might. But the hounds were too hot upon me and it was not until I was well away that I realized what had been under my nose the whole time. It seemed to me then, freshly escaped from both Ransley and the sea, a faint and threadbare hope, not worth putting my neck back into the noose for. I determined to make a new life." Ashburne's shoulders shifted. "I won't pretend I've never regretted that choice. But Roger had stood by me, helped me escape at great risk to himself."

Portia very nearly said something about Courtland, but he did not pause long enough for her to speak. It was just as well, perhaps. Roger was beyond anyone's grasp now, but Courtland could still be hurt by an incautious word. She regretted blurting out her realization as she had. It was no wonder he'd been frantic.

"I couldn't see the justice in returning to take everything away from him." Ashburne tipped his head back against the chair, his eyes focused somewhere over her head, cataloging cobwebs and moth-eaten drapes. A muscle in his jaw stood out in high relief. "I had no idea how badly under the hatches he was, nor what wanton destruction he would wreck upon the Hall. Had I known, I would not have stayed away."

"What led you to return, my lord?" Portia asked softly, certain if she spoke more loudly she'd bring him back from wherever he was, and he would never answer.

His eyes drifted down to her, but his focus had not yet returned from foreign climes. "A fellow I did business with thought I'd be interested in the news from England. He dropped me the scandal sheets every time one came his way. In one of them, I read of Roger's death. And in that moment...." His voice trailed off, and picked up again, almost too soft to hear. "I was overcome with heartsickness. It seemed an easier thing to risk my life in returning home than to stay away all my days."

And so the threadbare hope became strong enough to hang a life on. Desperation, Portia reflected, could make any man wager all for a poor shot at success. "Well," she said, and saw him blink at her vigorous tone, "I would be happy to help you look through these books, my lord." With his shoulder, it would take him a great deal longer than it had already if she didn't lend a hand. "But I think you'd have better luck with the people who were there. Someone must know something."

"What do you suggest I do? Ask up and down the high street?"

"No, but I could."

"Absolutely not. You've put me in enough jeopardy already. Not to mention the danger you've brought upon yourself." Ashburne got up and took a stack of books from her, including one she hadn't looked at yet.

She snatched it back and watched him shove the books on the shelf without regard to their proper places. "Someone other than you saw Lady Amelia go out. Someone saw whoever went out after her, or knows who was not in the house during the time she must have been killed."

"She might have been killed any time up to the moment I found her. Or after, if you believe the case against me," Ashburne said brutally. "We were all of us out of the house looking for her."

"Then someone saw them together, she and this lover of hers. You don't have to have the note to confront him. You may be able to trick a confession out of him by merely intimating that you've seen the note."

"And I may not."

"Someone knows who her lover was," Portia urged. No longer for her own sake, or even for his, but for the sake of Lady Amelia who, whatever her faults, had lain too long in her grave while her murderer walked free. "Perhaps even Ransley."

"No." Ashburne turned on her, a book tumbling to the floor, and took her wrists in a bruising grip. "You will not speak to Ransley again, do you understand me, madam?"

"I don't mean that he *knows* he knows her killer's name, just that—"

Ashburne gave her a shake. Her fingers were going numb. "I said leave him out of this. Do you understand me?"

"I understand." He was getting wise to her. Though his grip gentled, he did not release her wrists.

"You will remain inside the Hall. You will not go out. You will help me search the library, and you will do nothing else. Are we agreed, my lady?"

Portia glared at him, but he did not soften one bit, and finally she said, "Yes. I'll help you look for the note."

He released her. "Good."

She rubbed her wrists, the mark of his fingers red on her pale skin. "And if we don't find it?"

Ashburne glared.

Chapter Twenty-Three

THERE were pressed flowers and squashed bugs, dust and spiderwebs and the occasional spider, not all of which were dead. And then there were the little "gifts" from the mice, which had tried out their teeth on more books than Portia could bear to contemplate.

And there were notes. Scraps of accounts, betting chits, letters long and short. Market lists, passages copied into schoolboy copperplate, rude drawings. Love notes. Notes tender, notes marital, notes of bitter disappointment and dawning glory. Notes that Portia blushed to read (and then read again, if Ashburne was not watching).

Most Portia returned to the pages where she found them, feeling obscurely that they deserved to rest where they had for decades, if not centuries. Some had no salutation or closing, no names to identify them, and those she gave to Ashburne. After reading them, he stuck them between the pages of whatever book he had open, something in the writing or the content assuring him they did not suit. Others slowly collected in a pile on the table by his elbow, more out of a fear of somehow going astray, she thought, than any real belief they might be what he sought.

Afternoon passed into evening without any effect on the library with its drawn drapes and flickering candles. Mrs. McFerran brought in tea, kept Ellie away when she returned from her free day, though Portia would not care to guess by what means, and chivvied them into the breakfast room for supper, the dining room being still too dusty and mouse-ridden for use. Ashburne ate fast, with the manner of a man who did not taste what he put in his mouth. Portia, who had missed her dinner, dined well also, but with significantly more appreciation. The difference between this meal and the lackluster attempts she'd threatened out of the housekeeper was night and day.

"You have much to answer for," Portia told Ashburne as they returned to the library. "Turning even the servants against me." She was thinking of the conversation she'd overheard several days since and assumed to be between the housekeeper and her husband. She owed Mr. McFerran an apology.

He sent her to bed when the candles guttered and she began to nod over the books, unable to remember anymore whether she had Dante or Rabelais in her hands, though she had not yet stopped looking at the frontispieces, for how else was she ever to know the contents of this library. A library that would be hers only so long as Ashburne must hide. She tried not to dwell on the loss she'd feel upon going back to Rosewood's little book room, if she were so lucky as to manage even that. Yawning, Portia went up to bed, where Ellie scolded her over reading so long and tucked her up like a little girl, nearly asleep before ever her head hit the pillow.

She dreamt that he came in while she slept and watched her by the light of a guttering candle. And that when she opened her eyes and saw him there, he set the candle aside and lowered his body over hers and she wanted him more than she'd ever dreamed of wanting Roger.

* * *

And so it went for another day.

Portia managed, somehow, to forget her dream long enough to be civil to Ashburne at breakfast, though she did blush when he asked how she'd slept. The courtesy was clearly an effort for him, though whether because he was out of practice with them (or had never been *in* practice; he sometimes scowled as if he'd as lief spend the rest of his life skulking about, for ghosts never had to speak to anyone) or because his arm pained him, she could not tell.

When she went to the kitchen to fetch dinner, she found Ellie with Mrs. McFerran in her sitting room, the two of them plying their needles together like old friends. Returning to the library with a tray that held more food than Portia could eat in a week, she wondered if their new accord reflected Mrs. McFerran's growing acceptance of her mistress, or had more to do with Ellie's assistance in tending Mr. McFerran. As for Ellie, she had to find company somewhere, and mayhap Mrs. McFerran had been starved for female companionship, little though it had showed.

Mrs. McFerran turned Clary away at the door when she arrived sometime in the afternoon, though Portia only knew of it at suppertime. The woman swore she'd said nothing more than that Lady Ashburne was feeling unwell, and Portia had no choice but to believe her. Truthfully, it was as well she'd sent Clary away. The girl would otherwise have come bursting into the library, and the cat would have been among the pigeons for certain.

After that first day, Portia had Ellie lay out one of her old gowns. Her maid grizzled at her unfashionable choice until she realized just how much grime had found its way onto the gown Portia'd been wearing, then grumbled about that while she buttoned Portia into a gray morning dress so faded it was an odd shade of lavender. The frivolous girl who still lived somewhere inside

Portia's breast complained bitterly at attending Ashburne in such a dress, and withered into silence when he seemed to notice nothing more than that she was there. His black coat and trousers were soon so covered in dust they might have been gray. Portia decided they were even and tried to put the matter from her mind.

She could not, try as she might, put *him* from her mind. However far from her he stood, he seemed to fill up the space around her with his scent of heat and spices. His hands, when they brushed hers, struck sparks, and the slow whisper of his breathing filled her ears, even over the rustle of pages.

She wished she knew whether he was as aware of her.

* * *

It was damned difficult to concentrate with Portia in the room.

Much as Giles appreciated her help—his shoulder ached so abominably the first night he'd resorted to laudanum to sleep and woke muzzy headed and irritable—he could hardly see what was in front of him when she sat opposite. She need but shift minutely to break his train of thought.

He fought it by concentrating ever harder on the books. It was here. It must be here somewhere, though with each bookcase finished, his hope faded further.

He was standing on the library stairs to avoid having to lift his left arm to reach the top shelf when the pounding began. Startled, he wavered and Portia, who was waiting below for him to hand down the books, steadied him with a hand on his calf that he could feel long after she removed it.

Someone was hammering at the front door. Someone strong and angry and very determined. Giles descended the library stairs and listened—Portia's nearness, the delicate scent of her, filling his head—as Mrs. McFerran rushed to the door, her footsteps echoing quickly in the great hall. Her voice came, quick and angry and indistinct though the library door, then a man's, loud and quite clear.

"Don't give me that rot. I know she's here and I'll thank you to step aside."

With a cry of "Tony," Portia dashed out into the hall, the library door not quite closing behind her.

Cursing, Giles tripped a hidden catch and one of the bookcases swung open. He slipped into the secret passage, recent practice allowing him to easily make his way to the kitchen without a candle. Family lore was voluble on the handful of secret rooms and passages in Ashburne Hall, attributing them variously to hiding Catholic priests, smuggling, thievery, or sheer bloody-minded perversity on the part of previous generations. The "priest-hole" in the servants' quarters where Giles had spent entirely too many of his recent days was devoid of any religious symbol, Catholic or otherwise. For himself, Giles believed that unlawful and unfortunate activities were the long-ago start of the Ashburne fortune and he was now paying the price for his ancestors' crimes.

He ran lightly up the servants' stair to duck into a room that fronted the drive. All he could see at first was the man's mount, a nice bit of horseflesh, sturdy but not fancy. A moment later, the fellow appeared, his dark head bent toward Portia's. She hung on his arm, her face turned to his, and Giles knew that bright expression. He'd seen it bent on himself, perhaps once, perhaps twice.

He should have sent her to the right-about that first morning. He'd been trying for a fortnight to force her out by means both fair and foul. With someone trying to hurt her and the threat she represented to his safety, he ought to have had no difficulty packing her off, bag and baggage. He had not. He'd been seduced by her flashing eyes and quick smile, her blunt conversation, delicate stature and far from delicate beauty.

He had let himself forget what kind of woman she was, let her adultery, perfidy as great as Amelia's, fade to the back of his mind while she worked by his side, too grateful for her easy acceptance to let himself remember what he knew her to be. He'd forgotten this *Tony*, his letters, his cavalier assumption of her love, vows and reputation and Roger be damned. Portia spoke animatedly to her lover, touching his arm, his chest. He laughed with careless affection and swept her into an embrace. Giles' fingers ached where they gripped the windowsill.

He would not forget again. Portia Ashburne would not spend another peaceful night in his house.

Chapter Twenty-Four

"BUT however did you find me here?" Portia demanded, blinking in the sunshine, painfully bright after the dim library. "And why aren't you at Oxford?"

"I tracked you down." Tony took up the reins of the horse he'd rushed her outside to see. "And deuced difficult it was, too. I'm run off my feet, Portia, dashing from one end of England to the other after you."

"Not quite so far as all that."

"And this downy fellow's carried me the whole way, haven't you boy? Oxford to Rosewood to Ashburne." He rubbed the horse between his twitching ears and turned a brilliant grin on Portia. "Isn't he a corker?"

"He's a lovely horse," Portia agreed, stroking the soft nose, "but wherever did you get the money for him? I know you haven't the blunt to—"

"Don't come over difficult at me, sis! I ain't in dutch with the duns. I own Lightning fair and square, don't I boy?"

"I don't believe it. Stop talking to your horse," Portia snapped when he persisted in whispering in the animal's ear, "and have the courtesy to speak to me. How did you come by him?"

Tony sighed. "You're a perfect Gorgon, you know that? I won him in a card game."

"Tony—"

"Don't start. Don't start, I haven't gone off the rails, I promise." He turned a charming smile on her, wrapping his arm about her waist. "It's not a regular thing with me. I'm not Roger, I promise you that."

"You had better not be!" Portia slapped his arm. "And don't try any of your wiles on me, I'm not a schoolroom miss or upstairs maid to be melted by your smile. You still haven't said why you're not at university."

He was suddenly very interested in the fit of his horse's bridle.

"Tony..." Portia's throat squeezed shut. "Tony, please tell me you haven't been sent down."

"Nothing as bad as all that. Just... Just rusticating for a couple of days."

"A couple of days."

"A month."

"Oh, Tony..."

"Look, you can ring a peal over me later. I'm hot and I'm dusty and my horse needs tending. What's a fellow got to do around here to get his horse seen to?"

"The stable's around back, Tony. You'll have to tend him yourself, I'm afraid."

"Are you telling me there's not a soul to look after my horse in all this ruddy great house?"

"Mr. McFerran's broken his leg and there's no one else." She frowned at his expression, which had gotten him his way far too often in the past and looked idiotic on a grown man. "For heaven's sake, Tony, it's not the first time you've had to shift for yourself. Nor will it be the last, I trow. There's only the five of us here, and making faces at me isn't going to do one blessed thing to change that."

"Five?"

"Mr. and Mrs. McFerran, Ellie, me, and—"

"Me," Tony supplied when Portia stopped, appalled at her slip. "All right, Portia." He bent to kiss her cheek and took up the slack in Lightning's reins. "Come on boy, looks like we're fending for ourselves."

As he walked away, the horse nudging his shoulder with its muzzle every couple of steps, Portia tried to remember whether she'd seen any oats in the run-down stables. They'd have to get some from the Duck and Drake if there wasn't. What a good thing she hadn't spent the money from the silver yet. She hadn't intended to spend it at all—the last thing she wanted to do was take Ashburne's money, and she'd only spouted the silver in the first place for the sake of the staff and the house—but it looked now as if she'd have to. Goodness! She'd forgotten all about Ashburne. Portia turned to the house and a movement in one of the upper windows caught her eye. She couldn't see who was watching, but she could certainly guess. It was only her guilty conscience that made her think he was scowling.

Portia went back inside. Ignoring Mrs. McFerran's glare, she said, "I take it he's gone upstairs?"

"Who, my lady?"

Portia sighed. "All right, then. If you should happen to see him, tell him he needn't worry about Tony—Mr. Durose, that is—he's perfectly harmless. And I'm sorry, but I'll be needing the master's bedchamber, as Mr. Durose will be staying a few days." That should give him enough warning to remove his shaving things and anything else he oughtn't leave lying about. Mrs. McFerran glowered, but she didn't return to the fiction that the bedchamber's ceiling leaked; at least she wasn't fooling herself that Portia's wits had gone completely begging.

"I'm sure I don't know to whom you refer."

Portia bit her cheek to keep her temper. "I'm quite certain you *do* know something about supper. Pray see to it. We will be eating in a quarter hour."

"Of course, my lady." Mrs. McFerran stalked back to the kitchen, leaving Portia rubbing her temples, which were beginning to ache. She closed the door to the library, though Ashburne was clearly lurking about upstairs somewhere, and went into the morning room, leaving the door ajar so Tony could find her when he returned.

* * *

"There you are!"

Portia jumped. She'd been too busy fretting over Ashburne's reaction to yet another uninvited guest to notice her brother's return. Having Tony about was, she feared, far from the best way to stay on her host's good side. Tony came jauntily into the morning room, bent to kiss her cheek and plumped down on the couch next to her.

"You look better," Portia observed. His hair was brushed back from his broad brow, his face scrubbed clean of road dust, and his coat shook out. "You haven't been washing yourself in the horse trough, have you?"

Tony laughed. "No, but if I'd known what kind of Gorgon you had in the kitchens, I'd have done so, rather than beg washwater from her."

"That would be Mrs. McFerran."

"Pleasant soul. By the by, where the devil did you get that horse?"

She was used to Tony's sudden diversions, but even so.... "What horse?"

"That bloody great bay stallion. Looks like he'd be a real corker to ride."

Oh dash it all! *That* was what had started niggling away at Portia's mind when Clary said she'd better run for the surgeon as her horse was better than any Portia had. She'd had no time since to think about it, but it had sat brooding at the back of her thoughts. Now she knew why. A stable was supposed to smell like horse, after all, and so she'd taken no notice of the fact that it oughtn't smell like fresh dung when there hadn't been an animal in it for ages. Ashburne again, right under her nose, where he'd been all along.

"Thought you hadn't a feather to fly with, sis. Where'd you get the blunt for such a prime goer?"

Portia cast about frantically for an answer, thankful to find one ready-made. "I'm keeping him for Mr. Foxkin, the innkeeper at the Duck and Drake." With whom she was going to have words the next time their paths crossed—he thought the bay's owner was too optimistic about how soon he'd be able to come for the horse, indeed! At least *he* hadn't shared Ashburne's confidence that she could be driven out of the Hall quickly. "Apparently the bay unsettles the other horses in the inn's stables, so I offered to keep him here."

"Interesting. Didn't notice Lightning particularly minded. But then, I don't have him in the adjoining stall." He scuffed his boot across the threadbare carpet, raising a small cloud of dust. "I hope you had the sense to dun the innkeep."

"Of course. Now Tony—"

"If your help's not able to take care of him, I expect you'll have to send him back. Though maybe I could help with that, since I'm here and—"

"Tony," Portia snapped, more sharply than she'd intended, but she simply had to redirect his attention. Recognizing her tone of voice, her brother groaned and slid down on the couch until he was nearly horizontal. "What the deuce did you do to get yourself sent down?"

He sat up and looked about with a false air of expectancy. "When's supper? Country hours, I hope. I've been on short commons all week, and I'm half-starved."

"In a quarter hour and don't change the subject."

"Have I mentioned you look fine as fivepence?"

"I look a perfect quiz and you know it. Stop trying to turn me up sweet and just tell me."

Tony sighed. "Is there something wrong with wanting to be able to flash the screens on occasion, or at least look as if you could? Man doesn't have to *act* pursepinched, even if he is. Fellow was asking to have his cork drawn, saying I must have snabbled my new corbeau coat from someone with more blunt. He's lucky I didn't call him out for the insult."

"What did you do?"

"Planted him a facer." He flashed her a grin. "Broke his nose."

"Oh, Tony."

"Don't 'oh Tony' me. It's dashed unfair I got sent off to rusticate and he didn't. And you," he went on, not giving her a chance to give him the trimming he deserved, "how the devil did you end up here? Thought you were buried at Rosewood."

"Well James dug me up."

"And packed you off here? I didn't think that mealymouthed toad had the bottom to so much as look at you sideways."

"Well, Violet had a lot to do with it. That woman...."

"James is the only man I know who'd need a woman to help him find his bottom."

Portia couldn't help but laugh. "I'm glad you're here, Tony."

"I may not be." Tony wiggled his finger in a mouse-hole in the upholstery. "Is there anyplace safe to sleep in this house?"

"Here and there. If you don't mind mice. And ghosts," Portia added with a smile.

"Ghosts? Are you bamming me or have you gone all about in the head?"

"A little of each. Come, you must be starving." She rose and Tony scrambled to his feet, every inch her little brother for all his airs and his years.

"Told you I was."

Portia tucked her hand into the crook of his arm. "How long are you here for?"

Tony hemmed. Portia could see a flush rising from his collar.

"Pockets to let?" she asked, not without sympathy, as they went into the breakfast room.

"It's dashed expensive, traveling."

"Not to mention buying corbeau coats," Portia murmured.

Tony ignored her. "You know what a pittance old Burnsides allows me. I've gone through my allowance for the month, and I was hoping you could put me up for a bit."

"Of course," Portia assured him, though she was by no means certain Ashburne wouldn't come over difficult. Surely he'd understand she couldn't turn her own brother away.

Mrs. McFerran moved about the table with quick efficiency and such a mutinous expression that Portia knew the housekeeper had, if at all possible, burnt supper. It smelled acceptable. Perhaps Mrs. McFerran had had too little time to manage. The housekeeper shot Portia a vicious look and swept out.

"Mm," Tony said after he'd savored the first bite. "Now I know why you keep her around."

"Eat up, Tony. We can't have you leaving my table hungry." Not least because this supper, cooked with Ashburne in mind, might be the last edible meal either of them had at the Hall.

* * *

As much as Portia loved her brother, she was weak with relief when he finally blew out his candle. All through dinner and the nice coze they had in the morning room afterward, her skin had pricked with nervous anticipation of Ashburne descending upon them. She was as certain Mrs. McFerran had passed along the message that Tony was harmless as she was that Ashburne didn't believe it. Portia may merely have been oversensitive, but the Hall felt steeped in thunderous rage.

Portia had been surprised to see Ashburne's portrait still hanging in its usual place on the landing. Now any slip on Ashburne's part, any glimpse Tony had of him, would be dashed difficult to explain. Not that it would have been easy regardless, but if Ashburne was truly concerned Tony might give him away, he'd have been better off making certain Tony could at least not identify him.

"Dashed disagreeable looking man," Tony had remarked, and Portia looked at the portrait with surprise.

"Is he? I hadn't noticed."

Ashburne's features were harsh, uncompromising. He was not, in his own words, a "pretty fellow." But Portia had stopped noticing some time ago. Perhaps even before she met him in the flesh. Ashburne was, quite simply, Ashburne.

Portia uncurled herself from her uncomfortable position on the floor of her dressing room. She'd waited so long that the night's chill had made its way through even her flannel dressing gown, and she shivered in the still dark. It had taken Tony long enough, but the faint light under his door had finally winked out a moment ago, and she knew for certain he was abed.

Which meant it was safe to go looking for Ashburne.

Portia had been sitting in the dressing room so long her eyes had adjusted to the night, but she still failed to spot Giles Ashburne in her dark bedchamber, and nearly fainted dead away when his hard fingers closed on her arm.

"For shame, sir," she hissed, "you frightened me."

"For shame, madam," he rejoined, and she had no time to wonder what he meant for, though low, his voice rumbled through her, unsettling the action of her heart.

"Hush. You'll wake him."

"No doubt he sleeps deep," Ashburne said coldly, "satisfied to be reunited with you. However, if you fear rousing him...." He dragged her, unprotesting, out into the dark hallway and up to the servants' wing at such a pace she was forced to trot to keep up with him. Portia's outstretched hand brushed the tapestry by the head of the stairs. She passed into a lightless chamber and finally knew how he had so often contrived to vanish under her very nose.

Ashburne released her. There was the scrabble of tin and a hot metallic smell as he opened the shutter on a dark lantern. Portia nervously rubbed her arm, fighting back a shiver. The room was tiny, both bare and barren, its only furnishings a narrow camp bed and a small table that held the lantern and a few books. There was no window, nor even a rug to soften the place.

In such close confines, Ashburne's presence was like heat lightning, beating upon her senses. The room, or he, smelled strongly of tobacco and she felt like she was taking in some essence of him with every breath. Under the flickering light of the lantern, she saw the man from the portrait, standing stern and obdurate against even the elements.

"Well, my lady," he said finally. "What are we to do?"

Portia looked around the spartan room. "I'm terribly sorry to have put you out, my lord. I thought only to find Tony a room suitable for habitation, and I assumed you must have had some place to go, as you've only occupied the master's bedchamber the last two nights." She glanced about again, helplessness overcoming her. "If I'd known it was so—"

"Had you known, you would of course have put him farther from you," Ashburne said in a freezing tone that implied the opposite. "But why, when the master's bedchamber is so... convenient?"

Portia could feel his anger beating upon her skin, combined with something else she did not understand. "I know you would prefer not to have him here," she tried. "The last thing you need is more people in the Hall. But I could hardly turn him away. Had I known he was coming—"

"Of course you knew. You were so shameless as to write to him, madam. How else could he find you here?"

Portia could barely breathe. "I don't understand. I haven't written. It was James. James sent him on from Rosewood."

"And why should he do the puppy such excellent and understanding service?"

Ashburne's mocking was the last straw. "Because he's too much the skinflint to put my brother up for even a night," Portia snapped. "I don't know what you're about, my lord, but—"

"Your brother?"

"Of course my brother, who did you think?"

Ashburne made a small movement and the gathering tension burst at the gesture in some way Portia did not understand. Quite suddenly, she felt cold again, her skin crawling with a chill she hadn't noticed while in the eye of his anger. He sank slowly onto the bed and stared at her until Portia wrapped her arms around herself as much for comfort as warmth. "I... did not know you had a brother."

"For shame, sir," Portia said, finding it within her to smile. "Of course you knew; you have read my letters." She feared, the moment the words left her mouth, that he would task her with her own transgression. He did not answer for so long that the fear had ample time to grow.

"I suppose," Ashburne said finally, "I did not expect him here."

"Nor I." Portia's smile became rueful. "Had I known, I *would* have written. To fob him off." She hesitated, shifting from one cold foot to the other. "Now that he is here...."

His eyes drifted back to her, looking strangely dazed. "Yes," he murmured. Then, "yes," louder. "I suppose now that your brother...?"

"Antony," she supplied.

"Spared your father's Shakespearean excesses, I see."

"And Cleopatra," Portia said tartly.

What might almost have been a smile ghosted over his lips. "I stand corrected." He passed a hand through his hair, and Portia was surprised to see that it trembled. "As you so accurately point out, we cannot simply send him packing. I'll keep to the shadows while he's here. Did he give you to know how long that would be?" Ashburne looked startled when Portia finally lost the battle against her shivering. He cursed and stood, shrugging out of his coat. "Why did you not tell me you were cold?"

Portia shivered again when he wrapped his coat about her. It was so warm and smelled so sweetly of him. "It's nothing, my lord," she said, grateful her teeth did not chatter. "I was a long time in my dressing room, waiting for Tony to blow out his candle so I might safely come looking for you."

He dragged his hand through his hair again. "Is that what you were doing?"

"Of course. Why else would I linger so long?" Portia realized suddenly that the left sleeve of his shirt was spotted with blood. "Oh, but you're bleeding."

"It's nothing," Ashburne said carelessly. "I overreached myself."

"Take off your shirt and sit down, my lord."

"No need. Your sewing's still intact."

When Portia's fingers found his sleeve and the hard heat of his arm beneath it, he drew in a harsh breath. "Have I hurt you?" And yet, her hand was not near his shoulder. "What is the matter?"

He gave her an unconvincing smile. "Nothing more than before. Less, perhaps," he added under his breath.

"I do not understand you, my lord."

"It's nothing to signify." Ashburne gently removed her hand from his arm, and though his fingers no longer shook, his touch sent shivers up her arm. "I should go down to the library while your brother sleeps, and you should go to bed. You will no doubt need your rest to entertain your brother upon the morrow."

"You might simply join us for nuncheon, my lord. Tony's a bit devil may care, but he's not a care-for-nobody. He'd not knowingly hurt me."

"And how is that anything to me?" Ashburne asked, his voice soft.

"Just, just," Portia stammered, covered in confusion and aware suddenly that they stood so near she could feel the heat of him even through the coat. "He would not breathe word to a soul that you're here if I told him not to. He may be of some help."

"And then I should have two green geese poking their beaks into what's better left alone," Ashburne said, so gently Portia could not take exception. "No. I'll continue on my own." His fingers tightened briefly on hers, then slipped away, leaving her cold.

"You need not work by night, my lord."

"Portia—"

"I mean to say," she went on quickly, "that we may continue in the library come morning without fear of Tony interrupting. He's a dreadful lay-abed."

"Is he now?" Ashburne smiled at her, suddenly far too close.

And then his lips were on hers and he was not close enough. Portia knew she made some sound in her throat, her hands clenching in his shirt, but could not make herself stop, or care. Her hair came loose, tumbling down her back, and he wrapped it around and around his hand, stopping with his broad palm cupping the back of her head. He circled her waist with his other arm and lifted her off her feet as if she weighed no more than dandelion down. Portia's arms wrapped of their own accord about his neck and she drowned in his kiss, her fingers burrowing into his thick hair. He tasted of musk and spices and... brandy, she thought. Though Roger had never come to her bed without reeking of some libation or other, he'd never been partial to brandy. Nor to her.

He released her hair to fall heavy down her back, his clever fingers moving to loosen the ties of her dressing gown. His coat slipped off her shoulders, but Portia didn't miss it, so far from cold she couldn't remember what it felt like. Her dressing gown parted, the heat of his body seeping through the thin cambric of his shirt and the fine lawn of her nightrail. He crushed her against him. Portia gasped against his lips, the hard heat of him searing her breasts and belly. He broke from her mouth, a low sound rumbling from his chest as he nuzzled down her throat, pushing aside her nightrail to kiss the rise of her breast.

Her arms tightened around his neck as she arched to meet his lips. An aching thread of need ran from where his lips touched her breast to the molten heat between her legs. She struggled to simultaneously press her body into the heat of his skin and lift her breasts to the inflaming touch of his mouth, her back bent across his arm like a bow. Her arms shook with the strain, and he lifted her higher, his large hands spanning her waist, then sliding slowly down, fingers spread as if to claim every inch of her skin he could encompass, to part her legs and press between, her nightrail all that kept him from the most intimate part of herself. A desperate cry escaped her, and he stilled at the sound.

Slowly, Giles lowered Portia to her feet, gently lifting her arms from around his neck. He knelt and her breath came fast, but when he bent to her, there was only restraint. He pressed his face against her breasts and was still, except for the shaking of his hands at her waist. She could feel his breath through her nightrail. When she ventured to touch his bent head, he set her a little away from him and lifted her nightrail back onto her shoulders, then refastened her dressing gown, a tremor shaking his fingers. He picked up his coat and wrapped it around her again, then stood and stepped away.

"I think you had best go to bed." She shivered at the rough edge to his voice.

"I—" Her voice quavered unexpectedly.

"Go, Portia."

She went, finding her way by a kind of blind instinct. The need that throbbed in her breasts and between her thighs tried to draw her back to him, but eventually she found herself in her own bedchamber. She peered at herself in the dressing table mirror and felt vaguely grateful that Tony was abed and had not come upon her wandering the dark halls with her dressing gown askew, clutching a man's coat about her and looking very well-used indeed.

Chapter Twenty-Five

IF it weren't for the coat, Portia might have thought it a dream, though she'd never dreamt so vividly, nor felt anything so powerfully, awake or asleep. But she had gone to bed with his coat still wrapped around her, the scent of him filling her heart, and woke to Ellie's scolding.

"That boy ought to know better, keeping you up all hours. At least he had the sense to lend you his coat."

Portia stretched luxuriously, so pleasantly sleep-muddled she didn't even think to panic about what Ellie would make of the coat until after she realized her maid was talking about Tony. And thank heavens for that! Just one day ago, the sight of her mistress wrapped in a man's coat would have sent Ellie into superstitious palpitations.

"Shall I take it in to him, my lady?" Ellie didn't quite meet Portia's eyes, her cheeks slightly flushed. Portia smiled tolerantly.

"No, Ellie. I'll see he gets it back. No doubt Mr. Durose will be late rising today." Portia glanced at the window, relieved to see by the angle of the sun that Ellie had woken her at her usual hour. She nonetheless rushed her maid through dressing and pinning up her hair while she consumed tea and toast with a ravenous appetite. Though she knew she'd only get it dirty, she couldn't resist Ellie's new creation, a morning dress of dusty rose that flattered Portia's figure nicely if Ellie did say so herself (which she did).

Ashburne's coat folded over her arm, Portia descended the stairs to meet him in the library, quite unable to stop herself wondering if he'd be in his shirtsleeves, thick black hair just brushing his crisp white collar. Or perhaps he'd be wearing a waistcoat, turning himself into a striking study in black and white somehow more solidly *real* than any man she'd ever met. She realized suddenly that she was short of breath and plumped down in the middle of the staircase to give herself a good talking to.

Portia had long suspected there was more to the marriage bed than the rather unspectacular activities Roger had rarely bothered to engage her in. The very fact that he was so eager to disport himself elsewhere made it clear there was some savor to the act she'd failed to grasp. That the women he tumbled enjoyed the experience—and surely they must, else why do it?—had given Portia to believe that the fault was her own. After last night.... For the first time, Portia suspected the failing had been Roger's. The least of Giles Ashburne's kisses had filled her with a desperate heat Roger had never inspired with even the most intimate of attentions.

Portia squeezed her eyes shut and forced herself *not* to think of those attentions and Ashburne at the same time. She may have been a widow, but she was *not*, she reminded herself sternly, free with her favors and lost to all propriety. *Yet*, her traitorous mind added.

Ashburne was in no position to marry, even supposing he would want to tie himself to *her*. As for Portia.... Marriage to Roger had taught her a few lessons, the least of which was that she never again wanted to tie herself to a man. There was no member of that sex not guaranteed to prove himself an unprincipled rake, however much of a gentleman he might have seemed before the wedding. A few minutes of pleasure were not reason enough to forget that.

Portia stood and marched herself the rest of the way downstairs. The library door was locked and she turned the key with a feeling of anticipation entirely out of keeping with the task she was there to undertake.

At first, she thought the library empty and her heart sank within her, but once she closed the door, Ashburne emerged from an alcove near the windows. Despite all her stern words to herself, she was disappointed to find him more correctly dressed than at any time since she'd first seen him. His coat and trousers were closer to charcoal than black, though not this time from dust, his waistcoat steel-gray, his cravat snowy white and perfectly arranged. He looked very proper and even more unapproachable than his portrait, though for different reasons.

"Good morning, my lord."

Ashburne inclined his head stiffly. "My lady."

His mood communicated itself to her, and Portia found herself saying, "Your coat, sir," and extending it to him in the most awkward manner possible, when she'd meant to thank him prettily for the loan. She hoped she was not blushing.

He took the coat without touching her. "Lady Ashburne—"

"You've got started already, I see," Portia said brightly. Actually, it was clear he'd worked through the night, for he was now on a new bookcase. Portia felt bereft to think he might have found the note when she was not there and berated herself for so selfish a thought. She seated herself next to the largest stack and took up the top book.

Portia bent her head over the volume, so aware of Ashburne's eyes on her that she was unable to take in a full breath until she heard him begin to move about behind her. While she searched, Ashburne returned most of the books he'd already handled to the shelves. The tidy stack of questionable notes that had been on the stand by his chair was also gone. Portia thought it unnecessarily fastidious of him, especially when he'd never previously shown any concern about the mess he made of the library, but discovered how wrong she was when Tony's voice rang out in the great hall.

Portia jolted to her feet, her book sliding unceremoniously to the floor. She'd forgotten to lock the door! Her eyes flew desperately to Ashburne, who jumped down from the library stairs while she ran for the door, reaching it just as Tony pushed it open.

"There you are! I should have known you'd closet yourself in the library."

"Tony!" Portia exclaimed, hearing herself breathless and unable to do anything about it. She pressed her hands to his chest and tried to step out the door, wishing she was tall enough to block his view of the library. "I thought sure you'd still be abed. Are you hungry?"

"Starved." Tony stood his ground without seeming aware she was trying to push him out. It was only when Portia realized he showed nothing but curiosity that she thought to turn around and realized that Ashburne was no longer in sight. The man was quicker to vanish than an actual ghost. Though personal experience assured her that Ashburne was no longer in the library, or at least nowhere he could be found, Portia wouldn't feel easy in her mind until she got Tony away. She could not bear to think of Ashburne trapped in some tiny room like the one upstairs, unable to leave until they cleared out.

"I'm certain Mrs. McFerran could be convinced to shirr you some eggs." Especially if she wanted Tony out of Ashburne's hair. "Let's go see." Portia winced at her cow-handed effort, but Tony appeared not to notice.

He wandered into the library, surveying the stacks of books that still surrounded her chair despite Ashburne's efforts. "Just what are you up to, Portia?"

"Nothing. A little... project. Nothing that would interest you."

Tony seated himself on the couch and smiled at her. "I'm interested in everything you do, sis. It's been too long since our paths coincided." He patted the couch next to him. "Come, sit with me. We haven't talked in ages."

"We talked *for* ages last night. I thought you were hungry."

"I'm beginning to think there's something here you don't want me to see." Tony stretched to reach the book she'd dropped when she heard him coming and leafed idly through it. "You haven't taken to writing penny dreadfuls to eke out the pittance Roger left you? Or are you looking for a secret treasure map?"

Even to herself, Portia's laugh sounded forced. "Of course not."

"Pity. The problem with you, Portia, is that you're far too prosy for your own good. You need a little *adventure* in your life."

"I've had quite enough of that, thank you."

"I hate to break it to you, sis, but figuring out whether to plant turnips or cabbage is not adventure and dealing with a house full of mice is a mere nuisance." Portia itched to ask him what he thought of being haunted and shot at, but managed to keep her peace until he said, "I don't know why you married that dastard, Portia."

"Because," Portia said on a sigh, "I fancied myself in love with him, the more fool I. I thought you were hungry." She was decidedly not in the mood to discuss Roger, especially not somewhere Ashburne might hear.

"I am." He laced his fingers behind his head and stretched his legs out, crossing them at the ankle. "Get that gargoyle of a housekeeper to bring something in, why don't you? I'm comfortable here."

Portia scowled. "You're impossible." If she kept at him, Tony would only dig his heels in harder. A strategic retreat was called for. She would think of a way to budge him while he ate.

She hurried to the kitchen to order Tony's breakfast and tell Mrs. McFerran to keep Ashburne away, then rushed back to the library. God knew what kind of trouble Tony would find if left to his own devices. She only hoped the housekeeper, who she had left scowling into her cooking fire, would not think poisoning Tony's breakfast a good expedient to keep him out of Ashburne's way.

Very much to Portia's surprise, Mrs. McFerran brought in a tray so quickly the water could hardly have had a chance to boil for tea. Perhaps, like Portia, she hoped Tony would agree to take himself off once he was fed. Tony took his tray to the library table, threw open the drapes "so he could see what he was eating," and made himself comfortable. He then proceeded to make Portia very *un*comfortable, throwing out questions between bites, curious as a cat about the Hall and everything she'd done since she arrived.

He had eaten half his breakfast when Clary burst in.

* * *

"Oh!" Clary exclaimed, turning a virulent shade of red that actually looked good on her. "Beg pardon!" She dropped a neat curtsey, wobbling a little as she rose out of it. She was properly attired for once, the turbulent sea-green of her riding habit perfectly in keeping with her personality.

"Lady Clarissa!" Portia moved to take Clary's arm. "Whatever are you doing here? Come, my dear, let's move to the morning room where we can be comfortable."

Clary didn't budge from staring at Tony, who'd jumped up from his incomplete breakfast and was staring right back. He cleared his throat. "Why the rush, Portia? Your best bonnet's not on fire, is it?" Clary giggled. Tony grinned. "Go on, sis. Do the honors, won't you?"

Portia squeezed her eyes briefly shut. She was as good as dead. If Ashburne didn't kill her, Ransley would. "Lady Clarissa, may I present my botheration of a brother, Mr. Antony Durose? Tony, this is Lady Clarissa Seabrooke, niece to his grace, the Duke of Ransley."

Tony made an elegant leg, bowing over Clary's fingers. Portia thought it a bit much, but the chit appeared quite taken. "Enchanted, my lady. Portia, you shall have to get used to my rusticating, for I'm certain to get into a great many fights when I return to university. My fellows," he said to Clary, as if he were exchanging confidences, "will never believe that such beautiful blossoms grow in the country, and I shall have to defend your honor. Frequently."

"You had better not," Portia said over Clary's giggle. She supposed she ought to be grateful that Tony had such a salubrious effect on Lady Clarissa. The chit might be displaying a new line in bubble-headed giggling, but at least the painful shyness she'd shown around Courtland wasn't in evidence. Tony was doing rather too good a job of it, however. The last thing any of them needed was for Clary to develop a *tendre* for the dratted boy. Portia deftly freed Clary's hand and led the young lady to the couch. "Now, my lady, what's brought you here today?"

"I've come for my lessons." Clary twisted on the couch and smiled unselfconsciously at Tony, who naturally came over to sit in the nearest chair. "I'm hopeless, absolutely hopeless when it comes to society. Your sister's kindly offered to teach me."

Tony clearly thought to make some witty remark at Portia's expense, but changed his mind at Portia's glare. "I'm quite certain you've been misled, Lady Clarissa," he said gallantly. "You don't appear at all hopeless to me."

"You haven't seen me racketing around the neighborhood on my horse."

Portia bit back a sigh, wondering for the first time if Ransley had it right—perhaps if Clary never had a come out.... But no, even a duke's niece needs must marry and she could hardly make an acceptable match buried at Tynesfield. Courtland was the closest thing to a marriageable man in the area, sad to say, and a house party would be disastrous, even were it not completely out of the question after what had happened to her unfortunate cousin. If someone didn't take a firm hand with her, Clary would thoroughly ruin her own chances, either through timidity or by demonstrating her singular lack of concern for propriety.

"You should see Gunpowder," Clary proved Portia's point by adding. "He's a great gun."

"I'm sure he is." Hearing Tony's gently amused tone, Portia became very concerned indeed. As dearly as she loved her brother, she could not pretend he had anything to recommend himself. Ransley could hardly approve a fellow not yet out of school, without title or money. Their grandfather had settled an income on Tony contingent on his managing to graduate university without being sent down, but it would not be any great amount. He'd have enough to keep himself, and if he were clever in his dealings, he might make something of it, but he was no great catch, even had his connection with the Ashburnes not put him beyond the pale as far as Ransley was concerned.

"Would you like to see him?" Clary asked with all the enthusiasm and discretion of a schoolroom chit. "He's right outside."

"Lady Clarissa—"

"We can't have that." Tony turned a deliberately blind eye to Portia's speaking look. "There's no one *else* to tuck him up in the stables while Lady Clarissa makes her visit, now is there?"

"Oh, he doesn't need to be in the stables," Clary assured him. "Come see." She hopped up and raced out the door.

"Tony...." Portia laid a restraining hand on his arm. "Don't."

"Why ever not?"

"She's a green girl and she doesn't understand."

Tony gave her a look. "I don't think *you* understand. I like the chit."

"Her guardian—"

"Is no doubt a dragon. They all are. I'm sure I can turn him up sweet."

"I doubt your smile will have any charms for the Duke of Ransley. He despises the Ashburnes."

"Why?"

"Because he believes Roger's cousin, Giles, killed his ward."

Tony stared at her. "Hell and damnation. The fellow at the head of the stairs?"

"How did you—"

"I can read a brass name plate, sis. I've learnt that much at Oxford. But you've forgotten one thing." Tony dropped a kiss on her cheek. "*I* am not an Ashburne."

"I doubt that will make one speck of difference to Ransley." But Portia was speaking to an empty room.

"Hell and damnation, woman! Can't you keep your own demmed family in check?"

Portia spun around, her heart racketing in her chest, but the library was empty. She closed the door and planted her hands on her hips. "Come out, sir. I won't talk to thin air."

A bookcase swung silently open to reveal Ashburne, his expression thunderous. Portia quickly went to pull the drapes. While she was at it, she caught a glimpse of Tony and Clary strolling around the side of the house, Gunpowder in tow. Obviously he'd convinced her to repair to the stables, if only to see his own 'prime goer.' She needn't have worried that one of them would spy Ashburne through the windows. They were so engaged in conversation, they wouldn't have noticed a fire-breathing dragon. Portia sighed, remembering how she'd wished for some young gentleman to help Clary overcome her shyness.

This was not what she'd had in mind.

"How delightful," Ashburne said acidly. "Your brother and Ransley's ward. That will surely solve all our problems. All you need do now is inform the duke. I'm certain he'll be overjoyed at the prospect of allying his house with mine."

"Stop." Portia wanted to put a hand on his arm, but didn't dare. She forced herself to take a slow breath so she could calmly say, "That's not what's got you in the boughs and we both know it. There's no point in cutting up at me, my lord. You know perfectly well that if Tony hadn't charged in and driven you off before Clary came, she would certainly have stumbled upon us."

"You're not making the best case for yourself, madam." Ashburne picked up the book Tony had left on the couch and tossed it on the table. "Lady Clarissa's tendency to barge into my house without so much as a by your leave is as much your fault as Mr. Durose making free of it. And now, in case you've failed to notice, he's taking her around to the stables, where she will no doubt be making the acquaintance of my horse!"

"Yes, but—"

"But nothing. This is intolerable, madam. I did *not* come back so I could sit in a demmed hole in the wall and nibble away at my library like the demmed mice. Every minute I'm here, my life and everything I hold dear is in jeopardy. Every minute brings me one minute closer to the moment when—"

Mrs. McFerran burst without warning into the library. "The Duke of Ransley, my lord!" she gasped. "He's here!"

* * *

Ashburne said something singularly rude, which Portia sincerely wished she dared echo, and retreated behind the bookcase. Portia followed Mrs. McFerran into the great hall, locking the library door behind her.

"I saw him from an upper window," the housekeeper whispered. "Himself coming up the drive in his curricle."

"All right, Mrs. McFerran. I'll take care of it."

Very much to her surprise, Mrs. McFerran gave her a relieved look and scurried off to the kitchen. Portia hadn't thought she sounded all that reassuring. She certainly didn't feel it.

She took a deep breath, smoothed her skirts, and opened the door. "Yes, Your Grace?"

He recovered quickly from his surprise at having the lady of the house open the door to him, and before he'd even knocked. "I've come for my ward."

"Lady Clarissa? I don't understand." Portia hoped Mrs. McFerran had the sense to take herself off to the stables and warn the chit. Thank heavens Tony had insisted on taking Gunpowder to the stables or they'd be in the soup already. As it was, Clary could leave through the home wood with Ransley none the wiser.

"Don't try to bam me, madam, I know she's here. I know she's been here on several occasions. Now where is she?" He stormed into the great hall and stopped short, like a horse balking at a fence. For a moment, as he took in the destruction of the once-beautiful house, there was shock reflected in his eyes. Then he blinked and banished it utterly. "I am waiting, madam."

"You will wait a long time," Portia rejoined tartly, "if you expect to see her here." Pray God it was true.

"On the contrary, Lady Ashburne, I know well that she is." He stared her down, his pale eyes colorless in the dim hall. "Did you think I wouldn't get wind of her flouting my wishes? I'm certain I made it quite clear to you that she was to have nothing to do with you or this place."

"Whoever told you she was here is no friend."

"Not yours. And perhaps not mine, but I make myself certain he told truth. Where is my ward?"

"She's not in the Hall."

"You will not win, madam." Ransley's voice so soft it would have been inaudible if he hadn't loomed so close. "I will not allow Lady Clarissa to go the way of her half-sister, turning to Banbury tales, sneaking about under my nose—"

Portia shook with fury at the imputation. "If, sir, you find the same faults in both your wards, perhaps the problem lies in you."

"You dare much, madam!" Ransley snapped, eyes blazing. "I will have my ward, Lady Ashburne, and you will cease these outrages. I will countenance no further interference." He glanced about the great hall, and if there was a flicker of sadness in his eyes, it did not show on his face, which hardened when his eyes lit on Giles Ashburne's portrait. "I vowed I would never set foot in this accursed place again. I will not forget that you made me break my oath. Now produce my niece."

Portia lifted her chin. "You are under a misapprehension, Your Grace. Your niece is not here."

Just then, proving that God, in His divine wisdom, thoroughly despised her, Tony and Lady Clarissa came through from the kitchen, their heads bent close in conversation. They could not smell more obviously of April and May, and they couldn't have had worse timing.

"What is the meaning of this, sir?"

Clary gave a little shriek at the sound of her uncle's voice and instantly turned mute as a fish. Tony jumped at the unexpected address but acquitted himself surprisingly well, immediately sweeping Ransley a bow. "Your Grace, I presume. Antony Durose, Lady Ashburne's brother, at your service. I have just finished seeing Lady Clarissa's horse settled comfortably in the stables."

"Un-settle him, sir," Ransley snapped. "The horse and my niece will be leaving here on the instant."

Tony glanced at Clary, who had turned a rather unattractive shade of gray, then at Portia, who shook her head helplessly. He turned back to Ransley. "My deepest apologies, Your Grace, but you appear to be under a misapprehension—" Portia winced at his choice of words.

"Enough, sirrah. I do not know how long your acquaintance with my niece is—" His tone made clear he'd have Tony's head if it was more than a few minutes. "—but it is *you* who are under a misapprehension if you think I would knowingly allow my niece to pass so much as a minute with a member of this accursed family."

"To be fair," Portia said as mildly as she could with the undercurrents between the duke and her brother making the hair stand up on the back of her neck, "Mr. Durose is no relation of the Ashburnes."

Ransley paid her no mind. "Lady Clarissa, if you would." It was not a question and Clary went without a sound. Ransley turned on Portia. "I will countenance no further interference from you or yours, Lady Ashburne. You may make yourself certain of that."

The door closed with a hard slam echoed by a crash somewhere in the depths of the Hall. Out on the drive, Ransley could be heard shouting at his tiger to get Lady Clarissa's horse and get himself home.

"Tony—" Portia broke off at his glare. He stormed out the rear of the house, the slamming of that door at least not jarring anything else off a shelf somewhere. Portia went back into the library.

"Damn, damn and double damn."

Chapter Twenty-Six

"You swear like a fishwife." Giles kept a weather eye on the library door. He'd heard Ransley's carriage wheeling down the drive a minute ago, but wasn't certain where Durose had got off to.

"No," Portia said, though her cheeks pinked with embarrassment, "*Roger* swore like a fishwife. I have better breeding." She sighed and rubbed her temples. "Pray, sir, do not rip up at me, I'm in no wise equal to it just now."

Giles watched her sink down upon the couch and wished he could offer her a glass of something for her nerves. Portia looked as burnt to the socket as he felt. It was strange to think the greatest peace he'd ever felt was found working alongside her in the library the few days they'd had to themselves. Since her brother came, Giles had flown from one peak of feeling to the next, barely alighting before he was bowled over by some new event.

He'd been enraged when she dared install her lover in his bedchamber. He could not stop himself imagining the puppy going to her through the dressing room. He'd spent hours in that bedchamber himself, waiting for the laudanum to dull the pain in his shoulder while he stared at her dressing room door and thought of how very close she was. How very easy it would be to go to her. Only respect for her honor and his own had stopped him, and when Durose's arrival reminded Giles she had none, he'd been incandescent with rage and failed opportunities.

Giles wasn't certain even now what he'd meant to do when he went to her bedchamber, other than tell her to get out and take her lover with her. He'd waited nearly an hour after she retired, keeping an eye on her bedchamber door all the while, and when he entered to find her absent, there could be no doubt where she'd gone. Only a lingering shred of self-preservation kept him from charging into Durose's room and tearing them apart. He sat in the dark, suffering in Portia's lavender scent, and waited, his fury mounting. When she snuck back through the dressing room in the dead of night, he could contain himself no longer.

To discover, in the midst of his rage, that he'd horribly misjudged her so derailed him that he'd forgotten he ought still tell her to leave, and especially tell her to find some excuse to send her brother away. Antony Durose was a threat, and worse an impediment. Just when Giles had begun to make real progress on the library, he was shoved back into hiding. It was not to be borne.

And yet it must. How could he, his misjudgment of her preying on his mind, force her out now? Guilt, Giles assured himself, was what stayed his hand. Not the taste of her mouth, the soft give of her body. He dared not allow himself to think these delights were his to sample, whatever the momentary weakness that had given him that first taste. Nor could he risk keeping her near when he feared he did so only in hopes of repeating his trespass. He should not touch her again. Next time, he might not be able to stop. He might push aside the dress she wore so beguilingly, might taste her soft skin, might lay her down and himself upon her—

Hoofbeats pounded across the grounds. Giles twitched the drapes open far enough to look out. "Your brother has just galloped off on that chestnut of his. Is he fool enough to follow Ransley?"

"I don't think so."

Giles shook the drapes back into place and turned from the window. The puppy had likely only fled to the Duck and Drake to drown his sorrows. Giles seated himself on the couch, close enough to fill his senses with her, far enough he would not be tempted more than he could resist. "Portia Ashburne, I'm beginning to think having you around is more dangerous than strong winds and high seas."

She gave a watery laugh. "Only beginning? My lord, I'm sorry, I did not intend—"

"To pave Hell? That's the problem with good intentions, my lady. They can be so easily twisted from their purpose." He ought still be angry with her. She'd not only brought two innocent calflings down on him, but Ransley as well. "You realize," he said quietly, "that your brother cannot stay here." He could no longer ignore the folly of keeping them around. While she was in residence, there would be far too many people making free of his house without so much as a by your leave. The next time—and there would be a next time, for neither Portia nor Clary were anything but stubborn and Durose no better—could be his undoing. If Ransley even suspected Giles was alive, let alone in the Hall, Giles, and everything he loved, was lost.

Portia wrung her fingers around and around each other. If she'd had a bonnet or reticule, the strings would be in impenetrable knots. Giles put his hand over hers. "Portia."

"I can't. I can't just turn him out, what am I to say?"

"You'll say that you require his escort back to Rosewood."

Portia gave him a strangely wild look, an uncharacteristic giggle bursting from her lips. "Surely you're not serious, my lord."

"It's not safe for you to stay, Lady Ashburne." Giles realized he was leaning toward her and made himself release her hand and shift away. "I should have sent you home the moment it became clear someone meant you harm. I'm sorry, Portia, but you really must go." For her safety and his peace of mind. Now that he knew what she tasted like without the tang of fear on her tongue, he wanted so badly to taste her again that it was fortunate her brother had arrived to act as unwitting chaperone. Whatever Giles had once thought her, Portia Ashburne was not some shameless lightskirt, ripe for a meaningless tumble.

"Go, my lord? You're putting me out?"

"I see no choice in the matter."

"And where am I to go?"

"You are not attending me, Lady Ashburne," Giles snapped. "You're to go home."

"This is my home."

Giles stood and walked away for fear he would shake her otherwise. "Return to Rosewood, Lady Ashburne. You told me you've kept it up the last few years; it's surely more comfortable than the Hall. And no one will try to kill you there."

She muttered something that may have been "Are you quite sure of that?" Before he could demand to know what she was on about, she said, "If you would be so good, Lord Ashburne, answer me this: what shall I tell my brother-in-law?"

"Why, tell him the truth." Giles said, realizing only then that he'd never asked himself why she was really at the Hall after learning how wrong his initial assumption that James had sent her off as a punishment was. "Ashburne Hall isn't fit for man nor beast."

"You are much mistaken if you think that would make a difference to him. James Ashburne sent me here because his wife couldn't bear to share the house and title. He would not welcome me back."

Giles stared foolishly at her several moments before he was able to make sense of her words. "James always was a prating prig of a man; I've never met his wife."

Portia's laugh was far too harsh. "She is quite his equal, I assure you. Between them, they make Ashburne Hall a delight by comparison. Not that it signifies whether I wish to return or not. *They* do not want *me*."

"Then do not go to them. You're a widowed woman, Lady Ashburne. Propriety does not required you to remain under your husband's roof." But somewhere in Giles' mind, words he'd overheard Tony say were going round and round, growing louder and louder. *The pittance Roger left you. The pittance Roger left you. The pittance Roger left you.*

"I am a widowed woman, Lord Ashburne," Portia echoed with a mocking edge, "and have not relied upon my husband, or his kin, since the morning after my wedding, when Roger put me in a coach for Rosewood with a few pounds in my reticule and no idea where I was going. All the Ashburne wealth was not blunt enough for Roger. He thought nothing of letting the family seat go begging. What makes you think he bothered his head about doing the same to his wife?"

Giles cursed. "He made no provision for you? He left you nothing?"

Portia's gesture encompassed not only the library, but the Hall, cold and dank and crumbling around them. "What was there to leave, my lord?"

Giles strode to the door and back, jaw clenched and hands working. His cousins were fortunate, Roger that he was beyond Giles' reach, James that a trip to Rosewood was too dangerous for a man in Giles' circumstances. They deserved all the horrors of Hell for what they had between them done to Portia. No wonder she balked at his every request. His cousins had so tarnished the Ashburne name that Giles couldn't help but be blackened by the brush. His relations had blighted him in this woman's eyes before he even had a chance to know her.

"Pray do not take on so, my lord." Portia's chin was up, her color high. Impossible to tell if it was shame or determination that put the flags in her cheeks. "I have a small competence from my grandfather. It is enough to live on, so long—" She stumbled slightly and her blush deepened. "—so long as I'm not thrown completely on my own devices. I must have a roof over my head, sir."

"Durose, does he—"

Her chin inched up still farther. "He will have a small income once he graduates. It is not sufficient to support the both of us, and I wouldn't batten onto him in any case."

"My apologies, my lady." Ashburne sat next to her on the couch, all the wind taken out of him. "I did not intend to suggest you might."

He was falling again, tumbled off the prominence on which he'd thought himself secure. So these were the souls he'd taken unwillingly into his house and unwittingly under his wing: a stunning woman with more courage than coin and her hay-go-mad brother, sent down from university in what was doubtless but one in a series of rustications. How often had Giles hosted Roger in just such circumstances? Always the good excuse, the unforgiving master who wouldn't listen to apology or explanation, the other student who instigated it all. Over and over, Roger had come to laze about Ashburne Hall, ride his horse neck or nothing about the countryside, and sit in Courtland's pocket, the two of them drinking and carousing as if they were of an age. Just so had Roger spoiled his chances, running unconcernedly through his own small competence, always under the hatches, always relying upon Giles to bail him out. Until he'd been forced to tell Roger he wouldn't keep putting up the blunt to bail him out of River Tick. He'd taken that step, he realized now, but two months before Roger inherited the entire Ashburne fortune.

He'd never thought it more than a schoolboy's carousing. He'd dipped into such waters himself when he was in school, and his father had cut him off, just as he had Roger. Giles had taken the lesson to heart. But when the money was his, Roger had managed to make ducks and drakes of the lot, just as Durose would no doubt fritter away anything that came his way. And Portia? She would make excuses for her brother, give him money and pay his debts, and find herself in search of a rich husband or wealthy protector just to keep a roof over her head.

The realization curdled Giles' thoughts. No woman had ever wanted him for aught but his money. Even Amelia had been taken with the Hall, the silver, the family jewels. It was now painfully clear that Portia was no different.

"May we stay, then, Lord Ashburne?" Portia asked stiffly.

He had been silent too long. "You may, my lady."

It was not her fault. Roger Ashburne had left his wife with no option but to marry money, and James Ashburne had ensured, all unwitting, that the first eligible man she met after she was widowed was a wretch poor in everything *but* money. Giles had worked hard in exile and amassed a substantial pile for himself while Roger was busily destroying everything Giles loved. Or could love, it seemed.

Even as his heart sank within him, Giles could not blame her, could not call her a shameless fortune-hunter and banish her from his affections. The time for that had passed him by. He cast back through recent days as after a possession lost somewhere by the road, though what he sought was far less tangible than a misplaced handkerchief and could not be so easily recovered. There were those, even before Amelia's death, who called Giles Ashburne heartless. Though he did not wear his heart upon his sleeve, nor give it away easily, yet still he had one, and where he had bestowed it, he could not easily retrieve it. For this reason, he continued to shoulder the guilt of Amelia's death, though he was not the author of it. He'd known long before her death that he could no longer bear to wed her, but neither could he bring himself to denounce her. Had he done so, she might have been ruined, but alive.

Must he take on more guilt now? Guilt for Portia, her life endangered trying to prove *his* innocence. He'd money enough to keep her in any house or inn, but he knew her stubborn independence would allow her neither to take his money nor to leave. He was stuck with her, and she him. Once he did clear himself, what then? So long as she was trapped in the Hall, whether by a murderer or her own poverty, the choice was not her own to make. Locked in his dark room after he sent her to bed, his body aching for her, heart aching with a tenderness he would rather not feel, Giles had thought of offering his hand, and known he could not do so while his name was tainted. Now he saw that even clearing himself would not be enough—however much he wanted Portia Ashburne, he would not take her when she had no choice but to accept him. She must have the freedom to decide without the specter of penury hanging over her, though he couldn't rightly see how he could give her that choice without giving her money, which he knew she wouldn't accept.

Giles had not thought he could be more determined to prove himself innocent than he was when he first set his foot upon this path. Now, however, he must clear his name not only for his sake, but for Portia's.

Chapter Twenty-Seven

TWO days later, Portia still blushed to think of that conversation. It was not her fault Roger left her destitute, but she could not bear to remember how desperate she had been, how she'd begged Ashburne to let her stay. His pity crept under her skin and festered there.

For two days, Ashburne had been unrelenting in his search for the *billet doux*, his urgency stronger than ever before, as if he could not get rid of her fast enough. Once he'd proven his innocence and got back what was his, he would have two other houses he could cart her off to without marring his conscience. There was a time Portia would have liked nothing better than to return to Rosewood, but now she could hardly bear to think of leaving Ashburne Hall and its master.

They worked deep into the night, until Portia was nodding over her books and Ashburne set his aside to walk her to her room. She could certainly have found it on her own, no matter how tired she was, but some wanton spirit within her hoped for more of his kisses. But he was all that was proper, and the nearest she got was a quick brush of his chiseled lips, light as butterfly wings, and that only once. Her nights were restless, spent lying awake and scolding herself for wanting him when he'd made it clear he did not want her, or asleep and dreaming of him. Dreams that left her shaking with desire, her insides molten with the heat he had awoken in her. She was up early each morning, dressing and eating quickly so she could join him once more in the library, certain from the gray exhaustion creeping over his face that he'd not left at all.

He'd taken to smoking in the library when she was not there, the scent of his tobacco creeping out into the hall, and even when she was, a fine tremor overtaking his hands as he lit cheroot after cheroot. Portia said nothing about the impropriety of his blowing a cloud in her presence. She could feel his tension as clearly as her own. It grew through all the long hours in the dim near-silent cocoon of the library—drapes drawn, door locked, candleflames standing straight and steady in the unchanging dusk where words, if spoken at all, were murmured, the tone intimate even when the words were not.

And still they found nothing.

Tony continued supremely indifferent, even to the odor of tobacco that followed Portia about like the shadow of Ashburne's embrace. Portia, to her shame, was grateful for his distraction, for his galloping off as soon as he was up, not to return for hours upon hours. Portia hoped he was not out trysting with Clary. She didn't want to know about it if he was. She could only handle one problem at a time, and Ashburne was eating up all her energy.

When she found it, Portia didn't at first realize what she held.

Tsking, she straightened the bent pages of the book, part of yet another set of Shakespeare, this one bound in a rich royal blue. *Love's Labors Lost.* Between the bent pages lay a single sheet of paper, folded haphazardly in half against the crease of its original folding. Someone had treated both note and book with callous disregard. When she opened it, inured by dozens of misplaced hopes to the disappointment that inevitably awaited, her hands began to shake so hard she dropped the book.

Portia didn't know what he read in her face, but Ashburne reached her side in a moment, kneeling by her chair to gently pry the note from her shaking fingers.

"My dearest Amelia," Ashburne read in a hushed reverent tone. "This is it, Portia. This is it!" He kissed her, hot and hard and all too brief, leaving her shaken in every limb and disgusted with herself for wanting to draw out the feeling of his lips on hers. The scrap of paper that trembled between his fingers was what he'd searched for for the better part of a month. It was his proof, his freedom. Portia was a goose, wanting him to drop it—just for a moment—and put his arms around her, and kiss her as he had two nights ago.

She was a ninnyhammer, who'd clearly learned nothing from her loveless marriage with Roger, for she wanted this man. Difficult, uncomfortable, infuriating as Giles Ashburne was, she wanted him. She was so happy to have been the one who found the *billet doux* that she could barely contain herself. She needed desperately for him to see her as his equal, not some wretched woman who dangled at his purse strings, aided and housed and borne up out of no emotion softer than pity. He needn't even marry her, if he didn't want, so long as he was honest with her and didn't pretend at constancy when he abandoned her for the pleasures of London. If he did, which Portia doubted—where Ashburne gave his heart, he stayed. Less than a sennight had passed since they first spoke, it was true, but Portia had begun her understanding of Giles Ashburne the moment she stepped foot in the Hall.

Ashburne cursed viciously, his voice as flat and hard and furious as she'd ever heard it. He leapt to his feet and strode out of the library, the door banging behind him. Then another banging, the front door this time.

Oh heavens! Portia rushed after him. He wouldn't dare call the murderer out, would he? Or even... could he mean to kill the man with his bare hands?

She caught up with him on the drive, which he was taking at a ground-eating clip, gulping great draughts of air as if half-suffocated in the Hall. Portia grabbed his arm and was dragged several stumbling steps before he ground to a halt. The muscles of his arm were so hard there was no give at all under her fingers.

"Come back inside, my lord," Portia said, stumbling over the words in her urgency. "It's broad daylight. Anyone might pass by. Come back inside."

"Why?" he demanded in a voice like ground glass.

"Someone will see you." Portia tugged on his arm, but he budged not an inch. "You'll be seen! You'll be seen and Ransley will come for you and— Giles, please!"

He looked at her with the distant expression of a sleepwalker. "It doesn't matter." He held out the *billet doux*. "It's not signed."

"Not—? Give it to me," Portia pleaded, struggling with his white-knuckled grip. "Give it to me, do."

Giles released it suddenly and swung back to stare at the Hall. Portia looked first at the bottom of the page, then the back. There was no closing, no name, yet it didn't appear unfinished. She read quickly, mumbling aloud to herself in her haste. The writer begged his love to meet him on the picnic green an hour after dusk, ending with an expression of love and his sincere hope she'd meet him. But no name. Portia reread it, but her first impression remained unchanged: it was sweet and romantic and read more like a missive from a secret admirer than a satisfied lover.

"I must leave." Ashburne said it so softly that Portia nearly didn't hear him. "I must leave. There's no justice to be had here."

"Come inside, my lord."

He turned a little toward her, and she could see the small quirk at the corner of his mouth that was sometimes a smile and sometimes not. "You called me 'Giles' earlier."

"Giles, then. Come inside. It's broad daylight. Someone may see you."

Giles turned back to the Hall, and though she couldn't see his face, she could feel the intensity of his stare. As if he were eating up this poor damaged remnant of the estate he loved, tucking it away somewhere inside to sustain him in the years to come.

"Giles? Someone may—"

"It doesn't matter."

"It matters to me! I've had to sew up your hide once already. I don't fancy doing it again."

That woke him up. He took her arm in a hard grip and hustled her back inside, for all the world as if he thought someone might shoot *her*. Portia didn't protest the rough handling. He was no longer outside; that was all she cared about.

Giles didn't turn loose of her until the door was closed and barred behind them. Then he released her, walking away without so much as a glance, taking the stairs two at a time. Portia straggled after, finding him in the secret room at the top of the second staircase. He'd left the door open, or she'd have wasted ages looking for the mechanism to open it. She closed it behind her in case Tony put in an unexpected appearance.

A valise sat open on the bed, and Giles was filling it with a terrible hopeless resolve. Everything he'd worked for this past month and all the months before that was stripped away, his hopes dashed. Portia looked at the note she still held and folded it carefully along its original crease. She saw it as a setback, not the end. But then, she'd thought it a very thin hope to begin with and perhaps, not putting the weight on it he had, she was better able to weather the disappointment now.

"It is unfortunate," Portia said in a deliberately cool tone, "but not insurmountable."

Giles didn't look up from gathering his belongings. "I never took you for such an incurable optimist, madam."

"The failure of one sally does not guarantee the failure of the battle, let alone the war."

He didn't look up from the bag in which he was creating a valet's nightmare. "Nor did I realize you were such an expert on military matters. Or is it only useless platitudes you've got so conveniently at your fingertips?"

"Neither. It's *hope* I've got and you seem to have—"

"*This* was my hope," he growled, plucking the *billet doux* from her hands. "This was it, everything. The only way I could prove my innocence." He crumpled it in his fist and threw it against the wall. "Now I've got nothing."

"Nonsense." Portia planted herself on the bed, pushing his valise behind her, and glared up at him. Quite a long way up. Heavens, he was tall! "You've got me, and my help, and a man who lurks about the grounds at night and shoots at people."

"Thank you for reminding me, madam," Giles said, without even sarcasm, which would have at least made sense of the words. He reached over her for the valise, set it on the table, and pulled out a small leather bag that clinked when he handled it. "It's not much, but it will keep you at least a month. If you give me the name of your solicitor, I'll send more once I'm away."

Portia glared and refused the money, much too angry to feel humiliated at his charity. Giles growled and tossed the clinking bag into her lap. She adjusted her skirts, knocking it to the floor.

"Damnation, woman!" Giles knelt to pick up the bag. Portia put her hands behind her back. "Take the money! It's the only thing I'm able to do for you, damn you, and you *will* take it."

He had both arms around her now, trying to wrest her hands free. Portia looked at his flushed face, so close to hers, his eyes blazing with desperation, and felt her heart near to bursting. She pressed her lips to his. He jerked away, startled, then slanted his mouth hard over hers, pulling her tight against him. Her legs parted and he pushed through a froth of skirts to press himself against her, enveloping her in his heat. His chest was hard against her breasts, the thunderous beat of his heart driving hers. Giles locked one arm around her waist and tangled his fingers in her hair, sending the plaits cascading down her back. His tongue pushed between her lips and she opened her mouth with a gasp.

Portia wrapped her arms around his shoulders and pressed herself wantonly against him, half swooning in the grip of his ravenous kisses. It was not only her heart that ached now, and only the heat and hardness of his body could soothe the need that rose inside her. When he loosened her bodice and slipped it down to expose her breasts, she kissed him all the harder, whimpering when his lips left hers. Burning, they touched her breast and she arched, crying out his name.

Giles froze, his brow pressed hard against her collarbone, hot breath panting over her tender skin. She buried her hands in his thick hair and tugged, not caring if he returned his attentions to her mouth or her breast, so long as he did not stop. He lifted his head finally. "Careful, my lady," he rasped. "I could lay you back on the bed and make you mine."

Heat flashed over Portia's skin. "I would welcome you, my lord," she said boldly.

She did not have a name for the sound he made then; she only knew she wanted to hear it again. Then his lips closed over her nipple and she could think of nothing but the pleasure he gave her. The world lurched and twisted around her, the only solid point his body, the wet tug of his mouth pulling the fine, hot thread of desire tight in her belly and between her thighs. The camp bed was hard against her back and he was heavy atop her, his mouth ruthless upon her breast, the tug and pull making her spread her legs, making her rock against him. He lay half on her, and it was his hard chest she pressed herself restlessly against, so broad there seemed not room enough for him between her thighs.

Portia couldn't think. All of her, her very skin, felt hungry for Giles, yet she couldn't seem to get to his skin, her fingers tangling blindly in his hair, his shirt. Thank heavens he was at least not wearing a waistcoat; having his shirt and parts of her gown between them was bad enough. She slid her hands under his coat and tugged on his shirt until it pulled loose from his trousers. He groaned against her, muscles flexing as her palms found smooth, hot skin.

She whimpered. "Giles, please." She tried to pull him more fully onto her, seeking his weight, but he lifted away instead, shifting up to kiss her throat, leaving her cold and bereft. "*Please.*"

His hand brushed against her thigh, and then his fingers found her through the slit in her drawers. "Giles!" She quaked against him as he gave her more pleasure with his mouth and fingers, the two of them more dressed than not, than Roger had with his entire and naked body. "Please," she babbled, holding tight to his shoulders, aware of nothing in the world but him, "please," though she didn't know what it was she begged for.

"Portia." He lay fully over her now, one hand braced against the bed to keep some of his weight off her, though she wished he wouldn't and tried in vain to pull him down upon her. His free hand brushed the hair from her face. "We shouldn't. You shouldn't let—"

She lifted her mouth to his and surged wantonly against him where he lay between her parted thighs. She could feel him bare and hot against her. He surrendered with a groan, his mouth falling ravenously onto hers as his weight descended. And then he was inside her, and the world dissolved into fire.

It was shimmering still around the edges when she came back to herself and found he no longer moved inside her. He lay with his face pressed hard against her belly, and when she sought blindly for his hands in the froth of her skirts, she found them fisted tightly in the blankets. He shuddered when she called his name, and finally crawled back up to lay half over her, keeping their clothing resolutely between them.

"Giles?"

He kissed her, not as if he were no longer famished, but as if he'd determined to step away from the table with the feast unfinished. Then he tucked her resolutely against him, stroking her side as if to gentle what lay between them. "Forgive me," he murmured. "I had no right."

The languor was slow to leave her limbs, but righteous indignation began to push it out at his words. She tried to pull back to look into his eyes, but he would not let her go. "I did, and I gave myself you." Why did you not want me, she wanted to ask, but he was still shaking against her and she did not understand.

His embrace tightened. "I had no right to risk getting you with child."

She ought to be afraid at the thought of what they had nearly done. Would have done, had he been less in control of himself. If there was anything that could make her situation worse, it was bringing a child into it. Her reputation would be utterly ruined. But that all touched her with light wings, nothing to the specter of losing him. "I would lie in your arms a hundred times if it meant you wouldn't leave."

He groaned and buried his face against her throat with a shudder she could feel through every inch of his body. "Don't, Portia," he said against her skin. "Don't tempt me. Not when I must go."

"Don't. Don't go."

He drew back then, and kept his eyes lowered as he carefully and gently set her clothing and then his to rights. "There's no hope for me here." He reached for her as if he could not resist and stroked a finger down her cheek. "To stay is to court terrible danger. Not only for me, but for you."

"Me? No one is——"

"Don't come over the fool with me," Giles growled, swinging his legs over the edge of the bed and sitting up. "You can't have forgotten that someone tried to shoot you. You mentioned it yourself not half an hour ago. Why, if not to remind me of the danger?"

His tone was like a dash of cold water, rousing her from the dream of keeping him with her. Had it really been only a half-hour? It seemed she'd spent hours in his arms, or seconds. Certainly not long enough. She inched towards him, willing to forget the conversation and his unfounded scolding if only he would take her in his arms again, but Giles stood before she could touch him. She watched him step away from the bed, his back set against her, and felt cold without his heat. "Yes, I mentioned him," Portia snapped. "But not to remind you that there was peril in the woods. Nor to winkle money from you." She gave the bag of coins that had somehow remained on the bed despite their activities a push that tumbled it to the floor. "You cannot have mistaken his purpose in firing on us; you warned me off yourself the first chance you got."

Giles sighed and picked up the money, dropping it on the table. "I warned you off because you'd obviously stuck your nose into the business of someone who would not hesitate to harm you."

Her body ached with the pleasure he had given her, her heart with his withdrawal. The anger helped her to marshal her thoughts and argue when she wanted only to draw him back into her arms. "Someone who is either the murderer or knows who is. Catch him and you'll have justice for yourself *and* Lady Amelia."

"Do you think I haven't thought of that? What good would it do? I could prove only that he shot at you, and likely not even that. Common sense says it must have something to do with Amelia's murder, but there's no way to prove it." He put a few more things in his valise, almost absently, and Portia breathed a little easier to see he was no longer in an unholy tear to leave. "Besides, he's got all the home wood to hide in."

"He can only see the house from part of it. If someone were to draw him in——"

"No."

"I'd be in no danger."

"No! I won't have you putting yourself at risk. Bad enough my mere presence here endangers you. To court danger by exposing yourself..." He shook his head. "You will do nothing of the sort and that's final. I'd rather wander all the world alone the rest of my life than see you hurt."

Portia's breath caught in her throat, his words all the more precious for being muttered to his valise. "Can you not see that I feel the same?"

He seemed not to hear her. "If you stop poking into the murder, this fellow will surely leave you in peace. Nor will Ransley keep at you if you cease interfering with his ward. I'll send money to make Ashburne Hall livable. You'll do well."

"Banbury tales and trickery," Portia murmured, the thought striking her suddenly.

"What?"

"Ransley. He made mention of Lady Amelia's Banbury tales and trickery, of her sneaking out under his nose." She stared at Giles, not seeing him. "He knew something was amiss, even before she died."

"He could have been no less aware of the gossip than I," Giles said impatiently.

"But he might know *who* it was she snuck out to meet. He might know who killed her."

"Of course he knows who killed her," Giles snarled. "I did. Hasn't he told you that often enough?"

"But don't you see?" Portia demanded, too consumed with the realization that had burst on her like lightning to be irritated by his deliberate obtuseness. "We've been digging through every book in your library in hopes of finding the name of Lady Amelia's lover, when we might have learned it weeks ago if we'd only asked Lord Ransley."

"Excellent idea! Why not ask the man who'd have my head and your good name if he had even a suspicion that I'm still alive? Has it by any chance occurred to you," he went on acidly, not giving her a chance to speak, "that if Ransley knew who seduced his ward, he'd have long since taken a horsewhip to the man?"

"And besmirch what was left of her honor? With Lady Amelia dead, punishing the blackguard would do nothing but make public her disgrace. That Lord Ransley's done nothing doesn't mean he doesn't know who—"

"Enough."

Portia jumped to her feet. "Why are you so adamant about this? Ransley may know her lover's name!"

"What good would it do if he did? It's a long step from lover to killer if we have no proof to bridge the gap. Without his name on the note, we can't prove he was the one she went out to meet that night. For God's sake, Portia, leave Ransley out of this. If you infuriate him, he'll make it dashed difficult for you. How long do you think the shopkeepers would continue to serve you if they risked Ransley's displeasure in doing so?"

"I don't care a button for—"

"I do! Bad enough I have to leave you at James' mercy. I won't leave you in Ransley's black books too. And if that's not reason enough for you, then have a care for me. If you push him too hard, he'll start asking himself why you bother. Ransley's no want-wit, Portia. I should like time to get well away before he charges in to dangle me from the nearest tree."

"But—"

Giles took her shoulders and gave her a shake, his expression both fierce and tender. "No, Portia. I forbid you to have anything to do with the Duke of Ransley." He wrapped her in his arms, bringing her again into the heat of his body, the scent of him making her head spin. He pressed her close, where she could feel the vibration of his voice shiver through his chest and into hers. "Promise me you won't."

Chapter Twenty-Eight

PORTIA hurried away from the Hall, her cloak pulled tight against the wind. She'd waited throughout the long afternoon for Tony to return, but he didn't come and finally she could wait no longer.

The argument about Ransley and the gunman had gone round and round until Giles refused to speak of either any longer. He finished his packing, keeping always at a distance from her, then went down to the library and returned all the books to their proper places, ending with a lovingly worn volume that he settled in to read with an appearance of calm undercut by the tension she could feel snapping through him. He was waiting for full dark to leave, she knew, and that was all that kept her from running.

She walked quickly down the drive, daring to glance back only once she was hidden by the trees. There was no sign of movement and she hurried on with a sigh of relief. He hadn't seen her leave, and with any luck, he'd believe her off indulging in a fit of the sulks somewhere. He wouldn't miss her until he prepared to leave and she could only hope he would wait if she wasn't back before then. No, she must be back before dark. She wasn't entirely sure he *would* wait.

At the road, Portia turned toward Ransley's estate, Tynesfield. She had no idea how far it was, but it couldn't be less than five miles. Hopefully a carriage or wagon would come along whose driver she might convince to pick her up for the short distance. She couldn't possibly get back before Giles left if she must walk all the way.

Pity Tony hadn't come home. She'd alternately worried over and raged at him for that. If he had, she might have been able to borrow his horse. As it was, the only mount in the stable was Giles' great bay stallion, and Portia wasn't fool enough to think she could handle him.

She walked nearly two miles before a farmer came along on his way back from market, his wagon rattling empty behind him. He looked her over suspiciously when she hailed him, but his face cleared when she said she was on her way to Tynesfield, and he was quick to offer her a ride. She perched nervously on the bench beside him, trying not to sidle too obviously away from his stench of garlic and onions, and hoped her teeth would not be rattled loose by the time he put her down before the gates.

Dusk was coming on fast by the time Portia stood at last before the doors of Tynesfield. Elegantly groomed lawns spread out around her, each close-cropped patch of grass and neatly trimmed tree reminding her of everything Ashburne Hall had once been. The house was enormous, a sprawling edifice of pale stone that glowed in the fading light, its windows glittering red with the setting sun. Only at night did Ashburne Hall look so grand. By light of day, its time-worn façade and grimy windowpanes, many of them broken, were all too evident.

Now that she was here, Portia fought to make herself reach for the knocker. It was the only way; she must make the attempt even if it meant going against Giles' express orders. Ransley knew something—he must—and if she didn't try to find out what it was, she would regret it for the rest of her life. Though she would happily follow Giles into exile if he'd have her, he'd already made it clear he would not allow her to accompany him. Like Roger, he had bedded her, then set her aside. She didn't know what failing of hers made men desire her only until they lay with her, nor whether she hoped by proving him innocent to earn enough gratitude that he would give her another chance, nor even whether she truly believed he'd look twice at her once his title and lands were his once more. She knew only that she had to get Ashburne Hall back for him, even if doing so meant she lost him forever.

"Yes, miss— my lady," the butler corrected himself when he saw her squarely. "What may I do for you?"

"I should like to see his grace."

"Yes, my lady. If I may tell him who's calling?"

"Tell him Lady Ashburne would like a word with him."

The butler's austere face frosted over. "Very good, madam." She was surprised he let her in after that, let alone deigned to leave her alone in the drawing room while he went to inform the duke of her presence.

The room glowed with light, a dozen candles and the roaring fire squeezing every shadow from the room. After Ashburne Hall's dim and drafty rooms, it was too bright and nearly too warm. Or maybe that was just her nerves. She removed her cloak and laid it over the arm of a chair.

When the duke entered, the temperature fell precipitously. Portia wished she hadn't taken off her cloak. Ransley granted her a slight inclination of his head, the strange pale gray of his eyes making her think of a pond that had been iced over all winter. "I shall save us both time, Lady Ashburne, and inform you that you will have no better luck pleading your brother's case than he."

Portia'd come prepared to make the duke talk about Amelia by any means necessary and spent the long minutes she was left kicking her heels in the drawing room steeling herself to do just that. Ransley's declaration completely flummoxed her. "Tony's been here?"

"A fact you were no doubt well aware of when you came. I detest repeating myself, madam, but as you appear unable to grasp simple facts, I will tell you what I told him. Under no circumstances will I ever permit Lady Clarissa Seabrooke to associate with any member of the Ashburne family."

"Mr. Durose is not an Ashburne. He has no connection whatever," Portia protested automatically. "He was at school for the duration of my marriage and met Roger on precisely one occasion."

"That is of no moment to me, madam. This interview is over. You will inform your brother that if he is prepared, as he so hot-headedly announced, to see Lady Clarissa with or without my permission, he would do well to also prepare himself to be horse-whipped when I catch him. Good day, madam."

"Wait! I didn't come here to discuss Tony or Lady Clarissa. I came to talk about Lady Amelia." She quailed at Ransley's expression.

"Good *day*, madam," he snapped, striding to the door

"Word has it," Portia pressed on, "that she had a lover—"

He swung back around. "You dare!"

"—and you yourself mentioned her sneaking out. Do you know who she went to see?"

Ransley came back across the room so fast that for a moment Portia thought he'd strike her. "Do you think I'd have let it go on if I did?"

"There must have been someone you suspected," she said, surprised to hear no quaver in her voice, however much she shook internally. "Someone she may have gone out to meet that night."

"Has Amelia's reputation not suffered enough that you needs must drag it through the mud ten years after her death?"

"Whoever she met may have killed her."

Ransley could not draw himself up any farther, for he was already pike-pole straight, but his glare became something terrible to see. "You will cease this detestable exercise at once, madam. Whatever reward or advancement you hope to win by attempting to clear Ashburne's name is nothing to the consequences of my ill will. With a word, I can close every door to you, and if you think I will not do it, you are grossly mistaken." Portia realized she was staring at the diamond stickpin in his cravat and forced her eyes to meet his. Ransley's eyes glittered with a level of fury she'd have called madness if she weren't so certain he was stone cold sane. "You need look no further for the author of Lady Amelia's murder than the portrait that hangs over your great hall. Giles Ashburne murdered Lady Amelia."

"Lord Ashburne did *not* murder his fiancée," Portia rejoined hotly, remembering at the last moment not to use his Christian name. "He's all that is correct and honorable, and had besides no cause to do it."

"He had a fiancée who betrayed him with another man and he had a temper."

"You also have a temper, Your Grace. Does that mean you killed her?"

She'd gone too far and she knew it the moment the words left her mouth. Ransley looked at her, his expression perfectly unreadable. "I do not understand your persistence, Lady Ashburne," he said finally. "You will only harm yourself with it. Come, I will see you to your carriage."

It masqueraded as courtesy, but was no such thing. He took Portia's arm in a grip of steel and steered her out into the hall before she could get wits enough about her to object, and then it was too late, for he was marching her along too fast to breathe, let alone speak. "Thank you, Hailston," Ransley said to the butler. "I'll see Lady Ashburne out."

The duke guided Portia onto his front step and handed her her cloak. She hadn't even seen him pick it up and she barely had enough presence of mind to take it from him. It was full dark and Portia's heart rose into her throat. *Please*, she thought, *please don't leave yet*. Ransley scanned the drive, so obviously empty in the pale moonlight. "Where is your carriage, Lady Ashburne? You surely did not expect to be here long enough to send it around to the stables."

"Ashburne Hall does not run to carriages, Your Grace. I walked." Portia shrugged her cloak about her shoulders and did up the strings while the wind snapped at the hem.

"You shall not walk back in the dark."

It was the slightest of courtesies and tokened no true softening in him, but she was desperate enough to grasp at straws. "Do you truly not know who she met, Your Grace?" she asked softly.

He was staring down the drive still, a frown furrowing his brow, and scarcely seemed to be talking to her when he said, "If I did, he would not have 'scaped whipping."

He did not, he could not, know how he crushed her. He had been her last hope. There was nothing now. Portia started down the steps, her thoughts bent on the Hall and Giles. Surely he wouldn't leave without a goodbye. He'd wait until she came. Wouldn't he?

"Lady Ashburne, you may be as stubborn as you like. I will not let you go alone."

"That won't be necessary, Your Grace," Portia snapped, hearing the panic in her voice too late to hide it. She didn't dare make him suspicious now, not with Giles determined to leave the safety of the Hall tonight. He'd be in terrible danger if Ransley insisted on accompanying her. She composed herself with an effort. "I thank you, but I shall do quite well on my own."

"Hailston," Ransley called without turning, "call up a carriage and groom for Lady Ashburne. She will need an escort home."

Portia's heart eased. Of course he didn't mean to come himself. Why force himself into such close proximity with her, even for the few miles to

Ashburne Hall? A carriage. By carriage, she could reach the Hall in a few minutes. She fought to keep the relief out of her voice. "If you insist, Your Grace."

He watched her until the groom drove up in a neat little dog cart and hopped down to hand her in.

* * *

He would be there. He must be there. The thoughts chased themselves around her head, beating in cadence with the clop of the horse's hooves.

It was only after the groom turned into the drive that Portia thought to worry that he might catch sight of the "ghost." Had Giles realized she'd left? Would he leave the Hall to look for her? The Hall, when they reached it, was silent and dark, without any sign of life or movement. Portia descended without waiting for the groom to help her down.

He'd barely passed back down the drive when Portia heard a hollow crack that made the hair stand up on the back of her neck. It sounded like lightning, but she knew it wasn't. She ran around the east wing of the Hall and collided with Mrs. McFerran, who was wringing her hands in the dark by the kitchen door.

"Oh, my lady, he's gone out. He's gone out and I couldn't stop him. He saw a light by the old picnicking green and went out after it."

Oh damn and double-damn! Her fault, it was her fault. When he couldn't find her in the house.... She made herself think, ignoring the pounding of her heart. First things first. "Has Mr. Durose returned?"

"Not twenty minutes ago, my lady, drunk as a lord."

Drowning his sorrows after his interview with Ransley, no doubt. "Good. Keep him in the house." At least he wouldn't be blundering into Giles before she could find him.

"He'd sleep straight through to morning if a cannon went off under his bed. But Lord Ashburne—"

"I'll go after him." Portia tucked her cloak about her, turning in the white lining so it wouldn't catch the moonlight.

"Oh, my lady, I don't know if—" Was that actual concern, or simply doubt?

"Go back in the house, Mrs. McFerran. I'll go after him."

"Here." The housekeeper pressed something cold and heavy into Portia's hand. "Mr. McFerran loaded it for me."

And then she was gone, leaving Portia in possession of a pistol she had no idea how to use. She moved cautiously in the direction of the picnicking green, the gun held tightly in her sweating fist, barrel pointed well away from herself. She very nearly left the thing at the edge of the home wood, but bethought herself that Giles might need it and kept on, the gun weighting her arm with cold iron.

Portia stumbled through the tangled wood for eons, following the remains of an overgrown track by the light of a gibbous moon, terrified that she might at any moment hear another of those vicious cracks. Almost more terrified she'd find nothing at all, and Giles would be gone from her forever, without even so much as a farewell.

The wind curled and eddied around her, bringing with it the creak and sough of dancing trees, the whinnying of horses in the stables, the faint low of distant cattle, and other noises of less earthly origin. A night bird called nearby, the eerie noise making Portia's heart pound. Another sound grew slowly in her ears, now and again overcome by the rushing of the wind. It was a faint murmur that at first put her in mind of the chuckle of a brook. By the time she realized it was voices she heard, she was nearly upon them.

Portia couldn't imagine that a full house party had ever picnicked in the small clearing, though obviously the stand of saplings that choked the east end would not have been there ten years ago. Moonlight shone as clear as if day had lingered a little longer here. Portia drew in a quick breath and ducked behind the stump of a broad oak close on the clearing where a man held Giles Ashburne at bay, one dueling pistol gleaming in his hand, the other, spent, tucked into his belt. The hunter had run his prey to ground at last.

Chapter Twenty-Nine

"I doubt Ransley cares whether I produce you dead or alive," Courtland said, "but I should hate to have to carry your body all the way to Tynesfield." Gone was the jovial libertine. Gone, even, were the gaudy peacock colors, though the cut of his coat was no less exacting. The brown coat covered a white shirt and cravat, only Courtland's ruddy hair adding a dash of color.

Of Giles, even less could be seen. In his severe black, he appeared a mere shadow in the moonlight, poised too far from the edge of the clearing to run.

"You can understand my surprise when I heard you were back at the Hall," Courtland said conversationally. "You're lucky, by the by, that the rabble that frequent the Duck and Drake still hold you in such high esteem, or Ransley would have known within an hour of your arrival. As it was, it cost me a deal of blunt to ensure I would receive news of your return, should it ever come. I had an edge over the others, of course. I knew you weren't among the dead when that ship foundered. The shipwreck was a stroke of luck for you."

"Fifty men died, Courtland," Giles said in a strangely soft voice that raised the hair on the back of Portia's neck.

Lord Courtland seemed not to feel it. "Their loss. And your gain. No need to bribe some official to send proof of your death when your loving family could do it for you. Roger assumed you were among those whose bodies were not recovered. I wasn't so certain. I've been watching for you."

"You were the one who set Ransley on me."

"On the contrary! Had I thought he had even the slightest chance of finding you, I would never have told him his ward was coming over the common Haymarket doxy at Ashburne Hall."

"Why then?"

"A little mischief." Courtland smiled. "I couldn't resist. Though I must say, I was much relieved to see him leave without you, Ashburne. If I want to reap the benefit of your capture, I must encompass it myself."

"Benefit?" A laugh stormed from Giles' throat. "There's no reward for my capture. They all believe me dead."

"But Ransley *will* reward me if I bring him you. He'll strike me from his black books, Ashburne." Courtland's voice dropped and he moved closer to Giles, the gun hanging loose in his hand. "He'll fling such laurels about the shoulders of the man who delivers you to him that he'll even let a man like me court his ward. Lovely little thing, Lady Clarissa, quite as innocent as the chit Roger married, though a great deal plumper in the pockets. I wouldn't have pressed him to marry her if I hadn't been so misled as to the state of her finances. A delectable morsel, Portia. I'd have had her myself. Though not, I think, to wed."

Giles lunged, but Courtland realized his error in time. He leapt back, the gun coming up to press against Giles' breastbone. Portia held her breath, cold sweat prickling down her back, until Giles stepped back. She remembered her own gun suddenly and lifted it against the rough bark of the tree, but her hand wobbled with the weight of it. She'd never fired a pistol before and was by no means certain of her aim. If she hit Giles....

"Dearest Portia," Courtland murmured, a parody of affection. "How unfair of you to tell her I was trying to kill her that night, when I only wanted to frighten her off. I'd not have hit her."

"You hit me."

Courtland flashed a cold smile. "What a gift to spot you charging after her. I could hardly believe my luck. You ducked too quickly, Ashburne, or I should have ended it then and there."

"Dammit, Courtland! Why the devil are you out for me? You know I didn't kill Lady Amelia or you wouldn't have helped me escape the country."

"Of course I know you didn't kill her, my dear Ashburne." Courtland pressed the muzzle of his gun to the base of Giles' throat, tipping his head as if to whisper in Giles' ear, though the words carrying clearly to where Portia knelt in the fragrant loam. "I did."

Giles grabbed Courtland about the waist and jerked him off his feet. Portia's nails bit into rough bark, a scream caught in her throat. She raised the gun again, but couldn't tell one man from the other as they grappled in the dirt, heaving and grunting. Portia's scream nearly tore free when she saw the gleaming barrel of the pistol raise. It fell on Giles' dark head with an audible thump, and he rolled off.

Courtland staggered to his feet, breathing heavily. He brushed dirt from his clothes with one hand, the gun never straying from Giles. Portia might shoot him now, but she was afraid of missing or only winging him. He could so easily squeeze the trigger before he fell. If she hit him at all. She held her breath. Giles, groaning, rolled to hands and knees.

"You," Giles panted, "why? What did she do to you?"

Courtland chuckled as if Giles had said the most delightfully amusing thing. "Why nothing, Ashburne. Nothing at all. It was you I needed. Or rather, your money."

"Money?" Giles echoed, as if the word meant nothing to him. Perhaps it didn't, with his head still ringing with Courtland's blow. Even to Portia, it had the sound of a word she had once understood.

"Money, Ashburne." Courtland used the muzzle of the gun to lift Giles' chin. "Blunt. The ready. In order to pay off certain debts of honor, I borrowed money from some unsavory gentlemen who refused to be put off. They were most insistent I pay up and prepared to do me physical injury if I did not. And you, Ashburne, *you* had cut Roger off."

Giles twisted his head away. "Do you dare tell me you killed her for a handful of sovereigns?"

"Oh, a great deal more than that. Don't take on so," he added with false compassion. "Even if you hadn't refused Roger further assistance, I should soon have had to resort to such lengths. Roger would have given me anything I asked, but really, he had so much less to offer than you did. Until *he* became Lord Ashburne."

Giles lifted his hand to his head and looked at his fingers as if wondering where the blood had come from. He dragged himself to his feet, Courtland backing away. It came to Portia suddenly that, even while he held Giles' death in his hands, Courtland was afraid of him. "Why would Roger pay you so well once he held the title? What did he owe you?"

"Oh, everything, Ashburne. Everything. Roger and I were the best of friends. He'd have done anything for me, especially after I covered up the murder for him. If it had come out that he killed Lady Amelia—"

"You said you killed her."

"Oh, I did," Courtland said without the slightest hint of remorse. "But Roger was never able to remember what he did while in his cups and always so trusting of anything I told him. He was ridiculously easy to convince. All it took was the sight of his own handkerchief smeared with her blood."

Giles' eyes closed and Portia thought she saw him swallow. "Why? Why would you...." He faltered.

"Why? To have him in my debt, Ashburne. Forever in my debt. I have lived high and well these last ten years. My debts paid, my least desire fulfilled. Roger was a gambler, a rake, and a fool, but did you really think he could run through the entire Ashburne fortune by himself? I found him far less amusing once his pockets were to let. It was just as well he died when he did. He was becoming a burden.

"Then," Courtland went on in a sprightly tone that made Portia feel as sick as Giles looked, "just when I was coming to my wits' end—I even considered sticking my neck in parson's mousetrap, could I but find a wealthy chit with an inattentive guardian—I got word you'd returned. Why did you come back, Ashburne? So long as you kept out of England, I was satisfied to leave well enough alone." He laughed. "Oh, but you've done me the most marvelous turn. I feared you at first, but then I saw how to turn your foolhardiness to my advantage.

"Ransley would pay anything for his revenge, but I'm not interested in anything so crude, and ultimately limited, as a gift of his money. I'll take the hand of his niece and with it all her blunt and a nice chunk of his. Ransley's settled a pretty penny on the Seabrooke chit when he dies. He has to stick his spoon in the wall sooner or later—and sooner can always be arranged. I shall be set for life *and* have a fetching doxy of a wife. She can't be as innocent as she looks, not riding over the neighborhood in men's breeches. Some farmer or stable boy's surely already tumbled her. Even if she turns out to be dull as dishwater, well, there's always Lady Ashburne. No doubt Roger taught her a thing or two."

Giles sprang wildly at Courtland, who leapt away, brandishing the gun. "Don't make me shoot you, Ashburne." Giles didn't seem to hear him until the muzzle of the gun was against his head.

Portia's lungs ached from holding back a scream. Her fingers slipped on the gun. She must shoot. Courtland wasn't going to let Giles live. He couldn't afford to give Giles the chance to tell what he now knew. Oh, but they were standing so close and her hands shook so.

"Such passion," Courtland mocked. "A pity you didn't show it to Lady Amelia. She might not have been so easy to lure from your side. And she was, Ashburne," he murmured, the muzzle of his gun pressed against Giles' head. "So easy to woo with pretty words, to bring traipsing gaily into my arms in her flimsy finery. I almost regretted killing her before I had a chance to taste her charms.

"And you made it so easy. I'd prepared the field—gossip spreads like wildfire, you know, and by the day of the ball, the entire house party knew of Lady Amelia's infidelities—and I knew I could count on Roger's assistance in directing everyone's attention to you once I broke the sad news. But then you went and found the body.... Oh, that was too perfect to plan for."

"But you did. It was you who suggested she might have gone to inspect the grounds for the morrow's picnic. I made nothing of it then." A bark of laughter escaped him. "Obvious enough now. It was you who led me to her."

"Did I now? How delightful. One forgets."

"No, one does *not*," Giles said heavily, and Portia knew he was remembering the night he carried Lady Amelia home, blood soaking his linen. "You'll pay for this, Courtland."

Courtland laughed. "You seem to forget that I have the gun. *And* the man Ransley's despised for more than a decade. Who will look beyond you, my dear Ashburne? Who will bother? Take heart. You'll be too dead to care. Unless, of course," he said with sickening levity, "your spirit should return to haunt the Hall. Now that *would* be ironic."

It was then Portia knew what she must do. She laid the gun on the ground and stripped open the ribbons of her cloak, her hands shaking horribly. She cursed herself, infuriated that she couldn't accomplish even so simple an act as reversing her cloak without fumbling. It took only a moment to turn the white lining of her cloak out, but it felt like an eternity.

"You must understand, Ashburne," Courtland said carelessly. "It's not that I believe he'd listen to a word you said. But one mustn't take chances." He raised the gun and Portia, looking up from the struggle to get her cloak about her again, caught her breath in terror, for there was now neither amusement nor mercy in him. The sprig of fashion was gone. Only the murderer remained. "I really must thank you for coming back, Ashburne. You gave me a few bad moments, I own, but thanks to you, the rest of my life...." He smiled. "The rest of my life will be quite comfortable."

There was no time to prick up her courage or have second thoughts. Portia could see Giles gathering himself to leap on Courtland, for all he could not fail to be shot. Courtland could see it too, and he smiled as if to encourage Giles.

Portia picked up the gun and pulled the hood of her cloak as far forward as she could without blinding herself entirely. "Simon...." she called, striving to sound like nothing of this earth. Portia rose from behind the stump. "Simon, dearest...."

* * *

Courtland blanched. He half-turned, his mouth forming Amelia's name, but Giles couldn't hear him for the roar of his blood. For the first time in what was surely an eternity, he was not looking into the mouth of Hell through the black muzzle of Courtland's gun.

"Giles!"

The cry staggered him in mid-lunge. He turned toward Portia's voice and the moonlit specter threw something to him. Instinctively, he caught it, cold metal slapping his hands. More sensed than seen, Courtland swung back, leading with the pistol. Giles fired just as Courtland's gun belched flames.

Something hot burrowed into his side, a buzzing numbness spreading out from it like ripples on a pond. His legs went out from under him, and Giles crashed to his knees. He vaguely heard Portia cry his name from some murky distance. Then she was on him. At her touch, he surfaced with a great indrawing of breath that seared his side.

Courtland still stood, the pistol dangling from his hand. His eyes had a strange inward look and blood blossomed under his cravat, a crimson flower unfolding across white linen. He swayed and dropped the gun, but stubbornly kept to his feet. He coughed, and his eyes focused on Portia. "Little bitch," he said, his words coming thick and slow. "Should have shot you when I had the chance." His eyes drifted to Giles and he smiled suddenly, blood black on his teeth. "How will you prove your innocence now?" With that, he crumpled.

Giles stared at Courtland's body, triumph turned to ash in his mouth. There was no proof. No way he could demonstrate the truth of anything

Courtland had said. Ransley would certainly not believe Giles, nor Portia if she spoke on his behalf. It was done for good this time. He would leave England and not look back, though he left his heart behind him. For a brief shining moment, Giles dreamt of taking Portia with him. He could happily pass the rest of his life in exile if only he had her by his side.

"Giles! Giles, are you hurt?"

Giles found Portia's hand and pressed her delicate fingers. No. An exile's life was not for her. "Nothing to signify, though I'm afraid you'll have to stitch up my worthless hide again, love." He cursed the fate that decreed their last hour together should be taken up with blood and gore. But there could be no further delay. Courtland couldn't have resisted dropping hints to Ransley, who was far from a fool. The duke could even now be awaiting Giles' delivery on his doorstep. Or worse, have grown impatient and come looking for him.

"Where?" Portia pushed at his coat. He hesitated, savoring this last chance to feel her light fingers ghosting across his chest, then pushed her gently away and touched his hand to the bright pain in his side. She made a soft sound when he brought it out painted with blood, but his Portia neither fainted nor panicked. "We should—" She broke off when he lurched to his feet and wrapped her arms around him to help, seeming not to notice his blood staining her white cloak. She was so slight he didn't dare lean more than a fraction of his weight on her, but still he kept her close, to feel her small body pressed against his one last time. "Have you a handkerchief?"

Her hands delved into his coat, but Giles was unable to help her. Standing had driven the swarm of bees from under his ribs into his head, and the world had gone gray.

"Here."

A hard hand pushed against the wet agony of Giles' side. He hissed through his teeth and looked into pale gray eyes that had once been as dear as a brother's. Giles jerked, but Ransley had his shoulder in a hard grip.

"Your lady's visit made me suspicious," the duke said quietly, pressing his handkerchief steadily against the furrow Courtland's bullet had dug across Giles' ribs. "I came hunting for a murderer." He glanced at Courtland's body, then back at Giles. "It seems I found one."

Chapter Thirty

"HAVE you news?" Portia called to Foxkin as she turned into the innyard in a shining gig borrowed from Ransley's stables. Lady Clarissa rode alongside, which explained Tony, sprawled on the bench next to her. Portia wasn't fool enough to think he'd come along purely for the pleasure of his sister's company.

Foxkin smiled at Portia, settling the horse with the calming touch of his hand. "You would know better than I, my lady."

Portia sighed. "I had hoped you might have heard something." It was near two months since Giles and Ransley left for London and she'd heard little since. Clary had gotten two short letters from her uncle, saying only that their efforts were proceeding apace. Giles had not written.

Foxkin shook his head. "And you, my lady," he said to Lady Clarissa, whose horse stamped restlessly beside Portia's carriage. "May I compliment you on your fine sidesaddle?"

Clary beamed down at him. "You may, sir." She looked very becoming, outfitted in a proper riding habit and perched on a new sidesaddle.

"I'll send word soon as I should get any," Foxkin told Portia, slapping her horse on the withers to send them once more into motion. "Pray you do the same," he called after her.

"Shouldn't carry on with innkeepers," Tony muttered when they were out of earshot. He was slouched with his head tipped back against the squabs and his hat over his face, and it was impossible to tell if he was talking to Portia or Clary.

"Foxkin's no mere innkeeper," Clary objected. "Foxkin's... well, Foxkin."

"Excellent logic, my lady. And you, sis," he went on without moving. "Patience."

"It's been two months! Surely it can't take that long to clear Giles' name in the House of Lords. Not with the Duke of Ransley speaking for him."

"How long do you think it'll take to wrest the title and estates from James bloody Ashburne's greedy grasping paws? Roger helped conceal a murder and place the blame on Ashburne, but James had nothing to do with it. He inherited in good faith, I'm sorry to say. Every lord in the Committee of Privileges with a title that descends through an ancestor whose death was the least bit questionable is asking himself what he'd do if that bloke or one of his descendants appeared and demanded everything back."

"That's not fair."

"Life ain't fair, sis." Tony yawned and boosted himself upright on the seat, returning his hat to its proper place on his head. "Ashburne will get it back, of course. The entire peerage would collapse if the Committee of Privileges couldn't decide such a clear-cut case. Be patient, puss. Ashburne's too busy to come dashing down from Town just to have a coze."

Yes, Portia thought, but he could at least write. "I'm not a puss, Antony Durose. I'll have you remember I'm five years your senior."

"Yes, in your dotage already," he drawled. Clary giggled. "And you, my lady of the sea, you're nothing but a chick, still wet behind the ears."

"Chicks don't have ears." And they were off, engaged in the amiable arguing that was entirely too like flirtation for Portia's peace of mind. She set Tony down in front of Ashburne Hall and called Clary away from where she sat chattering, Tony's hand resting on her horse's shoulder entirely, and quite deliberately Portia was certain, too close to her knee.

The duke insisted Portia stay at Tynesfield for the duration, supposedly so she could chaperone Lady Clarissa during his absence. That lady's long-suffering governess could do as good a job as ever Portia could, and she suspected Ransley's insistence was more a matter of guilt than expediency. Rather than argue with him and risk damaging his new-found accord with Giles, Portia had thanked Ransley prettily and moved into a guest room at Tynesfield. Ellie was delighted with their new accommodations, and especially with the company, though she'd admitted when pressed that even the duke's underservants were inclined to come over snooty. Portia spent her days keeping Clary's flirtation with Tony to a minimum, her evenings exploring a library every bit as good as Ashburne's if less inclined toward spiders and mice, and her nights dreaming of Giles.

She might have withstood his absence better if she'd known he meant to return to her. But she didn't have that certainty. She knew now why Roger hadn't wanted her, having married her only for the money he thought she possessed. It was no fault of hers that he'd set her aside immediately after consummating their union. She ought to have been more sure of Giles, but she could take no comfort from how desperately he had wanted her. Giles Ashburne was not a man to be led around by the heartstrings.

Every moment that passed after Courtland's death, Portia had felt Giles withdraw from her a little further. The retreat had become precipitous when Ransley appeared on the scene. The duke had carried them away to Tynesfield and sent for Mr. Millbank to attend to Giles' wound, and Portia had never seen him from that moment to the day he left that he was not in Ransley's company. Now that she was no longer his sole ally, it seemed Giles had no further use for her, and Portia remembered too late that she could expect little justice and less consideration from the Ashburnes.

And yet, she could no more cease worrying about Giles and wishing for him than she could fly to the moon and back.

So Portia kept Clary reminded of the manners expected of Quality, shooed Tony away from Tynesfield half a dozen times a day, and watched for Giles. And waited.

Finally, after a sleepless night spent listening for ghostly footsteps, after sending Tony to the rightabout at least a dozen times, and after brangling with Clary for having been so cruel as to send him away, Portia collapsed on a chair in the library and realized quite suddenly that she was not just an Ashburne. She was a Durose, with the same stubborn determination that had led Tony to tell Ransley he'd continue to pay Lady Clarissa his attentions with or without the duke's permission.

Where had that willingness to defy anyone and everyone in the pursuit of what she wanted gone? Had Roger and five years of scraping by on what he left her blasted it, or James and a year of the contempt heaped upon a penniless relation nibbled away what was left? Certainly all the discomforts of Ashburne Hall could not have done it, and yet Portia realized she'd become prepared to make do with what was given her and not seek more.

Portia looked around Ransley's bright and gleaming library and realized three things. The first was that it would be an unjust world indeed if Ashburne's library did not one day look like this. The second was that she wanted to see it when it did. And the third, which went so deep as to be more an unearthing than a revelation, was that she simply could not rest until she'd seen it as no mere guest, but the mistress of Ashburne Hall. And *not* because she'd come to love the place.

Portia jumped up and hauled on the bellpull. "Hailston," she said when the butler appeared in the doorway, "prepare a carriage and groom for Lady Clarissa and myself and see to it that our bags are packed. We are going to London."

* * *

It was not nearly so easy as that, of course. Late the next morning, Clary's maid was still wailing about the impossibility of packing appropriate attire without two days to prepare and at least some idea what events were to be attended, the cook was insisting upon just another few hours to complete baskets for the travelers' sustenance, and the stable boys were fighting over who got to ride postilion. Or so Ellie told Portia as she did up her hair that morning, such brangling being carried out well away from the ears of the Quality.

The only thing that *was* ready was the coach: Ransley's traveling chaise with, at Hailston's insistence, a driver, postilion, and two outriders. It said something about how Ashburne's star had risen at Tynesfield that the butler did not by so much as the twitch of an eyebrow bristle at Portia's high-handed ordering of his grace's equipage.

Portia had spent the night mentally telling over the money Giles had left her—that same bag of coins he'd tried to push on her for charity's sake, which she'd found on her dressing table after he left. She had enough to keep them all in food and drink and lodge them until they got to Town. Once there, they'd needs must throw themselves on Ransley's mercy, but the duke could hardly turn aside his own ward when he had, according to Clary, a grand townhouse that, if he had not already opened it, might be made habitable in half the time it took to think about. By such stratagems, she managed to avoid thinking about what she meant to do when she got there. And how very wrong it might go.

She was pacing in the morning room, ignoring Clary's complaints that merely watching her was *quite* wearing her out, when the sound of a ruckus came from the great hall, a man's voice rising over all to demand, "What the deuce is going on here?"

Portia knew before she rushed out that it was Ransley's voice, but if he was back, then surely Giles was as well. She found the duke in the middle of the hall, still wearing his driving gloves and caped greatcoat. "Why are my best cattle fidgeting in harness on the drive while my household scurries around like demented rodents?"

"It's my fault, Your Grace," Portia said, her heart sinking in her breast. It was not fear of his wrath that disheartened her, though an absence of two months had not made Ransley any less formidable, but that Giles was not with him.

"Indeed?" Ransley allowed Hailston to take his greatcoat and began pulling off his gloves. "Would you care to enlighten me, Lady Ashburne?"

"I thought—"

"*We* thought," Clary piped up from behind her.

"—to come to Town, Your Grace. To, to see you."

"To see me." For a moment, Portia thought Ransley might smile, but she was clearly mistaken, for his expression only got sterner. "And what prompted this sudden desire?"

Oh heavens! "I—"

"What the devil is about?" Giles demanded, striding into the great hall with a face like a thundercloud. "Ransley, your servants have all gone mad."

"On the contrary, Ashburne. They are merely obeying the orders your— Lady Ashburne gave. They are preparing for a trip."

"A trip?" Giles scowled at Portia. Her nerves gave way to relief at seeing him so hale and hearty. The wound that had still been so painful that he had suffered Ransley to help him into the curricle when they left clearly no longer bothered him.

"Indeed," Ransley said. "Perhaps we might take a dish of tea in the morning room and discuss the matter. Hailston?" The butler vanished silently, and the duke ushered them all into the morning room. He hadn't been there five minutes—five rather strained minutes, Portia thought, though Clary seemed not to feel the tension—when he announced that he needed a word with his ward and ordered her to join him in the library. Clary didn't even have the grace to look nervous as she followed her uncle from the room. In fact, she tipped Portia a saucy wink before she closed the door, leaving Portia alone with Giles.

Portia folded her hands in her lap so Giles would not see how her fingers twisted together and didn't even try to prevent her eyes from seeking him out where he stood before the fire. His hands were clasped behind him and his eyes on the painting over the hearth, an insipid watercolor not meriting half so intense an examination.

"You appear to be in fine health, my lord," Portia said to Giles' back when he'd stood so for several silent minutes. "Your wounds no longer pain you?"

He didn't answer for some time and when he did, his voice was cold. "A trip, Lady Ashburne? Where, pray tell, were you going?"

Portia gritted her teeth. "Oh, I'm in blooming health, I assure you, my lord. Thank you for inquiring."

"Hell and damnation, Portia!" He swung around and glared at her. "Where were you planning to vanish off to? If I'd been a day later, I'd have returned to find you'd gone without a word."

"If it's a question of sending word, my lord," Portia said sweetly, forgetting that she had no claim on him, "might I assume that all your missives have gone astray?"

"Damnation, what was I to write?"

"You might at least have let me know you weren't languishing in Newgate Gaol."

"Unlikely, with Ransley there to speak for me. As for the rest..." Giles laughed without amusement. "Your blasted brother-in-law's as tenacious as a demmed lobster. Nothing escapes his grasp."

"Don't blame James on me," Portia snapped. "He's your kin."

"Aye, he's my kin," Giles growled. "More's the pity. And he's made some powerful friends, who're doing what everyone swears up and down can't be done. I don't know if they can block me forever, but they've done an excellent job so far." He dragged his hand through his hair and sat down next to her on the couch. "Truly, Portia, what was I to write? That I was free of Amelia's murder but still a landless, title-less corpse?"

Portia's heart gave a painful thump. "You're *not* a corpse," she said, reaching automatically to put her hand on his. He turned his hand over and studied the fall of her fingers against his, his manner almost detached. "You might have written," Portia said again.

He seemed not to hear. "Where were you going? Rosewood's closed to you and you haven't anything but the pittance I left you." The reminder of his charity closed Portia's throat and his face hardened when she failed to answer. "I forget I know so little of you. Perhaps, like Lady Amelia, you have a lover to fly to."

"Lady Amelia never had a lover," Portia said, finding in his accusation a kind of courage, for he seemed as hurt by the words as she. "And neither have I. She had only a stranger who fed her pretty words and lies. For that, I had Roger."

"Roger!" On Giles' lips, the name was a curse. "That double-damned blaggard—"

"I feel rather sorry for him, actually." As lowering as it was to discover Roger had only wed her at Courtland's instigation, it meant his coolness towards her was not her fault. It was nothing Portia had done that sent Roger to plunder his way through the demimonde, burying himself in the arms of every woman but her. "All those years fearing it would come out that he killed Lady Amelia, believing he could slit a woman's throat while in his cups—"

"It didn't stop him drinking," Giles said, his voice hard. "It didn't stop him turning himself into an unprincipled rake with a reputation as wide and murky as the Thames. The stories I heard in Town...." He shook his head. "I forget myself. If, then, it is no lover you fly to, Portia, where do you fly?"

Portia curled her fingers in his and took heart from the instant strengthening of his grip, as if he feared she'd withdraw her hand. "To Town." She took a quick breath for courage. "To you."

"To me?" His smile was charmed. And charming, she'd seen it so rarely.

"You had not written," Portia reminded him. "If your case is going so... slowly, how can you spare the time to travel to Ashburne Hall? Is there some proof you require for your claim or—"

"There is nothing I require at Ashburne Hall." Giles took both her hands in his. "I came to Tynesfield, and I came for what is right before me." His grip was so tight her fingers were growing numb, but she didn't care. "I hadn't heard from you—I'm not the only one to be scolded for not writing, madam— and I worried you'd left Tynesfield. I'd no idea where you could go, nor how I'd find you if you did. And I realized that I didn't..." He paused so long, she turned her eyes up to his, and saw a fire warming their depths. "I didn't care if I ever got Ashburne Hall back if I didn't have you. What say you, lady? I may ever be a man without title or home, but I've money enough to keep us in comfort. I'll never be a man of pretty words, but I promise, if you accept me, I'll keep you in my heart until the day I die. I—"

Portia pressed her fingers to his lips, lingering a moment at their softness. "I've lived with money and I've lived without. But I've never lived in a man's heart. Yours is the only home I'll ever need."

He let out his breath in a gust that fanned her face and gathered her against his chest, holding Portia so close she could hardly draw breath. Then, as if he could wait not a moment more than she, he drew back far enough to bend his head to hers. Portia met his kiss eagerly, a great bubble of relief and joy and passion rising inside her. She could have swooned in his arms and wouldn't have cared so long as he never stopped kissing her, never stopped holding her against him as if she were the dearest treasure the world possessed.

Finally, he set her from him, his black eyes bright. "If Parliament decides in my favor, you may yet be Lady Ashburne to a living lord."

"If it does not," Portia said, twining her arms around his neck, "then I shall be Mrs. Ashburne, and happy so."

FINIS

*Thank you for reading *The Lady's Ghost*. If you enjoyed this book, please think about leaving a review at your favorite online retailer.*

The Duke of Ransley's and Lady Clarissa's stories are continued in *The Duke's Despair*, available in ebook and print format.

And Lady Clarissa will finally find her heart's desire in *The Hoyden's Heart*, out soon.

About the Author

Colleen Ladd lives in the mountains of northern Colorado with her family, including three goofball dogs and two lunatic cats. When she's not writing, she is a volunteer firefighter and medical first responder. She'd never make it as a Regency lady at a fancy ball, but would certainly enjoy looking on from the sidelines.

You can reach Colleen through her website (www.colleenladd.com) where you can also sign up to receive notifications about new books.

Also available from this author:

The Duke's Despair

The Duke of Ransley despairs of getting his ward safely launched. She'll be lucky to make it through her first Season without permanently blotting her copybook. He's somehow managed to raise a perfect hoyden, and fixing that will take some doing. But he doesn't need the help of some marriage-mad woman using his ward to get close to him.

Althea Ravenshaw has neither the need nor the desire to marry. Her heart goes out to Ransley's ward, saddled with a fire-breathing dragon of a guardian, and she can't help trying to keep the girl out of trouble. *Someone* has to, for Ransley clearly isn't equal to the task.

Neither of them realize that someone is deliberately trying to ruin the girl, someone who will stop at nothing to send Ransley and his ward packing. And he has no objection to including Althea in his plot if she continues to interfere. If Ransley and Althea do not use all their wits, and find the will to actually work together, they will have something far more important than a reputation to despair of.